Bitter Oranges

Seamus O'Connor

Chapter 1

Big Sur, California — 2004

THE FIRST VISIT with the psychiatrist-monk had not started off well.

The man hadn't said a word, motioned Holland to a chair, then went back to reading the papers on his lap. The small, whitewashed office was furnished with only a table and two chairs. A gruesome modern crucifix hung on the wall behind the monk. Typical monkish affectation, this austerity, Holland mused as he looked around.

The monk looked up from the papers, eyebrows raised expectantly. "How a man like you can live with himself is beyond me — completely beyond me!"

Holland bit his tongue.

The little monk, rimless glasses straddling a thin shiny nose, glared at the rough-looking individual in faded work clothes.

"How in God's name could someone in your position be so irresponsible, give so much scandal to … to the faithful?" He demanded.

Holland was watching from the cave at the back of his mind—refusing to be provoked. Any lack of cooperation, and he'd be out on his ear. But his patience was wearing thin.

"Perhaps this will jog your memory." The monk held out a Xerox copy of a newspaper headline for him to read:

Controversial Cleric Embroiled In Heresy and Scandal—

He'd seen it before of course, the day the paper first hit the streets; when the ink was fresh and black, and he was a young man full of strength still. He remembered like it was yesterday how he'd felt then and how he had steeled himself against the pain of that day and the worse days that were to follow. He had managed to put it out of his mind until now. Annoying, having this stuff dug up and thrown in his face—and for what? For room and board? Jerry's face flashed for a moment in his imagination but he told it to go away—ghosts would be too much to bear on top of the other stuff this man was resurrecting. Staring at the floor in a semi-trance was all he knew to do to keep control.

Silence, thick and hostile as sour milk, filled the space between the two men in what had become a battle of wills. The monk took off his glasses and started polishing them meticulously.

"Well?" He demanded after a long silence.

"Oh! I'm sorry! Were you asking me a question, *Doctor?*" Holland asked. "I could have sworn you were still scolding me? Scolding was not a recommended form of psychotherapy — at least in the old days."

"You're right!" The priest admitted after a moment during which he fit the glasses into the deep grooves in his nose and carefully hooked each sidepiece behind an ear. There was a hint of remorse in his tone. "I was being judgmental. I'm sorry."

Holland shrugged which the other may have taken as forgiveness for he continued.

"Could I ask you, please, to comment on the reports in these newspapers?"

"I'd just as soon you'd leave all that nonsense from the past alone." Holland's voice had taken on an assertive edge.

"That is not an option my Superiors have given you, as I understand it." The little man's voice was brittle with indignation again. "This report in *The Minerva Chronicle*, for example." He waved a piece of newsprint accusingly. "It reports that you, John Holland, a Catholic Official, were removed from office, ...'for acts of willful disobedience to Church authorities.'" He paused and glowered over his lenses.

Holland had nearly had enough. How much was room and board worth in self-respect? And his inquisitor, cocky as a bantam rooster, demanding answers that were none of his damned business. He'd have to put an end to this nonsense soon.

"I'm merely trying to get to the facts behind the stories!" The monk persisted. "Are they true, these...?" He stopped, took a breath, then said, "Is it true you were "defrocked and excommunicated" as some of the stories report?"

Holland stood up suddenly. He was a good half a foot taller than the other man and outweighed him by sixty pounds.

"I've been thinking about this evaluation... or whatever you'd call it," Holland said — his voice stern and authoritative. "Waste of time for both of us. I'd just as soon head off down the road as stay around here rooting about in garbage." Gripping the back of his chair with both hands he lifted it a few inches then slammed it onto the wood floor emphatically. "And a bright young fellow like yourself must have a whole bunch of important stuff to be getting on with, like chatting with god and what not…"

"Why would you rather run away than look at your life, Mister?"

The monk's question took Holland by surprise — just when he'd put an end to the whole silly business. His fingers had begun to hurt from gripping the chair-back. He shook his head and turned towards the door. Time to leave.

"Why is it that you've never talked about what happened—not to anybody, ever?" After a moment's silence, he added, "Afraid to take a look at your life, are you, Mister Holland?"

Holland's jaw muscles rippled underneath the red, weathered cheek. He paused for just a second with his hand on the doorknob.

"Are you ashamed of what you did back then, *Mister* Holland?"

Had he emphasized the word, "*Mister*" a bit or was that just Holland's imagination? It was uncalled for—below the belt sort of thing — provocative. But, he had often wondered what it would be like, telling the whole story to a psychiatrist; seeing what a trained person would make of it. Was he maybe walking out on the chance to do that?

"If you're willing to tell your story to me, I'll try to be worthy of the confidence."

"Well…" Holland started to say, but the monk interrupted him.

"I *was* scolding and judgmental. I'm out of practice as a therapist. This is not an ideal situation for psychotherapy for either of us."

Without replying immediately, Holland sat back down in the chair, his large shoulders slumped forward once more. He was again staring at the grain of the bare wood planks between his boots. He would have to go off to a safe place in his head and stay there if he were to talk about those things. It was in that instant that he had made up his mind. Yes, he would go through with it no matter how painful.

"I never could get the whole mess straight in my own head," he said. The compulsion to make some sense of what happened had nearly driven him crazy in the years after he'd left Minerva. Yet, here he was breaking his own rule, one he'd made to save his sanity. He was talking to an inquisitive stranger.

"Maybe you'll have better luck, with your training, making sense of it." He could read nothing one way or the other on the man's face.

The monk raised his eyebrows and shrugged.

Friggin' android, Holland grumbled to himself.

CHAPTER 2

Derry, Ireland — 1953

"YOU'RE OUTTA' YOUR friggin' tree, maun!" McGarrity said finally.

We were heading for the Bishop's Walk—it was quiet and we could talk in peace there. The word had just leaked out that I'd been accepted into a seminary and he and I hadn't had a chance to talk all day. I was dreading McGarrity's reaction since I hadn't breathed a word to anybody—not even to him or Murray, my closest friends.

I decided to say nothing. Let him have his say.

"You're fucking coddin' me?" he said. A sidelong glance—to maybe catch me in some leg-pull.

"I am not!" I said.

Silence then for a long bit again.

The oaks that formed a Gothic canopy over the walk were fully leafed already and the gravely dirt was crunchy underfoot and dusty. It was near the end of summer term and we would soon be finished with St. Columb's.

"It's not as bad as it sounds, McGarrity—not if you go to Los Angeles or Florida—some place nice and sunny." I found myself trying to console him he seemed so upset. "People in sunny places need help too," I pleaded.

"Och, shite!" He took a sudden mighty swing then at an imaginary football and followed through like he was taking a penalty for Derry City. The stone he kicked hit the base of an oak and skited away down the grassy slope onto the football pitch.

"I thought at least you were goin' on the real foreign missions, like ta Africa — do somethin' worthwhile, like baptizing them wee pagans babies."

Was he annoyed that I wasn't going to be eaten by cannibals or die a horrible death from malaria or something?

"Och, I could go to Africa if I wanted to, I suppose. But the brochure says they mostly send priests to America and Australia—even England—places they speak English, like…"

"I wouldn't go ta no fuckin' England." He interrupted emphatically before trying the penalty again—this time sending a pebble hard against the corrugated iron gate at the end of the walk. The bang of the iron could be heard echoing off the little brick row-houses, back and forth, down the street outside.

"You might as well stay around this friggin' place in all the rain and shite, as do that." He paused. "I wouldn't mind goin' ta Florida myself though… or maybe Sydney—some fuckin' warm place—some place way palm trees."

We walked on a few more minutes then, out of the blue, he asked.

"It isn't true the fuckers castrate you before they ordain you, is it?"

"Don't be fuckin' ridiculous!" I retorted. I took a swing myself at a penalty kick for emphasis—skiting a stone off the iron railing at the side. "Where d'you hear that shite?"

"Me Uncle Willie told me about it—swore it was the truth, so he did." He pitched a flat stone along the path behind us making it skip along the dust like it was water.

"This wan night he had a few pints too many, he starts ta tell a bunch of us these stories about priests and nuns—fuckin' wild stories they were, too. Make your hair stand on your head, so they would."

He glanced over at me as we were walking along, checking how I was taking it, I suppose. I said nothing but I was clenching my fists so hard that later I could see where the nails had cut white crescent-moons into my palms. He went on with his story.

"Seems, wan time—och a long, long time ago—they were always playing hanky-panky way each other—these priests and nuns, you know. Climbing over the monastery walls and inta the dormitories in the convents and having it off and stuff like that way the nuns. You know what I mean?"

I looked at him to see if he was smiling but his face was dead serious. He glanced over at me again before he continued.

"Well, it seems nobody knew what the fuck ta do way all the wee wanes that were bein' born ta these nuns, you know. D'ye see the problem? In a fuckin' convent, all these wanes runnin' around interruptin' prayers and mass and shite. You know what I mean? It was a quare fuckin' headache for the Pope at the time—can't remember who the fucker was—Leo the something." He looked at me again to see how it was going down, but I was keeping my eyes fixed straight in front of me.

"No matter what the authorities tried ta do these fuckin' priests kept sneaking over the walls and diggin' these secret tunnels and shaggin' the nuns in these convents and the wanes kept coming—there was more wanes than nuns in a lot of the fuckin' convents. They were havin' a horrible fuckin' problem way it, you know. So anyway, this wan Pope—Leo or Julius or something—got in this wild snit at all a' this shaggin' and all the wanes way no daddies and what not. And the cost… Christ! It was costin' a fortune—just feedin' them. Next thing you know, hadn't he issued this law saying that every priest, before he's even ordained, had ta have his whole business cut off."

I said nothing and I was hoping he couldn't sense the ice-cold fingers that had suddenly raced up my spine—all the way to my neck hair. Not that I believed what he was saying for a minute, mind you, but it was the scary way he was saying it—as though he was believing it himself.

"Like that! Ffittt!" He made this cutting swipe with the edge of his hand.

"You're full of shite, McGarrity!"

He leaned over, hands still deep in his trouser pockets, and with his shoulder nudged me hard like the soccer forward he was, sending me staggering nearly into the railing. He grinned at me. We were still friends, is what that meant—him taking the piss out of me, as usual.

"You fuckin' deranged or what?" was Murray's first reaction.

What in the hell could have come over me? It wasn't like me at all, they agreed, going to a seminary. We'd been friends through everything together for six tedious years—they knew me far better than anybody in the world. Why would I decide to become priest, of all things? We were still virgins, through no fault of our own, but we still shared the dream of getting real sex some day. What in the hell was wrong with me?

But I had pressures neither McGarrity nor Murray knew about.

What was driving my decision was not some calling from the deity, as a pious person might assume. No! I had felt no pushing of the spiritual sap that drives young lads towards the religious life — not a nudge. And neither was I that Irish cliché: the child returned to God —ultimate adornment on his mammy's resume.

The priesthood was not nearly grand enough for my mammy. How likely was it you'd see a priest on the cover of *Time*? A Nobel Prize-winning scientist would be far more fitting.

"Ah, sure mustn't his mother have been an atrociously brilliant woman herself!" They'd be saying outside the chapel on a Sunday, after the eight o'clock mass.

My father had expectations of me too and he made no secret of them either: that I get a job, any job—the dole, even — so long as it got me out of the house and supporting myself.

"Afore I was yer age, a'd near finished servin' me time in the grocery trade—earnin' me own keep." He had heard they were hiring unskilled college boys in the local Nestle factory.

"Oh, be quiet!" My mother said as she snapped her sheet of rye crisp in two with a crack as definitive as a gavel. "Let's have no more of this balderdash about milk factories."

"Which is it to be: Queen's or Trinity?" She asked. "Haven't you made up your mind yet? Time is running out, you know."

She might just as well have offered Jupiter or Mars as options, for all the likelihood I'd get into either one. This next term I'd be sitting A Levels and I'd be unmasked then as an academic failure. My mother would be crushed.

"Huh!' My father snorted. He took *The Ulster Herald* and went off to sit in the other room.

"The McGintys, you know, all went to Queen's and took Firsts," my mother continued as soon as he'd gone. "Queen's was very good in my day too. I'd recommend you go there."

The damned McGintys — cousins on my mother's side—excelled in everything: academics, music, Irish dancing and, most of all, in their pious practices. They were the gold standard against which my sister and I were always judged. Funny then that it should be from them that I got the idea of going to seminary. And —talk about the nick of time —the idea had struck me the very day I was going back to school for that final, awful term.

My mother had had a letter that morning from Mrs. McGinty and she, of course, had to read it to us as we were having lunch. After reporting some of the usual McGinty stuff: doctorates and fellowships, recitals, etc., etc., the last page struck an usually wistful note. Not one of her children, she complained, had chosen to enter the religious life—not a nun or priest in the bunch—not even a Christian Brother. That very week, her youngest son, Liam—her last hope for a crown of laurels—had announced his decision to pursue pure mathematics rather than theology.

"Well! Woe is me!" My father exploded in a spiteful snort.

"Aw! The poor creature!" My mother murmured, shaking her head sadly and twisting her mouth—maybe to keep back an indecent smile. She frowned down the table at my father who was smiling a delighted smile. She returned the letter to its envelope.

"Ah. The single thing she wanted the most!" My mother keened. "The one thing that would have made all the rest of it perfect … Ah, sure isn't it very sad," she lamented as she returned the letter to its envelope after reading it for the third time.

Could this be a sign? I was asking myself.

My neck hair bristled from nearness of the Spirit. Pentecost—all but the dove.

"A nod is as good as a wink to a blind horse," my mother was fond of saying and I'd hate to think she had raised a blind horse!

Like the fox that will gnaw his leg off to escape from a trap, my escape strategy suddenly became clear: let them have your penis, jettison the testes—whatever it takes! At seventeen, what did I know? Seminary would take at least six or seven years—practically an eternity. Who could tell how circumstances might change before I should be faced with the really serious stuff: vows of celibacy and obedience and ordination.

All I'd have to do was learn how you avoid "sins of the flesh." There had to be some knack to it or so many wouldn't be doing it—Ireland was crawling with priests and nuns back then — some trick maybe they teach you in seminary. As it was, I was doing well to go more than a whole day—two at the very most. I'd friggin' never get to say mass at that rate.

We heard theories about how priests did it.

"They put saltpeter in their cigarettes," Murray had heard. "That 's why their fingers are always yellow with nicotine—smoking like fuckers, getting enough saltpeter inta them to kill the aul drive." This didn't reassure me a bit. His alternate hypothesis was even less comforting: "They're all fruits—no starch at all in them—like wee cuttics way cocks".

God I hoped that wasn't it or I was in awful trouble.

But, I had made my decision and, dammit, I'd go through with it no matter what.

To my great surprise and relief, less than a month after I applied, I received a letter saying that Holy Trinity College for the Foreign Missions would be delighted to see me on the second week of September. Four months should be time enough to get the hang of holy purity.

My decision had completely disarmed my parents of course. What could my father say to a future man-of-the-cloth?

My mother, being of the, "when life gives you lemons, you make lemonade" school, bragged to Mrs. McGinty and anyone who'd listen about my vocation.

"Wasn't it a far greater honor than any scholarship, a calling from God Himself, no less?"

She'd have given my right eye to have had a university scholarship to brag about.

CHAPTER 3

Holy Trinity Seminary, Ireland — 1953

THE RISING-BELL WAS clanging past our door. Could it be 6:30 already?

"Benedicamus Domino," shouted the bell-ringer.

Oh, Shite! I muttered to nobody in particular.

I had been six weeks in Holy Trinity College for the Foreign Missions already and still could not bring myself to yell, "Thanks be to God," at that hour of the morning. I swung my legs out into the cold of a November morning.

It dawned on me just about then that I had not heard my roommate's usual hearty *"Deo Gratias"* in response to the bell.

George was sitting on the side of his bed, his head bowed and his shoulders heaving from the deep sobs he was doing his best to stifle. I was jarred awake *instanter* — as they apparently said in ancient Rome — when I noticed the pajama bottoms crumpled on the floor around his ankles. And when I saw the blue hand-towel he had clutched in his lap, I sensed instantly what had happened.

Oh, Fuck! I prayed. Only the day before George had asked me about impure temptations, whether I'd been troubled by them since we'd been in Holy Trinity. I had happily reported the amazing fact that since September I hadn't felt so much as a flinch — not a flicker of the old libido. A gift, a veritable miracle! George, it seemed, had not been given the same gift.

"I came this close the other night," he said, holding thumb and forefinger a millimeter apart.

I had recommended the usual Catholic cure for such things: trust in God, three Hail Marys for holy purity and think about your mother and sister. That was yesterday afternoon. My remedy hadn't been enough — obviously.

I had to get out of there. I grabbed my toiletry bag and headed down along the chilly corridor to the showers and made washing-up last as long as possible. When I

10

finally returned to the room, George was standing at his washbasin shaving. Thank God for small mercies! He'd put his pants on.

I would have been content pretending that nothing out of the ordinary had happened earlier, that I had not seen what I had seen, and that he had not done what he had presumably done. But George was not the type to let something like that go. In the past six weeks I'd learned this much about him, he talked about everything — talked it to death.

"Dammit, Holland! Didn't I tell you it was going to happen? Didn't I? Didn't I, boy?" He turned around and faced me, accusingly.

"And it did, by God!" He turned back and leaned on the basin again, his head bowed deep over it—for a second it looked as though he might try drowning himself in it. He straightened up then and glared hatefully into the mirror. "You went and did it, so you did!"

Suddenly he turned towards me and reaching out, gripped both my shoulders, his fingers digging painfully into my muscles. I tried not to flinch as he stared pitifully into my face, his eyes brimming with tears.

"Tell me honestly," he asked. "Is this God's way of telling me to leave this place?"

"I don't think that's what it means at all." I lied. I realized that I'd been practicing spiritual medicine without a license. "What you need to do is go up after breakfast and have a talk with one of the Spiritual Directors." That gave him something to think about and I escaped while he was considering it.

I was relieved to see George take his place directly across the center aisle from me in chapel. You couldn't tell to look at him what he'd been through — except that he didn't go up to receive communion with the rest of us. How embarrassing, such a public confession of sinfulness. Interesting though — in a mathematical sense. Though George had already earned eternal damnation by the mortal sin of masturbation, he was suffering public humiliation rather than commit another mortal sin by receiving communion. I had always understood eternity to resemble zero and infinity, concepts that didn't admit of multiples, how then does one compute "eternity times two?" Must bring it up in Ethics someday. I had always followed the principle, that I might as well be hung for a sheep as a lamb. Perhaps I was missing something intrinsic to the spiritual life.

After lunch that day George took me by the arm and led me aside.

"I'm sorry about that business this morning, boy."

I mumbled that he wasn't to think anymore about it. What's the etiquette in situations like that anyway? Did you ask: "Was it good for you?" Or, maybe something more religious: "Hope it was at least worth the black mark on your immortal soul!"

Instead I asked, "How are you feeling now?" It was a dead safe question for he was looking like the cat that had just scarfed the canary.

"I had a talk with the Spiritual Director," he said. He couldn't stop grinning he was so pleased with himself.

"Great!" I vamped.

"Told me to put the whole thing right out of my mind, boy." George batted an imaginary pest right out of the air in front of his face. "God often tests our vocations, he told me, to see if they're the real article."

I nodded—not because I agreed but because I was thinking what a great line of twaddle this priest had. I made a mental note for use in my future ministry.

"There was this saint, it seems," he continued, very animated, jumpy with excitement about whatever cock-and-bull story the priest had told him.

"I don't remember the saint's name, but he was this wonderful priest—all the time giving alms to the poor and the lepers and a bunch of other misfortunates like that—and what do you think?" George grabbed a handful of material in the front of my cassock in his enthusiasm.

I didn't want to draw attention from the entire student body milling about a few feet away, so I batted his hand down. He hardly noticed anyway.

"And... wasn't this saint afflicted with the exact same temptation as myself, boy."

What could I say? A saint that whacked off regularly? "Fabulous!" And, did it matter if the story was true or not, the result was remarkable.

"Gave me absolution right there and then," he gushed. "I'm telling you boy, I feel like a new man."

He certainly looked reborn. It hardly even seemed decent, to recover so fast from eternal damnation. But, it got me thinking. Was George's elation the result, maybe, of a refreshing interlude after such a stretch of celibacy. And, how would it sit if I were I to treat myself to some of the same — a reward for being so good? Some day, say, when I had a doctor's appointment in Dublin. I could go to confession up there — not bother any of the seminary priests with the tawdry details — then I could resume my virtuous way of life and who'd be the wiser? I banished the thought almost right away.

George went along swimmingly for a few weeks after this, the picture of spiritual health, so when once again he hadn't hopped out of bed yelling *"Deo Gratias,"* I just assumed he'd received permission for a lie-in. I left for chapel and hardly gave him a thought till I was in the refectory and saw that he still hadn't come down. That had me worried. Could he have decided to pack it in—leave the place and tell no one? Could he be ill? As the students were filing into their places, I dashed up the center stairs and, with the most perfunctory of knocks, burst into the room.

George had not left. He was sitting on the edge of his bed, hunched over and staring intently at something in his lap. A blue hand towel lay on the floor by his feet.

Oh, shite! He's been at it again and I've walked in on him. But… out of the corner of my eye, as I was about to close the door, I noticed that there was blood on the towel. I hesitated.

"Sorry!" I mumbled.

At that moment, George jumped to his feet and dramatically whipped away another towel that had been covering his crotch.

"There!" He exclaimed triumphantly. "That will fix it for good! Won't it, boy? That'll take care of everything!"

The blood rushed from my head. Suddenly dizzy, my forehead clammy-cold, I grabbed the door jam to steady myself. I needed to sit down. I didn't dare look at him and that bloody, wounded thing again.

Just then I felt a large hand grip my shoulder. Oh, God! The damned senior Dean, of all people. I spluttered something apologetic.

"Mister Holland, what…?" His glare was withering but his eye must at that moment have caught sight of George, for he stopped in mid-outburst.

George, having sewn the ends of his uncircumcised foreskin securely closed, was tidying up excess thread, seemingly unaware of the Dean's presence.

I should have fled then but I was rooted to the floorboards.

The Dean had recovered his composure very quickly. You'd have thought they'd been holding regular faculty drills for such occasions: *Procedures for Management of Self-Mutilating Students.*

Rule One: — Limit the number of eyewitnesses.

He grabbed my arm, pulled me urgently into the room and closed the door.

Rule Two: —Don't expect to gain useful information by interrogating the deranged.

He never so much as glanced at George after that first stare; nor did he address him —not even to ask, "What in hell did you think you were doing, sewing that thing up?"

But for me, he had instructions.

"Mister! You're to get this man into some clothes right away—a cassock at least—and then take him to the infirmary. Use the back stairs and be quick about it. Do it while everybody is still at breakfast."

"Yes, Father."

"I'll have the doctor in as soon as possible and…" He wagged a finger right at my nose. "And Mister, not a word of this to anyone—now or ever. Do we have that clear, Mister Holland?"

He transfixed me for a long second with his infamous death-ray and I stared mesmerized at the white strings of spittle that stretched and contracted between his lips. I came out of the trance.

"Yes, Father. Not a word." It was very clear.

Another warning finger to keep me in line, then, without so much as a second glance at George, he swept from the room, his cassock creating dust eddies.

I closed the door behind him and, standing with my back pressed against it, I breathed deeply for a moment to exhale the tension that was threatening to paralyze me. I needed a smoke. I needed to get a thousand miles away from this loony bin.

George had remained standing by his bedside all through the Dean's visit, apparently oblivious to all the excitement he had created. His face had taken on a sort of radiance and a gentle smile was teasing the long dimples that framed his mouth. His eyes seemed focused on some distant place; a place, perhaps, from which the martyrs and mystics of the Church were smiling back at him.

I ought to get the fucking Spiritual Director over—have him clean up this spiritual mess. Doesn't he guarantee his work?

You'd better get going, I cautioned myself, or they'll be flocking out of the refectory just as you get him to the foot of the stairs.

Fuck them all! I never signed on for this shite. I should walk down the stairs myself and out the front gate, and keep on walking to England or California; get to someplace where people are saner. But I can't leave this poor bastard standing here — and him out of his mind.

"Last night God revealed what he wanted from me, Jack." George's voice was coming from some remote place, eerily calm and monotonous. But he was addressing me by name at least.

"Yes, George, I understand." Keep him calm, humor him.

"After I did that sinful act again last night, God showed me what he wanted me to do." He lifted his penis up and held it out in my direction. I focused on getting his clothes from the wardrobe.

He joined his hands together in a prayer-like gesture and then spread them out as in a blessing. "Isn't our God a good God, Jack?"

I agreed that his god was a fabulous god. I was trying to find some pants he might wear, the baggier the better, some drawers too.

I had a job to do and counseling George was not part of my assignment, but shouldn't I ask him whether he had maybe misunderstood some part of his god's instructions? George was actually quite a slow learner and in the six weeks we'd roomed together hardly a day had passed but he'd got some philosophical concept completely back-to-front. And George's Latin was so bad… if his god had spoken to him in Latin…

Another look, though, at the ecstatic glow on his face and I decided to forget questioning—it was far too late to appeal to reason. Get him moving before they're out of the refectory.

He had repelled my first effort at stuffing one of his legs into the drawers—reared back highly indignant and in a scathing voice demanded, "Are you ashamed to look upon what God hath wrought in me?"

"Right then!" I agreed. I would install lower garments later. I set aside the drawers. "You're right. A cassock would be far more appropriate." I suggested. "The very symbol of your dedication to God."

That worked better. I helped him button it up. It was encouraging having him so well covered but still, shouldn't we try for at least one undergarment out of modesty— there was usually a fierce wind whipping through those downstairs corridors.

"Now that I'm dressed, Jack." Suddenly he was speaking in a firm and resolute voice. "Let us go down quickly and join the rest of the house at breakfast."

Christ! I had to distract him quickly, had to capture the attention of what was left of his mind. But I could think of nothing that would keep him from going out the door. It is in that second which precedes imminent foundering they say a man's mettle is tested. It was in that moment of desperation that the god—or something like it—set my synapses crackling with creativity.

"You know of course the famous story of St. Elutherius?" I asked, trying to keep my tone conversational. I was lifting his foot up, trying again to install a pair of drawers and holding on to him to keep him in the room. He acted as though he hadn't even heard me. He was accepting the drawers though—he put the first leg into the hole.

"Reminds me a lot of the Elutherius story." I gave the saint another shot.

"Who? Who was he—this Elu... that you're going on and on about?" He sounded cranky but I'd got his attention at least and he was allowing me to lift the second foot into the drawers.

'Elutherius." I repeated. "Hundreds of years ago the famous St. Elutherius did the same thing exactly with his penis." Both feet in. There, we go!

"He did, really?"

"Absolutely! Exactly the same thing." I wasn't feeling bad at all about lying—it was for his own good.

"St. Elutherius, Pray for us!" He intoned as I helped him pull his drawers up. "Tell me more about St. Elutherius."

I was crouching at his feet trying to pull on a sock over toes splayed out and resisting. The name Elutherius was from a pamphlet I'd taken off a rack in Notre Dame Cathedral. I let my imagination have its head as I described a conversation on the subject of impure thoughts and acts of masturbation between Elutherius and St. Denis, the Bishop of Paris. The saint's repeated failure to control sins of the flesh and the resultant spiritual torment were not something I felt I could rush through. The story got George into the baggiest pants I could lay my hands on. Elutherius's foreskin stitching —strikingly similar, down to the use of medieval button thread— I described in detail as I was nudging him through the door and along the corridor.

"St Elutherius, pray for us!" George had taken to intoning this with every step. I was daring to hope the saint might get us the rest of the way safely.

"What did Elutherius do after?" George stopped walking and looked at me inquiringly. I tried desperately to think of something vivid, something lurid that would grab his attention.

"Jack!" He shook my arm urgently, as though he was afraid I had maybe lost *my* mind. "What happened to Saint Elutherius after that?"

I needed more material and fast. Think of Paris, I ordered my mind. Paris? Pigalle, Montmartre, naked dancers, Moulin Rouge... Ah, Paris! I was getting a picture.

"Picture this." I invited. "It's a sweltering-hot, August day about a year after the stitching..." I was tempted to add for authenticity that nobody was in Paris that day but the tourists, but thought better of it. George knew nothing about Paris anyway. But, my change of tone had got him moving again.

"Elutherius and Denis are walking down a steep, cobbled street and Elutherius is carrying St. Denis' severed head. Denis has just been executed on Montmartre — yet, miraculously, he's walking alongside Elutherius..."

"Carrying his head from Montmartre to where?" George interrupted — unimpressed, it seemed, by the miracle.

"To be entombed where the town of St. Denis is today, George."

"St Elutherius and St. Denis pray for us!"

By the time we had arrived in the lower corridors I had just about run out of interesting things for Elutherius to have done. I was in a ruthless mood and would have resorted to anything. I had even toyed with having him invent the croissant.

I cannot describe the relief I felt when we reached the infirmary and found Matron and the Dean awaiting our arrival. As I ushered George through the door and into their care I was barely holding myself together. I needed to get away from this place; I needed to scream my lungs out in a sulfurous scream. I was having trouble breathing for the great dark rage that was boiling inside me.

I fled the infirmary and raced to a remote corner of the upper fields. There, hidden from the walkways, I threw myself face down in the grass.

"Fuck your crazy superstitions that have driven this poor simpleton out of his fucking mind!" I lay there paralyzed and exhausted for I don't know how long. The bell rang for first lecture.

"Fuck your lectures!" I roared at the sky and the rage came tearing up from its primal pit again and I shouted it into the grass and the damp brown soil. I screamed and roared till I lost my voice and my mouth was green from the juice of grass — like it was the Famine. There wasn't a starling left on a telephone wire for miles around from my screeching. Schoolboys passing on the main road heard my screaming and started pelting stones over the hedges at me — as at a mad dog. I felt madder by far than George with his quiet deluded piety. I was mad with a great rage that would rip to pieces a god I didn't even believe in—yet hated passionately.

"You're out of your fucking minds!" I shouted back at the college.

The last I saw of George was when he turned to me in the infirmary and, taking both my hands in his, asked that I pray to St. Elutherius for him.

His family came over to Holy Trinity later that day and took him home.

CHAPTER 4

Big Sur, California, — 2004

ALL NIGHT THE wind-borne sheets of rain had howled in from the Pacific, Furies clawing at the windows screens. There was no sleeping on a night like this, not with the sea-god throwing the ocean itself at him—no point even trying. And in the past half-hour he had unleashed thunder and lightening bolts as well. It was enough to bring any sinner to his knees.

Come on you bastard! I dare you, Holland muttered

This monastery was situated on the mesa, high above the coast road that runs through Big Sur. And Holland's room, sitting as it did at the western edge of the monastery grounds, was buffeted more than any other by the full fresh force of the many storms that charged ashore between November and March.

He had been awake, tossing from side to side, ever since midnight when the storm had first come ashore. The older he grew the more bothered he was by these tantrums of what some called Nature. As a young man he'd been strong and fearless; had welcomed storms; loved defying them; enjoyed listening as they howled their frustration. He would snuggle down then, warm beneath an eider-down and send his imagination off to the snowy Russia of palaces and sleighs, of Anna Karenina and The Brothers Karamazov. But now—now he had grown old and weak—high winds frightened him and the rage of the gods set his stomach quivering. A tethered goat, awaiting the footfall of the cat.

He felt his way around the metal table in the center of the kitchen floor to the bank of great commercial refrigerators humming contentedly in that large still space. He took a bottle of Heineken from one of them. He lighted the first of the fifty or so Marlboro's he would smoke that day.

Out of the east-facing windows the faint outline of the monastery build-ings was dimly visible through the sheets of driven rain that swept the center quadrangle. A few of the monks had turned their lights on—nervous old men like himself. Pathetic, the lot of them! Sitting out their lives on this bleak mountaintop searching for the god.

"Haven't you heard: he's skipped, left no forwarding address—paring his fingernails in another universe." He shouted at them. He shrugged and took another pull on the cigarette. Shouting at the night like a madman.

They hadn't come of age in that bitter, godforsaken island, these monks, so how would they know the kind of god they're dealing with? Yanks and their sentimental daddy-god. Good for quieting peevish children. Swift was right, that pagan island bred either universal disrespect or paralyzing piety—nothing in between.

He took a long draft of the beer—the blood was starting to circulate at last. He'd have to start looking around for a job and a room in the next week or so.

Thoughts of his session with the psychiatrist-monk flitted about in his head. He tried relegating them to that holding tank where he quarantined unpleasant realities. But the tank was leaking badly.

It was the Prior, he was the real problem — damned bully. Though only second in command in the monastery, he had the old Abbot wrapped around his finger.

"This reprobate will be a source of scandal for the younger monks," the Prior had told the Abbot, right there in front of him that first day.

And the Abbot, sentimental old Rhinelander, had his own agenda: he was determined to save Holland's soul from eternal damnation and reinstate him in the priesthood.

"I haff good friends, Jack, in high places in Rome, you know," he'd say and wag a kindly finger at him.

Rome would rather legalize abortions than have Jack Holland within a hundred miles of a pulpit.

Though he was more or less paying for his keep by baking for them, it smelled far too much like running home out of fear—home to mammy. He was horribly embarrassed when he thought about it. He, who'd been so defiant, so adamant, that no matter what befell him: sickness or poverty—on his deathbed, even—he would never crawl back to her tit. And here he was, snuggling up and sucking like a bastard.

It was getting on towards five o'clock. He drained the last dregs of the beer, near time to move if he was to bake anything for their breakfast. He measured a few heaping tablespoons of fine-ground Sumatra into the coffeemaker and while it was dripping he went into his room and washed his face and hands.

Lavabo inter innocentes manus meas... The face in the little stained mirror pulled a grimace at him. 'Innocent my ass!'

From one of the refrigerators he pulled the tray of croissant dough that he had prepared the previous afternoon and upended it with a slap onto the table.

"The three men I admire the most... they've caught the last train to the Coast..." He hummed as he worked.

Baking, by which he had supported himself through the years, he'd learned from a kindly Swede during the three years he lived anonymously in San Francisco after his disgrace. Bo was not much of anything when it came to religion, but he'd kept Holland's secret — though he'd admit after a drink that he loved having a defrocked priest working his ass off at a baker's bench.

An hour later the oven and the croissants were ready for each other. As he set up the percolators for the monks' coffee and tea in the refectory, dawn was breaking faintly over the monastery roof. It was a gloomy, watery dawn with the sky still full of storm clouds. But the heavy rain had let up.

When he was satisfied that the monks seated around the long tables had all they needed, he went into his bedroom, pulled on his swim trunks and exchanged his apron for a plaid shirt.

In the carport his ancient pickup was cleaner than usual after the pelting it had taken from the sidewise-blown rain. With a shoulder to the doorframe he pushed the truck across the gravely yard to where the narrow unpaved lane plunged abruptly off the western face of the mesa. He ran alongside as the little truck gathered momentum and timed his leap aboard to the last possible second — saving the battery, his father had called it. He got the gearbox to accept third gear then let out the clutch. As the wheels bounced over the ruts, gravel loosened by the rains flew up and attacked the undercarriage in a deafening barrage. At the coast highway, Holland let a solitary early-morning car go by on its way to Monterey before turning south.

A beautiful, lonely stretch of road this that squeezed its narrow shoulders between the sheer rock face of the mesa on his left and the cliff's edge on his right—a breath-taking hundred foot drop to the ocean-pounded rocks.

After his nightlong assault the storm-god was catching his breath—the rain had stopped completely. Holland rolled the window down as he drove and inhaled the freshness of the juicy ocean air. He'd never liked that skinny-assed desert air in Minerva—scorched and wizened like a raisin by the baking valley heat.

The storm and its promise of rowdy seas had enticed a good scattering of surfers from the warmth of their beds and into clammy wet suits. He could see them off to his right as he drove, bobbing out in the breaks, sleek and black like sea otters.

He continued south about a mile beneath the steep brown cliffs, vibrant with yellow broom and the electric blue of ceanothus, before pulling in alongside a low stonewall that separated the beach from the highway.

Throwing his clothes on the driest part of the seat, he stepped onto the stonewall where he paused for a moment each morning to stiffen his resolve. He dropped then gently onto the grainy sand below—no heroics!

He broke into a stiff-kneed trot and let the momentum of it carry him into the water where the force of his will propelled him through the first cold shock. Scrotum-wilting! Fuck! It helped to curse it at the top of his lungs—helped keep his mind off the arctic cold numbing his legs. He pulled on his goggles and settled the eyepieces firmly to his eyes as he went. Fuck!

Sunny fucking California? Silly bugger! Any sense, you'd get a wet suit. Swear to Christ, it's colder than Bundoran! Fuck!

He strode high-kneed through the shallows out to where the water became intolerable as it crept icily up his flanks. There he finally plunged in and charged straight out through the breakers.

Take your breath away, the cold, the shock of it. Christ! And the sand all stirred up too this morning from the storm, getting in your mouth. The shortest way past the high towering breakers was head-on. Plunge into each of the fuckers as they came at you, hold your breath till you come out the other side, do it again and again till you'd finally got past the last of them—out into the swells. The worst part of the swim was getting out there.

Cuss enough and you'll get through it. Come on ye fuckers! He managed to shout before another wall of ocean collapsed on him. Grab a breath, quick!

Finally he'd made it through to where the deep swells were running, then caught his breath briefly before turning right and swimming parallel to the coast.

There was sand in the water even out here. It would float up unexpectedly in slow-moving, billowy clouds—a gritty bloom.

His body was becoming looser and his mind was free to drift off into the meditative trance that was a bonus of open-water swimming. He settled into the loose, efficient stroke he could hold for hours.

Yesterday, right after his swim, he got the call he'd been expecting.

"Father Prior wants to see you in his office right away."

Ominous, by the tone of it! He's got his way with the Abbot, was Holland's first assumption. I'm out on my ass this afternoon and it still winter.

But it hadn't been the expected kick-out, after all—well, not directly.

If Holland were to seek acceptance into the monastic community as a lay brother, the Prior told him, he could keep his room and continue baking for them pending an evaluation of his fitness.

A frigging lay brother? Holland almost exclaimed aloud. But he bit his tongue.

The sensible part of his mind went into survival mode: buy time, time to think, to plan, to create options.

"What do I have to do?" He hated himself for even asking, but if it would buy him time, a week—two weeks, maybe —time enough to get something lined up on the outside. But two weeks, at most.

"Father James will contact you," the Prior said. "He was a psychiatrist in New York before he renounced the world and he has agreed to assess your fitness as a candidate."

"Will this man be reporting what he and I talk about to you or anybody?" He'd asked.

The Prior had reacted with surprise as though he hadn't even considered the question.

"Oh, no. No, I don't expect so. Merely his conclusions." He'd frowned then and closed his eyes briefly —as though bored by the whole business.

Had he waved his hand in dismissal? Holland couldn't tell. The baldhead was already bent over a sheaf of papers on the desk. Holland was just closing the door when a voice from under the head said,

"You may continue using the apartment till this is resolved." He never so much as glanced up as he said it.

Holland didn't remember walking down the stairs nor crossing the quadrangle to the kitchen. Back in his room—*their* room — more depressed than he'd been in years, he was angry at himself too.

Fool! Ejit!! Giving some tight-assed priest the power to do this to you. He fumed at the mirror over the washbasin.

He'd gone into the storeroom then and for half an hour had beaten the stuffing out of a hundred weight sack of flour. That had helped some.

The rage that had been reawakened yesterday had very little to do with the little Prior and Holland knew it. The Prior hadn't been born when Holland had first experienced the soul-racking pain of living under a man's cruel control—powerless to fight back or even escape. If he'd been a drinker this would be the perfect excuse for a wild and raucous drunk.

Maybe talking to a shrink wouldn't be the worst thing he could do.

He'd gone outside then—over to the edge of the mesa and had sat on the wall there, gazing out over the ocean. It had helped, swinging his legs over the edge of the world.

The Prior wasted no time setting things up. Less than an hour later, a lay-monk had showed up at the kitchen with another message:

"Father James will see you at two this afternoon in room 204."

He could see the low stonewall where he had parked just ahead. More and more often recently he had swum up to his landmark and back without remembering making the turn. He headed in towards the shore, gratefully letting the waves carry him in to the shallows.

Best time of day, this: relaxed, tired from his swim strolling up the beach to the truck. He felt younger then than at any other time of the day; his hips loose and his shoulders free of pain. He got his clothes out of the truck.

It would be death, knowing the sea was here so close and being locked away up there a lay brother. He felt more at home in the ocean than anywhere these days.

It's too far from sea we've come —fish out of water, he often thought.

He finished dressing and got into the truck. Complications are all we've brought to the party since that first pair slithered up on the beach—Adam and Eve, or whoever—and started breeding and breathing in this sharp gas.

I wonder how long it was after they learned to breathe that they'd invented religion.

Those Indian medicine men, now there was a religion a man could get excited about. Give your parishioners an out-of-body sacrament every week. You'd have to limit church attendance to once a week.

"God's really present in the sacrament, no doubt about it, Father! Seen him myself, so I did!"

"I know, my child. That's the power of god acting through the sacrament, so it is."

"Father, I always feel so wonderful after communion!"

Holland shivered suddenly. The morning chill was seeping back into his body— and he was ravenous.

Back in the kitchen he cut a heel of fresh-baked bread and ate it standing by the window. A family of quail was pecking away over by the chapel while the cock, perched on the edge of the fountain, was keeping watch over them. He had drawn himself up to his full height—a force to be reckoned with, that rooster. Holland had watched in terror a couple of days before as a harrier had carried off one of the cock-quail from the same fountain. He was scared for the little family but they had started back pecking almost right away.

A great blessing that, not having memory—peck away as though the lost one had never existed. Better than religion, having no memory.

Two of his mother's sisters had died and there'd been no mourning time for them either —not even let home from boarding school. "Your exams are coming up," the Strabane nuns had said. No time for mourning —like quail — carry on with what you're doing. But it would come later, the mourning.

Holland sat down at his little typewriter.

"Tell me about your life," the monk had said.

He wouldn't mind vulgarity in the writing, he said. "Just write it as you would say it — so I get a sense of you," he'd told Holland.

He tried to imagine this American psychiatrist, trying to make sense of this tangle of shredded memories, this marmalade of a life.

CHAPTER 5

Dublin, Ireland — 1954

MICK PULLED THE Morris Minor to the curb in front of a curious building, the lonely survivor of what had been an elegant residential square before urban blight and the wrecker had leveled everything else that had once stood around the central green.

Doohan's, it said on the wooden panel that ran along the top of the large front window—a public house of some sort and an old one at that, to judge by the crazy tilt of the walls and windows. It was a miracle the place hadn't fallen over in a heap of rubble with every wall so far out of plumb.

I looked at Mick skeptically. Neither of us had spoken a word for ten minutes, at least. I was sulking—in retaliation for the wild-goose-chase he had taken me on—and Mick, I suspect, had become fed up asking me to be patient.

He nodded his head sideways in the direction of the doorway. I read the claim painted on the lintel in fake-Irish lettering: *"Dean Swift's Favorite Alehouse."*

"Tourist shite!" I grumbled. "Who else'd give a frig where the bastard drank?"

This was no way to spend Saint Patrick's Day—the only day in spring term they let us out from behind the walls.

"I was wondering when we might get around to having breakfast," I asked. I was not to be distracted from breakfast by some stupid, *"Tour of Literary Sites,"* or whatever the frig he thought he was conducting. All I had thought about on the ride up from Holy Trinity was getting one of the legendary mixed-grills they did in The Castle Hotel. So why were we all the way over on the wrong side of the Liffey, gawking at some friggin' wreck of a pub?

"So...?" I inquired.

"Oi just want ye ta meet some of ta bois first. Ah sure, just a minit s'all it'll take— den off to ta Castle—loike rabbits." He opened the car door.

He was deep into his "Jublin Jackeen" act, trying for all he was worth to humor me but I was determined not to be humored.

"Five minutes, then—at the outside!" I grumbled, as I got out of the car. But I was talking to the wind—Mick was already half-way to the door, paying no attention.

I ducked through a low doorway over a brass threshold that had been worn down to a sliver by generations of drinkers—though I seriously doubt the Dean had ever been among them. The tavern—it was too ancient and low-beamed a place to be called a bar—was a long, narrow, low-ceilinged room, dimly lit from the dingy front window and by a few ancient wall-sconces. An enormously long mahogany bar ran the length of the room; what was at the rear I could not make out for the blue fog of cigarette smoke that hung in the air. About twenty sports were propped against the mahogany bar gassing over pints of stout and cigarettes. Regulars, I supposed, by the ease with which they leaned hip-shot against the rail, and "well on their way," as the Irish say—though it was still the forenoon. Could it be some sort of rule that they must all dress in the same costume: tweed sports coat and gabardine trousers? Or was it merely from lack of imagination? In my black pants and the Fairisle jumper Mick had loaned me, I was as conspicuous as a whore in a convent.

He was still trying to soften me up; wanted to buy me a drink but I declined, on the grounds that I hadn't eaten breakfast; he introduced me to his friends but I barely acknowledged their nods and waves. I would not be amused. If I had been cranky before, I was crankier now—so totally out of my element. Perhaps Swift had been in this place, after all. Could it have been this tavern that had given him the notion of Gulliver, the alien? Mick had moved further down the bar where several men were huddled over the horse-racing section of the *Irish Press*.

Suffocating in resentment is not a pleasant way to spend a holiday so, after a few more minutes sulking, I had begun to feel more disgusted with myself than with Mick.

Grow up, I scolded myself. Do something—anything. Maybe an alcoholic drink would help.

I told the bartender I'd changed my mind. I would, after all, try a pint of his stout. I had tasted a bottle of Guinness once and it was about the foulest thing I had ever put into my mouth—ahead of even castor oil. But, at least the alcohol might relax me—the arches of my feet were cramping. As the barman pulled the pint it looked appetizing—the rich, creamy topping, the syrupy, puce-black liquid… surely something that looked so good couldn't taste too bad. Maybe in Dublin—around the corner from the brewery—it would be fresher, tastier than up in the North. I lifted the glass and drank a mouthful on sheer faith.

I had not been mistaken the first time—monstrous swill! I shivered as I forced myself to swallow. Disgusting! How could these men spend hours, even days, lapping up this horrible stuff? I lighted a cigarette to kill the taste. I prayed for the nerve to order an orange crush.

Mick whispered to me that he'd be right back. "Have to see a man about a dog." Before I could object, he was half way down the bar, heading towards the rear of the tavern.

That was Mick. Why had I expected him to behave differently? He had started with our class the previous September in Holy Trinity after ten years on the road selling Scotch whisky. He had decided on an impulse to enter the seminary. Something he'd mistaken for a vocation, had come over him one Saturday evening after he'd confessed a "bigger than usual load of mortal sins."

"Oi tink Oi was weak still, after shaggin' all night the night before, and when tat priest yelled at me, didn't oi tink it was Jazus himself was callin' me."

We had been friends from the first day and he had talked to me often about his old life and his old friends, the other salesmen and his many lady friends and how he missed them. Then one day shortly before the Christmas vacation, without a word to me or anyone else, he had walked out the gate, caught the Dublin bus and was back selling Scotch within forty eight hours of his last Scholastic Philosophy lecture. But, he'd kept in touch with me—in that he was reliable—and had visited me most Sundays, bringing a pack of Afton Major and sometimes a box of Black Magic. And it had been his idea, spending this Saint Patrick's Day together. The company had let him hold on to the car over the holiday.

"Might be nice, takin' her for an aul spin down through Wicklow," he'd said.

"Aye, after we've had one of those mixed-grills at The Castle," I had stipulated.

So how in hell had I wound up wasting the best part of the day in a hole like this? I was making wet rings on the bar with the stout glass and my precious hours of freedom were racing towards seven o'clock check-in. I'd had it with Mick and his friends and his whims.

I ought to leave, go to the Castle by myself; cut my losses. I could call a taxi—leave him here with his drunken friends. It would be the price of him, to come back and find me gone.

I was jarred out of my bitter rumination by the bartender.

"That Mick's a howl, now, isn't he?" He remarked as he gave the bar under my glass a long wipe with his dishcloth. I looked up from contemplating the black depths of my lukewarm stout, suspicious. Is he laughing at my predicament? Am I so ridiculously out of place?

But he gave me a slow, conspiratorial wink then—enough to convince me he was on my side; that at least one other earth person was at the Hatter's tea party. I could ask him to phone for the taxi. He'd understand my need to escape. But, before I could ask him anything, he tapped me on the wrist and raised his eyes piously to the low ceiling, just inches above his head.

"He says you're to go on up there now." He inclined his head towards the rear of the room and winked again. "The Mick boyo." He added by way of clarification.

What could I say? I hadn't the faintest notion what he was talking about but, happy to take any out, I winked back and scurried along behind the confederacy of drinkers at the bar toward the dark, slat-lined passageway that led off towards the back of the building. Twenty feet or so along this corridor a heavy maroon curtain hanging from large brass rings divided what lay on the other side from the bar. Behind the greasy curtain were two doors: the one straight ahead I assumed led out to the tavern yard, for a sign pointing that way to the toilets—a euphemism for a slate-clad outer wall running into a drain. The door on the left opened onto a steep staircase leading up and around a narrow stairwell. The pale blue, forget-me-not paper that covered the walls, though faded and smudged by generations of hands, gave off an unexpected feeling of domesticity. And the beam of dust-flecked daylight that streamed in from the tall narrow window to my right was almost dazzling after the dim-lit tavern. The stairs, covered in a thin brown linoleum with a Grecian border, creaked loudly as I tiptoed up.

On the landing straight ahead a door stood slightly ajar. I called out "Hello!" but no one answered so I pushed the door open and hesitantly entered what was obviously the parlor of someone's home. An upright piano stood against the wall to my left and a pair of fat armchairs—crochet antimacassars pinned on the backs and arms—squatted on either side of an iron fireplace that was directly opposite the door. Centered between the two narrow windows to my right was a small, spiral-legged oval table on which stood a pewter vase with the dried flowers we called "grandma's spectacles." An old-fashioned, oval-framed photograph of a thin, stern woman, all in black, hair in a severe bun, hung over the mantelpiece—a ferocious household goddess.

On the piano's music stand was the same Czerny Tutor that had me cringing every Friday when I was eight—it was open at page thirty six: *A Highland Lass My Love Was Born*. My knuckles hurt from the memory. The dread spinster in her creamy white room with the shiny grand piano—

"Slippers only, no shoes on my carpet. Finger change. Up! Up! Wrists up, wrists up!" Crack. "Stupid, Boy! All thumbs! Staccato! From the wrists, from the wrists—not the forearms!" Crack.

A door opened out on the landing and I hurriedly backed out of the parlor, guiltily—nosing about in somebody else's house was not nice. A woman stuck her head out, around the partially opened door.

"You Mick's friend, sweetie?"

I could only nod for my mouth was suddenly parched. She didn't have to draw me pictures. I had already sensed what this was about—though I hadn't dared let myself admit it.

"Come on in then," she said. She opened the door and made a come-on-in gesture. Was she a bit impatient with me already?

"Come on, now!" She urged, sounding more inviting this time. She was wearing a full-length, pink, satiny robe that was tied at the waist by a belt of the same material and on her feet she wore fuzzy bedroom slippers also pink—a lot of pink.

Oh God! What have I got myself into?

I fled then to the cave in my head again; to that refuge from which I could watch and control a fearful world. My perception shifted into its customary slow-motion mode. Did reality actually slow down at these times or was it, rather, that my thought process sped up? I should bring the question up in Epistemology.

Going into that room with this woman would definitely be a sin, my conscience —or the remnant of it not yet suffocated by desire and curiosity — was harping. Unlike those paltry touchings and delectations that I had let myself out of before, no amount of reasoning could let me off on this count, it screamed. This was going to be a grave sin—the gravest.

Or was there, maybe, another way of looking at the matter, a more enlightened way, suggested a convincing voice I hadn't heard in some time? Doesn't a blameless intention count for anything, Your Lordship—towards amelioration of the punishment at least? All the accused had been planning was to eat a delicious mixed grill and top it off with a helping of the sherry trifle for which the Castle Hotel was famous —gluttony, at worst, My Lord. After all, coming here had not been his idea at all. The fault was Mick's entirely. How was a foolish boy like this supposed to know what trap Mick had set? And, doesn't the fact that he's so obviously scared to death of the woman count for something? Any reasonable person would agree that he was hardly in full possession of his mind at the moment.

We had learned in first term Scholastic Ethics that moral guilt attaches only to what they called an *actus humanus*: an act performed with adequate knowledge and free will. It had all seemed so clear sitting in a classroom following along as Professor Kane was explaining Aquinas' reasoning. How had it become suddenly so muddled in my head? Equidistant between two forms of the *bonum* — the good of my soul and the good of my senses — like Buridan's ass I was paralyzed.

And what about the poor woman? The soothing voice suggested. This was, after all, her livelihood and time was money in any business. Shouldn't I just go ahead and commit the sin. And anyway, it wasn't every day that an opportunity like this presented itself to a body, particularly to a seminarian. I could always deal with the moral stuff later. The woman was becoming impatient I sensed—I'd better get on with it, quit dithering. Aquinas must have led a very simple life.

The woman reached out then and took my hand in hers. It was a soft hand, white and smooth—mine was hot and clammy when I dared open my desperately clasped fists. I was tight-strung as a fiddle string and my knees felt weak and jerky. She drew me gently but forcefully towards her and closed the door behind us.

This is it: "the big wan itself"— the thing we'd talked about so many nights back in St. Columb's, McGarrity, Murray and I. I couldn't believe I was actually going to find out about it in this room. I had almost panicked out there on the landing but now, with the door closed to the world and the woman's body so close to mine, I was becoming excited.

"Don't just stand there gawking." She was taking charge of the situation by her tone of voice—bossy but not unkind. "Take your shoes off at least," she added and with that she turned away to pat the pillows and straighten out the coverlet on the bed.

She wasn't terribly exotic-looking—for a whore. In fact, she reminded me a lot more of the postman's wife at home than of any whore I'd ever imagined. A very ordinary-looking woman, maybe in her early thirties, nice enough looking, with a squarish, innocent-looking face and mousy brown shoulder-length hair— an uncomplicated, average Irish woman. How somebody like her wound up in a business like whoring—not being the seductress type at all—puzzled me. It was hardly the thing she'd told the nuns she wanted to do when she grew up—back in Ballyhaunis or wherever she'd gone to school. And there wasn't so much as a trace of that deep red lipstick nor the heavy eye make-up that I'd been expecting either.

She wasn't at all the painted harlot those Redemptorist priests used to get all apoplectic about during the retreats in St. Columb's. In every retreat there'd be at least one talk on Holy Purity and there'd always be this story about a nice, clean-cut young fellow, well-brought up by his mammy, who gets seduced into a grave sin of impurity by an exotic female—very Genesis.

So, despite all the painstaking religious training, there I stood gawking at the woman, my immortal soul teetering on the very lip of the fiery pit itself and I could hardly wait to discover the mysteries that lay hidden underneath that pink robe and all the angels and saints in heaven could not save me from my curiosity at that moment. The threat of Eternal Perdition wasn't nearly the deterrent those priests had made it out to be.

She went over to a washstand that stood behind the door and with her back towards me she started fussing with something underneath her robe. Though I was impatient for the show to begin, until she was ready all I could do was learn about the woman from the room where she conducted her business.

Over the head of her bed there was the standard picture of the Sacred Heart that you'd find in any Catholic home and, on a little platform attached to the frame, there was the usual little red lamp—its flame flickering in perpetual prayer. Behind the picture frame she had tucked a St. Brigid's cross of woven reeds and a dried-up palm-frond from last Palm Sunday. A religious woman obviously, this whore—but then this was Ireland where even the whores said their three *Hail Marys* every day for holy purity.

I had pictured a more exotic creature than this for my first professional sin. I had envisioned a woman with redder lips, more Latin looking probably, eyes, "dark and flashing" as in the songs, and fishnet stockings — I had always seen her in black fishnet stockings — and garters that peeked down from underneath her wide-legged knickers as in pre-war German movies.

She had finished at the washbasin and seemed ready to give me her full attention. Suddenly my nervousness was back and my fingers were quivering.

"Mick tells me 'tis the very first time for you."

My mouth was so dry from nervousness my tongue kept sticking to my palate, I could hardly speak. "Yes, I'm afraid it is." I stammered.

For a fleeting moment I saw my mother standing behind the woman—by the iron bedpost—her hand cupping the brass knob, bringing a chalice of pain to her lips: a chalice she was being forced to drink on my account. And from dark holes in her pink palms, fat drops of blood welled up and dripped red onto the coverlet of the bed where I was longing to commit at least one sin.

I blinked my eyes and with a great effort of will I pulled my mind back from the brink of psychosis. To my immense relief I saw that the mammy and her blood had vanished as quickly as they had appeared. It would have ruined everything had she stayed and watched my tutorial.

The woman drew closer then and laid her soft round forearms lightly on my shoulders and looked gently into my eyes. I could feel the warmth radiating from her body and her breath faint on my cheek was sweet like the taste of the yellow primroses we sucked alongside the roadside as children. I had not stopped sweating and quivering, but all thoughts of the mammy had evaporated. My arms seemed to find a natural place for themselves around her waist as though they'd been there a thousand times before and my fingers were delighting as they traced the outline of her hip bones and pressed into the firmness of her waist through the silky gown. She had kind gray eyes and nice even teeth that showed very prettily when she smiled. Her lips were full and moist and inviting.

"What would you like me to call you, sweetie?"

"Ah….Jack." I said. She made it sound optional, the name you gave her.

"You can call me Vanessa."

I apologized then for being shaky but Vanessa poo-poo'd it.

"Ah 'tis quite common for young fellas to be a bit nervous the first time they do it with a woman, so it is." She looked at me and smiled. "No earthly amount of practicing by yourself could prepare you for the real thing." Her voice was very gentle and reassuring.

"The first time is always a bit disappointing, after all the build-up—but after that, sure you'll be the dab hand at it before you know it. T'will be a lot more enjoyable the second and third times too—gets better the more you do it."

This was great news for a man who was planning to be celibate for life after this one go at sins of the flesh

"And now you know where to find me…" She pushed me back a little as though to see me better and winked—a knowing wink. Then, without further preamble she let her robe drop to the floor.

Her body was so unbelievably beautiful my knees turned to water and the blood drained suddenly out of my head.

Oh god, I prayed, in your mercy let me not ruin this, my first and only chance for a shag.

Everything I had tried to visualize was there within easy reach of my fingers. It was not a dream.

Oh god, let me not spoil it by throwing up.

I could touch the black brassier if only I had the courage. Even the mysterious breasts themselves, delicate blue veins tracing along the translucent mounds, practically at my fingertips. And there too as in my fantasy was the garter belt and the black stockings that came half-way up her thighs, suspenders running up from them… up and up …

Oh my god! You've got no knickers on! I almost blurted out. It was logical I suppose in her line of work, but shocking to the first-timer—being confronted so abruptly by the object of his *delectatio*. My knees were going watery-weak again; my fingers had begun quivering again too; time had slowed down ominously—my mind was fleeing the scene again.

I cannot leave; it would not be right; what will she think? It's normal to be scared, confronted by a mystery. Take a deep breath, that's better—now another one,

Mysterium est.

Oh Lord, it is good for me to be here!

But I could never in a million years bring myself to touch those breasts nor reach down there into the *sanctum sanctorum.*

Oh god, help me to fuck this nice woman who is trying so hard to be understanding.

The *Memorare* is a prayer we were told never fails, I was trying to remember the words when the woman came to the rescue. She must have sensed the force-field that was inhibiting me, for she drew me close and held me there till the tension had all drained out of me and was replaced by a sturdy chemical response. Augustine, Aquinas and twenty centuries of moral theology had all the relevance of a Hans Anderson Fairy Tale for me at that moment. Lust, the big "L," that most-fun-of-all *appetitus sensitivus,* had taken charge. My inhibitions melted like an icicle on the hob-stone of hell.

Feeling strong and masterful suddenly, I enfolded her surprisingly delicate body in my arms and as I touched and stroked and savored the unfamiliar contours and textures of her, I decided to spirit her away for ever from that dingy room; to save and protect her… England, I could take her to England, far from my mother; to England where they had sex as quick as they'd look at you and nobody cared a frig what you did. She leaned her head on my chest then and through the strands of her hair, I found myself staring into the cold patrician eyes of Pope Pius XII.

She had a picture of the Pope hanging over her mantelpiece. I had not looked in that direction when I'd first come in the room—what a time to discover it. It was disconcerting to say the least, finding the Pope spying on me in a place dedicated to sins of the flesh. Was nothing sacred? The Sacred Heart and St. Brigid, now Pius the Twelfth in her whoring room? What's wrong with this one anyway? I was quivering again. Is she mental or something? A fucking religious fanatic? What does the crazy bitch think she's running here—the friggin' Lourdes grotto? Christ almighty! She'll be selling me relics of the true cross after we fuck. Doesn't know the first thing about being a whore. Hasn't read anything, obviously. None of the writers: not Miller nor Joyce nor Hemingway, none of them, had ever described the likes of this. Was this any way to run a whorehouse?

Beneath the Pontiff on her mantle shelf she had jars of Pond's Cold Cream and Vanishing Cream and a familiar Coty powder box decorated with the same little mushroomy things as the one on my mother's dressing table.

I'm sightseeing. This would never do. I'll never get the job done at this rate. Relax. I told myself. Forget them, the Pope and the mammy. Focus again on the woman you've been holding in your arms.

Vanessa had been crooning to me, endearments, all the while I had been off on my latest tack. She was a patient woman. Lucky for me, finding such an understanding novice mistress; one who understood my conflicts and was willing to work with me. Fortunate, really, having my first go with an Irish girl. Who else would go to such lengths to be helpful? She was a fucking saint, this whore.

Get on with the job, I prompted.

I began again touching, exploring, savoring the smooth white skin of her shoulders and stomach, of her thighs and hips. She helped me undo the tricky hooks at the back of her bra, then let it drop off her arms casually, playfully, as I watched fascinated. Nothing I'd seen in the Louvre could rival those freed-up breasts. Certainly nothing in any *National Geographic* had looked at all like what she was offering me. And the nipples, soft and pink and no bigger around than a boys, were so beautiful I wanted to taste them. I touched one lightly with my fingertips—a velvety flower—then I ran my fingertip over the other—she didn't seem to mind. I had never in my life felt anything as delicate.

I bent down and tasted a nipple with the tip of my tongue—salty; then I closed my lips around it—heavenly! Soft, almost buttery at first, but it became suddenly firm as I continued sucking on it. She shivered slightly.

She unfastened my belt and released the top button of my pants so that they fell around my ankles, then she pulled my drawers down till they too lay in the pile of clothes on the floor.

It was odd, undressing in front of a woman and not feeling the least bit shy about my nakedness. Not like me at all. Only hours ago I had taken communion in the chapel vested in cassock and surplice. Could this possibly be the same day? And in a few more hours I would be once again kneeling in chapel; again dressed in cassock and surplice. Odd, indeed but wonderful!

Amazing! I was euphoric standing there without my pants. I thought of my classmates and their mixed-grills.

This is really the aul biscuit, Mona Lisa! I hummed. And faintly in the background, very faintly, my Jansenistic soul was keening the *De Profundis*.

"Oh god!" I groaned aloud. I had never imagined anything could be so gentle and sensuous as the hand that took hold of my penis then. It was all I could do to control myself. *Appetitus sensitivus sunt sex*—friggin' right, *Domine*!

She was washing me with a soft damp cloth and the sensation was driving me closer to the brink than she perhaps realized. I hadn't felt this nurtured that I could remember but if I didn't send my thoughts off somewhere quickly I would embarrass myself.

And with her hair she dried his feet.

Ah, Magdalene. Wasn't it grand that you were there, girl—warm and fun lovin'. The poor auld thing, and him bored outta his skull with all the righteousness that was around him. Good girl yourself, Mary!

When she had finished drying me she led me to her bed and as I lay down she plumped another pillow for under my head. She wondered if I was comfortable. I said I was very comfortable indeed.

The sheets were clean but in the center crease there was a scattering of biscuit crumbs—digestive biscuits. So she lies here and eats biscuits between customers. A nice picture, innocent and familiar—reassuring. She must keep the biscuit packet in the built-in corner cupboard, for I couldn't see them anywhere. It would be funny if she gave the customer one at the end—like Carlin the barber with lollipops. No, she'd hardly. Does she read, I wondered, while she snacks—she'd have to pass the time somehow in such a small room and not even a radio. I could see nothing but a copy of *The Sacred Heart Messenger* on the bedside table underneath a water glass and the ubiquitous red and green box of Finnon Salts. Her other life: bickies in bed with health salts and devotions to the Sacred Heart of Jesus—not a very exotic life, especially for a whore—hardly how I'd pictured *la vie en rose*. Maybe she's the one learning the piano—trades, maybe, with a music teacher.

When she was satisfied finally that I had been made comfortable and she had draped my clothes carefully on a bentwood chair that was near the washstand, she kicked off the fur-trimmed slippers and stretched out beside me on the bed. Though my own nakedness and the proximity of hers no longer inhibited me, I was feeling a bit nervous again as the moment of truth approached—at the thought of what came next. I had only the faintest notion of the 'how' and the 'where' of what I was supposed to do and none at all of the 'when' of it.

I moved closer to her and took her into my arms for a start—hoping that the rest would follow naturally. The holding part was easy, so comfortable and natural—particularly when she returned the embrace and I felt her soft round arm lying under my neck—so gentle against my cheek. The woman-scent rising off her skin was filling me with a longing to get even closer. She snuggled her face into the curve of my neck and when she rested her thigh casually—companionably—over my hip I felt more at home than I had ever felt in my life. The soft roundness of her hip under my hand was so familiar I might have stroked it a thousand times in the past.

She permitted me a few minutes more of such indolent bliss, of holding and stroking and tasting, before she gently and firmly rolled me over on top of her. And she held me there between her thighs, kneeling and resting my weight awkwardly on my elbows. Those slender thighs were amazingly strong.

"Go ahead now Sweetie," she prompted.

Oh my god! *For this was I born. For this came I into the world.* The universe was calling upon me to do my manly thing, and I had no clue how to go about that.

For want of a better idea, I started into an instinct-driven spasm of thrusting. It was an act of blind faith really; faith that some infinitely clever creator would have eliminated the need for skill on the part of the operator. But my faith in that, as in so many other things he is credited with designing, turned out to be entirely misplaced. In the throbbing excitement that possessed me I seemed to have lost all sense of direction. I tried to recall diagrams of the female anatomy but it was hard to concentrate in that position. Even an exploration of the topography with my fingers left me in the dark. It was frustrating. But Vanessa to the rescue! Educator that she was, having allowed the pupil several attempts without guidance, she reached down then and guided him. And no knuckle-bashing either.

"Ah, there ye are now, darlin'!" She crooned. "It's not that easy to find the first time or so. But ye'r doin' grand, so ye are—just grand."

"Aah! Aah! Oh my god! Oh my god!" I replied.

I wasn't absolutely clear then or later what exactly happened at the moment of entry. I understood it in a general sense of course. I knew that I had entered a warm place that then embraced me like a strong, soft hand. And I knew, of course, that something very agreeable had occurred then, almost immediately. But the whole thing was nothing like my imagining. Where were the deep, pile-driver thrusts? Where was the piston-like endurance of my nighttime fantasy? Neither had there had been a sweaty wrestling match with an eager girl, half- crazed by her own moist lust. The reality bore almost no resemblance to the fantasy. Anything less like piston-thrusting could hardly be imagined. And as for the lust-crazed girl, Vanessa had hardly stirred at all during the entire fifteen seconds that my passion had lasted—not so much as a wriggle.

Oh god! What a colossal fizzle I've turned out to be! How can I ever look Mick in the eye after such a disgrace? And she's sure to tell him—probably tell him to never bring me back. Good thing I'm planning to be celibate.

"It will be a lot better the next time." She'd said earlier—but would she still say that. Maybe I'd improve if I were to practice; become expert at it like the men in novels, Slim Callahan and Hemingway—even old, neurotic Scoby in *The Heart Of The Matter* had probably been better at it. The first time would be disappointing, she'd implied—and she was the professional. Next time I would be better, I told myself—pepping myself up for I was becoming depressed. I'll do it one more time, I promised myself, after that I'll be celibate forever—knowing I've mastered it. I was starting to feel better.

How long did you have to wait between times? I was wondering. Was there something about waiting half an hour... or was that swimming after eating?

As I lay there, still held within her reassuring legs, a relaxing tingle had begun to spread through me at the thought of getting a second go. It was encouraging, knowing I'd be better next time. I must have nodded off then, for I was startled to feel the woman squirming underneath me. My weight, I suppose, had sagged on to her.

"Sorry!" I said.

"We must go now, darlin'," she whispered as she pushed me off her firmly. "Wasn't that lovely though?"

"Great!" I agreed as I swung my legs reluctantly out of the bed. I sat a minute on the edge collecting my thoughts—a little dazed still. Vanessa remained stretched out in the center of the bed, her eyes closed—taking a breather too.

Pope Pius was still there, still looking at us through his persnickety wire glasses—his expression even more disapproving now that I had actually done the sin. The woman was shaking me—I should get dressed. My pants and drawers were draped over the bentwood chair but I was reluctant to exchange the warmth of this woman's room for the harshness outside. She nudged me again, she wanted me to leave. Had she a customer, waiting out in the parlor? I didn't want to think about her with somebody else. I braced myself for returning to the cold March daylight and started pulling on my socks.

She'd have a lot of customers today, St. Patrick's Day and all—drinkers nipping up for an aul shag before goin' back to the wife and kiddies.

Vanessa lighted a cigarette from the pack of Woodbine that had been on the mantelpiece underneath Pius XII.

"Now don't forget," she said. "Before you go back into that college, run down the quays to the Franciscans... for confession, you know—won't take a minit. Grand and human, the Friars, oh aye."

"Oh, god! You're right! Before I go back in." I could never tell a seminary priest about this. They'd order me to leave immediately.

I was about to step into my drawers when Vanessa held her hand up to stop me. She wiped my penis off with the same damp cloth that she'd used before and then dried me with a towel. It felt so good I was getting aroused again; would she suggest maybe that I take a mulligan?

But Vanessa was unimpressed.

"There now," she said when she was satisfied I wouldn't soil my clothes. "Ah sure look at that little thing, all perky again—sittin' up and takin' notice."

Would she suggest the obvious remedy? She pulled my drawers up, over it.

"It'll go down by itself as soon as you hit the cold air on the street." She was so matter-of-fact.

Good Catholic that she was, she would be thinking that I ought to have progressed to the perfect contrition stage of sex and that, rather than thinking about breasts, I should be working on a firm purpose of amendment. Even Irish whores were Jansenists. I got into my pants then.

"I go to Father Anselem, myself—a wonderful, wonderful little man he is and no questions. Gives a body a dacent little penance then and ye'r all done." A consumers' guide to the absolution market was just part of being a full-service Irish whore.

I was already on the landing when I remembered the money—she would of course be expecting money in a transaction like this. I hadn't been that good she'd be giving it to me free of charge—unless she gave complimentary ones to the clergy. They wouldn't have been getting free sex, would they, all this time and never letting on? Hardly. Not in Ireland anyway, they wouldn't.

I hadn't the slightest idea how much they'd charge for a service like that. And were you expected to tip the operator? What would be an appropriate amount? Would it be considered a ten or maybe a fifteen percent sort of thing? Or, was the tip maybe included already in the bill, as they'd started doing recently in the restaurants? My mother had been a stickler when it came to good manners, but some situations she hadn't prepared me for.

I stood for a moment, dithering. But I needn't have worried—she'd been reading my thoughts.

"Mick took care of all the money stuff, sweetie."

She took my arm firmly and led me to the top of the stairs. It was clearly time for me to go. As I went down the stairs I heard the door of her room close. I hadn't looked into the small parlor, better to keep the illusion that I was her last one for the day; that she'd spend the rest of Saint Patrick's Day eating biscuits in bed and reading *The Sacred Heart Messenger.*

Mick was at the bar still, talking and laughing with his friends, when I came down. I walked right through without stopping and out the front door, into the damp, still empty square. A feeble March sun was glistening through a light misty rain. I waited by the car till Mick came out finally and didn't mind the wait—the drizzle was soft and cool on my sex-flushed face.

We went directly from there to the pictures in one of the O'Connell Street cinemas and much later had dinner in the unaccustomed grandeur of Jury's Hotel. I hadn't been hungry all day and I definitely wasn't in any mood for an evening in The Castle Hotel lounge listening to the monkey-chatter of a hundred seminarians.

"Down in Maynooth, we always …"

"But, in All Hallows we …"

"Did you hear that in Carlow they… ?"

"In Trinity you see, we …"

The trivia of seminary life—in-house gossip:

"Did you hear whosit's in a big combo with little whatsit?"

"Go away!"

"Really!"

"Serious?"

"Spend every minute together—practically holding hands—talk of the house down there."

"Oh, my dear!"

"Did ye hear so-and-so got clipped again last summer?"

"No! My goodness—one more and that's it for him."

No, thank you. Not after the morning I'd had. Even the great mixed grill wouldn't have been worth that. We drove out to the Phoenix Park after the pictures and wandered around in the zoo for a while. On the way to Jury's for dinner I had him stop at the Franciscan church to make my confession. Several times that afternoon I tried to bring up the subject of Vanessa, at least to thank him for paying the fee, but he wouldn't let me talk about it. Put his finger to his lip in a knowing way each time to stop me. He dropped me off at the gate and I waved to him as he drove off in the little Morris Minor.

Was being with a whore something men of the world never spoke of afterwards? I had so many questions. I'd have to find out at least about the cost if I was to have one more go. I'd have to give up the fags probably, to afford it, but it would be worth the sacrifice just knowing I was good at sex before promising celibacy — giving informed consent —and better for my health too. I'd ask him next visiting day.

At night prayer I thought of nothing but Vanessa. I was too excited to sleep and, after lying wide-eyed for a couple of hours, I finally gave up on it and got out of bed. Standing by the open window of the darkened room I lit a cigarette and blew the smoke out into the night. The near-full moon scudding briskly across a mottled ocean of clouds was throwing fast-moving shadows on the meadows and hawthorn hedges that stretched off for miles on every side. This same blue, magic moonlight had excited me on summer nights as a child, prompting me to steal out and play hide-and-seek around moon-shadowed haystacks with my friends.

It was this moon too that had lighted the night for a distant forefather—a creature untroubled by our latter-day pieties—on the last ice-age glaciers. Weary and cold, I saw him struggle along the glittering ice field, slipping and sliding under its blue light, longing with every step for his bed behind the flickering fires, longing to be warm again with his woman and safe from the saber-tooth and the wolf pack.

I thanked the moon-god of my fathers' for a glimpse of my humanity. I could not find it in my soul to repent what I had done that day—that human thing the Christians' god considered sinful.

I could hardly wait for Mick's visit the following Sunday, there were so many things I had to ask him. But he got in first with a question:

"How are you, boy?" He inquired as soon as we had left the visitors' parlor and begun our usual stroll down the driveway. "No ill effects, no burning sensations nor unaccustomed discharges?"

What was this? I blanched as I remembered the intense glow of well-being I had felt that night standing by the window; could that have been from some venereal disease? My mind raced off to stories of syphilis and the dreadful pock-faced deaths in Tudor times.

"I don't know..." The panic must have been evident from my voice.

"Oi'm only havin' ye on, aul son!" He laughed and nudged me with his shoulder. "Sure Vanessa's the cleanest girl on god's earth—never a trace of burning nor dripping would you ever find on any of her fellas."

I couldn't help thinking that, despite his disclaimer, he had in fact been concerned about diseases. We walked on in silence after that for a minute or two.

"Should I go up to Dublin, maybe, to a quack up there and have it checked out, d'you think?" I asked.

"Arrah, I don't think ye need worry yer head about that. Sure, if ye'd caught anything it'd be so bad by now ye couldn't stand it—ye couldn't so much as take a piss without screaming."

That was reassuring.

"So?" He looked at me, a questioning grin twisting his mouth. "How did you survive the deflowering?"

"Och! I survived it fine." I said. I found talking about it was actually a bit awkward—even with him. "Thanks again." I said but then I wasn't sure how to pose one of the questions that had been on my mind since Patrick's Day. "Maybe I liked doin' that more than being in here. You know what I mean?"

He gave me this long appraising look out of the side of his eye before he answered.

"Are ye thinking that it's maybe worth leaving over? Is that what yer getting'at?"

"Aye. Something like that."

"Was it so great ye're thinking that doin' it would keep ye occupied for the rest of yer days or what?" He cut his eyes sharply at me and grinned.

I could think of nothing to say to that.

After a minute he added. "Sure ye'd have ta get out of the fuckin' bed sometimes me aul bucko. Ye know what I mean?" He nudged me with his elbow and laughed.

I couldn't help smiling at how ridiculous he made it seem.

"Else the friggin' thing'll fall off and then where are ye?" Another hard nudge and I laughed along with him though I wasn't that amused really.

"But seriously..." I wanted to ask what I'd been planning all week to ask. "I've been wondering if you think I should pull the pin here? It's all that's been on my mind this past week. I loved being with Vanessa a lot, ye know—more than a future priest should." I was praying he would take my quandary seriously and he did.

"Good!" He said. "You're fucking meant to enjoy it." He had become unusually stern and was speaking very emphatically. He caught hold of my arm then and we stopped walking, right in the middle of the driveway. Other students and their visitors were having to walk around us—Mick seemed neither to notice nor care.

"Isn't it precisely because you enjoy something that you're asked to give it up?" He started jabbing my chest hard with his forefinger. "It's like Lent:. You don't fucking give up cabbages and turnips and shite like that for Lent, do ye? Nobody in their right minds likes that garbage anyway. No! You only give up the stuff you enjoy, isn't that right: shite like sweets and cigarettes and the booze and women?"

He was glaring at me, demanding a response. I could think of nothing to say.

"So." He poked me with his forefinger again. "My answer to your question is an emphatic ' No!' I don't fuckin' think you should leave and become a layman. You'd be a hopeless fucking failure at being a layman." He was snorting, he was so intense.

"Look at you, the other day in the bar there—a fuckin' fish out of water. A born, friggin' priest if ever I saw one. I knew it from the minute I first set eyes on you over there by the Junior House door, that first day in here."

I couldn't believe it. Here was somebody that ought to know; a real man of the world. And he's telling me that I'm a born priest and that I'd be a fuckin' washout as a layman.

"Well, shite!" I exclaimed more to myself than him as we resumed the walk. "Shite!" We walked then all the way to the front gate before he spoke again.

"Don't you go disappointing me, boy," he demanded. "I'm friggin' bettin' on you getting ordained." He jabbed me one more time in the chest— punctuation. "Full stop! No argument!" And with that valediction, he headed out the gate. There was still an hour or more of visiting time left. It was the first time he'd left before the vespers bell.

I had forgotten completely to ask him about another go with Vanessa or even how much it would cost.

"A fuckin' born priest!"

I only saw Mick one more time after that day: on Easter Sunday. The week after Easter he left for a new job in London—a job with a bigger firm and better pay. When the bell for vespers rang that day I walked with him down the driveway to the gate and we shook hands, goodbye. He promised to write and send me his London address—but I never heard from him again.

So I stayed on in Holy Trinity. It wasn't simply because of what Mick had told me, though it weighed heavily with me at the time, but principally because I found that living with a dubious vocation was less confusing than the uncertainty I would face on the outside. And I sensed he might have been right: I would never make it as a layman.

CHAPTER 6

Big Sur, California — 2004

WITH HIS HOMEWORK assignment under his shirt for protection, Holland hurried across the quadrangle to the monastery, a stiff westerly wind on his back carrying him along. The usual flock of grub-hunting birds around the fountain had taken the morning off; water from the fountain was flying in horizontal sheets across the lawn. He shivered as he stepped inside the building and closed the door; the cold bite of winter was in the wind still. He climbed the stairs to the second floor office. He was surprised to find he'd actually been looking forward to the session with Father James.

No greeting — a tight nod of the head.

"You've been writing, then?" The monk indicated the sheaf of pages in Holland's hand.

"Yes. I surprised myself how much poured out once I got going."

He waited self-consciously as the priest leafed through the pages. It had been so long since he'd written anything Holland was suddenly stricken by insecurity. Was it what the man had intended? The language and all—rough, the way he remembered it, but… The priest looked up from his scanning. He held the pages up.

"Did you find writing about this difficult?"

"A bit, at times, yes." Holland shuffled his feet. The man had not asked him to sit down.

"I went on and on a bit about some things—probably bore the pants off you."

"No, no. It'll be fine." The monk had started reading—apparently engrossed — didn't even look up. Holland waited until the man turned the page — kept reading. It was disconcerting. Had he been dismissed?

"Should I go on with the writing… or what?" Holland asked finally.

"What else do you think you should be writing about?" The man finally looked at Holland.

"I don't have a clue. What are we trying to accomplish anyway?"

"You've never been in therapy before, Mister… Jack?"

Holland shook his head, no.

"This is how therapy proceeds: discovering and unraveling. It may seem very indirect and slow at first. Try to be patient with it for a while."

Holland was prepared to be patient—at least till the weather got a bit warmer. Keep the man satisfied. Postpone his eviction. He nodded.

"Good." The monk said and looked up from the reading. "Why don't you leave these pages with me. We'll meet tomorrow at this same time." He resumed his reading

"We're not having a session today then?"

"No, we're not." There was a pause and the monk looked up. "Are you disappointed?"

"Ah! Not at all!" Holland took a deep breath and shook his head. "Well, yeah, I suppose I am disappointed, a bit. I thought we had agreed to meet again today." He paused. He realized he was annoyed at the change. Or, was it with himself for looking forward to the meeting?

"Yes, I was counting on us meeting," he said.

"I'll see you tomorrow and by then I'll have read all this. Keep up the writing."

A sudden listlessness swept through Holland and he walked slowly out of the office without looking back at the monk. He hurried down the stairs and across the lawn to his room.

Fuck him! He closed the door and threw himself into the armchair. Why was he shocked at being let down by that fuckin' wimp of a monk? Should have known better than to trust somebody like that?

He couldn't sit still. He went over and stood by the window.

Fuckin' ejit, thinking that "hoor of a friar" was there to help him. Oldest trick in the book: informer posing as confessor. God damn! You'll never learn.

He stewed in the bitter juices of hurt and anger until he finally grew tired of the self-pity and drama.

Get over it, he scolded himself. Pack your friggin' bags if you don't want to be in their power. Who's keepin' you? A fuckin' volunteer, is what you are. Hit the road, why don't you?

He needed fresh air and a lungful of smoke to settle his head down. He went out through the kitchen and crossed the lawn to the low stonewall that ran along behind the kitchen, a place where he felt safe from the inquisitive eyes of the monastery. A good place for a man to come when his perspective needed calibrating.

Sitting on that wall, your legs dangling over the escarpment edge, you could look right down the cliff face into the ocean and get a glimpse of yourself from a different point of view.

Far below the wall, toy cars and trucks were scooting importantly along, while further down still the waves were pummeling the same rocks they had been smashing against the day Friar Serra had ridden past, plodding north on his mule. Hell! When those Asiatics had passed by going the other way a few thousand years earlier, those same waves on the same friggin' rocks. Insignificance was relaxing.

The breeze was fat with moisture and, though the rain had stopped hours before, he could feel its damp softness brush his face and arms. There was something about that wet west wind on the skin—something familiar and calming in its cold caress.

He lighted a cigarette, sheltering the match in his cupped hand, and as the drug caressed his temples he felt the remaining bitterness drain out of him.

Childish friggin' sulk! Pounding on your highchair!

The monk likely couldn't help it—something he'd been ordered to do by his superiors. Get over yourself, he'll see you tomorrow. Not the center of the man's universe. He went back to his room and put a fresh sheet of paper into the typewriter. Now for the really hard stuff. He took a deep breath, lighted a cigarette and started writing.

It was barely light enough to see the page when he finally took a break. He was reluctant to turn on the light —it would be incongruent somehow with his mood. The wind had turned blustery again now the light was fading and hard-driven raindrops had begun sporadically pecking at the corrugated roof of his room.

Get out of the room for a bit, breathe some fresh air or you'll spend another sleepless night ruminating on the past.

He pushed his truck quietly out of the carport and let it run down the hill. At the highway he turned north, towards Monterey. The wind barging in from the west was driving the rain in heavy slanting sheets across the roadway, like squalls, on and off. It buffeted the old pickup intermittently and made steering tricky

He cut off Highway One before Munras and took the winding road that climbs up through the wooded hills above Pebble Beach then heads downhill into the town of Pacific Grove. He kept on Forrest Street till it dead-ended at the cove, then, turning left, he drove along the sea front for a mile or so more. He turned in at the parking area across from the golf course. For years this had been his favorite spot on the coast. He found a measure of contentment parked there where waves breaking on the rocks sprayed salty foam onto the windshield, where the air was rich always with the ocean's smells. And on a stormy day like this it was the best place he knew for watching the white horses race each other madly for the shore, their frothy manes flying wildly, whipped into a fine drifting mist by the crosswind.

On a day like this too there were few tourists to distract him as he sat staring over the bay towards the Santa Cruz shore, the lights of Moss Landing appearing and disappearing through the rain-squalls. A cormorant patrol skimming the water in single file, necks low and straight, flew past on its deliberate course. An unruly flight of pelicans too, heading for shelter struggled past battling the stormy crosswind.

His mind was a jumble of images as he listened to the familiar rhythms of the ocean. The writing and those sessions with that monk had been digging up the dead—forcing him to think about that strangely matched couple that were his parents and their bizarre contests for dominance. The promise of their wedding picture, in their going-away finery: dapper groom, tall and confident, enamored of the slender beauty on his arm. So happy, so excited, off on their motoring honeymoon.

"Those poor children," he said aloud, picturing the two of them that brilliant day and the tragedy that was already poised to strike them.

The spume off a particularly ferocious wave splattered the windshield and slapped the hood hard, startling him. It had jarred him out of his reverie. He lighted a cigarette and rolled the window down an inch. The air was cold but the rain had let up for the moment. Twilight had dissolved into darkness and the seabirds had left for their night-roosts

The same young woman, older-looking now than in the wedding photo, and a little boy barely three, were kneeling on the concrete curb that enclosed a grave. Two glass domes, with wax flower bouquets inside them, marked the head and feet of the baby girl who had died at two and a half from meningitis. Every Saturday afternoon they came, the woman and the boy, to weed and plant flower seeds for her. And as they weeded the grave she would tell him about his sister, about the joy their first-born had been to his father and her. He had wondered about that for he had never seen the man anywhere near the grave nor felt any joy in him.

At times the woman would grow distant for no apparent reason and the boy would watch in dread as darkness clouded her face. He would run to her then and, standing in front of her where she was kneeling, he would clutch her face in his small cool hands and start frantically kissing it. He would stare deep into her eyes to hold on to the remnant of her and keep that from leaving too. And holding his cool pink cheek against hers, smelling her Coty powder, he would pray to Jesus, till he was sure the darkness had passed over. She would hug him then and say she was fine and that he was her big strong boy and that he was not to tell daddy. He lived in dread of the day she would go away and nothing he could do would bring her back.

His sister had died five months after he was born, but more than two years later his parents still missed her awfully and nothing he could do seemed to fill the void. When her name was mentioned their faces would light up for the moment, remembering that magical time—the time before that awful January when their lives had been plunged into a sadness that had changed them forever. She had taken the best parts to the grave with her and left behind, for him, a place ruled by a sour and jealous god—a demon guaranteed to snatch away anyone you dared love.

It was in the religion of their demon-god that he had been raised—no trace of the nice-daddy god others talked about, not in that house. Why else would a child steal into his parents' room at night, crawl along the floor to her side of the bed and listen there to be sure she was still breathing? How else could a boy reassure himself that the bastard hadn't struck again? And wasn't it belief in this same demon that had killed her love for him when at eight he had contracted osteomyelitis? Like yesterday, he remembered her face, cold and white, turning away from him—refusing to look at another dead child—as he was carried out to the ambulance. The demon had struck again, she'd felt his icy breath. Love had once again enraged the fucker.

Holland shook his head. The cold chill that caused him to shiver had returned him to the present. The storm seemed to have blown off to the east. A half-moon was sailing calmly through an ocean of rippling clouds. Time to be heading back. Time, finally, to brace himself and write about Jerry.

CHAPTER 7

Holy Trinity Seminary — 1956

"DIDN'T YOU THINK it odd that I *just happened to have* a pair of tights in my suitcase?" Jerry looked over at me quizzically.

"Huh?" I'm sure I must have looked as blank and puzzled as I felt, for he quickly added.

"Women's tights—in my suitcase? Didn't it strike you odd—that I had them?"

"Now that you mention it, I suppose…"

He was still staring at me—expecting more.

"Aye! I suppose it is a bit odd, in a way—if you think about it." I was trying to seem interested in his tights though my mind was still out there with the bombers of the Dam Busters. Would we all make it through the anti-aircraft fire? Bomber Command and I were holding our breath.

We had been rooming together for about two and a half months when Jerry decided to trust me with his deepest, most embarrassing secret. We had come a long way in a short time, the two of us.

The years in undergraduate philosophy had taken an unusually heavy toll on our class: of the thirty we had started-out with, a mere seventeen had made it to graduation. And it was when this remnant moved over to the Senior House to start Divinity that Jerry Egan and I were assigned as roommates. We had no way of knowing that September how the relationship we would develop in the subsequent year would color the remainder of our lives for by total coincidence we had each chosen the same diocese for our future ministry: Minerva, California.

Things had not looked at all promising our first week rooming together. We started off being almost painfully polite to one another, each of us deferring constantly, and generally walking on eggshells around the other. For my part, I was already in awe of Jerry's intellect and personality long before we had been assigned as roommates, so that, finding myself living in close proximity to such a paragon, I felt out of my depth socially and intellectually. What did you talk about to such a brain anyhow? On the other hand, Jerry—he admitted this to me later—had perceived me as a go-along-to-get-along empty-head and spent those first days cursing the Fates that had inflicted me on him.

Our period of uneasy formality was suffocating both of us, it was clear—I had had my fill after just a few days and I suspected that Jerry wasn't doing any better. Something had to be done about it. So one night a week or so into term, with my characteristic subtlety, I lobbed a bomb into the brittle atmosphere of the room.

"Aren't we the right aul pair of ejits?" I said—totally out of the blue. Jerry looked over, an eyebrow raised in question.

"Yeah, us two ejits," I elaborated. "Volunteers on friggin' Devil's Island; like friggin' Greek widows in our long black dresses; memorizing definitions in a dead friggin' language—what a way to squander our youth?"

There was a great silence then—it must have lasted all of ten seconds—during which I held my breath.

"Friggin' right!" Jerry shouted. He started laughing then and couldn't seem to stop and I got caught up in it too and we both laughed till we were helpless. He dried his eyes finally, leaned back in the chair and stared at the ceiling as though reading something that was written there.

"A pack of castrated sissies is all we are! A raging pack of pansies! Pansies preparing to be pompous, prissy priests!"

We laughed then off and on till the end of study. And even later, during the *Silentium*, when we caught the other's eye we couldn't help but laugh. We were fast friends from that night on.

Jerry was not only the most brilliant member of our class by far, but he was philosophically liberal as well—a rare combination in that conservative and intellectually undemanding school.

What a gift, to have as a roommate someone both intelligent and humorous. What a contrast to poor George who had been neither. Suddenly, life in Holy Trinity had begun to look up and as those autumn days shortened into the darkness of another dreary Irish winter, I grew to appreciate Jerry more with each day that passed.

The fourth floor of the Senior House dormitory was a miserable place to live even in the best of weather but when the bitter winds of winter came whistling into our room through the weather-warped windows, it became an icy Purgatory. No amount of extra clothing—cassocks and overcoats, gloves and scarves—could keep a body warm. Throughout that freezing winter though, for the first time since I'd come to Holy Trinity, I had a companion who would daydream with me—as McGarrity and Murray had dreamed with me in St. Columb's. And Jerry, I found, shared with me the dream of a mythic place where skies were always blue and oranges grew wild alongside the road; of a land where palm trees swayed and clacked beside white beaches, where soft Trade Winds blew in off warm oceans. We agreed that Hawaii and Tahiti were close to idyllic but, since they were not looking for Irish priests in those islands, we hoped that in our California diocese we had come close. The very name, "Minerva" seemed to augur well: Pallas Athena, goddess of the arts, sprung full-grown from the very mind of Jupiter. What growing boy would not be drawn to a place named after such a beauty?

Though we both considered ourselves liberals, there was an enormous difference in what each of us understood by the term "liberal." Jerry's liberalism described his stance in life—the result of principles and values that he had consciously adopted after much reading and study and thought. For me, "liberal" was a name I gave to the vacuum that existed where my principles should have been. Jerry did not understand how I could have been so long on the planet and still be so rudderless. He would poke me and prod me, trying to elicit some evidence of a conscience. "Kicking a dead cat," I called it.

"But how do you feel about that?" He would ask and, on finding me searching his face for an answer that would satisfy him, he would become frustrated.

"But you must have some reaction… some feeling inside yourself… something telling you whether you feel good or bad about it?" He would insist. Gently, persistently, he nudged me into adopting a few rudimentary moral principles. They might come in handy, he suggested, in case I ever got tired using fear as the basis for decision making. It was disconcerting, living so close to a man who could see through me like that.

Similarly with study. The notion of intellectual research, outside of that prescribed by the professors, had been an altogether foreign concept to me before that year. Jerry took it upon himself to be my mentor, my guide to the library stacks, my devil's advocate and my Socratic goad. I was sort of a pet project for him—his tame ignoramus. And as a result, when he came to trust me of all people with his deepest secret, I was flattered out of my skull that he should consider me trustworthy.

It was during second study on a night in the cold drear of that November of our First Divine year. We were at our desks as usual, doing everything we knew to keep warm: overcoats pulled around our shoulders on top of cassocks, gloved hands deep thrust into pockets and scarves wound tightly around our necks and faces. It was another night when the frigid east wind like a knife sliced down on Ireland from the Steppes of the Ukraine, penetrating every seam of the ancient woodwork of the Senior House. To avoid chilblains on our feet we kept our legs elevated above the freezing draught that blew under the door from the vaulted corridor outside. Two lukewarm hot pipes running along the wall underneath the window were having no success at all mitigating the cold. As usual, I was trying to get my mind off the present misery by losing myself in a novel and so I was taken completely by surprise when Jerry staged his little theatre piece.

I was flying wingman that night to Guy Gibson, the wingtip of my Lancaster just off his starboard elevator. The rapture of hypothermia was something the entire squadron had to guard against on a night like this—clear and frosty. The 617 Squadron had set course for the dams finally that night after months of preparation. We were flying low, about five hundred feet above the surface and had maintained radio silence since crossing the English coast. Any second now we would be running into the flack, bright with tracer rounds, rising from the German batteries as we crossed the Dutch coast a few miles north of the Belgian border.

Suddenly Jerry jumped to his feet sending his chair scraping across the floorboards.

"I don't even care at this point what you'll think of me! I'm so friggin' cold I can't stand it any longer."

That was all he said. No explanation accompanied the outburst.

He stomped over then to his bedside and slung one of his suitcases from the top of his tin wardrobe down onto the bed and snapped it open.

I was so taken by surprise I still hadn't said a word, though I had begun thinking the worst:

He's pulling the friggin' pin! Fuck it! Finally I have someone I really like as a friend and he's decided to leave the friggin' place—and me. Wouldn't you friggin' know it!

"Here! God dammit! I'm past caring what anybody will say!" Jerry was holding up what looked to me like a pair of tights, black woolen tights.

Why was he being so emphatic about a pair of tights—what was he on about? Had I missed something—something that would have explained the significance of what he was saying? I said nothing.

"I don't see why I shouldn't wear the friggin' things if they keep me warm!" It sounded for all the world as though he was having an argument with somebody— and I was the only one present. It had to be about me. And it obviously had something to do with the tights, for he kept holding them up and shaking them angrily.

"I don't see why not." I said.

He pulled up his cassock then and, after stepping out of his pants, he sat on the edge of the bed and pulled on the tights.

Something like that would be nice and warm, I was thinking. I should get myself some long-johns at Christmas.

The crisis seemed to have blown over. Jerry put his pants back on and returned quietly to his desk. Thank god, I prayed, he's not pulling the pin—whatever else is going on! It was safe to direct my full attention once again to the Ruhr Dams.

It was a tricky proposition: running the gauntlet of anti-aircraft fire over the dams while maintaining exactly the right altitude, then releasing the bomb at precisely the right moment. I had just ordered my bombardier to re-check the fuses for the fifth or sixth time when Jerry interrupted my war again with the question: Didn't I think it odd, him having tights in his suitcase?

I should make an effort, I told myself. Get your head out of the book. Pay attention to your roommate. Jerry had complained that I wasn't really "present" often, when he was talking to me— it made him feel invisible, he said.

"How did you come to have them anyway—in your suitcase?" I asked. A good question, I thought — showed interest.

"Odd? You did think it was 'odd' though? Didn't you? Admit it!"

"All right!" I went ahead and stepped into the trap. "I suppose it did seem odd—a bit."

"How odd?" He was pinning me to the wall.

"Oh, I don't know, really." Christ almighty—how do I get him off this? "My first thought was that you've had them from some of the plays you've been in— over in Junior House."

This was a pretty reasonable assumption, I thought, for he'd been involved in every play that had been put on by our dramatic club since First Philosophy. If there was a play being produced —Shakespeare, Gilbert and Sullivan or Christie — there was Jerry playing the female lead. *Ubi… ibi….!* as they're supposed to have said in Rome.

"There's more to it than that, you know—than just wearing them in the plays," he said.

I looked over at him and I was shocked to see that he had turned white and his eyes… I recognized immediately what it was I saw there: it was fear. But what did he have to fear?

"You like dressing up as a woman? Is that it?" A shot in the dark—what else could it be?

"It's more than just "liking" to do it!" I could feel his eyes examining my face.

"You… I just don't know, so there is no point in my guessing." I shrugged helplessly. "Can't you just tell me? You know it'll take me ages getting it, if you don't." I was never good at picking up on subtle hints and suggestions and he of all people should know that. "I mean, if it's not too difficult to talk about." I added that in case I was riding over some sensibility I wasn't aware of.

Jerry's face seemed to relax then after one final searching look into my eyes.

"I don't even know if I can explain it," he began. He looked away from me, as though telling me would be harder if he had to watch my reaction—a flinch or something that might show revulsion.

"I have never before talked about this… whatever it's called—this 'obsession'—never before to a soul." He glanced briefly over at me and paused for a long moment. I could see tears welling up in his eyes and nearly overflowing the lower lids. I wanted to reach over and touch him then, but of course I didn't—there was a force-field between us that would have never permitted such a thing. I was making a conscious effort to not look away from him—as men usually do when other men cry. Maybe it's been since Noah that men can't gaze on another man's nakedness.

"I have always dressed up secretly in women's clothes," he began and his voice had the determination of someone taking a cold dip. His knuckles, I noticed, were white from gripping the arms of the chair.

I kept my gaze steady and erased all reaction from my face. It must have worked for, though his eyes had been searching my face, they had detected none of the emotional flinch that coursed through me. He continued.

"First it was my sisters' things and then, when I got bigger, my mother's." He paused and took a breath. This was hard for him. I didn't have a clue what to say. Best be quiet, I advised myself.

"Every time I had the house to myself for a few hours, I would dash up to their rooms and put on their clothes, underwear and stockings, jumpers and skirts, even my mother's bra and corset sometimes." He paused and seemed to be having trouble with his chest. He was pressing his hand against it hard—up near his throat.

He's not about to have a heart attack — I was worried.

"Jack, I'm so embarrassed telling you this I can hardly breathe. I can't even believe I'm telling somebody about it. But... I know I can trust you."

I nodded and again I felt a surge of compassion for the pain he was in. I wanted to touch his arm and reassure him—but was unable to break through that barrier. I wanted desperately to tell him something that would help but I couldn't think of a thing to say that would be any use. God damn it! I scolded myself. Can't you come up with at least one intelligent thing to say?

"I was always scared to death somebody would come home suddenly and catch me at it, you know." He shivered thinking about it.

Just being there, saying nothing, listening and looking at him, was as much as I could think to do.

"God! They'd have flayed me alive—good Christians that they are—if they'd ever seen me doing it. Dragged me up to some idiotic parish priest, probably—I'd have died of the shame. So I was very, very careful and put everything back exactly the way I found it."

He paused and looked over at me, waiting for some reaction.

"Was this like a sexual thing: something, you know, that aroused you—turned you on—looking at yourself dressed as a girl?" It was the best I could do—and I had to admit that I had forgotten all about the Ruhr dams.

He said nothing for a moment but I noticed that his cheeks were flushed. I have ruined everything with my inquisitiveness—bull in a friggin' china shop—I scolded myself. But, whatever he was feeling, he answered me calmly.

"I was dressing up in girl's clothes as early as three and four—long before I even knew what being aroused felt like. Even as a teenager, it didn't get me horny or anything, doing it." He had sounded a bit hurt sure enough. "You're thinking about the dirty old men playing with their mammy's knickers, aren't you?" He was sounding a bit argumentative, even.

"Jerry, I know nothing about this sort of thing at all and I'm afraid I'm doing a lousy job of discussing it with you. If I ask you anything at all, it'll likely be something else really stupid and it'll hurt your feelings too—and then I'll never forgive myself…"

He smiled. "It wasn't a stupid question at all. It's just embarrassing, hearing you say it." His knuckles were still gripping the chair arm and dark rings I had not noticed before discolored the skin underneath his eyes.

"It wasn't connected to masturbating." He was determined, it seemed, to get everything out on the table. "It was different from anything I'd read about. After I've dressed up, I find I am more relaxed—as though I'd taken a sedative."

Now I was being too quiet for him it appeared.

"Don't feel you're stupid or that you'll hurt my feelings if you say something. I'm as puzzled as you about the whole thing."

But, try as I might, I could think of nothing to say to fill the silence. After about a minute in which he seemed to be staring at his desk-top, he added. "I probably don't belong in a seminary—a mental hospital, more like. I shouldn't have come here in the first place."

Now that really scared me—the thought of his leaving. I don't give a shite whether he likes dressing up in women's clothes or not just so long as he doesn't leave?

"For god's sake, man! I wouldn't worry my head about bein' a bit nuts. Sure nobody in his right mind would be in this friggin' place anyway." He smiled but I could see that tears were not far behind.

I was feeling protective of him again. He shouldn't have to apologize to me or to anybody for the way he was.

Fuckit, anyway! I thought.

"Look Jerry." I demanded his attention and the change in my tone caused him to turn and face me. "I have no problem with you wearing anything you want to wear. And I hope you feel free to do it with me in the room—that you don't have to go sneaking around to do it."

My awkward attempts at putting him at ease obviously moved him. He could no longer look me in the eye. His battle to contain his tears had been lost again. He turned his face away from me, back to staring at the dim reading light on his desk.

I waited a bit then, but he seemed to be done with the conversation and I forced my mind back to the frustrations of Guy Gibson and the Dam Busters: the hedge-hopping had already claimed one Lancaster—downed on powerlines.

My mind kept drifting off to Jerry. He had hardly moved since we had finished talking—sitting motionless, staring at an unopened book on his desk.

The squadron droned on in the nighttime German skies, rocked occasionally by flak from the anti-aircraft batteries as they approached the Ruhr. The pilots and bombardiers were tense, worrying about the defenses they'd run into over the targets; about how they could keep their Lancasters at just the right altitude so the bombs would bounce right up to the base of the dams.

All was quiet in our room except for the occasional sniffle. Jerry's head was down now, resting on his arm on the desktop. His shoulders would heave occasionally and his body shudder from all the misery that had been bottled up inside.

I forced myself to read for the next twenty minutes or so, though half the time my mind was nowhere near the Ruhr. Jerry lifted his head finally.

"Jerry!" I said. He seemed startled by the sound of my voice—had he thought I'd left, I wondered. "Yes, I'm still here! As far as I'm concerned, you can wear anything you like just as long as it's attractive. I'm warning you though, the day I come in and see you slopping about in an aul housecoat, your hair done up in rollers, we'll be havin' another talk."

I was rewarded with a faint, thankful smile. For a moment I felt he might even reach over and touch me. But that impulse slid into the void which swallows most male tenderness.

Jerry's proclivity for cross-dressing remained our secret. Now that I was in his confidence, he showed me the extensive wardrobe he had collected over the years, under the rubric of doing theater. By year's end his dressing up had become such a routine part of life in our room that I hardly noticed whether he was wearing a cassock or frock.

I confided in him the whole messy dilemma that had led me to choose the priesthood and he hadn't been a bit shocked. His own decision, he said was driven at least partly by a desire to avoid the social stuff—dates and dances—mating rituals, the very thought of which terrified him. Like thousands of confused young men and women through the centuries, he had fled into the religious life—a haven—safe from the heavy-handed marriage and breeding agenda raging outside.

"What are we anyway?" He asked me one day. "Are we viruses compelled to mindlessly spread our species throughout the environment?"

Good question.

Jerry felt deeply about many things, but especially so about social issues outside of Ireland. My mother had been interested in the greater world too—had subscribed to *Time* and *The Sunday Times* for as long as I could remember—but it had been more of an academic interest, without a trace of Jerry's emotional investment in the people and their causes.

We were at our desks one night for example,, each immersed in his own book, when I heard sobbing. Jerry, I realized, was crying—mopping his cheeks unashamedly, a handkerchief bunched up in his fist. What could he be reading that would bring such a thing on?

"You all right?" I whispered.

When he turned his head, he looked for the entire world like that woman in the head-cold advertisement—the one with red and swollen eyes and a nose raw and angry from rubbing. His cheeks were splotchy and wet with tears. He nodded and smiled a watery smile to reassure me. He pointed to the book he'd been so absorbed in and shook his head in wonderment.

"*Treblinka.*" He said it as if the name should be a full explanation.

"Treblinka?" I repeated. The blank look on my face told it all.

"The camp. Treblinka. I'm reading about what it was like there and the exterminations: the gassing and the incinerators."

"Oh?" I said.

I had read what little there was in the news about the concentration camps: The Allies discovering them when they invaded Germany and Eastern Europe; the skeletal inmates—DP's they were called in the news reports on the *Pathe Gazette* and in *Time*. But there hadn't been much talk about extermination up until that time in the British Isles—no popular books about it—though there had been a flood of war stories on the book-shelves. Heroic stories these were mostly: British spies in occupied France; Fighter Command and Biggin Hill saving London; British POW's outwitting Nazis in Stalags—Douglas Bader *sans* legs in Colditz Castle and

Ronald Searle drawing the fattened cat in that Japanese camp in Burma. I'd read all of them. But I hadn't seen a word about Auschwitz or Sobibor or Treblinka up until that time.

He loaned me the book when he was done with it—I'm not sure if it was merely called *Treblinka* or if it had another title. I began reading it—it was unbelievable. I would read particularly affecting passages aloud to him as I came across them and we cried together at the heartbreak of the families. And together on St. Patrick's Day that year we searched in Dublin for other books on what became known later on as "The Holocaust." We had no name for it then.

"Where was the Church in all this?" I asked him one night. "Couldn't they have stopped it?"

He shook his head.

"What?" I asked, frustrated at his inscrutability.

"Don't rock St. Peter's barque and he won't rock your boat." He said.

"That was the deal with Hitler and company?"

"Always has been the deal—since Constantine."

"Fuck!" I exclaimed. I was shocked. For the very first time I had caught an inkling of how naïve I had been: thinking all along that I was the sinner; that I was the one not worthy—not living up to the mark. The fucking mark was being adjusted all the time, depending on whose ox was being gored.

"Shite!" I exclaimed and banged the desk. "The fuckers knew about all those camps—and the Jews?"

"You've finally got it, huh?" He said.

"What are we doing in this fucking place, then?" I was shaking with indignation. "Why are you in this friggin' church then? What is somebody as smart and well-read as you doing in a place like this—if you've known this stuff all along?"

"What is a nice girl like me doing in a place like this? Leave the money on the dresser, ducky."

"We're whores? Is that what you're telling me?"

"There've been bad priests and there've been good priests in every religion. Any one of us can choose which sort to be. Catholic is my tradition—so why not make the most of what you've got? Be one of the good Catholic priests."

I was still in shock though. I had no idea till then how completely I had swallowed the party line about Luther and Calvin—even about Henry the Eighth and

Elizabeth. What if they were right in doing what they'd done? And what if it wasn't done out of pride and lust?

I wanted more answers than the course of studies was providing and it was then that Jerry took my education in hand.

From him I acquired the habit of using the library—pathetic and inadequate though it was—to research questions for myself. Jerry had little use for the prescribed theology textbooks. "Pre-chewed theology for the hard-of-thinking," he called them.

So, he and I followed our own reading list of theologians and when we weren't reading from these and discussing what we had read, we were spending study time reading worthwhile novels—the more banned by Church and State they were, the more worthwhile we considered them.

When we moved up to be Second Divines and no longer had to share a room, Jerry would still invite me over, now and then, and model a new outfit for me. It was a lonely world indeed that he inhabited.

Our mutual trust and self-revealing had cemented a friendship about which I have much more to tell. But, even as we went on through Divinity, I wondered how I had come so far in life without having Jerry as my confidant. When I told him one day how much I valued his friendship —an act of incredible vulnerability on my part —he smiled but said nothing. That night when I got to my room for second study, I found a single sheet of paper and in Jerry's handwriting, written diagonally on the page:

"ME TOO—I am so glad you are in my life. Thanks."

Jerry continued to appear as leading lady in each of the plays our class staged right through Fourth Divinity. In the Fourth Divine *Jack*, on Ascension Thursday—a month or so before we were ordained—he had more fun than all the rest of us put together. As Sadie Thompson, he seduced a series of recognizable faculty members, each priest lured to her bed by his particular, notorious weakness: food, drink, erudition, adulation and even moralizing—all to the drumming of a tropical rain storm on a tin roof.

Yes Father. Jerry was definitely a transvestite and he was also the finest priest I ever knew.

CHAPTER 8

Holy Trinity Seminary — 1957

I GOT MY first love letter in Second Divinity—it was from a boy.

The boy, in First Philosophy, lived in the Junior House while I was on the other side of the ecclesiastical Grand Canyon, in the Senior House—no fraternizing, no talking, not even eye contact permitted. For the most part, seniors didn't even know the names of the undergraduates. A few times every week these anonymous boys would troop into senior chapel for spiritual talks and for high mass on Sundays. They would file into the front rows on either side of the aisle and, as soon as the exercise was over, out they would troop, back to their compound—never a word passing between us. Yet Tommy Corbett said he'd been in love with me since before Christmas.

I didn't know Tommy Corbett from Adam.

We had met, he wrote, over ice cream in Caffolla's on O'Connell Street the day we got out for the Christmas vacation. "I was attracted to you immediately that day and haven't been able to stop thinking about you since."

From a boy… and from someone whose face I couldn't even picture? I remembered the group in the café that day vaguely — but couldn't see him. I was shocked a bit by what he said—but more than a little tantalized, I had to confess. In fact, I couldn't wait to see who he was—what he looked like? Was I flattered? Definitely. He loved my eyes, he said. I looked at them in the mirror—they were blue eyes with a fleck of yellow—well, I suppose… but could he have even seen them from across the wide aisle of the chapel?

He hoped that his letter did not offend me. His cousin, Jimmy Corbett, had assured him, he said, that I wouldn't mind. Jimmy was a year senior to me who shared my interest in pop music, but how on earth had he decided that I would be open to something like this?

Tommy had enclosed a picture of himself taken the previous summer at some tennis club: a very handsome, dark-haired boy in white shorts and shirt, tall and slight, tanned and athletic—a nice cheeky smile. For the life of me I couldn't remember ever meeting him. But he'd certainly got my attention. In fact, I thought of little else that night but Tommy Corbett.

But then sometime after lights out I had this paranoid thought: what if it's all a hoax—a letter written by somebody having me on?

I zeroed in on Jimmy Corbett the following morning right after breakfast.

"I had a letter from your cousin…" I began—trying to be casual.

"Ah! So, he finally got up the nerve to post that letter." He sounded very matter-of-fact about the whole thing.

He knows about it? I was relieved—but a bit shocked too.

"What do you mean, 'that letter'?" I was suddenly paranoid again. "You've read the letter?"

"Hey! I didn't have anything to do with it," he protested, holding his hands up—a mime's wall—in defense. He took a deep drag then on his cigarette and exhaled the gray smoke slowly into the frosty air before he continued.

"All I know about it is this: he wrote a letter to you and tore it up half a dozen times during the Christmas holidays. And, no, I never read it—though I have a fair idea what was on his mind." He looked me in the eye as though defying me to doubt him. I felt he wasn't lying to me.

"I just told the kid he should go ahead and post the damn thing—he was driving himself nuts thinking about it. I told him you wouldn't be offended even if you weren't interested."

"What is he like anyway, this cousin of yours?" I asked. "I don't remember much—we didn't talk that day at all—before Christmas." A truthful person might have said that he remembered nothing at all, but then…

"He was nice enough till he came across you!" He punched me on the arm then playfully. "Before that, he was this nice pious boy from a good Christian family, then all of a sudden one day…"

"Seriously?"

Jimmy dragged hard on his cigarette. "Seriously: beginning on the train ride down home that day, he turned into this little pain in the arse. All during the Christmas holidays, every time we met, all I heard was: 'Jack Holland this…' and

'Jack Holland that…' 'What is he like, this Jack Holland?'— obsessed, he was. And then 'Would he be offended if I wrote to him.'"

Jimmy and I were only a few yards from where the mail was being called and where a hundred or so divines were milling about. Jimmy moved closer and in just above a whisper added.

"Finally, I told him to write telling you how he felt and post the friggin' thing—get it off his chest. Give my ears a rest at the same time."

"You're not coddin' me then?"

Jimmy looked at me and blew Sweet Afton smoke over my head.

"I would never do that, not about something like this and especially not about Tommy."

He was being so serious—no trace of his usual bantering manner—that I had no doubt he meant every word he said.

The juniors were due in our chapel that evening for the dreary weekly talk by the Spiritual Director—a leisurely ramble through his thesaurus of religious clichés. For the first time in my seminary career I was excited at the prospect of leaving the novel I was reading to listen to a spiritual talk. Tommy had said he could look right across at me which meant he was on the opposite side of the great center aisle—that was good. I was hoping I'd recognize him. What if he doesn't look like the snap-shot?

But I needn't have worried, the minute he came through the door I spotted him: a very striking boy with dark hair and pale skin, he looked taller than his five foot nine, being so slightly built. Lithe as a cat he genuflected and watching him I remembered that tennis had been his passion—"till you came along"—he had written.

He knelt for the customary minute pretending to pray before sitting back on the seat. As he leaned forward on his arms I caught his eye for an instant—he was frowning and seemed anxious. I smiled and suddenly his face lighted up, he smiled in response and immediately bowed his head bashfully. I felt a tripping in my chest I had never felt there before.

Suddenly it was I who felt self-conscious. Could someone sitting nearby have been watching us? I risked a sideways glance at the faces on either side and I was reassured. They had mostly lapsed already into that state of anesthesia that enabled one to survive an hour of the priest's droning voice. Tommy had been watching me check around and grinned mischievously as I then shrugged for his benefit. He blushed suddenly and immediately covered his face with both hands—a gesture that might be mistaken by an onlooker for contemplation. But I had seen the blush before he covered it—and very becoming it was, too!

Crushes, or "Particular Friendships," as they were called in *The Rule*, were, I imagine, a common feature of most enclosed religious institutions down through history. *The Rule* advised that even in taking walks around the grounds there should be at least three —never two: *"Numquam duo, saltem tres"*— bad for community spirit, hanging out with one person so much. In our 1950's innocence, I doubt that anyone in an Irish seminary would have expected such a relationship to result in anything sexual — far, far too shocking.

That evening in study my mind swung from obsession about Tommy to confusion that I — whose every fantasy since puberty had involved girls — should be feeling this way about an eighteen-year-old boy. I was not ready to let my mind even begin to imagine where this obsession might lead. If someone had suggested that first night that I had begun a homosexual love affair, I would have denied it indignantly—vehemently.

While I could not let my thinking cross a certain awful threshold, my emotions, on the other hand, were not fooled for a second, they were stirred up as they had never been stirred up before. I spent that night and many subsequent nights at my window, smoking and staring out at the night sky and the shadowy fields and thinking about him.

We exchanged letters by the post, probably three or four each, over the next ten days or so. Mine were more inhibited, my statements more cautiously worded than his by far; mine expressing generalities while his were explicit and vulnerable. He wrote of how he loved my eyes, my face, my hair; how he lived for my glances and smiles in chapel; how I made his day merely being in refectory or anywhere else he could catch a glimpse of me. He was forthright in describing his passion and how he longed to spend even a few moments with me. Never had anyone rejoiced so in my very existence.

I had to talk to someone—someone tolerant and understanding and non-judgmental. That ruled out all of the faculty and most of the students. Jimmy Corbett had shown himself surprisingly broadminded in this matter but, as Tommy's cousin, he was hardly the one in whom I could safely confide. Only Jerry, my former roommate, could be counted on to be tolerant and understanding; only Jerry did I trust absolutely. I told him about Tommy and asked him to read the letters.

"He's really in love with you, I'd say." He glanced over at me briefly between letters.

"I think so too—scares the hell out of me half the time."

"And the other half...?" He raised his eyebrows as he looked at me.

"Oh god! The rest of the time I'm like a teenage girl—obsessed." Only to Jerry could I be that honest. "D' you think maybe it's just a fierce crush, maybe that's all it is, a crush?" I was half-hoping the answer would be yes—and at the same time dreading that.

"Love or a crush—where's the difference? Don't they feel the same when you're in the middle of one?" He continued reading.

"You've been in love then?" I wondered how he knew so much.

He seemed to give some thought to what he would say next for he was silent for a long moment before he waved his hand at me and said. "Never mind about that—sometime when I'm further removed from it, maybe I'll talk about it." He glanced away and I thought there was sadness in his voice.

But he gathered himself together almost immediately. "At the moment though, it's you I'm wondering about—what are you feeling about this boy? Do you feel the same—or are you just flattered that he thinks you've got such nice eyes?" He looked into my face very intently as he asked this.

"I can't think of a friggin' thing these days except him." That was about as forthcoming as I could get—even with Jerry.

"Then, I'd say you've both got it, and a pretty bad dose of it too."

"What the frig should I do, though, about it—that's what I want to know?"

"Well it all depends..." He was infuriating when he turned Socratic. We walked along in silence. Was he pondering what he would say next or was he eliciting some reaction from me by his 'all depends...'?

Finally I could take it no longer. "Depends on what?"

"It depends," he said, "on whether you're in for a penny or a pound."

"What the fuck's that supposed to mean? A penny or a pound—I mean, in this thing, what's what?"

"If you go on any further..." He paused then and began again. "Remember that you're hearing this from a romantic, from someone who invariably roots for the lovers in any story, who cheers them on as they run away to the forest green; from someone who gets misty eyed when they live happily ever after. So, consider the source! But I'd say, if you two go any further into this you're probably in for a wild ride. And often on that kind of ride somebody gets hurt."

"I should break it off then, you think?"

"I didn't say that and I probably wouldn't myself, if I was lucky enough to have somebody feeling like that about me. I'd probably run away and live in sin with them or something very shocking—but I wouldn't throw it away."

I was too confused by all this to say anything, so we walked along in silence for about a minute before he spoke again.

"Myself, I probably wouldn't break it off, but I don't have the foggiest what you ought to do."

"I'm more confused than ever." I sounded whiny even to my own ears as I said it—as though it was Jerry's job to resolve my dilemma. "I still don't have a clue what I... Well I do know what I should do, but...Fuckit!"

"It'll come to you. And you'll survive being in love—we all have." He punched me on the arm affectionately. "At least, I'm pretty sure you will."

"You're a big help!" I complained as we headed back for second study.

Tommy, in his letters, had begun pressing me to set a time when we could meet, up in Dublin, under some pretext: a doctor or dental appointment. And, after a lot of backing and forthing through the tedious postal route, we agreed finally on a day. We would both schedule appointments for that day with the same dentist in Dublin and have some time afterwards to talk. At first I was excited at the prospect—a tryst, how adventurous of me—but as the day approached I grew increasingly apprehensive. I was scared of being caught but I was even more terrified that in person I wouldn't live up to the image this boy had of me. What if he realized he'd been mistaken in that first impression—we'd hardly said a word to each other that day in Caffolla's. I spent the entire night before our meeting, standing at my window, smoking cigarette after cigarette, till the *Benedicamus Domino* rang through the corridors.

When I told Jerry about the dental appointment—he simply rolled his eyes to heaven.

My head dropped with a bump on the desktop during the Dean's Sacred Liturgy lecture that morning—a dead give-away that I hadn't found his dissertation on the reredos exactly riveting. Jerry kept me awake the rest of the day by jabbing me every few minutes with his elbow.

"I can hardly wait till you've got the marriage all arranged—decided on the children's' names or whatever..." He scribbled on his notebook and turned it so I could read it. I had just awakened myself with a snore in dogmatic theology. I looked over at him and he shook his head sympathetically.

"It's beginning to sound like a Doris Day movie," he whispered.

Tommy was already in the dentist's treatment room when I arrived but I didn't have long to wait before he returned to the waiting room. Up close, he was shorter than he had seemed in the cassock. He was startlingly good looking though: dark hair and very dark eyes contrasting with unblemished, winter-white skin, high cheekbones and features that were cut into dramatic planes. Not nearly as athletic-looking as in his tennis photo but more vulnerably attractive to me—and very shy as we shook hands. He would wait for me there, he said.

That was all either of us said before I had to accompany the dentist into his surgery for my completely unnecessary oral examination. In less than fifteen minutes Tommy and I were on the sidewalk in Merrion Square—alone together finally. Typically, I fled immediately to a safer place leaving Tommy my almost vacant body for company.

I noted how skeletal the trees around the Square looked against the gray, late winter Dublin sky. I took in the nearly infinite variety of Georgian doorways we were passing and the brass plates of every imaginable medical specialty and I saw the same streets peopled by characters a lot more colorful than those doctors and dentists. They were more vivid for me, these characters real and fictional, than was the boy walking beside me. Wilde and Swift, O'Casey and Behan, even characters from the minds of O'Casey and Behan were more real at that moment than Tommy; Sheridan and Burke, Maude Gonne and Yeats, Beckett, Padraig Colum and AE—all more vivid than this boy who loved me. And, of course Joyce—Joyce the Church-forbidden. Jerry and I had spent hours the year we had roomed together squeezing *Ulysses* and *The Portrait* for every drop of Dublin juice. Bloom—now there was somebody I could talk to.

Tommy and I were shouldering our way through the crowds of evening pedestrians along Nassau Street. Time had been doing its slow-motion trick on me again: my thoughts racing like the mind of a madman, while time seemed to be frozen.

A couple of minutes at least must have passed since we'd left the dentist's door and neither of us had said a word. I began to frantically think of something to say.

"Maybe we should go and have a coffee in Caffolla's?" I managed, finally. O'Connell Street was nearby enough and on the way to our bus anyway.

"Back to the scene of the crime?" He looked at me as he said it and we both laughed—more a release of tension on my part than amusement.

"What?" He asked—as though suddenly afraid I was laughing at something he hadn't caught.

"I don't really know 'what'. I'm just glad I'm here, is all. Glad you suggested it—relieved that we've made it. I wasn't sure—I was nervous about the whole idea," I said. "I'm babbling… I'm tense as all get out… But I am glad you suggested it."

"'Suggested'? Twisted your arm, you mean. I was so relieved when you showed up. I'd have felt like the right ejit if you'd stood me up, now wouldn't I?" He smiled at me and I was tongue-tied again. We crossed Nassau Street at the foot of Grafton Street

"I was worried you'd be real cross—think I was a nut case," he said.

Goldsmith and Burke looking down at us from their pedestals at Trinity College gates took more notice of us than did any of the Dubliners hurrying past in their headscarves and raincoats. Had Wilde in his splendificence been there he would almost certainly have noticed—and understood perfectly.

Once seated in Caffolla's we ordered coffees. He put a shilling in the jukebox and picked Lonnie Donnegan and Carl Perkins. As he studied the titles in the selector, I was noticing the clean, severe line of his jaw and the almost feminine grace of his neck. His hands, as he put the coin in the slot, were narrow with long slender fingers.

"What did you think when you got that first letter—honestly?" He spoke as though he had already planned exactly what he needed to ask. "Did you even remember at all, who I was?"

"Och aye, I remembered you all right." I lied. "I just couldn't imagine why you would be writing to me. I'm still not sure why you picked me to write to, though. Was there something… ? My first thought, honest to god, was that maybe Jimmy was pulling my leg."

I wanted to touch his hand as it rested on the table beside his saucer but thought better of it—sitting in a cafe before god and man and in the capitol of

Inhibitionland. Instead I touched his leg with mine and was thrilled to feel a recip-
rocal pressure coming from him.

"I told Jimmy you probably didn't remember me from a hole in the wall. 'Sure
he'll think I'm the right aul ejit', I told him, 'writing the man love letters,' you know.
Down there in Mullingar being in love with a man felt even weirder than it does up
here. I mean it's a pretty ridiculous idea if you think about it, isn't it? I mean being
in a seminary and all and two boys… 'What the frig is he going to think?' I asked
Jimmy."

"It took a lot of courage—more than I'd have." I told him.

"It took a big raging crush, and a right bit of insanity, now didn't it?"

He was so exposed, taking all the risks. And somehow, though I wanted to tell
him that I was every bit as obsessed as he, I couldn't seem to find language in me
for saying any of it.

"Tommy." I began. I had been feeling so bad at not being able to express
myself and he must have seen it in my face. He had turned suddenly even paler than
before—frightened maybe. Afraid that I might hurt him.

"Tommy. I've been repeating your name over and over again to myself for the
past three weeks like it was some holy invocation—like in a litany or something—
and all I've been thinking about for weeks is you. I've so badly wanted to be with
you but, at the same time, far too scared to do anything about it." Again I wanted
to reach over and touch his hand but again I restrained myself and went on with
what I had to get out.

"And I've never before looked forward to being in chapel as I have since your
letter. I can't explain how even the slightest contact thrills me—makes that day
worth living. You're what I think about first thing in the morning when I hear the
Benedicamus Domino, and when it's lights-out, thoughts of you *are* my night prayer…
If this is not being in love…"

He gave me a sympathetic smile and, reaching over the table, very briefly
touched my hand with the tips of his fingers. Excitement raced up my arm and down
the length of my spine in a flash of electricity. Suddenly Caffolla's glowed with vivid
colors, the people in the café were warmer, O'Connell's Street was suddenly shimmering under a mediterranean sun. I wanted to leap on the tabletop and tap-dance
like Astaire and shout at the top of my voice that I'd found love. But—being only a
clerical student in full penguin drag—I was forced to maintain the proper demeanor.

"Oh god!" I groaned.

"But, do you think we can ever really be together?" He almost whispered it.

And, though I heard him well enough, it took a few seconds for the meaning of what he'd said to sink in.

"Oh! God no! No! Never anything like that. You mean… Oh God, no! Aah, aah! It would never lead to anything like…" I was babbling again. My denial was fighting a half-hearted rear-guard skirmish. I was still reeling from the mere touch of him. "Oh no! Never anything like that!"

But even as I was protesting, in my mind I was already holding him in my arms and nuzzling the softness of his neck above the white shirt collar …

The harsh voice of our waitress taking orders at the booth behind me jarred me back to Dublin and reality.

"No! We could never be …" I agreed shaking my head.

"I know you're right," he said and shook his head regretfully too. "You would never want to be with me like that, would you?"

I avoided the question.

"Have you ever been with anyone?" I asked.

"No. No, I haven't. Have you?"

"God, Tommy! I don't know where in hell this is going. I don't know what it is about you but what I'm wanting is scaring the bejazus out of me. I mean what if somebody were to catch us… together?"

Even as I said it I could hear how cowardly I sounded.

"Ah! So you have no real problem with being together—only with being caught?" There was no note of censure in his voice. But he smiled—a satisfied smile—as though he had just won a point.

"Well. I suppose you're right. God, I wish…" I couldn't put that wish into words.

"You wish what?" He asked.

"Don't you have any problem with it… like morally?"

"Of course I do. Who wouldn't? But then, it'd be no more a mortal sin than if it was a boy and a girl, would it?"

"But it would be a mortal sin." I wasn't even convincing myself.

Tommy's only reaction to this was a cynical flick of an eyebrow.

He looked at the clock—it was good one of us had his feet on the ground. We had just time to catch the bus back, report in and change before first study bell.

We left the money on the table and hurried over to the bus station. It was getting dark as we walked from the bus stop and, just outside the gates, hidden by dense shrubbery from the college buildings, I pulled him to me in a hug. It was a very tentative embrace till he wrapped his arms around me. We held each other then for just a moment but before letting go he kissed me gently on the cheek. Once inside the grounds, *The Rule* forbade us to speak, so without another word we — observant seminarians — each headed to his own dormitory.

I changed into a cassock and reported to the Dean — still in a daze.

"Yes, Father. He thought I should probably have two of them filled in the near future." "No, Father. It doesn't pain me any longer." I reported to the Dean and sowed the seed of a future trip to the city. "Yes, Father. He is a very good dentist. Thank you for the recommendation."

I could feel his lips soft still on my cheek hours later, during night prayer. Had they imprinted an indelible mark there, a character like the one baptism or ordination is said to leave on the soul? "…or mortal sin?" My mother's voice taunted. "Mortal sin leaves a mark on the soul too—a black mark!"

It was two nights later and I must have been asleep for a couple of hours already when I was awakened by the distinctive click of the doorknob being turned very softly. I froze. Nobody dared enter another's room at night—not even the Dean. The room was brightly lit by the wintry moon streaming in through the high Gothic casements. In a dark tracksuit with the hood pulled over his head the effect was eerie—a haunted abbey.

"My God! What in hell …?" I sat up in bed. For him to be found anywhere near Senior House meant immediate expulsion and, if caught in my room, we would both get the *ipso facto* boot. To say I was scared would be a massive understatement—I was frozen with fear.

"Shhh!" He breathed, as he closed the door very quietly behind him.

He came over to the bed and very deliberately pulled the covers off me. He sat down on the edge then and slipped off his tennis shoes. Though I was terrified of being caught, I lay on my elbow watching him—as in a dream. I tried to remember later what I was feeling then but I couldn't remember feeling anything, good or bad. I must have taken off for my round tower again. Still in his tracksuit, he stretched out beside me on the bed and I lay back and surrendered to what I had been dreaming of for weeks. I must have returned to my body about then for I remember that my heart began pounding at the touch of his face against mine and the feel of his body. I responded by enfolding him tightly. I pulled the covers over us.

We held each other, more like lonely children than lovers, hugging fiercely and kissing each other's faces. His breath was warm and child-fragrant on my neck but his body and face were cold from being outside. The curve of his neck where my face was nestled was as soft as I had imagined it that day in Caffolla's and it smelled of him—the smell of water and soap and boyish skin. We held each gently, hardly stirring, for half an hour before he kissed me gently on the cheek and slipped out of bed. We had not spoken a single word since he had come into the room.

I stroked his back under his shirt as he sat on the bedside tying his shoes. I ran my fingers along the fine bones of his shoulders and traced with my fingertips the narrow taper of his ribs to the muscles of his firm waist. When he'd finished dressing he bent over me and kissed me lightly again—this time his lips brushed mine. I let myself fall back onto the pillow holding his head with both my hands and pulled him down on top of me.

"I must go now," he whispered after a few moments and struggling out of my embrace he stood up.

I sprang from the bed then—desperate to hold him one last time. Embracing in the cold moonlight, in that cold bare room, I told him that I loved him. Against all logic and caution I wanted him to stay with me till the morning.

"I'll come back again in a few nights," he said as he gently disengaged himself from my arms. A smile flashed in the moonlight, then quickly, softly as a cat, he slipped out of the room.

The room had never seemed so empty. I was afraid for him as I pictured him stealing through the dark corridors—back to Junior House.

"Do not harm this boy," I prayed to the monster-god that destroys everyone we love. "If you must destroy someone for this love, destroy me."

I stood at the window and blew cigarette smoke out into the night. My self-conferred vocation hung in tatters—it had been a ragged disguise for inadequacy even at the best of times—but now... Everything I had been working towards for the past five years had been suddenly blown away and, to boot, I was involved in what was considered the most unthinkable of sins — a "perversion" even. But my spirit had never felt so joyful. How long could I keep feeling this way? How long before the priests in black gowns began making their rounds? Blake had battled these same demons.

It was not until I tried to sleep that the bitter cleric in my head became properly provoked.

"You had better not go to communion tomorrow—not with this vileness on your soul." He carped. "Even you cannot excuse this, surely?"

"And the ignominy," he mocked, "of kneeling in your place while the others step over you to go to the altar."

"Wear a sign, why don't you?" He taunted.

"And what faculty priest, do you imagine, will absolve this perversion?" He mocked. There was no possible way—not for another week at least—to fake a dental excuse so as to visit the friendly Friars on the Dublin quays.

For a good hour I let him torment me until finally, enraged at how he was poisoning my joy, I banished him to hell and set the moral housekeeping aside for a later time. I allowed myself instead to recall the love and tenderness of the moment when Tommy had lain in my arms—in that same narrow bed.

Next morning when I awoke to the shouting of *Benedicamus Domino* and the rising bell's clanging along the hollow corridor outside my door, the previous night seemed hardly real. I surfaced reluctantly from the most peaceful sleep I had enjoyed in months, feeling fresh and energetic—and wonderfully untroubled by my sin.

I remembered George and how full of vigor he had been following his "wonderful experience". Could it be that sin is so much more invigorating than virtue? Could they have had it back to front all these years? I felt particularly alert in chapel too and my mind had never felt so in tune with the sentiments contained in our morning prayers.

This was verily the day that the Lord had made and I did rejoice and feel very glad indeed in it—a day full of hope and promise—the divine spirit had truly renewed the face of the earth—you'd hardly recognize it—and yea verily, ours was a good and beneficent god that encouraged love.

During meditation, in place of my customary nap, I wrestled with the issues of moral theology that related to my situation: whether what Tommy and I had done constituted the elements of a mortal sin. I listened patiently to both sides as they made their presentations—the black-gowned clerics, for the prosecution, of course—made a good case for eternal damnation, I had to admit; but counsel for the defense—a charming gentleman in a scarlet cape—argued the law most persuasively for the other side. And, before meditation was over I had arrived at a verdict: "Not Guilty." I had done nothing mortally sinful, not by the strictest interpretation of the law—we had done nothing that had involved the genitalia after all and wasn't it true that penal laws should be interpreted narrowly? Very, very good point! No mortal sin having been committed... ablative absolute—nothing in heaven or earth barred me from communion.

I was the first out of the seat after the *Agnus Dei*. Surely I had persuaded the Lamb in the previous half-hour of casuistry, as I had persuaded myself. Wasn't this the god who supposedly loved me more even than I loved myself? Fabulous!

I don't believe I crossed the Rubicon that morning in my relationship with the Church but I had certainly waded a bit further into the water than when I had created my own rules regarding *delectatio* and *masturbatio*.

That night Tommy came to me again and for the three nights after that as well. On each occasion we grew progressively more relaxed and intimate till by the third night we felt free to undress completely. That night we also broke through every remaining inhibition, tenderly at first, then with greater and greater urgency, and finally we allowed our passion to erupt in wild explosions of released energy. The echo of our feral groans seemed to surge like waves along the vaulted corridors and reverberate around the silent grounds, ricocheting off handball courts and caroming around the quadrangle. Surely no one could have slept through the electrical storm we let loose in that sterile barn; surely dark phantoms plucked angrily at the black-gowned priests in their chaste beds.

He did not return the following night and, though I had tried to discourage him from the terrible risk he was taking, I was frantic when he didn't come.

Had he had been frightened off by the intensity of what was happening? Things had moved so rapidly it was only natural to be frightened. And what he was doing, coming over from Junior House ... It was better that he not take the chance. Yet, it was so lonely without him, I spent most of that night standing at my window, smoking, worried that he no longer wanted to see me.

I pictured myself stealing down the four flights of stairs and sprinting along the miles of dark corridors to Junior House...

What if I run into the Dean? What could I say? Immediate expulsion, disgrace. What do I tell them at home when I arrive, suitcases in hand—a spoiled priest stinking up their doorstep? And kicked out for what?

I dragged myself through lectures and spiritual exercises the following morning, barely able to keep awake in chapel or lecture hall. We had the Dean for dogma that morning and naturally he called me—nothing escaped his eye—and naturally I hadn't a clue. I tried to fake it by babbling vague generalities. He cut me off in mid-babble.

"That will be all *Domine.*"

He called me aside afterwards. He had been noticing recently that I had seemed distracted. Was I not sleeping well? He stared at his little well-shined shoes while I denied both suggestions. He'd been getting reports recently from other faculty, he said. And the faculty was concerned—it was not typical of me. Backhanded compliment noted. If something was troubling me I should speak to someone.

I assured him it was nothing serious—"maybe a bit tired, Father."

He gave me permission for long lie-ins the next two mornings. Two less bad communions. Two less sacrileges—the Catholic tabulator rang up.

That evening the juniors would be in our chapel again for the weekly Spiritual Talk. As I sat in my place awaiting their arrival my stomach and thigh muscles were clenched with anxiety. Had he become frightened, dangling out on that precarious moral limb, I fretted? Had he, maybe, fled from the danger—back to the high ground staked out by the Church? It would not seem in character, given his courage—but he was very young and very vulnerable.

I held my breath as the familiar graceful figure came through the door and I watched anxiously as he walked up the aisle to his place and knelt down. He pushed back onto the seat finally and looked over towards me. To my intense relief, he smiled.

No sooner had he smiled and brought the light back into my void than I became annoyed with him for worrying me, and instead of smiling back I sat frowning at him. I was sulking—punishing him. But, how long could I hold out? In less than a minute I returned his smile.

He came to me again that night and after we had made love tenderly and passionately he whispered that he had decided to quit Holy Trinity. He had to leave, he said. He couldn't in good conscience live with such dishonesty. He had been doubting his vocation even during first term—even before meeting me at Christmas—but now he was certain the priesthood was not for him.

Oh god! I'd been afraid of something like this. Not everyone was born with my talent for living a conflicted existence.

Would I leave too and be with him? We could go off to England together, he said. We could live there in a city where nobody would know us or care what we did. He had it all thought out. He would get a job and I could go to school for something. It would all work out if we were only together.

I was shocked. What could I say? His logic was faultless, and though terribly romantic, his plan was so much more grounded in reality—not to mention integrity—than anything I had in mind. What was it I had in mind anyway, I wondered for an instant? Study theology during the day and enjoy well-deserved sin at night? For how long could that last? But I was shocked by his plan for us.

He must have sensed my involuntary recoil and become frightened, for he slipped out of bed right away and began to get dressed. Neither of us said a word for several agonizing minutes. I lay on my elbow watching him, knowing I had disappointed him and wondering if he was so hurt he was leaving me for good. I rubbed his back gently, my fingers moving over the now-familiar contours of his spine and ribs. He did not look around at me nor respond as he had always before.

Only when he had his tennis shoes tied, did he turn and meet my eye.

"Just think about it, between now and summer," he whispered. "No rush." He kissed me gently then. "See you tomorrow night," he promised.

And he was gone noiselessly out the door.

It was lonely always when he left but that night, after his announcement, I felt particularly desolate. I settled in for a night gazing out into starless night; sleep was unthinkable.

He had said he would come again the following night and that I had till the end of the year to make up my mind. Anything might happen before the end of the year. I might even get courage.

A light drizzle was falling and it felt cool and clean on my hot skin when I leaned far out the window. Clouds were covering the stars and in the distance across the plowed fields, a lonely dog was barking continuously. It was dark out except for the faint haloed streetlights on the road that ran alongside the playing fields off to the north.

Could I ever live alone again?

What Tommy was proposing was of course the fulfillment of every fantasy I'd had since he had come into my life, but it was also the scariest, most unthinkable cliff I could imagine leaping off.

I was far more practiced in living with unresolved moral issues than Tommy. Habits of avoidance, perfected over many years, allowed me to enjoy life one day at a time while ignoring impending disasters.

"A veritable field trip in moral theology," was how Jerry described my life around that time. I had told him so much about my emotional ups and downs and had gone on and on so much about Tommy that he had begun referring to him as his "sister-in-law."

Tommy, on the other hand, struck me as someone who did not consider a life of lies and accommodation as an option; nor was denial preferable to reality for him. He might have come from a different planet his values were so foreign to me—he reminded me a lot of Jerry.

I already knew in my soul what I would have to do—though I had no idea how I would break the news to Tommy. How could I tell him that I was too cowardly to follow my heart's prompting and that I was too frightened to follow my conscience. I had to tell him that I was just too afraid—afraid of what my mother and the neighbors would say about quitting —not to mention my running off to England with a lover—and a boy-lover, into the bargain.

"You must come home and meet my mother—you'll just love her!" I could just see it.

"Mammy, this is Tommy, your daughter-in-law."

"We had hoped you and daddy might come over and visit us in our new place."

"A baby? No. Not really any signs of that yet, mammy."

The thought of leaving Ireland and finding work in England, while frightening, wasn't nearly as terrifying as the thought of facing her. Still, being in the world as a man who loved another man was a terrifying prospect too. I would rather hide out behind the Church's skirts—and I suspected that Tommy already sensed that.

After breakfast the next morning I was standing outside the refectory waiting for mail-call when Jimmy took me by the arm and, without a word, pulled me away from the mob. His face was pale and there were dark shadows under his eyes I had not seen before—as though he hadn't slept. His mouth had an unusually grim set to it as I waited for him to tell me what was on his mind. He did not look at me but kept looking around the rooftops of the college and heaving deep sighs as though seeking strength.

"Tommy's been expelled," he whispered finally. "Or did you know that?"

"What...?" A bolt of fear charged through me at the news—the hairs rippled on the nape of my neck and my entire body shuddered suddenly. My shock and dismay must have made it apparent that I had no prior knowledge of anything of the sort.

"When?" I managed to ask. It couldn't have been more than four hours since he had left my room. But of course Jimmy had no certain knowledge of that—I hoped. He was looking at me curiously though—suspiciously, I thought.

"What the hell happened?" I asked lamely—my fear already knew and had known it to be inevitable since the first night he'd come to me.

"He was caught crossing from Senior House back to the Junior House around half-past-four this morning." Jimmy stifled a sob. There were tears now on his cheeks that he tried wiping away with the sleeve of his cassock.

"Oh, my God!" I exclaimed involuntarily

"I got to see him for just a few minutes in the visitors parlor while everybody else was at mass. He had asked to see me," Jimmy said. "He's left already." He lighted a cigarette and took a deep pull off it.

"Where did he go, d'you know? Did you get to speak to him alone?" The questions tumbled out of me.

"Apparently, they convened an emergency meeting of the Consultors—at half past five—and decided to have him leave right away."

As I listened to Jimmy my self-serving fear was struggling to assess my own risk and the questions I didn't dare ask were racing about in my head. Had he told them where he'd been—who he'd been with? Surely they'd guess what he'd been doing—they weren't total imbeciles. Had they pressed him to reveal his senior accomplice? Had they caught him near my room or well away from it? Had he made it back again into Junior House before they caught him?

"The Dean came to my room before the rising bell." Jimmy's hand that held the cigarette was shaking. "He told me to be in the visitors parlor around half past six. I didn't know what the frig was wrong. I thought somebody at home was dead or something and they were going to break the news. Even when I saw Tommy there, I thought the same: something's wrong at home."

Jimmy's voice was beginning to break and great involuntary sobs were interrupting what he was saying. I led him away a bit further from the milling crowd around mail-call.

"They left me alone with him in the parlor—he told me then that he'd been expelled and about being caught over here last night and about the Consultors meeting and all."

"Oh, Fuck!" Was all I could think to say. I pictured Tommy there in the polish-smelling parlor.

"He said he was thinking of going over to England instead of going home—I don't think he wanted to face them at home. Borrowed some money—for the boat, I suppose."

"D'ye think that's where he went then?"

Jimmy had been staring intently into my face—as though trying to read something there. I wished he would take to examining the rooftops again for it was making me uncomfortable. I was so full of guilt I had trouble keeping my voice from quivering as I asked the question.

"Yeah." He said, through a mouthful of smoke. "I think he went straight from here to the North Wall." He looked down at his shoes and kicked a piece of gravel angrily—was that me he was lashing out at?

"He gave me a message" Jimmy continued and there was definitely anger in his voice now. "Told me to give it to you right away." Jimmy looked grimmer than ever but his eyes looked sad, brimming with unshed tears. I was afraid of what he was thinking and of his anger.

"I don't want to know why he was over here or if it was with you." He was exercising great control to even talk to me, I realized. "But I know what I know."

Jimmy kicked another piece of gravel before he continued. He refused to meet my eye.

"If I find out that he was over here at your suggestion... You'd better not have done something to hurt him, I'm tellin' you."

Jimmy's anger and his bitter words would stay with me for years adding to my guilt. I had no reason to fear Jimmy physically for I was so much larger and stronger, but I was frightened by the power of his emotion. What could I say to him? I should wait, I felt, for some of his emotion to subside before trying to explain.

"Be that as it may." Jimmy continued. He had taken a deep breath and a few last drags on his cigarette before crushing it fiercely under his toe. His voice seemed more resigned when he spoke again.

"The message he gave me was this: 'Tell Jack I have said nothing to anybody and that he's to stop worrying.'"

His message had relieved my fears but in the process of doing so it had aggravated my shame. For years I would be haunted by the picture of that young frightened boy stealing along the dark echoing corridors while I, by my window, sat contemplating my betrayal speech. I see him: a lonely boy, already saddened by my reluctance, surprised in the dark by the Dean, accused, convicted and the summary sentence of expulsion delivered—all in the dead of night.

I had never even been to his room. I had never seen where he'd slept and studied; the bed he had left and returned to every night and where he had packed his hurried luggage the last morning. Neither had I been with him in the early morning darkness as he walked down the crunchy gravel of the driveway, through the gates to the bus stop: nor did I accompany him to North Wall for the early Liverpool boat. And I would not be there as his partner in the new life he was beginning. I have never forgiven myself.

I arranged for another dentist appointment the next half-day. It had been a mere four weeks since the day Tommy and I first met and had coffee in Caffolla's. When the dentist was done, I walked down along the quays. In the confessional I told the kindly friar all about my sins of the flesh and the sacrileges I had committed by receiving communion in the state of mortal sin but mainly, I told him about my cowardice and the most recent betrayal it had caused. He was a good man and he listened to everything I said and he was very gentle with me. He understood too, I felt, when I told him how I was far more troubled by abandoning this boy who loved me than I was about all the sins of impurity and sacrilege. I made it clear that it was this sin, alone of all my many sins, that troubled my conscience.

I was to say a rosary for penance, he said, and as he droned the Christian words of absolution: *Ego te absolvo a peccatis tuis…* I asked the god of love to forgive me.

I knelt awhile, staring at the altar but nothing was stirring in my soul. Out in the damp of a dusky Dublin evening I walked along the quays to O'Connell's Bridge where I stopped. The river below slithered by, a rainbow-sheen of oil shimmering on the surface—watered silk like a bishop's bellyband. The rain was turning heavy and water streaming off the brim of my hat was splashing onto the bridge parapet. The sky above O'Connell's Street was grey-black, threatening a long drenching. Before long it would be dark.

Already, lights were coming on in the dark little shops along the Walk and Peterson's Pipes on the corner was lighted up like a space ship. The clock on the bank said it was five to five. The green double-deckers from the Pillar, splashed past me heading for College Green and Dame Street carrying Dubliners home for their tea. I must soon catch my bus too.

Returning to voluntary captivity was depressing but freedom had become even less attractive. Wasn't there a third option, some safe hole, where I might mark time till I could decently die. Confession had not only failed to lighten my soul, but in begging absolution I had perpetrated the ultimate betrayal.

My spirits had soared for a moment with him—then I'd looked down. That's what had spoiled everything — reality.

But Peter, seeing the winds and the waves, became afraid.

Walking on water —no trick to it when the water's calm.

CHAPTER 9

Big Sur, California — 2004

"I'VE JUST FINISHED reading what you wrote about your relationship with the boy in seminary."

"I was afraid of that," Holland said. He had pushed the pages under the priest's door this morning early, before his swim, and had been on edge since thinking about the discussion it would provoke.

"It can't have been easy—writing about it." The monk's tone was sympathetic, but not patronizing—definitely not patronizing. Holland's antennae had been on the lookout for that.

"I relived the shame of it last night as I was writing about it. I had blocked it out of my mind till we started this… this exploration."

"The 'shame'. . . ? Could you say more about that?"

"What I said in the writing there: being ashamed of my cowardice mostly and the abandonment. Last night I was writhing in the shame and guilt all over again— it might have been yesterday not forty years ago it happened."

As he spoke Holland had slouched forward, his forearms resting on his knees as though weighed down by the depression of the previous night. He looked up briefly when he'd finished but his eyes did not seek out the priest's eyes.

"And you haven't forgiven yourself in all this time?" The monk asked.

Holland was staring at the floor between his weathered boots; he shook his head slowly from side to side in agreement.

"You loved him—Tommy—didn't you?" The priest's voice had a softer tone than Holland had heard in it before.

It was startling, hearing the words spoken by a man he hardly knew, and a monk at that. He looked up and for an instant thought he detected compassion in the pale face across from him—the face rearranged itself quickly.

"I did, I loved him." Holland almost whispered the words. "We walked into the trap, he and I, and the jealous god became enraged and ripped us apart."

It was odd talking about such intimate matters after talking to nobody for years—nobody since Jerry.

"After a few years in seminary I had almost forgotten the jealous bastard and how we provoke his rage if we dare love another mortal. I had bought into the Christian myth: where the daddy-god and the mammy-god and the little baby-god—the love-gods—want everybody to love one another. But after losing Tommy I came back to the god I knew to be the one true god: The Lord of the Psychopaths." Holland took a deep, labored breath and leaned forward again, forearms on his knees. His head seemed to fall forward under its own weight.

As Holland was speaking the little monk's face had become grim and his lips even more tightly pursed than usual. When he spoke finally his voice was sharp and angry.

"I don't see why you feel it necessary to blaspheme to get your point across. Just because we don't share the same faith, Mr. Holland, it hardly means that we are fooling ourselves."

"Oh, really? I think if you look hard enough you'll discover that you and I both believe in the same god—you're in denial, maybe. How else explain the so-called virtue of detachment? Why else would a human being renounce every kind of natural human love, except to appease a jealous bastard that flies into a rage when faced with competition? I recognize a true believer when I see one."

"Aren't you being more than a little judgmental? I don't see how you can pretend to know so much about someone else's faith." The priest said.

There was silence for a long moment then. Finally, the big man straightened up and stretched his cramped back out to its full length. His eyes lifted till they met the priest's; the wiry gray brows were gathered into a puzzled frown as he began to speak.

"So, even though you've thrown your body on the altar to placate the jealous god, my saying so is too 'judgmental'?" His tone was angry, defiant. "Well then. How about the man who, every time he kneels down, creates a little god for himself, cobbled together from scraps of myth and theological speculation that he's drawn from books; this composite idea he projects then onto a little screen in the back of his brain and he prays to it; and as he prays, he pretends that his shadow-puppet will answer his prayers, and that it loves him and watches over him. He even tells himself that this creation of his mind is the creator of the universe. Yet, this god exists only so long as he is keeping it in existence by thinking about it; the moment his mind turns to something else, it vanishes like a candle flame—poof! 'Put your toys away when you're done playing with them'."

Holland paused to catch his breath; a blue fire was blazed in the eyes set deep underneath the heavy brows; the tight-wound intensity of a Savonarola or a Luther was pulsating in his voice and body. Holland's tirade seemed to have stunned the little monk for he was still staring open-mouthed at him.

"So what sort of faith would you say that is, Father?" Holland asked before collapsing forward onto his elbows again, exhausted by the burst of fervor—his head too heavy for his neck, sagged.

"Maybe faith cannot stand such a searingly honest examination—it isn't science after all." The monk suggested.

"So? Are you a man who believes in the god, Father?" Holland looked up at the priest.

"I have to wonder now, after what you've just said, whether I can say that I do or whether…" The monk was staring at the wall behind Holland's head—looking at it intently as though expecting something to appear there. He seemed to have forgotten what he was about to say. Holland straightened up and looked him in the eye—a question in his raised eyebrow.

"You've got me questioning myself. Perhaps I've been constructing a god in my own head and calling it 'The Creator.' Though I frankly don't know how else one can find God."

Holland stretched his long back against the chair back, bringing his shoulder blades together laboriously—he winced at the muscle ache. The little chair creaked dangerously from the strain.

"Very well." The priest suddenly held up both his hands as though to bring himself back to the therapist role from wherever his mind had been roaming. "Interesting!" He added in a voice Holland understood to mean, "I'm bored."

"Sorry I went on and on like that." Holland apologized.

"I think that's all we have time for today." The monk was suddenly all business. "Continue with your writing and we'll meet again the day after tomorrow— same time?"

Holland was bewildered by the man's sudden change of tone. He stood up and looked for a moment at the tortured figure hanging by his finger-bones on that gruesome crucifix and then, without a word to the priest, he strode from the room.

Poor stupid Jew! Waste of a bloody life, that! He was muttering to himself as he went down the stairs. Dying so these bastards can run up here, away from the world.

Stay away from these priests if you're planning on coming back—they'll do you far worse the next time—now they've got all this new technology.

Walking back across the lawn he held his face up to the fine mist that was drifting gentle as muslin over the soft grass. It felt good, cooling on his hot face.

Right little fucker!

Shite! I let him get to me again—too sensitive by far; too needy.

In the room he dried off his face and looked at himself in the little mirror—the grim face lined and weathered.

Pathetic is what you are, Holland. Fucking pathetic! In spite of itself the face in the mirror grinned ruefully back at him.

Get back to your writing—it calms you down at least.

CHAPTER 10

Holy Trinity Seminary — 1959

STAYING AWAKE IN Sharkey's lecture was always a challenge—but one for which Jerry and I had devised a solution.

"Yes, Domine Egan. You have a question?"

"Father is it true that the Church may begin ordaining women in the very near future?"

"Domine Egan!" The priest shook his little close-cropped head sadly. "How on earth could you even imagine such an abomination?"

"But why not, Father?"

"*Mister* Egan. Can you just imagine the commotion if a woman were to come out on the altar of your local parish, all vested up to say mass on a Sunday morning? Shocking! Absolutely shocking!" He spluttered

"I don't understand what you mean, Father." I chimed in, careful to keep a butter-wouldn't-melt expression.

"Completely unthinkable!" Sharkey was trembling with outrage and indignation. He grabbed a glass of water off the podium with shaking hand.

"To think of a woman someday handling the sacred host is just terrible, terrible!" His narrow body shivered at the very thought.

"Why is that, Father?" I persisted.

"Mister Holland. Don't tell me that you too… This is just terrible, terrible! Such a nasty business, nasty business!"

"I don't understand what you mean, Father?"

"Blood, you silly boys! That's why. It's because of the blood. Can't you see that? Do I have to explain everything to you silly boys?"

"Blood, Father? Do you mean the blood of Christ?"

"Oh God, give me strength!" He implored the ceiling of the classroom. Jerry and I hardly dared a sideways glance at each other.

"What blood do you mean, Father?" Jerry asked innocently.

The rest of the class sat tight in their seats—half of them as outraged as Sharkey, the other half trying not to laugh out loud.

"It's their blood. Oh, this is all such a nasty business. Very nasty business all together!" He had splashed water over his notes and was mopping it with his handkerchief.

"It's their monthly bleeding—that's why. Let's make an end of this whole conversation now. Turn to page …"

"Father. Is it then because they have menstrual blood that they cannot be priests?" I asked, keeping my face open and innocent—pencil poised over notebook—a seeker of truth.

"Yes indeed. That's it. That's the main reason of course and it should be plain to everybody with half a brain in his head." He fussed finding his page, tut-tutting under his breath. He had found his place finally.

"Just wouldn't be fitting at all, at all. Now come on! We shouldn't be talking about this nasty stuff here. Shouldn't be talking about it at all. Terrible, terrible! Let's move on…"

"Father!" Jerry was so persistent it was almost embarrassing. "Didn't the Blessed Virgin menstruate?"

Sharkey glared at Jerry over his glasses—a hateful look.

"And didn't she have Christ inside her body, let alone touch him with her hands?" I had to deflect his attention from Jerry—*El piccador*. Sharkey aimed his death-ray in my direction.

"And didn't she breast-feed him too?" Jerry was upping the stakes.

"She did nothing of the sort!" Sharkey banged his fist on the rostrum, rattling the empty glass. "Christ was conceived immaculately. None of those other disgusting things were involved at all." For a moment I was worried he would have a heart attack—he had become pale and his hands were shaking badly.

"And don't let me hear you suggest any such thing again, Mr. Egan, or you'll find yourself out there—in quick order." He waved vaguely in a generally southwesterly direction that might have signified County Kerry or Brazil.

"And, are you saying that she did not even menstruate, Father?" I would not be deterred. "Yet she was truly a woman?"

"Because she was not tainted by Original Sin." Sharkey was speaking through clenched teeth; desperately controlling himself. "Consequently, she did not have any of these afflictions of the children of Eve."

"I didn't know that, Father." Jerry was humble in his acquiescence. "Where could I read up on that?"

"I'll get you references tomorrow. And now finally, let us resume the point I was making about…"

By then the class would be almost over—at least we hadn't totally squandered the hour.

Jerry and I were brought up before the Rector and the Board of Consultors once in Third Divinity, "On Suspicion of Modernism," was the charge.

"Modernism," for those young enough to have escaped its scourge, was this frightful heresy—condemned in no uncertain terms by a succession of Popes—that had raged through the world like the Black Death. It advocated using Reason as a vehicle for arriving at Truth. The abominations a twisted heretical mind will devise to mislead the faithful boggle the imagination!

Jerry was all for challenging the faculty—Luther style—to a classical *disputatio,* but my more thoughtful approach prevailed—we lied. It was my considered opinion that, in a case such as ours, "Truth" would most likely not set us free at all, but would almost certainly get us into a whole lot of trouble. By claiming that our errors had arisen out of our ignorance and naiveté—rather than the much-dreaded "intellectual inquisitiveness"—we had given them the excuse they needed to absolve us. And, of course, by absolving us of the charges they happened also to be serving their own best interests: it allowed them to fill the quota of new bodies that had been ordered and paid for by our American diocese.

The Catholic slave trade was a growth industry in Holy Trinity, as indeed it was in most Irish seminaries and novitiates of that era. Young Irish men and women were shipped by the hundreds each year to American dioceses as priests and nuns, young people who would work for little more than their keep—indentured servants—cheap teachers and clergy for rich American Catholics.

The loss of two men in Third Divinity would mean a serious financial loss for a seminary, but where both men were being paid for by the same diocese, it could be a disaster—the diocese might take its business elsewhere. And with that business would go all those lovely Yankee dollars down the drain. It is always easy to convince men who are eager to be convinced—a little lie, a little contrition— we were off the hook and they were back in business. Exactly how far our beliefs diverged from orthodoxy they were not eager to discover.

As Third Divinity ended I was ordained to the order of Sub-Diaconate, noteworthy as the occasion when one was required to begin the celibate life. Some men were so agonized coming up to this watershed that they fled the night before ordination.

"Maybe I should bail out, before it's too late? What d'you think?" I asked Jerry. But I would sooner renounce sex for life than face my mother's wrath— nothing much had changed in the years since St. Columb's and I was now within a year of ordination.

The scene: my homecoming, having quit the seminary.

"Hello there!" I'd sing out cheerfully as I'd sling my suitcase in the back door.

"And where did you come out of, pray tell?" She's wiping her hands on her apron as her worried eyes scrutinize my face—worried, and sharp with suspicion.

"Och, I just walked over from the bus, you know."

"But you're not supposed to be home for another week yet—wasn't it the seventeenth you told us was subdiaconate?"

"Och aye, it was. But… Mammy, I just couldn't go through with it, you know."

That was as far as my imagination would venture into the scene. I hadn't the nerve to imagine the disgust and recriminations. And all my father's resentments, so successfully checkmated by my going to the seminary, unleashed then with the interest accrued over six years.

Oh God! The embarrassment.

My mother would have to stop going to Sunday mass from the shame of it: her son, suddenly appearing in the chapel dressed in layman's clothes.

I could hear them cackling, the aul biddies with the headscarves tied tight under their white-bristly chins, in the chapel porch after the eight o'clock mass.

"And a few days before taking the vow of celibacy, if ye don't mind." Nudges with sharp elbows in the crones' aisle.

"Aye. God, save us!" Signs of the cross dusted hastily on their droopy chests— to ward off sexual filth.

'A tarrer he couldn't control hisself?" Knowing looks—woman to woman—eyes cut quickly sideways and back. Nobody within earshot but the select circle. And who knew better the depravity of men's durty urges?

"Eh? Eh? Why else d'ye think they got rid of him, and after all them years in there?"

"And him prancing about dressed up like he was a priest already and all the time behind closed doors he's . . ."

"Jesus, Mary and Joseph, Mary Ann, d'ye think...!"

"Och aye, Bridie dear. Why else?"

"'Tis well they caught thon wan in time, so it is."

"And what d'ye think herself's goin' through?"

"Ah now. Sure the poor crathur beeta be beside herself, so she beeta. Wasn't her whole heart set on havin' a priest?"

"It's a tarrer, so it is. Och aye! 'Tis indeed."

"Kill her, it could, too."

"Och, aye it could, right enough, so it could."

Jerry's reaction to my talk of quitting was typical of him.

"I don't see why you should get off the hook, leaving the rest of us to do the dirty work. You're no worse than any of us, so quit braggin', will you."

"You don't think I'm out of me mind, taking this on, do you?"

"You're not whackin' off much are you, or buggering some wee boy-friend in your bed these nights—or at least not regularly, are ye?" He cocked his head inquiringly—about half in fun.

"It's not even about the sex thing, really. It's just that none of it seems real—like it's all happening to somebody else and I'm just an observer. And I'm still not sure I even believe in much of anything. But it's all creeping up on me like some great machine that grabs hold of your leg and drags your whole body inexorably into the mechanism."

"'Inexorably'? Nice image—was it 'Modern Times,' you were picturing? But far too dramatic. Why don't you just keep showing up like you've been doin' for the past six years."

"And...?"

"Maybe that's the only way we know what it is we really intend—the thing we keep doing, day after day, over a long period of time?

"But I'm not sure why I kept doing it. Couldn't that have just been lethargy—or cowardice?" I was determined to indict myself.

"If you'd bought a car six years ago and you'd been driving it every day, as old Rogers might say, 'what's the best evidence of your intention?' You'd have a hard time arguing 'lack of intention' in that case now, wouldn't you?"

"I suppose so."

"Besides, who the frig else would hire you?" He nudged me with his shoulder to jar me out of the seriousness.

Jerry and I walked up the aisle, side by side to face the bishop and together we recited the formula by which we voluntarily abandoned what neither of us had any right to forswear, given our ignorance. And so we entered our final year of Divinity.

As Fourth Divines, in addition to theology, canon law, scripture, sacred eloquence, history etc., we began practicing the rituals of the church in endless dry-runs. A *practicum* with the Senior Dean—punctilious *obersturmbanfuhrer* of the liturgy —was one of the most daunting hurdles we faced. It was nerve-wracking. At the slightest hint of either sloppiness or flamboyance in a gesture the unfortunate candidate was flunked forthwith. I took a dry-run in front of a panel of my classmates before submitting to the Dean's gimlet eye. My diligence paid off, I passed first time. Next loomed the Faculties Examinations, the most torturous examination of our time in Holy Trinity: oral and written comprehensives on everything covered in the four years of divinity. By studying hard for the month or so before, I survived that too. Nothing now stood between me and ordination to the priesthood.

As they said in those old-fashioned detective stories, "the jig was up".

CHAPTER 11

Holy Trinity Seminary — 1960

ON A SUNNY Sunday morning in the middle of June of that year I was ordained a priest.

My family came up from the North for the big event; my father—stiff and awkward in a new suit; my mother—red-eyed and proprietary; my uncles and aunts—milling about with cine cameras, unconvincingly jolly; my sister—barely containing her skepticism; a half dozen male cousins—there for the party mainly, but awestruck too.

Despite all my misgivings about the Church and particularly about becoming a priest in it, I was weeping as we walked down the aisle to the singing of *Veni Creator Spiritus*... Jerry and I—seat-mates for life it seemed—emerged from the chapel together as priests. No longer something that chewed on cabbages, I had emerged from the cocoon a fully-fledged priest.

That *Veni Creator* kills me still, just hearing it.

It was a very emotional occasion, the whole thing: sweaty boy morphed into "Other Christ"—awesome spiritual powers: bread and wine into body and blood, sins forgiven; the dying prepared for another life and on and on. This was not just another meaningless minor order I had received; not another insignificant ritual after which I would go off on the long vacation, off to hitchhike on the Continent or to spend lazy days drifting on the fat Moselle. This was the start of adulthood— the real deal, finally.

Maybe I wouldn't feel so phony in California—isn't that where Tinsel Town is located? I would have more than ten weeks to get through at home first though, ten weeks of trying to act as people expected a priest to act, before I could escape to California.

...*sacerdos in aeternum*... A priest forever? Christ!

The following morning was my First Mass, an event ranking up there with weddings and funerals in the Irish culture of the time. I had arranged to say the mass in a convent chapel on St. Stephen's Green in Dublin. The reception afterwards was around The Green a bit in The Shelbourne Hotel. I must have walked through that morning in a haze, for very little about it registered in my memory.

Later that summer, one of the cousins collected the product of a dozen cine cameras and sent me the resulting montage of confusing and repetitive images. It showed an endless family nightmare filmed in incessant drizzle—a dozen eight millimeter versions of a nervous young man with a facial tick, dressed like a priest, thin and ill at ease, never without a cigarette, posing awkwardly with overdressed aunts and jolly uncles, all being especially artificial for the camera. My father, false teeth falsely smiling; my mother, a serene and tearful, *mater dolorosa*. In a few candid shots she could be seen fondly gazing at her unsullied lamb unwittingly sacrificed. Pieta!

Pythonesque!

It can't have been as grim as it looked in those pictures, though I know I felt darker that day than the Dublin sky.

Ah, Leopold. 'Twasn't that far away from Grafton Street itself that it was all happening either. We could've run for it now, so we could, instead of standing there in the rain outside of Loretto College and The Shelbourne, and maybe had a jar with some of the boyos. But, no thanks, not the kidneys fried up in butter and tasting faintly of piss. Nice! But thank's all the same—I have to fast for mass, you know—a wee jar woulda been nice, though!

My mother had scheduled me for two more First Masses: one in our parish church at home and another in the town church, where many of the relatives lived.

"I hope you don't mind, but I told the nuns in Omagh you'd go up there and say mass for them too. And I told Mrs. McSorley you'd come by and see her—she has trouble, you know, getting out these days," and on and on and on. My mother might not have extracted the academic success she needed from me but she'd wound up with a priest and by god, she was going to get what mileage she could from it. It wasn't a Nobel Prize—but when you're stuck with a lemon... That summer my mother fairly strutted her lemonade.

They had set up an altar at home where I could say daily mass in the house—when I wasn't booked into some other venue. My father had rigged it up from a table he'd raised to the proper height by putting a two-pound tin of *Tate and Lyly*

Golden Syrup, under each leg. My mother had then draped it with the white damask table cloths she kept in the small parlor cupboard for when we had company.

God! My parents were so in awe, the boy they had raised turning bread and wine into the body and blood of Jesus by his words. I could hardly stand it. Imposter, and a poor actor at that, surely they could see it was a sham. I couldn't wait to leave for California.

I was asked to baptize infants, marry people I had been in school with and bring communion to shut-ins. I was treated as a holy man by people who should have known better, by classmates from St. Columb's and by girls I'd danced with and fantasized about. I could no longer have a conversation with anyone like an ordinary man.

I felt like screaming.

Only my sister, though religious in her own way, was unaffected by my change in status. She had never overcome her skepticism about my decision to go to seminary and after ordination she continued to treat me with the same reservation as she had before. I would miss her when I left for America but she had effectively disconnected herself from me years before.

That summer dragged on painfully—Rome Olympics on the new TV in the sitting room—cake and tea endlessly in the upper rooms of farmhouses—pounds and ten bobs notes in envelopes, masses and prayers paid for. I was a priest all right.

CHAPTER 12

Big Sur, California — 2004

HOLLAND WAS STRUGGLING. He'd made half a dozen false starts but scrapped them all. The fresh page in the typewriter had been blank for most of an hour. Try as he might he couldn't remember anything she had said to him that last morning.

The old man and he had sat at the table in their usual places but his mother in her frayed, blue candlewick dressing gown wouldn't sit down. She was frying eggs and bacon and sliced tomatoes on the cream-colored cooker or she was toasting bread. But she would not look at him directly.

"Did you put in the extra razor blades?" The old man asked.

He had glanced towards the old man at the head of the table, slurping his tea—yellow beads of butter floating on it from the dipped toast. He had looked older that morning. Holland had never noticed before how gray his skin had become. The wattles below his chin and the purple-hued cheek-jowls were saggier—wrinkly too. And his prominent nose, where it flared out at his cheeks, was shot through with more broken capillaries than he had noticed before. And his eyes, pale-gray and watery, seemed weighed down by the large shiny bags slung underneath them. He must be over seventy by now.

He remembers noticing the old man's ears with their gray, wiry hairs but he could not remember anything she said that morning, nor could he picture her face, there in the kitchen that morning. Except for the blue dressing gown moving around behind him, cooking, he could not recall what she looked like at all.

He remembered going around the corner—over past the cabbage patch to take a piss—and noticing the beads of dew on the tea rose outside the front door—of all the roses, her favorite. She would cut a perfectly formed bud on her way to school, to help her make it through the day, she said. He remembered the dew drops like it was yesterday.

The old man had driven the four miles from Aghybeg Cross into town. It was seven more miles from there to the station at Victoria Bridge. They both stared straight ahead as they went along the familiar road, the silence broken only by the old man's checklist conversation.

"How's the time doing?"

"Do you have enough change for the porters?"

"I think the weather's going to pick up finally."

It had been a miserably wet summer, one of the wettest on record—that last summer he was at home. Hardly a day you could go out without a raincoat the whole time since he had been ordained. Finally he was off to California. Thank god! Another half-hour and he'd have left it all behind him.

"I think the weather's going to pick up," the old man repeats. "Aye! That's what they were saying on the radio."

As though it matters to me, he'd thought.

The old gray Vauxhall Velox fussed along between the high hawthorn hedges— vines of wild woodbine tangled around the thorn branches. "Honeysuckle," she always called it.

The roads were narrow up in that part of West Tyrone and the rare time you met anybody you could hear the ferns and brambles rasping along the doors of the car. They'd met the early bus on its way up to Aghybeg crossroads and he could remember the rush of air as they passed on the narrow road and the brambles scratching the metal.

He got out of the car at the curb and jumped up to see the bank clock through the window of the Hibernian Bank in Castlegorm. They were still in time for the Dublin train.

"Morning Father!" Mrs. McMenamin, the Sexton, was coming out of Gas Lane by the side of the bank, on her way up to open the chapel for the seven o'clock mass. She was a pale hunched over creature in a cloth raincoat and headscarf. He'd swear it was the same coat and headscarf she had worn since he'd been an altar-boy.

"And are ye off then today, finally, to the States?"

The whole town depended on Mrs. McMenamin. It was her tolling of the chapel bell that let everybody in town know, no matter what denomination they belonged to, that it was a quarter to seven in the morning. And when she began a continuous pealing on the bell, they knew it was already five to seven. The driver and conductor of the seven o'clock bus to Derry via Victoria Bridge, Sion Mills and Strabane, finished up their ham sandwiches and tea at the wee milk bar on John's Street when she began pealing the bell.

"Time tae warm her up, Jackie."

"Aye! Beeta be near seven—thon's the chapel bell."

"God Bless you then, Father. Ah beeta be goin' now!" She checked the bulky man's watch she kept on a leather leash in her handbag.

He remembered what Mrs. McMenamin said that morning and he'd never liked the woman.

Victoria Bridge was a no more than a stop on the Derry—Belfast line, no café, not even a news kiosk in the place. He bought a "single" to Dublin—it was liberating not buying a "return" to Tyrone. The porter told him — as he'd told him twice a year for seven years— that he needed to be on the other platform for the down line, and to be careful crossing the tracks.

Forty years later he still remembered the screenings, stained dark from the engines' steam and smoke, and the crunch of them under his shoes as he crossed the tracks to the down line platform—even the tufts of grass between the sleepers, he remembered noticing.

The old man shook his hand after he had handed the suitcases up into the carriage. That was it between them. No fond farewells. No hugs. No tears. Nothing mawkish; nothing but his father's stiff-fingered handshake and tight-pursed lips.

"Safe journey!" He'd said. Like going off to school for another term or for a week at the seaside—not off to America for life.

Nothing soft or sentimental like: "I may never see you again," or "I'll be looking forward to the day in four years when you can get your first holiday at home," and certainly not, "I'll miss you."

Neither curse nor blessing; no fierce tears.

"Safe journey!" Covered the subject.

Nothing like the silent, head-bursting pain that had finally erupted from behind her eyes at the very last minute, standing bowed over the Aga cooker. He had hugged her tightly as she stood there trembling in her blue candlewick robe, silent—her face distorted from feelings she couldn't speak. He did remember that her face was all scrunched up then, unrecognizable and shiny with tears. She had clung to him, her fingers digging desperately into his back. He felt the power of her love as he had not felt it since he was a child of eight. The icy wall that had slammed down between them that Friday evening as his father carried him past her to the ambulance had melted suddenly. It had been her protection against hurt but it had suddenly failed her.

They'd held each other then until he'd had to leave. The old man had come back in from the car twice shouting, "We'll miss the train." She had sobbed and he could feel her slight body quiver like a scared thing and he wanted to stay with her and keep his arms around her forever.

She looked tired and older than fifty-five as she stood at the top of the lane, waving him goodbye—till the car had passed the first corner.

She was still standing by the front door, her hand raised above her head, when they had pulled out of the lane onto the main road and he had waved to her till the high bushes around the first laborer's cottage cut her off from view. Standing, waving after him in her faded blue dressing gown was the last he'd seen of her.

He had waved once to the old man before the rusty girders of the bridge blocked sight of the platform. Had he raised his hand in response? It was hard to tell. He had looked around him as though uncertain whether his son's wave was meant for him, though there was no one else on the platform except a porter loading goods onto a hand-truck.

Funny the stuff you remember decades later. He remembered everything but her voice and how her face looked as she went about the kitchen while he was trying to eat the bacon and eggs and fried tomato she had cooked for his *viaticum*.

The winter after he left for California she no longer had the strength to face what she called the "long dark tunnel" of winter behind that god-forsaken hill. Winter had depressed her for as long as Holland could remember but that winter her condition was much more serious. She had become so paralyzed by depression she couldn't leave her bed. The doctors, unable to help with medication, recommended hospitalization. She rejected the idea and insisted she would pull out of it on her own. For two months she lay facing the wall — neither speaking nor eating. Suddenly, one day in December she returned to life. After months of depression, she was suddenly and for no apparent reason in high spirits, planning Christmas gifts and decorating the house. She announced that she was going to stay for a week or so in Bundoran after the New Year.

"The sea air will work wonders for my spirits," she'd told his father and sister.

"Breezy, Bracing, Bundoran." The brochures and postcards proclaimed.

"Bundoran in January?" The old man had understandably asked.

The sister had written to tell Holland of her death. She had died of a heart attack in a boarding house in Bundoran.

The light was failing in the room and still Holland had written nothing about that last time he'd seen her.

Just put the bare facts on paper, let the monk ask questions if he needs to know more.

He turned on the lamp, lighted a cigarette and started typing.

CHAPTER 13

Big Sur, California — 2004

WHEN HE'D FINALLY stretched out on the bed around two-thirty, his back aching from typing and his eyes burning from the cigarette fog that hung in the room, he still couldn't sleep for the thoughts that came crowding in; always the same demanding, clamoring thoughts that had been hounding him since he'd come to this place — gulls squabbling over a crust. He had started thinking about the Jew before getting into bed last night. That was a mistake.

An hour or so of turning and twisting, too hot, too agitated, and he'd finally written off another night as a dead loss. He got out of bed then and groped his way into the kitchen, put on a pot of Sumatra to brew and lighted the first Marlboro of another day. Another night at the kitchen window, another night smoking, drinking coffee, and staring at the dark horizon—the voices in his head jabbering.

God Almighty! He complained to whatever inhabited the vastness stretching out to the west. The nights I've wasted wondering in the dark about things — about the mysteries — the truly important puzzles. Was there really something like a god, somewhere in this frigging universe — some being that really gives a shite about us? And what about all that afterlife stuff? Was that just a myth they'd made up to keep the poor from killing the wealthy?

And always there was the puzzle of that frigging Jew: whether he was what they said he was or just one hell of a con man. If he was a fraud he was the world's greatest failure; pulling off the greatest scam in all of history and dying on a cross before the payoff. Or had someone who'd come along later invented the scam?

He poured some coffee and savored the smooth, heavy flavor of the Sumatra.

If I could just get the damned Catholic virus out of my system, he grumbled to himself. If only I didn't give a shite about any of it. But always the dilemma: can't be a Catholic, can't not to be a fucking Catholic.

And then, what if it was true and that Jew had, in fact, been some kind of a god?

What if he'd actually done the things they'd reported, like raising the dead and curing the sick? In that case a body would have to take it to heart, wouldn't he — maybe see what he ought to be doing and hurry up about getting it done?

C.S. Lewis was right in the way he laid it out: the Jew was either who he claimed to be or he was a total fried egg. No middle road made any sense. God or fruitcake, a world-class, fucking dilemma. He poured another mug of the heavy coffee and lighted another cigarette.

The ocean far below the monastery was peaceful, reflecting rippled light from the near-full moon that was coasting smoothly across a mottled sky. It had been an artist's sunset last evening — aqua streaked across a magenta field — with another beautiful day promised to those who'd get to see it. The bell summoning the monks to chapel pealed in the stillness, time to get some clothes on and begin the morning's baking.

An hour later, as he was waiting for the croissants to rise, clutching his latest writing he walked across the dew-moist lawn to the monastery. He shoved the pages under the monk's door and hurried back to the warmth of his kitchen. The ovens, he noted with satisfaction had come up to temperature and the croissants had risen to puffy perfection.

Resurrexit sicut dixit, alleluia!

"Good morning, Jack!" The priest glanced up from his reading and immediately returned to the pages on his lap —pencil poised.

Holland took his seat.

He had been looking forward to this session despite feeling hurt by that abrupt dismissal last time. He'd been wondering about that too last night at the window. Could he be "getting something out of it," as he'd heard people say about their psychotherapy? Or was he just another loser needing an ear; needing somebody who'd hold still for his version of "A could'da bin a contender"? Maybe that's all you got out of therapy anyway, a captive audience.

"So. You came to America already a priest?" Holland said nothing.

"How old were you then, when you got here?"

"Just turned twenty four — a baby priest!" He didn't look up

"Hmm!" The priest was flipping back over the pages on his lap. "I read what you've written about that last morning — when you left home — and your mother...?"

Holland stared at the floor and found nothing he wanted to say — wasn't it all there for the man, on the paper?

"And her death…?" The monk probed.

"God dammit, man! She committed suicide — I should think that would be obvious to you." He had never said that about her death to anyone before — not even to himself.

This time it was the monk who was laconic. "Really?"

"This was a woman who'd been an open-water swimmer all her life, they can't tell me she just drowned off Rogey Rock — no friggin' way!"

"I thought you said it was a heart attack?" The monk was thumbing through the pages.

"My sister wrote and told me she'd died of a heart attack. It was only later I discovered she'd been pulled from the ocean, dead, by the Bundoran lifeboat."

"Still… It could have been an accident, couldn't it?"

"On the same day and month as my sister, January 19th? When I saw the two identical names and the identical dates of death, one below the other on the tombstone, I got it. She had finally surrendered to the monster-god — he would not be fooled."

"Say more about …" The monk prompted.

"About the monster-god, our family's household deity? I've told you about that bastard before. She thought she could deflect him — pull the wool over his eyes — by hiding her feelings for me. But he knew! He knew all along!" Holland straightened his back up and stared at the priest with such anger in his face the priest recoiled in his chair. "To love someone with a demon-god watching is to stake them out in the clearing like a goat — bait that draws the predator."

"Don't we have a choice? Can't we decide to find a better god to believe in — one that loves those we love?"

"Father, I think that god you're talking about is the god of rich Americans, of people raised without the blight of dead children and famine — it's a sentimental god that could never survive in most of the world." Holland was still agitated, not so much by anything the priest had said, as by the truth of what he had admitted: his mother had committed suicide.

"Tommy…?" The priest said.

Had the priest asked something? Holland was preoccupied still and couldn't be sure.

"Tommy...?" The priest repeated. "Do you not then — to be consistent — think it fortunate that he escaped?"

Holland had no response to this. His thoughts were with the woman swimming to her death off the strand where they had spent every summer of his childhood.

"Why don't you continue with the narrative from where you left off. Your arrival in the Minerva diocese, how was it for a young Irish priest coming to a strange country? Did it all seem very foreign to you, being in America? How was your first assignment? Things like that. And, of course, when you first went off the rails, so to speak?"

"It took a while before the wheels came off totally, but I was never very 'on' the rails." Holland cautioned.

"I know. But still. There must have been a period when you were trying?"

This didn't seem to require an answer.

"Any questions?"

Holland shook his head. It felt as though the session was over. He had an aversion to being dismissed by these priests — something from his background, he was sure they'd say — so he had resolved to end the sessions himself. He stood up.

As he had never done before, the little monk stood too and walked out of the room with him to the head of the stairs where he offered his hand to the big man.

"I've been very impressed with the effort you're making in this matter and your patience too, Jack." He didn't look Holland in the eye.

Embarrassed at paying the compliment, Holland thought to himself. He was amused, seeing that in the shrink. Out of his element — this emotional stuff — for a monk.

"You may think you're an atheist but I must say I'm not at all convinced of it."

Holland, a little embarrassed himself now by the compliments, muttered something about continuing his writing and edged towards the stairs.

"Day after tomorrow then, same time?" The priest called after him.

Holland waved agreement. He started down the stairs without looking back.

Holland had the kitchen to himself. It was cool there among the acres of stainless steel, the refrigeration purring, compressors cycling — real things. You could touch and feel things in a kitchen and when you made a good bread with whole grains and a nice rough texture, that was real too — you could get your teeth into it and taste it.

He had gone to mass a few times over the years. Why go, he would ask himself? Was it from some guilty burr deep in his soul prodding him, or could he be seeking still some magic he'd been promised as a child? What was its appeal? What about it had 'wowed' the crowds in Corinth and Ephesus and Rome?

"Hey, you Corinthians. I have some incredibly good news for you: You will henceforth be going to Hell for masturbation."

"Citizens of Rome, come, join us! We Christians have a new improved concept of Hell."

"Listen up! You people of Ephesus! We Christians have far more fast days and mortal sins than those followers of Diana."

The "Good News" must have lost something in the translation.

Or, had it been from the start just another story, one devised to make life and death less terrifying? A myth to pacify those half-starved creatures in their clay and wattle hovels, half their children dead before their tenth birthday?

"Send one of those ragged friars down to keep the serfs in line, bishop."

"Yer aal so lucky for havin' such a generous master. Look at the nice table scraps he's sent down to yez from the castle table."

"Ah sure won't tings be great for yous aal later in the world to come."

"Your banquet table is already being aal set and after yous is dead, yous'll have a wonderful time."

"Keep your chins up! Keep at the work, now."

"Those dead children? Ah sure aren't they the lucky wans? They're sitting up there way Jazus himself, so they are, having the grand aul time of it. Like little lords and ladies, they are. Aren't they the lucky wans, when you tink about it?"

Oh, to not give a shite about any of it!

CHAPTER 14

Minerva, California — 1960

THE NIGHT WE arrived in Minerva we came into town over the old drawbridge, into that god-forsaken part of the city that lies alongside the river wharfs. Drunks hunkering in doorways with bottles in brown paper sacks, streets dusty and trash-strewn, cars out of *The Grapes of Wrath*; khaki mud-splattered bus disgorging brown-skinned men at a cantina. Sudden blast of mariachi trumpets on a sudden shaft of light, blaring out into the dark street when the doors open — ceasing just as suddenly, taking back the light. Darkness again even darker. Men displacing their own volume in sound and light. Archimedes has been here.

Eureka! It was the State motto of California, I'd read that in a Chamber of Commerce brochure. I never forget what I read in brochures.

It was our first night in America.

We drove slowly past the foreign-looking, dusky men leaning against walls in the shadows of dark sidewalks, angry-glowering men, eye-whites cutting at us, wary.

Cannery Row, Tortilla Flats. I've been here before; I've met these men before; reading, shivering in that cold, damp Irish dormitory — they'd been exotic then. But Second Street wasn't the book *"America"* nor the movie *"America"* — not the Disneyland *America*, certainly. The bell would not ring for night prayer tonight and the covers of my book would not shut on these men tonight, freezing them in place till tomorrow — not Steinbeck's word-people; not toys-to-go-back-in-their-box-people. Real people.

"Checks Cashed," "Rooms for Rent." Empty wine bottles, wind-blown newspapers wrapped around lamp posts; urine running off crumbling walls to the gutter; brown children play jacks in the shadows, dark liquid-eyed children — nothing like them in West Tyrone — playing in the dark streets behind the whores on the corner.

I had not pictured California this way at all. I had devoured Steinbeck's novels of dust and heat and passion, huddled in the wet chill of Ireland's winters — at least it was dry in Oklahoma. How bad could things be if the days were hot and dry enough to raise the dust? They had been hard, those times he'd written about, with drought and prejudice and poverty. But nothing like that existed in the modern Golden State, not now, we'd been told by the Bishop — not since the Depression.

Pat O'Reilly, from the class ahead of us in Trinity, had met us at San Francisco airport that evening and driven us out to Minerva. Jerry sat on the huge front sofa between me and the driver.

"It's the fuckin' Queen Mary!" I'd said when O'Reilly pointed the car out to us in the parking lot.

Now that DeSoto was the real America; the *braceros* on skid row belonged in a different book entirely. Salmon-pink and gray, colorful and extravagant, a set designer's fantasy car. Not an earth-bound car at all, as our Vauxhall Velox was a car, but an *auto-mo-bile*. From its great flamboyant fins flaring to the heavens, to its gleaming, grinning chromium snout it had streamed out of a Hollywood musical surely. Row upon ivory row of buttons for magically changing gears and getting heat and playing music; creamy steering wheel with silvery horn-rings and yards of dashboard chrome, it was straight from M.G.M. It was Vera-Ellen in tap pants, Debbie Reynolds in a yellow slicker, it was Ginger and Fred. Nothing of its kind had ever come out of an English car factory — no Austin or Morris or Hillman had ever looked anything like this. And its likes had never graced the narrow roads of Tyrone. And the blackberry briars — that had scratched the old Vauxhall's paint down to rusty metal — would never have laid a thorn on a goddess like her!

I'd have to get my hands on one of those DeSotos, I decided that night, riding out to Minerva.

Coveting thy neighbor's car. So began my California ministry.

"A back-stabbing, son-of-a-bitch." That was how several of the priests at our welcoming dinner had described the Chancellor of the diocese.

"Watch what you tell the bastard," was something else they seemed to all agree on.

Name, rank and serial number; ask no questions, volunteer nothing, I cautioned myself, as I sat with Jerry and three other new, Irish priests in the front office of the Chancery the following morning awaiting our assignments. Only Jerry and I were from Holy Trinity; the other three had that florid-faced look of Gaelic football players. They'd fit in perfectly with the men we'd met at the reception — probably their uncles or cousins anyway. Neither Jerry nor I had had a relative in the clergy within living memory. We were strangers in a totally strange land.

After we had cooled our heels on the bench for at least half an hour, a young white-faced priest — an American, from the way he spoke through his nose — came out and shepherded us into a large conference room. He told us to be seated — Monsignor Fitzwilliam would be with us presently. Aha! The ogre himself.

When he did finally come into the room, the frail, smiley man with the slicked-back hair and tobacco-stained teeth looked more like a seller of French post-cards than the chancellor of a diocese. He was a big letdown after the Fitzwilliam I had constructed in my head. He was hardly inside the door before he started rattling off the first in a string of very lame jokes he would treat us to in the next five minutes. He looked so ill at ease and foolish I began to relax. What a pair they made: Fitz, with the concave chest and sallow cheeks of a consumptive, telling his moldy jokes and the young Yankee priest laughing, sucking up for all he was worth. Pathetic. The assistant was still giggling as he was passing out the handbook of diocesan regulations, long after the last punch line.

Watching two such inept politicians — apparently the in-crowd in Minerva — a bizarre notion flashed across my mind: I could take this place over with one arm tied behind my back. Though I banished the thought right away, I could feel a residual tingle of excitement, the frisson of power. Minerva might turn out to be a far more interesting place than I had imagined driving through the squalor of Second Street the previous evening. A new game had suggested itself — one I knew how to play.

Fitz cleared his throat — the hilarity part of the program was apparently over. He started in lecturing us then on the behavior expected from Assistant Pastors: obedience mainly. He strongly suggested that the consequence of disobedience might well be the cancellation of our permanent resident visas.

Oh God, no! Not back to Ireland! Anything but that! Van Demon's land, Devil's Island, some place warm at least. Please! I said none of this out loud of course.

Next he gave each of us a document saying we were priests in good standing of Minerva and then an official letter appointing each of us to a parish. None of us had the foggiest where his new parish was located nor who the Pastor was, but nobody was about to attract attention by asking Fitz any questions either. The letters of appointment lay on the table like so many unexploded bombs for the remainder of the session.

What if they send me up country, to some god-forsaken mining camp in the back of nowhere or to some dreary lumber town? Suddenly I was in the power of other people again, the feeling of excitement drained out of me as though a sluice gate had opened. I needed to leave.

Tahiti? How much farther west could it be anyway? How much did a Pan Am ticket cost?

We would be paid the lordly sum of sixty-four dollars a month, Fitz said. That was a lot more than it might seem, he said, since we had our room and board free and clear from the parish.

We might be straight off the boat but did that mean we were mentally defective too?

Sixty-four Yankee dollars a month? Paddies for peanuts.

Finally, after we had endured an hour or more of Fitz and his point-by-point exposition of diocesan regulations, the door flew open and, with a sound "as of a great rushing wind" the Bishop himself entered the room.

I was suddenly on the edge of my chair. What a presence! Rocking back and forth, heel to toe, a great bay-window stomach corralled by a silk purple bellyband, he filled the room with his voice and energy.

He was very, very happy to meet us, he said, and very, very excited at the prospect of getting to know each one of us and working with us in the Minerva diocese. He even looked happy and excited as he was saying it — that was his art. More personality by far than Fitz and even more full of shite. No wonder this man was a Bishop.

Even we, the greenhorns, knew he hadn't the slightest intention of staying in that backwater diocese a minute longer than he could help. He had written already to Santa Claus for a big new toy: the Archdiocese of San Francisco—and everybody knew it. But there he stood in front of us that day, giving us his sales pitch: the changes he'd made, the millions he'd raised for schools and the dozens of new parishes he'd built. A well-polished resume. He'd probably delivered the same litany to every Roman official who'd stood still for ten minutes during his last *ad limina* visit — that and a suitcase of cash for your favorite charity, *Monsignore.*

What an opportunity was ours, he said, what great good fortune to serve God in such an "abundant vineyard" as the Minerva diocese. My brain was so massaged after ten minutes listening to that stained-glass baritone that I caught myself believing he was really interested in getting to know me. And, with a perfectly straight face he described the five year building program he and the Chancellor were getting very excited about.

Wow! I thought. Maybe he is going to stay.

The priests had told us the night before that he'd slit both his wrists if Rome left him in that sleepy valley town for another five years.

But, even knowing it was all a lie, still you couldn't help but believe the man, he had such a wonderfully convincing manner. What Roman could resist a great big handsome American like this blowing smoke up his ass? What Roman could resist that big sincere smile, that lovely voice, that intimate, caring handshake — and a nice big sack of money for your favorite charity, *Monsignore?* What a gift. He would of course be given San Francisco, at the very least — maybe even Los Angeles and a cardinal's red hat, he was that good. Fitz, on the other hand, would live and die in Shitsville — that I could see right away.

I was assigned to a new parish in the suburbs of Minerva, to a Pastor, Harry Flood, with a reputation for being hot tempered and hard to get along with. Jerry was appointed to a college town about a hundred miles up the valley — I would see him only infrequently during that first year till he was reassigned to a parish in Minerva City the following summer.

Father Flood and I got along great. As close to being an honest man as I have ever met, Harry had no need to impress anyone at all, bishop or parishioner. His temper was hot and his fuse short but when I showed that I would engage him in battle, he grudgingly respected that. We had some great fights, the two of us, and I discovered the perverse joy of being charged to the gills with reckless rage when my temper was aroused. Harry would fuss and fume about my lack of respect for my Pastor when I would engage him in a shouting match and he would avoid me then for an hour or so after we had finished yelling, red-faced, at each other. But I discovered the rush of that rage, standing in the middle of my own adrenaline, to be a powerful thing that I had not known before — I could slay dragons with my bare hands while it lasted.

"Yer' a hot tempered little bastard, now. Aren't ye?"

When I would shrug in response he'd throw his great white mane of a head back and, snorting then like a winded horse, he would laughingly grumble. "We're a foine pair, the two of us, now, aren't we?" He'd run his fingers through both sides of his hair to tame it.

"That son-of-a-bitch Fitz put us together, ye know, so we'd destroy each other. Good riddance, he'd say the day they'd find the bodies."

After I was there a while and had grown to trust him, I hesitantly told him about the doubts I was still having about my vocation. He listened and nodded.

"The way I look at that is this…" He lit one of the many Camel cigarettes he smoked every day and ran his finger under his roman collar, wincing as though it was choking him.

"Who the hell knows for certain what's what?" He took a great, noisy drag of smoke deep into his lungs and exhaled it in streams from both nostrils and his mouth, like some sort of steam calliope about to burst out in circus music.

"Anytime I meet a man that's too sure what God has in mind, I check to see that my wallet's still in me pocket." He laughed his throaty laugh then and broke immediately into a fit of red-faced coughing.

"Damn!" He exclaimed — his face beet-red, his eyes watering. "That's what these damn Camels will do to you. Pluhering, day and night, they have me. But, God! I love the bloody things. The only friggin' smoke worth killing yerself for."

He had been raised on a rocky little farm in County Cavan, as backward and forlorn a piece of Purgatory as a man could escape from. He spoke with the accent of that county still, after thirty years in California. He had never become Americanized and the results were obvious, from the 1949 Plymouth coupe he drove, to the one shiny suit, stained and dandruff-dusty that he threw on every day.

Where was Father Flood's DeSoto with the lovely fins and the chrome and the rows of ivory buttons?

We went out together car shopping and he bought a new Ford Falcon station wagon for me from the sparse parish funds — one with tough plastic seats, embossed with little longhorn skulls, a tin dash, rubber mats and just enough power to pull your socks off. The dealer, whose wife was a Catholic, threw in an AM radio — a ridiculous luxury in the eyes of our parishioners when they found out about it.

When it was over one hundred degrees in the great Central Valley and I had spent a day driving Mexican children to and from catechism classes, bringing communion to shut-ins and running other parish errands, I had little longhorns branded onto both cheeks of my ass.

The two of us ran the parish and got along so well it must have totally confounded Fitz to hear us speak so highly of each other. But delightful as Harry was, after a year or so of parish work I was bored out of my mind by the routine. Jerry had been drafted to full-time teaching when they'd transferred him back from the hills so, to relieve the tedium, I volunteered as a part-time teacher in the same Catholic high school. Often I was teaching subjects I had barely passed in St. Columb's — keeping a page or so ahead of my students. I was willing to try anything that promised to stave off a desperate boredom that was feeling more like depression every day.

Because I had taken on additional work — rather than polishing my golf game — I was considered an "up-and-coming young'un," by the Chancery. When it came to politics, though, I was playing a fairly competitive game — without seeming to suck-up. I made a point of excelling at the flashy stuff like raising bags of money for diocesan building funds and assembling a record-breaking class of adult converts for Confirmation. That was impressive stuff.

Confirmation, you see, was a lot like the Super Bowl of parish work. The quarterback with the longest string of adult converts for the bishop to confirm got the trip to Disneyland —figuratively speaking. You could hear gasps of dismay from all the neighboring pastors seated in the sanctuary when I lined up my new Catholics. They counted heads — the line stretched all the way down the aisle to the rear doors of the church. They couldn't believe the numbers. That night there'd be a lot of red faces in neighboring rectories when the pastors returned and took it out on their assistants.

And after dinner when all the clergy had gorged themselves to bursting point on our standing rib roast — the official food of priests — the Bishop would make a little speech of congratulations — salt in the other pastors' wounds. What a wonderful job Father Flood was doing raising money, he'd say. And what an incredible turnout of converts. I hope you other men are taking note, he'd say. Then Father Flood would stand up and very decently give Father Holland all the credit and say he was the one had done all the work. Father Holland, he'd say, "...has such a knack with those convert classes and... a tiger at the fund raising."

Bishops are far more impressed by a priest who produces lots and lots of converts and raises lots and lots of cash, than by a man whose specialty is holiness or some similar intangible. And much the same values apply in the bishops' dealings with Rome. A bishop who piles up good statistics; lots of schools and churches and seminaries, gets the lollipop.

As everyone had suspected, our Bishop — Mister Personality — hadn't long to wait for his reward. Before I was two years in Minerva he was promoted to the Archdiocese of San Francisco. And, needless to say, a lot of my hard work done for his benefit went down the river with him. I started working on the new Bishop right away.

CHAPTER 15

Minerva, California — 1962

THE INSTRUCTION CLASS for adults interested in converting to the One True Church had twenty sign-ups that spring term, my second year in St. Joseph's Parish, and on the first night of class all twenty hardy souls braved the drenching February rains to attend. I had arranged for them to meet in the all-purpose room of the school — it was the only one heated in the evenings. There they sat, smelling like wet dogs, their big middle-class bodies crammed into the child-sized desks.

It was my third time teaching the instruction series but I was pacing, restless, as I waited in the Principal's office next door. It wasn't the teaching itself that had me on edge, it was the people. Would there be someone out there this time itching for a battle of wits on theology, some militant Protestant, armed to the teeth with scriptures, waiting to challenge me on papal infallibility, or transubstantiation, or confession of sins? They were all still Protestants of some sort, raised in hostility to the Church of Rome and everything she represents. Surely it would raise the hackles on at least one of them, having some Papist priest ram his outlandish superstitions down their throats. Surely there would be one brave soul who'd fight a rearguard action for the sake of Luther and Calvin before surrendering to the Great Whore. The prospect of such a tussle both frightened and excited me.

It was seven thirty on the dot. I took a deep breath and went in to meet them.

"Good evening, everybody!"

"Good evening, Father!"

And so it began again, another convert class.

There they sat, those cheerful and docile Protestants, thirsting for my Church's teachings — not a single skeptic, not a disputative soul in the bunch; not for these smiling faces the intellectual wrestling matches Bishop Sheen reported with the likes of Claire Boothe Luce. As with the two previous classes, these folks would accept even the most difficult teachings of the Church without a murmur, doctrines I almost dreaded bringing up for fear of ridicule, gobbled up, swallowed whole — not so much as a burp.

Could it be they weren't understanding the full implication of what I was telling them?

Was there maybe a language gap?

But, when I quizzed them they would invariably dish the material back with apparent understanding. And still, they had no difficulty accepting …?

What was wrong with these people? Wake up, I felt like shouting at them. It's the twentieth century, for Christ's sake! People don't swallow shite like this without batting an eyelid, not in the age of science.

Was the reputation of the Roman Church still so frightening, the memory of the Inquisition and its methods of persuasions still so vivid, that these heretics were afraid to question anything? Were they afraid it would brand them as troublemakers and I'd then refuse them membership in the One, the Holy, The Catholic …?

"Questions are good," I told them repeatedly. "Questions will be regarded as showing interest — a good thing in a Catholic." Liar, I told myself

The first time I'd taught the convert class I'd become so exasperated by their lack of participation in the question and answer sessions that I'd brought it up with Father Flood.

"Are they just not interested in what I'm telling them or don't they understand the implications?"

The old priest looking at me quizzically.

"Is it maybe ye don't believe it all that much yerself, Jack?"

We were having a drink together at the dining room table. Flood gave me a look that might have been compassion, then drew in a great deep drag off a Camel. He exhaled after what seemed too long a time for the brain to live without oxygen.

"Could it be with `yer own faith ye're having the biggest problem, ye think?"

Flood was right of course; I didn't believe much of what I was supposed to be representing and was constantly conflicted by my own lack of faith when I'd see the faith of the laity.

But how could anybody with half a brain not have some doubt about these stories. How could a person accept what they said about this Jew from the Galilee: that he was God, that he'd been conceived by a virgin through miraculous fertilization by something called a "holy ghost," or that a priest could turn bread and wine into this Jew's body and blood at mass?

As a child even, I'd had to shut off the doubts that plagued me in church.

Pray for faith, they'd said. But faith was a very tricky commodity, even for an adult.

One stupid boy in St. Columb's had caused a stir in Form IV, Religious Knowledge, by admitting that he had some doubts about the Resurrection. We'd been reading the story of Doubting Thomas when this McLaughlin boy said he was sympathetic with Thomas' dilemma — it was a hard thing to swallow, resurrection from the dead.

All three hundred pink pounds of Father McDuffy quivered violently at this — a great indignant strawberry Jell-O. Apoplectic with offended piety, he dug deep in his cassock pocket for his leather strap and when he'd given the infidel six of the best on each hand, he then frog-marched the wretch up the Senior House stairs to Big Mick's office.

That saintly man had slapped the boy firmly across the face several times for his impudence, whaled at him for a while with his strap till his hands were bleeding and would probably have thought up something else to do to him had not a forgetful god rushed the gift of faith to the unfortunate boy.

"I believe, Father, I believe!" We heard him scream.

The rest of the class waited quietly in their desks while McDuffy was gone — wildebeests, relieved that the lion had taken someone else — listening to the sounds from the floor above. McDuffy was no sooner back with the newly converted Mc Laughlin than I had raised my hand.

"Father?" I heard myself say. Though terrified of McDuffy, my stubbornness couldn't let the matter rest there. McDuffy glared down at me.

"What do *you* want, Holland?"

"Father, I was wondering... If faith is a gift, given only by God, and if God has not given it to McLaughlin here, what I was wondering, Father, was, how is that McLaughlin's fault?"

"Hold out yer hands, and I'll teach ye ta have a smart mouth." McDuffy dished out three on each hand with the stiff leather strap. I tried to not flinch — to annoy the thick bastard.

"D'ye want to be goin' up the stirs thir ta the President's office too?"

"No, Father." I met McDuffy's eye. "I was just wondering though about…" I began.

"Hold out yer hands again." Six more and I was still not flinching, though my hands stung something awful and were bright red except where the strap had raised buttery white welts — those would be puce by tomorrow morning.

"Are ye still wonderin' now about sompin'?"

"No, Father. Not anymore."

"That's good." He glanced over the class. "Anybody else having a crisis of faith?"

I tucked my hands under my armpits for they were tingling from the two lickings, coming so close together.

I had just learned a basic lesson about faith though: you pretend to have it and everyone else pretends they have it and, if someone is stupid enough to say he hasn't got it, you punish him — or kill him. And, when teachers are telling you something you may think is too farfetched, you look up at them, dumb as a sack of hammers, and nod your head.

So here was another group of eager Protestants just dying to fill in the blanks so they could become Catholics — defectors from the Reformation — their big American arses squeezed into those tight little desks.

"Tell us what to believe and we're yours," they seemed to be saying.

Their questions, when they did ask any, were about the simple things: the candles and the bells — the religious trivia. The vestments in particular fascinated them and it was an easy class, the night I took them into the sacristy and showed them how each garment was worn and explained its symbolism. They loved it when I would reenact the ceremony of vesting for mass. God almighty, these Protestants were starving for ritual — that was their problem. It wasn't dogma they were seeking at all but theater. The poor old Huguenots would spin in their austere graves at the betrayal. And the colors — they loved memorizing what each of the colors stood for, what season or occasion.

"Ah, yes. That's so right, Mr. Rasmussen. White vestments for a virgin not a martyr.

No wonder they loved Halloween — the friggin costumes. God help them; they loved every bit of Catholic trivia and the more outlandish the dogma the better they liked it.

> *I wish there had been Four of them,*
> *So I could believe more in them.*

"Yes, Mrs. Schlitz?"

A question from the tall attractive brunette whose silky, shapely legs I had been trying for weeks not to be caught staring at. Sometimes she'd cross her legs and it was all I could do to remember the names of the Trinity. She looked so bright and interested as she raised a graceful, well-manicured hand.

"You had a question, Mrs. Schlitz?"

Finally I would have an intelligent question — one with a bit of philosophical depth. She had been raised an Episcopalian, so maybe the validity of Anglican orders would be troubling her. She might go on then to inquire whether an Anglican mass was a valid mass. It would surely be something meaty coming from such a beautiful mind.

"Father, is it true that after you take communion you're not supposed to let your teeth touch the host?"

"Yes. Mrs. Schlitz, that is the custom."

"And is it true, Father, that we shouldn't wear lipstick when we go up to receive Holy Communion?"

"Again true, Mrs. Schlitz."

"Please call me Julia, Father."

She made a careful note in her journal of the crucial points of doctrine she had just cleared up and then looked up alertly, on her toes at the net, ready for the next subtlety. Disappointing questions from someone who looked so intelligent and who was always taking such extensive notes in her linen covered notebook. She had such a charming smile though, and the greatest fucking pair of legs you ever saw in black stockings, legs that just went up and up … It was hard to be impatient with such a person.

Sister Mary Gerard, the school principal, knocked and stuck her head in the door.

"Is it warm enough in here, Father?"

Sister was from Ireland, close to my age and had already taken her Ph.D. in philosophy at UCLA. She was ridiculously overqualified for an elementary school, but, as she said, "What's a nunny bunny to do?" Her school was consistently the highest rated school academically in the diocese with the result that she was something of a star within the diocese.

Father Flood thought her a stuck-up little bitch with a big head about herself but I admired her intellect and spunky personality. Over the previous 18 months she and I had become friends and allies in dealing with the more reactionary elements in the parish. On the nights I had convert class she and I would meet afterwards for hot chocolate and gossip in the principal's office. We'd chat often for hours about subjects ranging all over the lot from the parish, to Ireland to, of course, the Church. And it would often be time for night prayers in the convent before we'd realize it and she'd have to rush over to chapel composing as she ran some new excuse for the Mother Superior. Never in all the time I'd known her had I noticed even the slightest hint of instability or mental illness so, it came as a complete surprise to find her behaving suddenly in what was definitely an odd, if not a totally irrational way. The incident that worried me happened late that winter on a night I was holding my convert class.

As I drove up to the office door that evening I wasn't terribly surprised to find that the school was still in darkness. The weather gods were flinging a real gullywasher at the Central Valley and sheets of wind-driven rain were drenching the parking lot. True, Sister usually opened the classroom and had the lights on but who'd come out on such an evening if they didn't have to. No problem! I had my own set of keys. I took a deep breath and dashed from the car to the shelter of the office doorway. I unlocked the door and turned the lights on in the outer office. For a second I didn't notice Sister Gerard standing back in the deep shadows behind the reception counter, as though hiding from someone. Pale and wild-eyed, she was shaking as though she'd seen a ghost.

"What the hell…? I started to ask.

She put a finger to her lips then and beckoned me to follow her into the principal's office.

What the hell is she up to, lurking like that in the dark, I was asking myself? I turned the lights on in her office.

And what was this thing she had about not turning on lights? Was she losing her marbles? It was just too weird!

"I was waiting for you to get here," she said.

What do you say to a friend whose suddenly acting so strangely?

She took hold of my sleeve as though afraid I'd try to escape, keeping her eyes riveted on my face.

"I wanted to give you a piece of advice about your present convert class," she breathed urgently. "Don't let yourself be taken in by that Schlitz woman. She's not to be trusted as far as you'd throw her."

"Well, I don't …" I started to protest but she cut me off,

"Don't for a second think you know what she is, that one!" She stomped her little black shoe on the linoleum floor. "Oh, it's only too well that I know women like her." She went behind her desk then and busied herself arranging the pens and pencils in the little pot she kept them in.

What could I say?

"She hasn't got me fooled—not for a minute!" She looked up from her desk and glared at me. "Maybe she's pulling the wool over her husband's eyes with this conversion nonsense! Mark my word, she'll be no addition to the Church unless I'm far mistaken."

She's going over the edge, was all I could think.

"Isn't that pretty judgmental?" I ventured — trying to put a stern edge on my voice.

She had merely shrugged then. "None of my business really, what you do, Father." She gestured for me to leave her office — a truly peremptory dismissal.

I went next door and waited for my class to assemble. Even half an hour later when I started teaching, I was still reeling from my encounter with a strangely bizarre side of someone I thought of as a friend. It was not the fact that she was being critical of Mrs. Schlitz that was shocking. I had seen her critical side in action many an evening in her office when she good-humoredly sliced and diced some parishioner, or Father Flood and even some other nun. On those occasions she'd have me in stitches. But what had just occurred had the flavor of insanity to it and I was worried.

The class was small that evening due to the storm but I decided to go ahead anyway and give them my prepared talk on the role of the Pope. My mouth was rattling on about the authority of the Pope but my mind kept drifting back to Sister Gerard and the sight of her standing there in the dark and the fear I'd seen in her eyes. Could I be reading too much into it? Could it be that she was merely trying in some wildly misguided way to be helpful. It took all my concentration to keep even half my mind on my convert class and on Papal Infallibility.

Julia Schlitz had of course braved the storm that evening and was in her usual place in the front row and writing away assiduously in her notebook. Despite Sister's warning and her insipid questions, I still felt Mrs. Schlitz was a good and sincere convert. I respected even the innocent sincerity behind her questions and was impressed by the close attention she paid in every class. And those legs. I was trying to keep my eyes from focusing on those graceful, black-stockinged legs folded so demurely around one another in the front row. It was a meager joy that I looked forward to one night a week — just the tiniest touch of *delictatio* — as compensation for the dreary celibate life I led the rest of the time.

That night after class Sister Mary Gerard was back apparently to her usual self. She helped me lock up as usual and acted as though nothing out of the ordinary had happened between us earlier. She was, in fact, more than usually playful that evening, telling funny stories about her days in secondary school in Monaghan, kidding me about putting on a few pounds and even taking the cigarette gingerly from my mouth and puffing on it — getting the end all soggy — before returning it. And when it was time for her to leave and I had walked with her to the convent door under my umbrella, she touched my hand gently as she whispered goodnight. Whatever it was had possessed her earlier had seemingly blown over completely.

Mrs. Schlitz called the Rectory the following morning just as I was finishing breakfast. Might she have a private conference about a very confidential and somewhat embarrassing matter?

"Of course, Julia!" I said.

It was the first time I had seen her outside a classroom setting and she looked, if anything, more stunningly beautiful. She was dressed simply: a floral print dress that stopped a few inches above her knee, black stockings and pumps, yet she looked as cool and elegantly innocent as an Audrey Hepburn. I showed her into my office. She crossed her legs and my heart skipped a beat. I tried to keep my eyes on her face so as to focus on the problem she was trying to explain.

Her trouble, it seemed, was with the Church's ban on artificial birth control. She'd told her husband about her doubts and now he was worried too. What if she couldn't accept the teaching at all, would that mean she couldn't convert? And how would her husband take that news?

"As you know, he's a very strict Catholic, Father."

It all came pouring out of her then, all the conflicting emotions she'd been living with for months. She'd been using the Pill since the last baby was born and not telling her husband about it. He'd kill her if he found out, she said. Every time the subject of birth control came up in class she'd feel so guilty she'd become sick with worry. On the other hand, she was totally adamant that she would never under any circumstance go through another pregnancy.

"Does this make me an evil person, Father? Does it mean I can never become a Catholic?"

I said I could certainly sympathize with how miserable and conflicted she must have been feeling. Perhaps, if she and I were to have a few extra sessions between classes we might discuss the morality of forming one's personal conscience where that conscience and the Church's teachings diverge. She didn't quite get what I was saying at first but, when I'd explained it in a bit more detail, she brightened up considerably. What I had just explained, she said, had given her the first ray of light she'd glimpsed in the whole matter of joining the Church. It sounded a lot like what she'd learned as a Protestant about integrity. Perhaps she'd been a good Catholic all along, she said. I hoped she wouldn't spread the word that Father Holland was a good Protestant all along.

Might she smoke? She asked.

"Smoke?" My mind had been drifting. "Of course you may smoke!" I'd been dying for a cigarette myself. I offered her my Camels but she took a pack of Benson and Hedges from her purse. I held a match for her. As she guided my hand to her cigarette I was aware of how cool and soft her fingers felt — a long time since I'd felt the warmth of a woman's fingers on my hand. Her nails were painted just the lightest blush of pink. And when she lowered her eyelids the faint green of her eye-shadow provided a dramatic setting for her large, deep-set brown eyes. I could willingly get lost in those eyes, I realized. I felt such a rude bumpkin, so big and thick, beside such delicate beauty.

I got a hold of myself then and did my best, given my delicate condition, to explain the reasoning behind the Church's teaching on contraception. As with so many other aspects of the Church's teaching, I even drew some satisfaction from elucidating the elegant reasoning upon which it was all based while privately regarding it as a nearly total fiction. I sympathized with the young Dublin Artist's view totally, that Catholicism was a` "… brilliantly logical and coherent absurdity."

The time flew and before I knew it she had to be off — meeting a friend for lunch. Pity, she had to leave just as I'd been leading her, hand-in-hand, down the exquisite staircase of logic that would culminate in the Church's position on birth control. How could she tear herself away just then? Hadn't she been on the edge of her chair as I was carefully unfolding the syllogism? She must have sensed my frustration for she added that she could hardly wait to hear the rest of it next session. I had the distinct impression that we'd made real progress. I was mollified a bit by this.

"One more session might do it," I told her as I saw her to the rectory door.

As it turned out, it had taken several special sessions before she phoned one morning to tell me that the problem had been cleared up for her —"Just like that, something clicked!" —the result, apparently, of something I had said in our previous meeting.

What could I possibly have said that had brought about such an effect? I was afraid to ask. Who was I to question the mysterious workings of some god I didn't much believe in. And, since the whole fuss about birth control was ridiculous anyhow, maybe she'd been struck by some divinely inspired common sense.

Had we gone in for such a thing, Julia would have, without a doubt, been named valedictorian of the spring convert class. She had taken far more notes, learned far more prayers by heart, and asked far more questions than all the rest of the class put together.

On the day of her Baptism, her voice rang out clear and loud above the others in the baptismal responses:

"Do you renounce Satan?"

"I do renounce him." She announced.

"And all his pomps."

"I do renounce them." She proclaimed.

CHAPTER 16

Minerva, California — 1962

I CLOSED THE sliding glass door behind me. The fierce valley heat of July rising in ripples from the sticky tarmac was oppressive after the air-conditioned cold of the office.

We had driven around for hours that morning, the two of us, torn by indecision, refusing to put into words what we both intended. We'd talked in code about finding some place, a restaurant or cocktail lounge maybe, any cool place at all. We had spent an hour or more lying on the hot dry grass, in the meager shade of a live oak, eating our picnic lunch: a chicken sandwich, most of a bag of potato chips with ridges and a warm can of Fresca. It was hot and uncomfortable there on the parched dusty grass alongside that back road in the foothills, twenty miles from the nearest town and air conditioning —our breaths and fingers greasy from the food.

Driving around half the morning avoiding what was uppermost in our minds had made both of us irritable and depressed — a stupid game in which neither was willing to make the first overt suggestion.

When I'd finally spotted the sign, *Flamingo* and underneath the promise: "Refrigerated Rooms"— vividly illustrated by blue ice-capped letters —I swung the car decisively into the parking lot and pulled up to the office door. I had become fatalistic by then. Anything was better than what we'd been doing, even discovery and public humiliation; anything but the frustration of driving around, our backsides frying on the plastic seats of my Ford Falcon, waiting for the other one to make a decision.

It was a terrible sin, taking a woman to a motel for illicit sexual purposes, and yet in the actual doing of it somehow it didn't feel nearly as sleazy as they'd made it seem in moral theology. And the gravity of this was infinitely greater than with the poor woman in Dublin: I was now an ordained priest and she a married woman; sacrilege *and* adultery. I'd been embarrassed always when Graham Greene's Catholics committed adultery or when his priests led dissolute lives. Funny how doing something yourself made it more respectable.

Getting the room key had been much less of an ordeal than I'd feared. The man behind the counter was sitting with his feet up watching TV when I walked into the frigid air of the little office.

"Seven dollars, fill out the card." He had barely looked up.

If the rooms were as cold as the office, what a blessing. The man was engrossed in the baseball game on the TV. I filled in a false name and occupation on the card and inverted the numbers in writing down the license. The guy was oblivious.

Childish, the feeling of accomplishment when I showed her the key. We were getting somewhere, finally. What if a parishioner should recognize the parish car? I was nervous as a cat.

The room was large and very cool; heavy drapes drawn against the fierce sun left it pleasantly dim-lit — a relief from the intense valley glare.

Once inside, safe from the eyes of the world, we held each other, clinging tightly more from relief than passion. I had fantasized about this moment — it was all I'd thought about for days — but the hours since I'd picked her up had been so filled with frustration that physical desire had withered on the vine.

She had never done anything like this before, she said. She was very scared by this whole thing that was happening —very vulnerable.

I assured her it was not the sort of thing that I'd made a habit of either and, if she was scared, I was paralyzed.

I'd been thinking about that earlier, as we'd been driving around, how inexperienced I was for my age. I mean, once in my entire life and that so many years ago — on that wet St. Patrick's Day — and with an Irish whore. To even mention that drab poor thing in the same breath with this elegant creature felt almost sacrilegious.

And the thought of taking my clothes off in front of this one… Christ! Holding her was enough to drive a man out of his mind. Where would I even begin? A body couldn't just reach underneath her dress and put his hand up there, into her knickers —too forward by far — downright unmannerly. I'd keep on holding her, something was bound to develop; some approach would surely suggest itself. Wasn't there anything I could do to get things moving? Prayer? Hardly! A body could go out of his mind from the stress of waiting for his libido to return.

Luckily, or perhaps by the grace of a friendly god, Mrs. Schlitz turned out to be a good scout and had not come to the camp-out unprepared. With a playful flourish she made a little square bottle of Jack Daniel's, Black Label, appear from her purse. Magic — a rabbit from a hat! Glasses with their little paper bands from the bathroom, a tiny splash from the faucet to baptize the sour-mash whisky and, before you could say "Father Robinson," my nerves were on the road to recovery.

We undressed each other slowly, savoring every newly revealed nakedness as gourmets relish every nuance of a complex dish, tasting the sauces, inhaling the fragrances, savoring the textures. She giggled delightedly at each new unveiling. Naked she was gorgeous, tall and graceful but surprisingly full-figured and shapely; lightly tanned all over except for the shadowy evidence of a very spare bikini bottom.

The more we relaxed the more sensual she became in her sex play, nipping and licking and teasing. I was more aroused than I'd ever thought possible as we lay in each others arms, gently touching and caressing each other.

The next several hours flew by in a crimson blur of passion interrupted only by brief interludes of playfulness. I had never dreamed that lovemaking could feel so childlike.

Late in the afternoon, sated puppies, we were lying, sprawled amid the wreckage of the sheets, legs and arms entwined, exhausted, when someone knocked on the door. We froze.

My worst fears leaped full-blown into my mind: her husband in a ferocious rage, brandishing a gun. Or, the Chancellor —the parish car had been recognized and reported. I am drummed out of the diocese, my green-card revoked — I am deported. Oh God! Not that! Not back to Ireland!

In my terror, I heard myself call out, "Come in." She put a hand over my mouth to stop me but, too late, a key was already turning.

Braced against the worst, we pulled the sheets up to our noses and stared at the door frozen, fatalistic — reconciled to whatever retribution an offended god might be hurling at us for our delicious sin.

A man's head appeared around the door — a stranger with skinny neck and gaunt cheeks. He sidled into the room. "*William*" was stitched on his grey overalls.

"Won't be but a minit folks — sorry. Just emptyin' the Magic Fingers box." His voice was hesitant. "Be rat out a your hair in a sec. Apologize!"

He came over to Julia's side of the bed and with a key opened the cash box of the electric vibrator system that was part of the bed. A torrent of coin rattled from the Magic Fingers into a bulging canvas sack. Did people really use that thing? Several coins escaped the sack and had to be rounded up.

Julia and I had at first been lying paralyzed, following this man's every movement anxiously, but, once it became clear that he was no threat, Julia had become playful, tickling me under the sheets so that I was in agony keeping from laughing.

"Much obliged, lettin' me get this last one here done. Won't have ta come way back out ta catch it tomorra!"

I signaled acknowledgment with a hand barely poking above the covers — fingers waved in greeting.

Almost at the door the man stopped. Very deliberately he dug his hand into the canvas sack, selected a single coin, then hurried across the room and with a florish inserted the quarter into the Magic Fingers.

"Just punch that button thar when ya're ready and have yarse'ves a good time with tha Magic Fingers patented re-laxation system." He rattled this off as he was walking towards the door.

"Thank you very, very much." Julia called out as he was closing the door.

Julia, in a fair imitation of the man's Central Valley Okie accent, allowed as how we needed some Magic Fingers patented relaxation, rat than and thir. She punched the button as William had instructed and the bed started into a bone rattling vibration, shaking us simultaneously north and south, and east and west. The result on systems already taxed by sexual excitement, guilty fears and a pint of Jack Daniel's, was probably predictable. My stomach was the first to go. I made it to the bathroom barely in time. The sound was enough to set Julia's off too and for the next half hour we took turns at the bowl.

Finally, after standing together under a cold shower, we gathered what tatters of energy we had left and braced ourselves for our return to reality. Outside the door lay a world of heat-shimmering tar and air crackling dry from the fierce valley sun; outside too was the world in which people expected me to act like a priest.

The Falcon was an oven and the plastic seat hot enough to brand steers. Weak and disoriented still, I merged carefully into the evening rush hour — merged with people who'd spent their day in honest work —people on their way to innocent dinners in innocent homes. I took her back to the shopping center where she had parked her car — it must have been days since I'd met her there. We were both tense, silent. Logistics.

Let her out on the opposite side of the department store from where she had parked.

She would walk to her car through the store — less conspicuous.

No affection in the parking lot.

"How was the game? Must have been a scorcher?"

The Pastor was in the hallway as I came through from the garage. Oh God! Don't let him stop me

"Too hot for golf really," I said and kept walking towards the stairs.

I closed the door of my suite, shutting out the world. I needed time by myself, time to think; to make sense of what was happening to me. It felt like love. But what would that mean; what would I do about it?

And guilt. A normal person would be feeling guilt, given the circumstances, but I wasn't feeling any. Fear and confusion, yes. I was filled with both of those — guilt would maybe come afterwards. I poured a whiskey and sat down in my armchair. I had to think it out.

In the month since her Baptism, how had such an innocent friendship got so wildly out of hand? And going to bed with a newly converted woman — and a married woman at that. That was as out of hand as anything I could imagine. Hell of a shepherd, you are, gobbling the lamb chops.

When I had first told Jerry about the feelings I was having and particularly when I told him about that Friday evening she showed up for Benediction, he had warned me. She was already intent on getting me, he predicted. But I had been excited by the danger of it all and flattered — definitely flattered that someone so glamorous might be interested in me.

"I was coming down the altar steps when I spotted her sitting in the front row; sitting — not kneeling like everybody else — and she had on this very short red skirt, and it was riding up on her thighs… Christ! I could see her stocking tops; and garters…I could even see her friggin' knickers… Shite!"

"Not blue garters, I hope — B.V.M. blue garters?" Jerry interjected.

"Fuckin' dead on! How d'you…?" I was stunned. "Oh, shite! Fuckin' Joyce! She's fuckin' read the bastard."

"Of course she's read him. Perfect bait to set for some pretentious Paddy like yourself. Set him frothing at the mouth. It's what I'd have worn myself." Jerry shook his head in mock sympathy. "Pur wee cub! Sure ye hae nae bit o' resistance in ye at a' now, hae ye?"

Hearing him confirm what I had hardly dared let myself believe was at once fearful and incredibly exciting. Nothing had ever thrilled me as did the thought that this woman might want me. I didn't, at that moment, care about anything but having this woman.

"You didn't go and get yourself all sticky like poor auld Leopold, did you?" Jerry added.

"No! At least not during the *Tantum Ergo,* I didn't. That'd be awful, wouldn't it, kneeling with that gold embroidered cope around my shoulders, and all sticky. Awful!"

Jerry smiled. "Isn't it awful, the things come into a body's head when he ought to be sayin' his prayers."

The whiskey was helping my perspective. True, people who heard about priests having affairs were always profoundly shocked, but I had come to love this woman — sincerely. Didn't that change everything? Of course I was bewitched by her beauty and her playful sexuality, but I was in love with her and what sin was there in loving someone? And what we had said and done was something real — not some night-fantasy that would have disappeared with the dawn. What we had begun now demanded some hard choices and decisions. It called for commitment and I was ready.

The phone rang — it was Julia. Her voice was sweet and loving. I would gladly spend my life with this woman, making love to her, giving her everything she'd ever dreamed of — making her happy.

She was home safe, everything was fine; preparing dinner for her husband and children; staying home tonight.

"Any regrets?"

"Not a one!" She replied.

"Me neither, "I said. "A little scared but very much in love."

"I'm scared too, scared half to death," she was giggling. "Let's scare ourselves again — really, really soon!"

"I'd love that," I told her.

She would love it more, she said — tongue-in-cheek — if next time there could be less driving around in the heat before checking in. "But, once you did. Va–Voom!"

I was in awe of her.

"Bye honey! Have to go," she said.

"You're wonderful," I told her but she had hung up already. Somebody must have come into the room.

I had to talk to Jerry. It was all far too exciting and stressful to bear alone. Though I resented his cynicism about the blue garters, he was the only one I could trust on something so crucial.

But it was hard, even with Jerry, knowing how to start. I could hardly look him in the eye when he sat down. We were in Messina's, the pizza joint with the Roaring Twenties theme. I spent time studying the menu — a short list we had both long ago memorized. We talked about what pizza to order and debated pepperoni versus sausage.

"Well, Jaques? Jerry said finally, when we had ordered our usual pizza and the gun moll had set a large misty pitcher of beer on the table between us. "How fareth thy barque? Goeth it well with the many-limbed Julia?"

I didn't know where to begin.

"We may have a two-pitcher night on our hands," I temporized.

"That bad?"

"Bad? No! Gut wrenching, exciting, scary as hell, maybe. But not, 'Bad,' definitely."

"Ah! Storm-tossed on the wine-red ocean of passion…" Jerry's bantering was not meeting with the usual response from me and he looked up, startled. "Sorry," he said.

I took a deep breath and launched into my confession:

"I spent the whole afternoon in bed with her today, in a friggin' motel."
I blurted that much out — to get it said and over with. I was studying Jerry face,
vigilant for his reaction. Not a muscle flinched in his face.

I went on:

"I'm in such a fucking daze: I don't know anything anymore and don't much
care either. Mind-blowing! I do know one thing. I want to spend every minute of
every day of my life making love to this woman — my immortal soul be damned!"

"You do have a sort of unearthly look, the look of a man deep in lust, now
that you mention it." Jerry looked thoughtfully at me. "But then, you've always had
a sort of sleepy-eyed charm: what a woman or the gentler sort of boy often finds
attractive — bedroom-eyes. Bowled me over I know, the first time I saw them."

"Get serious!" I was staring at the untouched slice of pizza on my plate,
seeing nothing.

"This has to be love — the way I'm feeling — don't you think?"

"Is she as head over heels as you?" Jerry asked.

"Oh God, yes! But she's married and to a pretty nice guy, and they have the
kids and a home and everything — good money — bought her a new Thunderbird.
I mean, how could I expect her to leave that — and me penniless."

"I'd give it a bit of time maybe — see what develops." Jerry ventured. "Not to
throw cold water on your enthusiasm or anything, but sometimes decisions become
clearer with a bit more time."

"I'd say 'yes' if she asked me to leave tonight — no hesitation."

"You'd run off — just like that?"

"Like a shot —fuck the consequences. Sounds adolescent and crazy, but …"

"Hopefully then, she won't propose taking off tonight. Give that old spoilsport
'reason' a chance to enter the equation." He looked with what seemed to be sympathy at me but, just as I was beginning to resent being patronized, he added: "You
know that whatever you decide will be OK with me."

I nodded, grateful for the pledge of friendship. "Just give it some time,
you think?"

Jerry said nothing.

"I should have gone off the last time someone was in love with me." I told him.

"With Tommy?"

"I've never got over my guilt at letting him down." I was beginning to
feel the beer —I hoped I wasn't slurring. "Broke my heart, abandoning him

and him so in love. Heading off by himself that morning, down the drive-way. And in the windy cold, at the North Wall alone, waiting for the friggin' Liverpool boat. Friggin' Liverpool, shitehole — dirty, rainy armpit — bad as fuckin' Derry." I found that tears were trickling down my cheeks. "I can't let that happen again."

"Tommy wasn't the only one in love, if my memory serves." Jerry smiled so there would be no bite in his words.

"I know. I was head over heels too. I have sex with them once and I'm a goner." I said sheepishly. "The sort of tart you find in cheap novels."

"Now he tells me …" Jerry teased.

"For Christ's sake, Jerry…"

"If I were to recommend that you never see her again, I suppose you'd say, 'Yes Father' and the whole matter would be resolved."

"I'd tell you, 'Boil your fuckin' head'!"

"Ah! I thought so. Plan B, then: make no decisions of any sort for a while — no matter how strong the provocation. How does that sit with you?"

I agreed to that and, in the numerous phone conversations I had with Julia in subsequent days, I did restrain myself admirably. But for how long could I keep my dreams a secret from her?

She phoned right after breakfast the third day. Could she come over — she just had to talk. I was excited, it would be the first time since our big day. I took her in my arms as soon as we were in the office — it was heaven, holding her again. The words teamed out of me in a rush of pent-up sentiments and dreams and plans: things that had been churning inside me waiting for the sluice-gate to open. Finally I stopped talking for want of breath, long enough to notice that she'd been pushing back from me— her hands, I realized, were pressing gently but firmly against my chest. I looked into her eyes and what I saw there frightened me.

"What…?

She placed her fingers on my lips very gently.

"No! No! Don't say anything more! You mustn't…" she whispered urgently.

"But I love you and… you love me and… Don't you… ?"

"Of course I do. But please…"

She pushed me back into one of the chairs in front of the desk and, going around it, she took the chair used by the priest in counseling sessions.

"Look Jack!" She made a calming motion, patting the air with both her hands.

"We have to settle down now and use our heads." She spoke in a tone she might have used with her kids, slow and emphatic. She placed her graceful fingertips on the desk edge, studying her nails as she spoke. They were painted a pale pink — not the deep red she'd worn the day we'd made love.

"It's just not possible for the two of us to carry this on any further than it's already gone." She covered her face with both her lovely hands. For a moment I thought she was crying, but she placed her hands on the desk edge again and continued, her voice strong and determined — no trace of tears in her eyes.

"I never dreamed you were going to react like this: getting all carried away and obsessed with me — like some teenage boy."

A leaden weight dropped in my stomach and the first wave of a dark hopelessness washed over me.

"I suppose you've had so little experience in this sort of thing." She paused as though expecting a response; an admission maybe that I'd done something in extremely bad taste — acted like an oaf in loving her.

"But I thought it was so much more than a … one-time fling? Something beautiful…" I was begging and hating myself for it.

"Oh, it was really lovely, honey." She splayed her fingers, wiggled them and scrutinizing her nails. "I mean that very sincerely." She stood up then, took her purse off the desk, and smiled at me — her chore was almost done. "In other circumstances, there'd be all sorts of possibilities."

She had come around the desk and was now standing over me. I could smell the familiar scent of her mingled with Chanel and the smell of her freshly ironed dress —the fresh smell of Saturday nights after Mrs. McGowan had done the laundry. *Saturday Night Theatre* on the BBC Home Service at ten past nine — in bed after my bath.

"But honey, as you well know, I have a husband and a family. I couldn't risk losing that over a bit of fun you and I enjoyed one afternoon." She was looking at me, her eyebrows raised in query.

"Wouldn't make any sense at all, would it?"

I looked down at the carpet then —numb.

"I know that when you think about it you'll agree, this is the only sensible course for everybody concerned."

I was not following her. What was it she was saying? Was she telling me that this was the end of our dreams?"

I pressed my fingertips hard into my temples; the pain of it helped keep down the shame that was welling up inside me— shame for my foolishness. She bent over and stroked my head very gently.

"Jack! Father, baby!" She bent down so that her mouth was right by my ear. "If things were different, running away with you and doing all the things you said would be wonderful. I really, really mean that."

She placed a gentle kiss on my forehead.

I sat staring at the floor long after she had quietly let herself out by the front door. I had listened and heard the Thunderbird start up. Was the motor idling out there longer than usual; could she be changing her mind? My heart stumbled with hope, but the car roared off then — decisively. I listened till the sound faded and the street was dead quiet again. I sat in the office that smelled of her for a long time.

CHAPTER 17

Big Sur, California — 2004

HOLLAND KNOCKED ON the partially open door of the monk's office.

"Come in, come in."

He sounds awful chipper, Holland reflected. For a man that's just been read-ing about the scandalous behavior of a priest and his newly converted parishioner.

Holland had brought the most recent pages over much earlier that morning, as had become his custom. He found that when he did that, the monk would have read them and been prepared to discuss them.

"So, Jack, how are you this morning?"

"Besides being full of the usual trepidation and embarrassment after revealing some hidden shame…?"

"Hmm!" The little man nodded his head but didn't seem inclined to add anything. So Holland continued:

"Writing all that about Julia last night was painful and I've been thinking about that all morning. You know, I'm not sure whether I'm more in pain from seeing how naïve I was — thinking that woman would leave everything and run off with me — or from letting you see how sociopathic I was with regard to sex."

"You think you were, or are, a sociopath?"

"Jerry used to accuse me of being one sometimes. I've tried to understand what it was that was missing in me — what sort of restraining conscience — and I never could figure it out."

"Interesting, you should think of yourself that way."

"Well, you're the doctor. What's your diagnosis?"

"Well, to begin with, you went into a seminary having neither faith nor the divine calling. These are the gifts that have enabled other men to restrain themselves when faced with an occasion of sin. So, is it surprising how you responded in those situations?" The monk paused and started wiping his glasses with a white handkerchief as he continued. "Then, upon coming to America, you were exposed to even more temptations and again you had no grace to resist. I would see the problem as one arising from your presumptuousness in entering the religious life. What do you feel about that?"

"You may well be right." Holland did not find this a satisfactory analysis at all. Hadn't the man been a psychoanalyst? Where were the deep psychoanalytic insights?

"Don't you think, Father, that my actions were maybe driven by some need, maybe by some deprivation that I suffered in my childhood? Isn't that how we humans are inclined to behave, trying to find something we've lost or to heal some wound?"

"You've watched too many movies, Jack. Hollywood loves the facile, cause-effect explanation of complex issues. It was a constant irritant to me as an analyst, the glib, pop-psychology tying up of ragged emotional ends. The wisest mentors I had steered me away from the illusion I could 'solve' people."

"So then, Father," Holland began, "what would you say was causing me to be so promiscuous?"

"Sexual desire. The voracious male sexual drive uninhibited by the grace of God."

"Could it be that simple?" Holland shook his head.

"When it comes to sex, nothing surprises me."

"I have to warn you," Holland said. "I haven't got to the worst incident — the most scandalous —yet."

"And you're preparing me for it, so I won't be so shocked."

"Oh, you'll be shocked all right. I'm finding it hard to know how to tackle putting it on paper. Maybe I should just tell it in a session and be done with it."

"No!" His voice was emphatic. "I feel there is real value for you in writing these down. Takes them out of the wispy realm of thoughts, lends them a certain concreteness."

Holland nodded and stood up. The monk accompanied him to the head of the stairs again and there they shook hands.

Amazing, he even speaks to me after that, Holland mused.

Chapter 18

Minerva, California — 1962

"I USED TO smoke Sweet Afton in school — in the dorm at night, you know, before I entered the convent." Sister Mary Gerard blew out a stream of smoke.

Helping me smoke my cigarettes had become a regular feature of our evening visits in her office while my convert classes had been in session. That night we had just brought the latest project — a parish building fund drive — to a very successful conclusion. Father Flood had left earlier, the parish volunteers had had their celebratory drinks and gone to their homes and she and I were having our customary hot chocolate.

"You, smoking cigarettes in the boarding school? I don't believe a word of it." I said. "I see you more as the sister's pet, cleaning blackboards, telling on the boys in primary school."

"Far from it! I was a shockin' bit of hot stuff in me day. You should have seen me at the Palais de Dance in Kilkee. Curled *your* toes, I'll bet."

"And did you get the ends of your cigarettes as soggy back then too?" I grimaced at the wet mess she had again made of my Camel.

"If you're going to be that way over a bit of spittle, I'll smoke me own." She pulled the pack out of my inside jacket pocket. I handed her the lighter.

She looked so adorably inept trying to get the lighter to work I reached over to help and before I realized what was happening I had taken her in my arms.

She glanced quickly up at me and then rested her head cozily on my chest. Her arms tightened around me. She smelled of face soap and the outdoors and blackboard chalk. It was heaven, standing there holding her. But a voice began to nag inside my head: What in hell are you up to? Trying for the Most Serious Sins In One Month Prize? And you bleeding still from being dumped by Julia? Are you out of your friggin'...? Mary Gerard looked up into my face at that moment and I kissed her full on the lips. She hardly hesitated before eagerly parting her lips and pulling my face down closer to hers. Her lips were full and moist and her breath was sweet behind the faintest trace of cigarette. The tip of my tongue touched hers and immediately a thrill of excitement electrified me. I desperately wanted to make love to this woman.

Suddenly, with a single movement and without interrupting our kiss, she yanked off her veil and the starched white frame that surrounded her face, — all of one piece apparently — and threw it casually across the room onto the desktop. It was the first time I'd seen her hair, auburn, thick and full, cut in a short bob. Like most Catholics I had pictured nuns with hair cropped to the skull like prisoners. We stood for an age holding each other and kissing and when she finally pushed me back gently it was to check the time.

"I have to collect myself before going back over there," she said.

Then, in what I feared was embarrassment or even remorse, she retreated behind her desk, sat down and covered her face with her hands.

Watching her, I was stricken by guilt over what I had begun and a cascade of apologies poured out of me.

"I don't know what to say. I took advantage. I am so sorry." I told her I would never forgive myself for hurting her and that I had shocked myself by my impulse.

Sister Mary Gerard looked up at me then, dry-eyed and grinning. "You must be kidding?" She dismissed my remorse with a wave of her hand and continued looking at me and grinning as though there was some joke I was not privy to.

I couldn't make out what was going on with her. Had I been so foolish a lover that she was laughing at me — a pathetic lecher, a deluded Lothario? Or, could she be so cynical that she'd merely been proving something to herself — some female ego thing?

"You're not upset?" I couldn't think what to say.

"Upset, me eye!" she almost snorted in derision. "Sure I couldn't be letting that bitch, Julia Schlitz, have you all to herself without so much as a murmur, now could I?"

"Oh come on. Stop it with that nonsense!" I was shocked. What did she know about me and Julia? How could she know? She was just guessing, I decided. Don't be too defensive.

"It would have been comical if it hadn't been so pathetic, watching her reel you in like some big dumb, willing fish — and you no more seeing through what she was up to than …than a bloomin' pike."

Mary Gerard must have been referring to Julia's fawning over me in general rather than anything specific. She couldn't possibly know about anything else. That was just my guilty conscience. Don't fall for it — she's just faking you out. Don't admit a thing.

"That's just…" I began to protest but she brushed the subject aside with an airy wave of her hand. She didn't want to talk about Julia.

"So, are you planning to attend this year's Educational Conference in the city?" She had shifted gears abruptly and seemed eager to put what had just happened behind her as quickly as possible.

The Catholic Education Conference was the biggest event of the school year for teachers in parochial schools from all over California — priests made only token appearances, as a show of support rather than as participants.

"I was thinking about going down — maybe for a day." I hadn't given it much thought really, though I had gone the previous year. "Most of it's way out of my depth — all that educator stuff."

She seemed intent, studying the calendar on her desk — though I thought I detected just the faintest trace of a smile. She stood up then as though she had resolved something in her own mind and came around the desk.

"Well I don't know about all that education stuff you're referring to." She looked at me— straight in the eye — defiant. "We might find something else worth doin'— if you're up to it, that is."

"God almighty, sure we'd never get a minute alone around that bunch." I couldn't imagine her having a minute's privacy with five hundred other nuns traipsing about the hotel and conference center. I was delighted though at the invitation for it meant she hadn't regretted the kiss. At least she wasn't mad at me for my impudence.

"It would be no trouble at all, getting away," she explained. Sister Mary Joseph — her companion and roommate for the outing — would be only too happy to spend the night in another room with some of her other friends. That was, of course, if I'd even care to come and visit her.

The prospect of going to bed with another woman so soon — any woman — was terrifying. But with a nun? What in god's name did I think I was doing? The fear must have shown on my face.

"So? Is it scared of me ye are now, me foin boyo?" She teased.

"No! No. It's nothing like that, at all." I was so thrown by the tack she had taken I didn't know how I felt about her proposition. "It's about the fact that you and I are... I mean a nun and a priest..." I was stammering. "You can't be serious?"

"Never mind all that pious stuff. Are you on for it or not?" She was posing with the back of her hand resting on her waist — defiant — brassy as a Dublin fishwife. "Or, would you rather maybe, it was the darlin' Julia herself that was after being in it?"

The two of us would often go in and out of that sort of exaggerated Irish idiom and mocking brogue when we were kidding around together. To many Irish-born, talking like this to each other was a way of being light and humorous or, as in this case, challenging without giving too much offense. I didn't think for a minute she was kidding around now. This was a challenge.

"God, yes! I mean, no! I'm game for it, is what I mean. Of course, I'd love to do it." Even as I was saying it I knew it sounded lame and unconvincing.

"Well good, then! We're on."

"We're on." I tried to sound more delighted than I felt.

"Oh, I know what!" She suddenly punched me playfully on the shoulder. She was stronger than she looked and her small fist stung the muscle where it landed.

"I've just had a far better idea!" She was looking at me quizzically, a smile teasing the corners of her mouth.

"If you have the nerve to come to the back door of the convent tonight after everybody's asleep you could come and visit me in my room."

"You must be kidding?" I was truly shocked — stealing into a convent. Shite! What is she trying to do, push to see what my limits are? It's like she's walked off the page of some medieval novel.

"You are kidding, aren't you?"

"You come over to the kitchen door, at one o'clock tonight and you'll see whether I'm kidding or not."

"I don't doubt you for a second. I'd put nothing past you." I said that but at the same time I was sure she was just daring me, playing chicken. I'd dealt with her likes before and the only remedy was to push it to the very limit and, in turn, frighten them. I decided to tough it out, see how far she'd take it.

"And then what? What happens when you let me in by the kitchen door?" I acted defiant even sticking my chin out at her. "Are you going to be pourin' me a cup of tae then when I get to the back door, or what do you have in mind?"

"All that for a cup of tea? Isn't it the cheap tart ye are yerself! Don't be ridiculous avic! I'd never go to that much bother for an auld cup o' tae. No indeed! I'll let you in, if you're man enough to show up, and I'll invite you to visit me in my bed for a couple of hours."

'That's friggin' crazy!" I had shouted out — in spite of my resolution to play it cool. It was truly the most insane idea I'd ever heard of. She couldn't possibly mean it. And what if Mother Annunciata or one of the others should see us? It'd be curtains for the both of us.

She sat back down in her principal's chair then and grinned up at me wickedly. Without the veil obscuring her graceful neck and head she was indeed very beautiful in a tomboyish way and the short auburn hair added somehow to the daredevil challenge that rode on her grin.

"I wouldn't have thought of you as such a timid wee soul." She stuck her chin out at me in defiance. "You can't tell me that it's because you're such a holy wee fella. And it certainly isn't moral squeamishness that's stopping you. Maybe it's just that you don't find me attractive enough to bother with. Could that be it?"

"All right then!" I'd retorted. Two could play that game. "So what time do you want me there?" I'd call her bluff for I believed, or at least fervently hoped, that she was bluffing. I'd watch her find a way to back down from the limb she crawled out on.

"Great!" She said and clapped her hands. She was either intending to go through with one of the most insane ideas a nun had ever devised — sheer madness— or else she was a lot better poker player than I'd imagined.

"You'll be at the kitchen door then at one o'clock sharp." She demanded.

I couldn't help laughing. "You're on then," I fired back. She'd never be crazy enough to go through with it; putting everything on the line for a stupid dare — she wasn't totally insane.

I went around the desk intending to hold her again but she pushed me away.

"You go on now and leave me alone. I have to put myself back together, get ready for chapel like a good little nun!" She swung the headpiece over her head and was suddenly transmogrified back into a nun.

"See you later," I said.

"One, on the dot, mind," she called as I left the office. "See you're on time. I'm the sort of woman that doesn't want to be kept waiting in her bed!"

She was enjoying the role of *femme fatale*.

"I'll be there all right." I left her in the school office looking for all the world the innocent little nun once again. If the parishioners could only see the two of us— certifiable lunatics.

I still half expected —and prayed for — a call from her under some pretext as late as 10:30 when I was having a night-cap of Old Grandad with Father Flood. But the phone never rang — no last minute reprieve.

Earlier in the evening as I was reading the prayers of Compline more than half my mind was on what lay ahead of me that night.

Noctem quietam et finem perfectum concedat nobis... A quiet night and a good ending... hardly!

Sobrii estote et vigilate: Quia adversarius vester diabolus tanquam leo rugiens circuit, quaerens quem devoret... Testosterone prowling like a roaring lion seeking whom he might devour.

Resist him, *fortes in fide!*

I am fucking crazy! I should have known better than to challenge her. There had been something in her voice and in the set of her jaw that I'd seen years before when my sister would turn competitive. I had learned then to never underestimate this recklessness, this to-hell-with-caution female fearlessness, this willingness to push things just that bit further than I thought prudent.

The News-at-Eleven came and went, and still no phone call begging-off. The Pastor said "goodnight" and went upstairs to his suite where he would remain — short of an earthquake — till morning. I checked the doors and turned off all the lights as usual. Another whiskey would settle my nerves — but, then, more whiskey, I decided, might affect my judgment.

Affect your fuckin' judgment? The voiced of sanity screamed at me. What sort of ejit are you to be talking about judgment? And you waiting — no, lurking — around like a fuckin' thief for the chance to get into some wee nun's knickers. And you're talking about whiskey affectin' your judgment.

I sat at my desk and watched *The Jack Paar Show* as the clock crawled uphill towards one o'clock.

Like a commando sneaking in the dark behind enemy lines, I slipped guiltily out of the back door. It was important that I be very quiet for the old housekeeper would be full of nosy questions in the morning if she were to hear me go out at that hour.

It was a bright night with a near-full moon that glazed the trees around the grounds with a brittle metallic sheen. Only the barest breath of wind was gently rattling the fronds of the towering windmill palms on the lawn behind the rectory. I crept along the crunchy grass verge of the short driveway between the rectory and the convent, keeping as much as possible to the long moon-shadows cast by the palm trees and the row of flowering peaches that led to the convent's kitchen door. To all appearances the convent and its occupants were asleep — not a glimmer of light showed in any of the windows. The far-off roar of trucks carried in the still night air, the surging and subsiding, braking and gearing up at the traffic lights out on the boulevard.

Anyone watching from the houses that bordered the parish property would have seen a figure sneaking furtively from shadow to shadow and would have decided he was up to no good and they'd have been right. All around the neighborhood good people of middle America, many of them devout members of the parish, slept, unaware of "the awful deeds afoot that night," as a Victorian detective might have said. "Awful deeds," indeed.

It wasn't as though the moral issues were of no consequence to me, but at that moment morality was an abstraction that took a back seat to the very concrete risk of being caught with my pants down violating the cloister of a convent. Neither the time nor place for moralizing — far too late for hair-splitting anyway. Time enough for philosophizing afterwards sitting with a drink — provided I survive.

I hadn't told Jerry about any of this and was it any wonder? It took a lot to annoy Jerry but this would set a saint off — coming as it did hard on the heels of the whole Julia debacle.

Just as I got to it the convent door opened silently. Of course! She'd have been watching for me, maybe hoping that I'd have chickened out and she wouldn't have put her career in jeopardy on a silly dare.

A white clad figure beckoned me impatiently and, as I stepped tentatively through the doorway, it hushed me to be quiet. The moonlight flooding through the window gleamed on the highly polished linoleum floor and lent an eerie luminescence to an already bizarre scene. By its light I noticed that it wasn't Mary Gerard who had opened the door but her friend and co-conspirator, Sister Mary Joseph. Good thing I noticed, for I'd been on the point of putting my arms around her. In the white gown, who could tell one nun from another in the dark? That'd be a fine start to the evening — hugging the wrong nun!

Like there was a right nun to be hugging! I could hear Jerry's voice.

I had been startled and embarrassed seeing Sister Mary Joseph. The moral issues involved bothered me far less than knowing this third party had a role in our foolish intrigue. It would be hard facing Mary Joseph after this and knowing what she knew about me.

Mary Gerard emerged from the shadows of the hallway just then and, grasping me firmly by the arm, led me quickly and silently in the pitch darkness down a long narrow hallway and into her bedroom near the far end.

I had never before set foot in this the *sanctum sanctorum* of a convent. Neither priests nor laity were ever permitted behind the doors that separate the nuns' living quarters from the reception and office areas.

She didn't turn on any lights, even when we'd reached the safety of her room and closed the door, but by her flashlight I could see how tiny the place was. It couldn't have been more than eight by ten— a tin wardrobe and a small desk were situated one on either side of the window; a three-drawer chest stood against the near wall and a single bed no more than forty inches wide — a cot really — was right behind the door.

She closed the door with a sigh of relief and immediately threw her arms around my neck. We kissed passionately for a moment before she pushed me back a bit and stroked my face.

"I wasn't sure you'd come." She seemed very pleased I hadn't let her down.

"You're glad I did?"

"Very," she said. She pulled me over to the tiny bed then.

"Would you lie down beside me for a while?"

Without waiting for an answer, she climbed into her rumpled, slept-in bed, gamely bundling her full-length cotton nightie up under her armpits till she was practically naked. She wriggled farther over towards the wall to make room for me. It was very narrow for two people but I peeled off my clothes and stretched out beside her.

My hands were cold against her warm skin but she didn't flinch when I touched her. She felt warm and her skin was powdery smooth and smelled like a newly bathed baby. Her body was strong and athletic, lean with sturdy bones and long, firm muscles — nothing fragile about her. Nothing fragile about her approach either. She took me firmly in her arms and pulled me over on top of her, gripping me firmly — her strong legs folded up over my backside.

"This feels so nice!" She whispered into my ear.

The pillow at my face was erotic with her girl-smell —I could have stayed there for ever, in an embrace at once familiar but not remembered — home finally after years of lonely beds in college and seminary.

Starved for such closeness, merely holding each other was enough to arouse us both to a pitch that quickly became unbearable for me to sustain. The mad urge to complete what we had begun —I was poised at the very threshold — was proving almost too much for my will-power. It could spell only disaster for us both and I had barely enough mind left to think through to the consequences. The tension inherent in the situation was at once perilous and wildly titillating.

I tried to escape the vice-grip legs before I let slip what little control I still had while she, on the other hand, seemed determined to keep me right there. The best I could do in the circumstances was avoid an actual consummation. I was at first terribly embarrassed by the mess I had made until she assured me that she loved feeling it there, warm and intimate — a keepsake, she called it, for after I'd gone.

We explored each other's bodies for the rest of the hour that Mary Joseph had agreed to keep watch, touching and kissing, endlessly, tenderly, intimately, maddeningly — arousal, explosion, exhaustion. Her body spasmed and quivered; I held her and soothed her. She had cried softly afterwards and clung to me fiercely. She was more vigorous in her sexuality — so much more physical in every way — than Julia. I was astounded by the volcano of sexual energy that had been smoldering underneath that habit.

Sister Mary Joseph tapped lightly on the door to signal that our time was up. Mary Gerard, after a final squeeze and kiss, scooted out of the bed past me. Pulling her gown demurely down and smoothing it around her legs, she stole quietly out into the hall. I dressed quickly.

When she returned, satisfied the coast was clear, she led me by the arm once again, back along the narrow corridor, and hustled me out through the kitchen door. Not a word had been spoken since we'd left the room and there was no sign of Mary Joseph — though she was surely lurking nearby. A blow-by-blow account, the reward for service above and beyond her vows.

From the shadow of the nearest palm, I glanced back. The door had been closed, but I knew she would be watching from the window over the sink. The convent looked as it always looked at night: a dark and peaceful place, austere and sterile, nuns sleeping the sleep of innocence on chaste cots. She would be watching till I was out of sight.

Walking again in the long shadows of the palms back to the rectory, I experienced once more a feeling of the unreality of my life — the sense that I was moving through the world but was not really *in* the world, as others were apparently in it. That I had stolen into a convent in the middle of the night and had, less than five minutes ago, been locked in the most intimate embrace with a beautiful, sensual nun could not be happening in any real life. Was this how psychopaths felt?

In seminary, the more progressive of us had passed around copies of the *Decameron* to be read in secret and wondered at. The sexual exploits of those medieval priests and nuns and their disregard for solemn vows had shocked and titillated us innocent priestlings. But those men and women had all seemed unreal — certainly not people I would ever meet.

CHAPTER 19

Minerva, California — 1962

"A nun?"

"Shhh!" I looked around guiltily at the nearby tables but no one seemed to have noticed Jerry's outburst. I'd better not say anything — let him vent.

After a long silence he said it again:

"A nun?" His voice sounded distant and vague to me for I had taken myself off to a safe place in my mind. And a few seconds later the voice droned: "You slept with a friggin' nun?"

Sitting, my head bowed over my beer, I sensed rather than saw the look that must have accompanied this indictment and I refused to look up at him.

"Are you out of your fuckin' mind?" Jerry leaned over and whispered urgently. But, after glaring at me for another long moment and, maybe seeing the fear in my eyes when I finally did look up, he shook his head slowly then and smiled a bemused smile — taking the sting out of his reaction.

I had been bracing myself for much worse —I didn't know what — and, having finally coughed up the leaden lump that had been weighing me down, I was starting to feel some of the tension seep out of me and it felt safe to return to my body. I'd been acting like a fugitive for days, avoiding Jerry's increasingly urgent phone messages and isolating in the rectory to such an extent even Father Flood had become concerned. And the stress of living with my secret had taking a toll on my health as well, I hadn't eaten a decent meal nor had a full night's sleep in over a week. The greater part of most nights I had spent smoking at the window, ruminating on the wreckage of my life. I had no choice really but to set up this meeting and unburden myself to my best friend.

I had arrived at the restaurant ahead of time and taken a table off a little to the side — nobody could overhear any part of tonight's conversation. I had watched —my head thrumming with nerves — as Jerry wound his way across the crowded restaurant, squeezing between tables of college students, sidestepping the gun-moll waitresses and beer-slinger wise guys.

Don't be scared, I reminded myself — he's your friend. He must have been just as worried about my reaction when he admitted his homosexuality to me last summer on vacation. He had since told me how relieved he was it had not affected our friendship. Still, knowing he would be angry and worried, I braced myself.

Jerry had pulled out the chair opposite and stood for a moment looking down at me, studying me. Not a word. He just stood there shaking his head and grinning.

"What?" I demanded.

Jerry shook his head, sagely, regretfully. "Oh my God!" He sighing dramatically. I watched his performance and bit my tongue.

"Yerra, 'tis the fierce lookin' wreck of a man dat does be in it!" He pronounced with a self-satisfied smirk —a cat-that-ate-the-canary smirk.

I would let him have his fun, let him run down like a cheap watch. I was in no rush to launch into my confession anyway.

He took a long pull on the beer before continuing.

"You want to invite me to perform the wedding, is that it? Or, would it be the holy sacrament of divorce, maybe, for the darlin' Julia we're on about today?"

"Will you shut up for a second!" I pleaded. "It's not Julia that's on my mind at all."

"And here, haven't I been excited all day, thirsting for another dizzying chapter out of your celibate life story. It's not going to be about prayer, fasting or alms deeds — or what we laughingly refer to as your 'spiritual life,' is it?"

"Well it is sort of *de sexto*, but not really about adultery …" I took a drag on my cigarette, temporizing — never taking my eyes off Jerry's face.

"If it's not about Julia and it's not about adultery as such! Hm! There's an explanation coming I'm sure — perhaps it's so as to achieve a greater dramatic effect eventually — but for the life of me I can't see why you have to be so damned elliptic?"

"It's because I'm embarrassed, telling even you about this one — that's why I'm having such a hard time coming out with it." I explained. Now I wished he'd shut up and let me get on with my confession — before I lost my nerve completely.

"Well now." Jerry was still in a playful mood. "Let's see if I can help — make the birthing of it easier on you. Am I right in assuming that it's not my turn yet? Ah! I see by your dour expression that you haven't yet succumbed to my many charms. Ah Well."

I poured beer for both of us from the pitcher, took a long pull and made a cautious start.

"It's somebody I've become involved with, totally unexpectedly. And it's even more complicated than Julia…"

"More complicated than sleeping with a married woman from your own parish whom you've just baptized and received into the Church? *More* complicated than that?" Jerry was frowning — the playfulness had left his voice.

"Far more."

"Bigger than a bread-box?"

"Bigger, more complicated, more scandalous …"

"Let me guess! You've met a boy, reminds you of Tommy — he's a minor still but you've been having it off with him anyway and he's an altar boy — and a convert too — and you're running off to Mexico, the two of you — to be married by that drunken priest out of Graham Greene's novel. Right?"

"Worse — much worse!"

"Worse?" Jerry rubbed his jaw thoughtfully and gazed for inspiration at the black bullet-riddled sedan that was suspended from the ceiling above our heads.

"Well, I was half hoping you might have come to your senses after that whole Julia debacle and that I'd be in the running, finally. But no, I can see it all now: I'd be far too simple and straightforward for you. Not nearly risky enough to turn you on." Jerry paused for a minute. "Worse and more complicated than Julia — and not a boy? I'm stumped."

He had thrown his hands up in the air then and reached for his cigarette pack.

Then I told him the story: how a semi-teasing plan to meet at the San Francisco educational conference had spiraled downhill into this crazy, career-wrecking, soul-destroying, dare.

"What am I going to do with you?" He smiled then and shook his head.

I was so relieved I was having trouble breathing.

"Let's get out of here," he said. We had finished the beer but neither of us had so much as tasted the pizza.

Standing by our cars in Messina's parking lot, he made me promise, at the very, very least, never go to visit her in the convent again and I had given my word on that. He hadn't thought a rendezvous in San Francisco with a nun such a brilliant idea either.

"… but then," he admitted cheerfully, "who do we know that's a rock of sense all the time?" He had draped his arm over my shoulder companionably. "Prancing about the Castro district all tarted out like a two dollar whore in my best frock, hardly the one to lecture anybody on prudence."

Ironically, until the business with Julia, it had been Jerry's cross-dressing that had most often been the worry and it was I who'd been the worrier on those occasions. Since we'd been in California, Jerry had progressed from the closeted transvestite he'd been in seminary to something of an exhibitionist, driven it seemed to put everything at risk about once a week. One traffic-stop by the Highway Patrol, any night, returning from San Francisco… I was terrified, imagining the disaster something like that would trigger.

It was puzzling, I reflected as I drove home from the restaurant that evening, how little we had been able to influence the other's behavior — despite our closeness. Oddballs among a clergy whose recreation ran mainly to golf and card games, Jerry and I preferred jazz clubs and art house movies.

We had rented a cabin the previous August in an antiquated motor court near Asilomar State Park and had spent our entire three-week vacation exploring the Monterey area and lazing by the ocean.

Once, our curiosity had led us up a steep path to investigate a new monastery I had heard was being built on the mesa above the Pacific Coast Highway. We were greeted, as soon as the car came to a stop, by a German monk about our age who introduced himself as the Guest Master. He apologized for the construction mess and the poor facilities for entertaining us. The kitchens and refectory would be built, he said, over near the cliff's edge where we had parked. To the east of where we were standing the main monastery building and the chapel were already taking shape. Would we like to visit the temporary chapel? Would we like to join the monks for lunch and stay for the singing of The Small Hours? He was eager to show himself a good Guest Master but we declined his invitations and headed back to the car. Good thing we hadn't told him we were priests or we'd have had to at least visit the chapel and pretend to pray.

The view from where we'd parked was spectacular. A few hundred sheer feet below us cars — like ants—crawled along in the shadow of the massive rock face. Looking directly west, my imagination could easily make out Hawaii and Tahiti.

"They always pick great views, don't they, these monks," Jerry whispered when we were out of earshot of the Guest Master. "All over the world the best views have monasteries perched on them — closer to God, maybe."

"Still, views or not, I'd hate to live in a god-forsaken spot like this." I shuddered at the thought as I slammed the door and started the car down the steep rutted lane to the highway.

"Nonsense!" Jerry teased. "You'd love it up here. They'd elect you Abbot inside a year — king of the hill, monarch of all you survey."

For those three glorious weeks we had eaten and drunk and talked, often far into the night, in an Arcadian interlude that had flown by only too quickly.

And it was during those weeks under Jerry's coaching that I had finally overcome my fear of the ocean — a fear that had plagued me since childhood. Patiently, Jerry had coaxed and bullied me into the water at least once a day, till by the end of the three weeks, I could accompany him, swimming parallel to the beach for a few hundred yards in each direction. It was then I began to understand what the ocean had meant to my mother; what it was she had wanted to share with me those early August mornings in Bundoran when she would shake me gently awake — quiet so as to not wake my sister — and whisper:

"Wouldn't you like to come down to Rogey with me — it's a lovely morning?"

Through sleepy eyes I would look up at her — bathing suit already on underneath her raincoat — and, though I would have done anything else in the world to please her, I could never bring myself to do that one thing. It had frightened me too deeply, those dark green waters churning beneath Rogey Rock. Overcome with remorse for having failed her — the door clicked as she quietly left the room, off for her lonely swim — I would cry then into my pillow out of shame.

After dinner every night Jerry would dress up and we would walk together all the way from the Asilomar beach to Lovers' Point and back; the dark, slender girl and her tall, husky fellow stepping out at a nice fast pace, enjoying the bracing, seaside breeze..

"Ah!" My mother would say as we'd walk around the cliffs by the Fairy Bridges, "The ozone — can't you just feel it? So bracing!"

Sister Mary Gerard and I never kept our rendezvous in San Francisco — nor anywhere else for that matter. I think we knew, even as it was happening, that our time together was merely a hiatus from vows and obligations and roles — the vows being perhaps the least of these. And, though we never discussed the matter, we seemed to have agreed tacitly to take matters no farther. Though we were together in that parish for the next three years and remained the best of friends for years afterwards, neither of us ever referred to that night's escapade

CHAPTER 20

Big Sur, California — 2004

"I've read your latest pages." The monk looked up from the folder he had balanced on his lap.

Holland was sitting bolt upright in the little bentwood chair; his back was more comfortable that way though the position became quickly tiring. The unusual trepidation he had felt walking over from the kitchen today had eased somewhat but it was still there in his fluttery stomach and in the tense muscles of his shoulders. Ever since he'd slid the pages under the monk's door he'd been in a funk.

Though the synopsis he had written for the monk had covered only the highlights — or low-lights — of both affairs, still, what was on those pages was unthinkably scandalous. How would a monk react to such goings-on by a priest, and with a nun too…? Horror, probably. And the business with Julia, and her a new convert… Awful! These were the stories they told to scare seminarians into saying their prayers.

"Awful stuff, isn't it?" Holland ventured.

"How do *you* feel, revealing all this to me?"

"I was worried after I'd delivered it this morning, that you mightn't want to see me today at all. Worried, embarrassed, foolish — to answer your question." He slumped forward, arms resting on his thighs.

"Well, I'm more puzzled, than anything else." The monk was staring off behind Holland's head, he rubbed both hands down across his face, massaging carefully under his glasses with his fingertips. "What I don't understand is the nun, why she did it."

"Not sex?" Holland ventured after he'd let a moment pass.

"No! I don't think so, not from what you've written about her otherwise. No! I'd definitely say it wasn't about sex."

"Jealousy or envy, maybe? Of Julia?"

"Hmm, maybe jealousy, in a way." The little man leaned forward towards Holland then — their heads were no more than two feet apart. "Let me speculate for a minute. You tell me whether this rings true or … if I'm way off the mark." He paused and frowned thoughtfully — as though carefully organizing what he was going to say. "Is it possible that Sister Mary Gerard had detected what was happening between you and Julia?"

"Possible, yes. And with her antenna … Likely even, I'd say." Holland agreed.

"And, isn't it likely that she had detected it long before you yourself recognized what was happening?"

"Possibly." Holland agreed skeptically.

"And, isn't it possible that she wanted to save you from…"

"From myself?" Holland interrupted.

"From leaving the priesthood, would be my guess." The monk looked at Holland, his eyebrows raised in a question.

"To save me from leaving the priesthood, she had sex with me?" Holland couldn't hide the sarcasm.

"Well… perhaps by having sex with you she hoped to save you from being seduced by the other woman, by Julia."

Holland didn't know how to respond to this. The little monk, he reminded himself, had come to the Church and the priesthood with the idealism of a convert. He hadn't experienced the "anything goes" 1960's in the Church either — a time when even men and women of faith had gone off the rails.

"Amazing!" The monk shook his head. "'Greater love than this hath no man…' A truly amazing thing to do."

Holland could hold his tongue no longer. "Father, I don't quite know how to say this, but — with the deepest respect for your brilliance as a psychiatrist —I think you're the one this time with the facile explanation. Talk about your 'Hollywood pop-psych'."

The monk frowned and was silent for a few moments. When he did speak, Holland was sure he detected some resentment.

"So, Mr. Holland, what would your interpretation be?"

"Well, let's pin point my motivation in sleeping with her, first. That was, of course, a product of the 'sexual voraciousness' you so cleverly identified in our last session." Holland looked up at the monk before he continued. The other man was not rising to the bait. "Now, as far as the nun's motivation," he continued. "I'd be inclined to think that — pardon my infernal ego for thinking such a thing —she was truly attracted to me and, on sensing Julia's interest or designs, she decided to mark her territory."

"Oh, I can't see that at all. I just don't see a woman in her position acting in that way. Just unimaginable." Father James gathered his habit tighter around his legs. The chilly draft of contradiction, Holland speculated.

"I'm afraid you're right," Holland began. "It probably is unimaginable to you from where you sit. You'd have needed to be in the Church as a priest or nun in the mid-60's to understand the cataclysmic changes that were taking place. Never since the Italian Renaissance had clerical discipline so disintegrated as between 1965 and 1975."

"Well, as we discussed the other day — and as you have just brought to my attention —there are few easy explanations of any human behavior, let alone of something so complex."

It seemed to Holland he was ending the discussion. He painfully straightened his long stiff back against the chair-back. "The doubts about my suitability are more than confirmed, I imagine."

"Suitability?"

"Isn't it my 'suitability' that you're supposed to be assessing?"

"Funny you should say that." The monk responded. Again that nervous reflex Holland had witnessed a few times before: a few quick pulls of his thin, prominent nose and a scratching along the underside of his jaw with his thumb — like a dog with fleas. No sound had emanated from him — or none at least that Holland could detect. He waited for the hilarity to die down.

"You see, Father Prior has stopped inquiring about our progress and without that prod I find that I have slipped back into the role of psychotherapist. I think I'm enjoying that role more."

"More than Grand Inquisitor?"

"More than anything else I've done recently, maybe. I was pretty nasty there for a while. I'm sorry, Jack."

"So what's your excuse for being in a place like this — sitting out your life, on top of a hill? Not that it's any of my business, of course."

To Holland's surprise the monk responded almost eagerly to the question.

"When I converted to Catholicism from a sort of WASP paganism, I was already in practice in New York and for a while being a Catholic had seemed enough — more than enough. Then, one day a patient lent me a book by Thomas Merton and…"

"The Seven Story Mountain," Holland supplied.

"Exactly! That book spoke to me — to my hunger. And from then on the monastic life drew me like a magnet." He stretched out his hands, palms up — as though helpless in the face of greater powers. "And here I am, still, almost ten years later."

"You came by your vocation honestly then, called by God—the genuine article. Fabulous!"

"Yes, it is."

"I hope you haven't been too offended then by the stuff I've written about the Church and the priests."

"Not offended… No." The monk paused and looked up towards a corner of the ceiling as though carefully assessing his reaction. "A bit shocked maybe. Some of your honesty has hit me like a bucket of cold water. But it has forced me to think about some basic things — more than I have in the ten years I've been here."

"So?" Holland seemed to have assumed the role of Inquisitor. "What are we to do about all this…" He spread his hands in an all-encompassing motion, "… this assessment business?"

"Let's continue with what we're doing, at least for now — unless there's some place with sunny skies and warm beaches calling out to you."

"I'm in no hurry. My little routine here: the baking and the swimming, and the writing, it all suits me fine for the present." Holland looked up at the little priest's face and realized he had been staring intently at him. "And it's still chilly out there — even down in San Diego."

The priest raised his eyebrows in a question.

"I have a confession to make." Holland hurried on with his thought before the priest could say anything. Somehow it didn't feel fair now, stringing the man along.

"This whole writing and therapy thing, I started it as a sort of scam, you know — buying myself some time."

"I think I knew that." The monk smiled one of his minimalist smiles and again Holland witnessed the frenzy of nose pulling and jaw scratching that seemed to indicate monkish joviality.

"Not totally a scam, mind you, but... a bit at first." Holland added.

"And now?"

"Now, I'm not really sure why I'm doing it. I am certain of one thing though: that no matter what you report, I couldn't possibly become a lay brother here, ever. I'd starve to death before I'd take any more vows." Holland chuckled then "And the Prior would never let me stay on unless he had some hold on me, like a vow of obedience '...a bad, bad example ... a proximate occasion ...etc.' So, sooner or later, I'll be heading off to where the ocean is warmer and where you just reach up and pick an orange any time you feel like it."

"Oh, that place...?"

"Since I was ten years old, at Foynes — as Shannon Airport was called then — I would listen as they called out the stops for Pan Am Route One. Every name in the litany sent a thrill up my spine. I wanted to be one of those cosmopolitan characters in the boarding lounge — elegantly casual, leather bags plastered with exotic stickers, Turkish cigarette smoke, expensive cameras. I longed to leave with them for London and Frankfurt, Cairo and Delhi, Singapore and Pago Pago, Tahiti and Hawaii. And when the Clipper lifted off without me and I watched till it had disappeared into the Irish clouds, there was nothing for it then but to go back home, to that wet hillside in County Tyrone."

Neither of them said a word then for what seemed a long time. Holland was embarrassed at having rambled on longer than necessary — typical old man thing, he scolded himself.

"In the meantime," the priest broke the silence finally. "Why don't we continue what we've been doing. My guess would be, from the chronology, that you're within a few sessions of completing the history?"

"About that, I'd say."

"And, we'll see where we go from there."

Holland nodded and, without saying anything else, he got up and walked to the door.

"Day after tomorrow, Jack, same time?" The monk asked.

Again Holland nodded. He had said too much already today and was looking forward to the silence of the kitchen and his rooms. Thing about living alone, your ears got tired of words, your own or anybody else's — but mainly tired of your own.

Elected Silence sing to me. Hopkins, faintly recollected in tranquility.

A lot to be said for the contemplative life, but was it any good as a remedy for a fidget?

Chapter 21

Washington, D.C. — 1965-1970

"I will not tolerate the use of alcoholic beverages nor drugs of any kind in Caldwell Hall."

The Dean glowered around the room.

Good luck on that one! Four of us who had met for the first time in the gym that morning had just killed a fifth of J&B scotch before coming to the refectory.

"Back in friggin' seminary!" Jack from Vermont grumbled under his breath.

It was the evening of my first full day at Catholic University and, after spending most of it in sweaty registration lines in the gym, I was now in the refectory where the Dean, Monsignor Steele, was formally welcoming the incoming class of priests to Caldwell Hall.

"I will insist on each one of you men conducting himself as a gentleman and a cleric at all times."

He had been protecting the virtue of unruly young priests like us, he told us, for more than twenty years and, by God, he wasn't going to falter at this stage of his career — no matter what was happening to discipline in the rest of the Church. He was not a fan of the liberalization following Vatican II and he made no bones about it.

After the five tedious years I'd spent in parish ministry, the Bishop had finally responded to my strenuous apple-polishing. He had decided to send me off to graduate school, to The Catholic University of America, in Washington, D.C. for a Doctor of Canon Law degree. This, most bishops believed, was the perfect preparation — spiritually and mentally — for promotion to a high office in the Church. And what a perfect candidate for higher office they had in me, a man unshackled by either religious conviction or scruple. A canon law degree was surely gilding the lilly.

Ambition is a funny thing when you think about it: seeking promotion for promotion's sake — an addiction to recognition at any cost. Why on earth, a reasonable person might ask, would someone like myself — a priest with so little respect for the Church — work so hard for promotion within it? Why would a man who considered the Church a Rube Goldberg, seek promotion from being an axel to the loftier responsibility of a pully? It was a question that has always puzzled me too. If it had been merely a matter of holding on to my meal ticket, I could have done that with half the effort and none of the frustration required by my ambition. No, it had to be something else. I could never make up my mind whether it was some cuckoo-like incubus —implanted in my soul most likely by my mother — or... just plain boredom that drove me. But, whatever it was, I jumped at the chance to kick the dust of "Shitsville" off my shoes. I would study canon law and gladly — if that was the price I'd have to pay for five years in Washington, D.C.

"Priests in Caldwell Hall are required to dress in clerical garb at all times, on and off the campus." The old man read the next item on the yellowing sheet of paper he'd typed out ten years before.

The Catholic University Of America for most of its history had been a staid, conservative place where pious young men and women from pious Catholic families had been sent to receive a staid, Catholic education. But in the mid 60's all that changed. The placid campus, located in the Northeast sector of the District of Columbia, had become a cauldron bubbling over with rebellion against every kind of authority, inside and outside the Church.

Hundreds of the brightest young priests and nuns from all across the United States — mostly in their twenties — had come there for graduate studies, as had hundreds of priest and nuns before them. But things were different this time. These young nuns and priests were enraged and frustrated by the intransigence of the old men who controlled their church and their country and they were determined to make their voices heard.

It was a yeasty mash then of Church reformers, civil rights activists and Vietnam war protesters that sat around the refectory tables in Caldwell Hall listening as the little white-haired Monsignor laid down the rules we were supposed to follow. Fat chance, I thought as I listened to him give the same speech he had probably been giving every one of the twenty years he'd been Dean.

"We will not tolerate public statements critical of the Church, our Holy Father or the American Bishops, by men in this residence hall. Any such actions will be dealt with most severely."

God help you! I thought. One of the men at the next table had just had an article published in that week's issue of *Look* magazine — anonymously, of course — entitled: *A Modern Priest Looks At His Outdated Church*. Everyone there knew who the author was — except Monsignor Steele.

The cauldron was boiling over and neither the Pope nor the American bishops — not even Monsignor Steele — could put the lid back on.

What a fun place for someone like myself who had just endured five incredibly boring years of youth groups, fund-raising and catechism; for someone who was seeking a refuge from boredom. I couldn't believe my good luck.

John XXIII had died the previous year and his once-promising Vatican Council had already devolved into a stylized mime by the Fall of 1965. The Church bureaucrats had sung a *Te Deum* — their god had removed that old meddler in the nick of time. And they'd seen to the election of Paul VI: someone devious enough for them, a man who'd make a show of continuing John's work while quietly blocking every change. Paul VI was Pius XII reincarnate —absent the aristocratic cachet.

If the Roman *monsignori* had not feared a second Great Schism in the Church they would have closed the Council down the very day the nice little fat man cashed his chips but, for public relations purposes they had kept the inert body of a General Council breathing on a ventilator for quite a while after they'd murdered it. This subterfuge gave the American bishops a reprieve — anything was better than returning from Rome and trying to explain to their angry laity and priests why they had done nothing during their three very expensive years in Rome. They were bragging that they had changed the liturgy into the vernacular, as though they had needed three years in Rome for that — the Pope could have done it with one executive order. Hadn't Elizabeth Tudor done that very sensible thing five hundred years before for the English Church and with a mere stroke of *her* pen — and been roundly condemned for it too by Rome?

The reforms they had not tackled were legion: unification of the Christian churches, equality for women in the Church, ordination of women to the priesthood, ordination of married people to the priesthood, election of bishops by the priests and laity of a diocese, returning marriage and sexual morality to the forum of individual conscience where it had resided for the first millennium of Christianity, taking a leadership role in racial and social justice matters around the world — instead of being dragged reluctantly along. The list of issues they had avoided was endless.

Night after night we watched these old gray heads on the TV News — decked out in their lace nighties and red frocks — lines of them waddling to their seats in St. Peter's. And the longer they stayed over there the more anachronistic the whole circus looked to us in the university.

Didn't they realize they were creating a hornets' nest of angry young priests and nuns in places like Catholic University? And the more sincere, the angrier they were becoming. Martin Luther would have seemed a conciliator had he been a resident in Caldwell Hall in the late 60's. With so much discontent I was beginning to feel right at home.

"No priest in this hall is to participate in any form of political activity or protest. To do so will mean immediate expulsion from the university and return to his religious community."

I had already been recruited, on my way into dinner in fact, as a sign-painter by a group of young people who said they were planning a big civil rights march in The Mall that weekend. They needed lots of help and bodies, they said. I was to report to the college theatre the next morning and there I would join the team that was building and painting the placards.

Our processions would make the evening news too — lines of us with placards, shuffling in front of the Johnson White House and posing on the steps at the Lincoln Memorial. It was far more fun than teaching catechism and counting collections.

"No resident of Caldwell Hall may, for any reason, invite *a female of any age* to his room." He pounded the table so hard on the word "female" that the empty dishes rattled.

This time the snickers were hardly even muted, for at least half of the young men listening were as gay as the Fourth of July and this prohibition contained no restriction on their activities at all. Funny how unintentionally progressive the Church could be at times. Steele's eyes swept around the refectory — defying any man to contest his authority with another laugh.

"Each of you is expected to celebrate a private mass each morning in the Caldwell chapel and no one is to be absent from Caldwell Hall overnight without my express permission." He thundered.

"I will be in constant communication with your various religious superiors and, upon my recommendation..." He glared fiercely at our table where some J&B snickers were simmering. "Any of you may be withdrawn from this university at any time and returned immediately to your community or diocese for reassignment."

"Oh no! Not that!" someone at our table exclaimed.

We stared resolutely at the tablecloth, the six of us.

"No booze!" Ray from Vermont whispered.

"No women in your room?" I inquired in a loud whisper.

"Cheap Bastard! Take her to a motel — least you could do for the girl!" Dick from Minnesota never so much as moved a lip muscle as he said this — and the old priest practically looking down his throat.

"You will not have telephones installed in your rooms ..." He went on with his list after a tense pause.

"Have I made myself perfectly clear on all these matters?" Monsignor Steele's eyes swept over the assembled priests one last time before he turned neatly on his heel and glided out of the refectory.

"I don't know about the rest of you, but I need a drink after all that." I told the table.

I got five takers immediately. Not wanting to seem defiant of the old man, we thought it best to lurk about the front door steps for a few minutes after his talk — rather than sprinting directly to the Holiday Inn at the edge of campus. We must have waited a full five minutes before going over there and already half the priests of Caldwell Hall were working on their second drinks.

Poor Monsignor Steele! He might have saved his breath to cool his porridge, for before Christmas break the vast majority of us were ignoring all of his rules and, by the following Spring, tee shirts and shorts were the standard attire in Caldwell;

everyone had a phone in his room; and nobody would dream of asking anybody's permission to stay away overnight. And, as for sex… The smell of sweaty feet in the dorm and the legendary male disinterest in housekeeping, were probably a far greater deterrent to fornication than Monsignor's rules. But those were the years when one wore a flower in one's hair in San Francisco and love was everything — so, no one who was interested in sex need have gone without for long.

The faculty of the school of Canon Law was pretty evenly divided between the naïve, who were still hoping the Vatican Council would reform the Church; and the traditionalists, for whom even the word "reform" reeked of sulphur and Martin Luther. And none of them was even remotely liberal in the sense of tolerating opposing opinions — the progressives least tolerant of all. Success in exams, in such a philosophical mine-field, called for the skill of a tight-rope artist. Sincere or scholarly students were understandably frustrated and discouraged by a system where the top grades went to any student who could regurgitate the professor's notes verbatim. But the set-up might have been especially designed for someone like me. I pranced along that high wire with the greatest of confidence and, thanks to an exceptional memory and an almost complete detachment from the issues, I got excellent grades in all my courses.

At the end of my first year, I gassed up my newly purchased Galaxy 500, bought a Rand McNally roadmap and with a light heart headed for California by the slowest route I could devise. I avoided freeways as much as possible and spent a little over a week meandering through small town America. I had to see the stuff between the coasts. I found some of it interesting but I could never live that far from the ocean. The evening I crossed the Utah border into Nevada and had my first Mexican food in months, I decided that I could wait no longer; I drove all night and by noon the next day I was parked at Land's End. I had missed the Pacific and its fresh winds more than anything else in California.

"Can't you be more discrete?" I pleaded. "Dress away to your heart's content but stay in your room where it's safe?"

"But passing in public is the whole point of cross-dressing — the ultimate fantasy. Totally safe, behind locked doors? That'd be simply weird," Jerry retorted.

I was back in Minerva for the summer and Jerry and I were once again relaxing over frosted mugs of Messina's beer.

"Isn't there some place… some sort of transvestite club?" In my arrogance I'd hoped to come up with something he hadn't already considered.

"Of course there's places like that."

"So?"

"A whole room full of men dressed up like women? Disgusting! Not my fantasy at all!"

"But without the risk…?"

"But it's the very riskiness of being out in public that's half the charge." He was sounding just a little frustrated, that after so many years I still hadn't understood this. "It's the thrill of walking down the street, looking very Grace Kellyish, and turning the heads of heterosexual men. That's what's addictive. It's not about attracting gay men — it's nothing to do with gay men really." He took a thoughtful drag of his cigarette after delivering this harangue.

"So!" He smiled at me finally. "You see what a twisted poor thing I am!" He drained his beer glass.

We were at our usual table in the pizza joint. A Charleston was playing frantically from somewhere and the black, bullet-riddled Ford still hung suspended above our heads. The place was filling up with young people from the nearby State College and the chatter was getting louder by the minute.

"So what happens if somebody takes a fancy to Her Serene Highness, while she's out there trolling in The City?" I asked.

"I don't have the slightest… But, in my fantasy at least, we'd have this long and romantic courtship: travel on the Continent… opera in Milan, dining in Paris, art museums and concerts and picnics, of course, in the countryside…

"…under sycamores, in wildflower-strewn meadows…" I supplied.

"… a light white wine, Mozart…"

"Bee-loud?" I suggested.

"Naturally!" He agreed. "And a cloth laid out on damp-fresh grass, a basket of crusty bread…"

"… strawberries and clotted cream…"

"… cool moisture on the hock glasses …"

"*Et in Arcadia*…?" I suggested

"Exactly! Very middle-class and pure."

"But, *that which dares not breathe its name*…?" I prompted.

"Not even contemplated — we are Catholic, after all. But of course I'd be so swept away that I would go with him and I would yield to him and do whatever he desired me to do."

"And it would be all his doing — morally speaking?"

"He would make all the decisions and take all the initiatives …"

"Tramp!" I pronounced.

"But what a lovely tramp!"

"And Prince Charming doesn't mind finding no vagina … at the end of the yellow brick road?"

"He doesn't mind a bit. Delighted, in fact, with what he does find."

"Mister Charming could get mean, if he's gotten all worked-up and …?"

"Not in my dream he doesn't."

"And your conscience?" I probe.

"A few drinks would take care of it at the time and… I'd call you next morning, Doctor."

"So, you haven't been with anybody yet, then?"

"Never had the nerve." He shuddered. "The thought terrifies me. Rejection… God!"

Another steamy September in Caldwell Hall; another academic year; a year that would leave America with scars that have not yet healed completely.

Washington had never experienced anything like the riots that followed the assassination of Martin Luther King — at least not since the Civil War. The veterans' protests after the Great War and those staged by the desperate during the Depression were orderly affairs by comparison with what we experienced in the spring of '68. Angry crowds rampaged up and down and all around the North-East section of the District of Columbia — the quarter where Catholic University was located — setting fire to buildings and cars and in some few cases beating up white men who dared stand in their way.

Young priests in Caldwell Hall, scared little white boys, we huddled in our dormitory and watched fretfully out the windows that faced towards North Capitol. Most of us considered ourselves liberals, some had even been in Selma and Montgomery with Martin Luther King, but regardless of our political leaning, every one was desperate to escape the District while the racial rage possessed the streets.

As we packed our cars that first night, preparing to flee at dawn, the skies over the university were flickering orange from a hundred businesses burning along nearby Fourteenth Street. Black flakes swirled like snow in the air settling as a gray dust on the cars and streets and windows — the smell of fires was in my nose for a week afterwards. Everyone had an evacuation plan that night: drive north into redneck Maryland or, south by the parkway into sedately traditional Virginia. I planned to ride out the storm in the Fredericksburg parish where I served on weekends, if I could only make it safely to Route 95.

In the morning the radio said the District had cooled off, evacuation would not be necessary, so we unpacked our cars, embarrassed by our panic. But the army was everywhere you looked that week: convoys of huge, ugly trucks, siren-urgent jeeps, row facing row of grim men in helmets, M16's clutched white-knuckled.

The riots had not lasted that long, considering the depth of the rage, and the fires had burned out in only a few days, but pale ones would never again stroll around the Fourteenth Street clubs after dark as they had before. No longer would they tumble down those steep winding steps to the low, lacquered tables and bathe their souls in the world's best jazz in the Bohemian Caverns.

I was already back on the Interstate that June morning in 1968 — on my annual commute to California — when I heard on the radio that Bobby Kennedy had been killed. I wasn't that surprised, not after they'd got his brother and Doctor King. We are vicious monkeys, we humans when someone messes with our food dish!

The Fall elections that year had brought us Richard M. Nixon and his band of merry pranksters with their solution to the war and the Democratic Party. Jerry Wilson, the DC, Police Chief, rounded up hundreds and thousands of war protesters every weekend and the students in the five area universities did everything they could to frustrate him.

Protesting had become the new religious service for the young and students from all over the country flocked into town every weekend to worship. It was a time of intense emotion and reckless behavior. It was the end of the world. We were in the final age of time and nothing that came from past ages had value or relevance any longer — nothing mattered but the moment. It was a blur of marching, protesting, smoking dope and fucking, marching and protesting and smoking more dope. Vague recollections of trampling over out-of-towners in sleeping bags on the floor of my room Friday and Saturday nights; of Sunday midnight collections — bail money for detainees in the Armory. There was never enough money for bail and taxis. A painful, wonderful time of maudlin, stoned parties listening to the Draft Lottery —death sentences — Russian roulette on the radio. A time of singing, crying, fucking, praying. A great time to be young and alive and able to feel pain — and in retrospect, it was even a great time to have been a priest.

Folk-masses were all the rage with students then, and priests were in great demand for leading the celebrations. With six universities and countless smaller colleges in the immediate area, hardly a day went by but someone, somewhere, was organizing a folk-mass — usually in an off-campus digs. It was the students' way of making common cause with each other over the issues of the day: civil rights, freedom, and opposition to the war and its draft — all worth fighting and praying for.

A gallon of Gallo, several loaves of home-baked bread and a vagrant priest were the only requirements. Details, such as religious or denominational differences were irrelevant, Jew, Catholic, Muslim or Protestant, made no difference.

A loaf of bread, a jug of wine and Wowie! Read one invitation to a home mass that I remember.

Everyone sat on the floor while the priest — distinguished only by the rainbow serape thrown over his shirt and jeans,—led the improvised celebration: guitars, folk songs, great hunks of broken bread swilled down with cups of Modesto red — laughter, tears, love. Was it perhaps that much-touted Christian fellowship we were experiencing for the first time in our lives?

After mass, more wine, more hugs, a few hits off a joint and Lo…! Jesus walked amongst us. Verily! Alleluia!

"I finally had a religious experience." I announced to Jerry the following summer in Minerva.

"A friggin' miracle!" He pounded the table making the beer jibble in the pitcher. "You've been to Lourdes?"

"This bottomless pit of disbelief can report a sighting of the Very God." I said.

"Verily! My faith in prayer is restored," he averred.

"You've had me in your prayers?"

"Relentlessly."

"But I have a confession to make, Father." I continued.

"It was too good to be unalloyed."

"It was while saying a mass where I was stoned out of my gourd on pot…" I confessed.

"Not exactly Padre Pio or John of the Cross, then."

"More grass than cross, I'm afraid. Surrounded by girls, also nicely christianized by wine and pot…"

"Ah! Not water and the Holy Spirit?"

"Wine and pot and god-given hormones."

"Once again you've smoked out the Very God from his usual hiding place: between some girl's mystical thighs?"

"No, no!" I protested. "This was different. A much more spiritual thing than with Julia."

"But, in your religious fervor, you slept with some of them … or, I suspect, with all of them?" At times Jerry was so intuitive it was spooky.

"But it was all very spiritual."

"I do not doubt that for a minute."

"You had detected that — that it was a purely spiritual act of love? You must be gifted with the second sight or else… in league with the Power of Darkness?"

"Father of Lies —Lord of the Flies."

"You don't believe I was after having a spiritual breakthrough then, Father, do you?"

He smiled tolerantly.

"Seriously though," I said. "I do wish I had even a little faith."

"A little faith's no use to anybody. It's worse than none at all."

"I don't really want to go out and get an honest job pumping gas or digging ditches, but shite…!"

"Whatever else you do, don't go praying for faith. It'd be the death of you."

I said nothing and he went on.

"If you were —and this is a purely hypothetical situation, mind — if you were to get even the slightest morsel of faith, they'd kick you right out of Canon Law school. They'd take back your *Codex Juris Canonici* and strip the covers off it in a public place, a warning to any others who might be tempted to go down that path, so mind yerself, boyo!"

I said nothing — not wanting to interfere with his rant.

"And divil the bit of use you'd be in the Chancery either, afterwards — if you ever got faith." He took a long pull on his beer. "You're the perfect man for the job as you stand, so watch you don't go ruining everything."

"I should just stick with wine and pot then?

"There ye go, boyo!"

"Worked better than any prayers I've ever said — better than any of the sacraments — far better than Holy Orders. Put me into immediate contact with that saving God they've all been talking about — the mystics and the Kerrymen. I had started thinking they'd made it all up —Teresa of Avila and John of the Cross and that bunch — all that stuff about experiencing the God, but now I get it. Having met him in person, now I see their point."

Jerry exhaled cigarette smoke — blowing it into my face as he intoned:

Though I walk through the valley of the shadow of death,
I shall fear no evil for Thou art with me . . .

"It's the fucking truth! I never felt such peace in my life as at those stoned masses." I said.

"Great!" He exclaimed. "Now you're indulging in something more insidious by far than faith: rigorous honesty. And, while that's of enormous importance for someone seeking the God, there's nothing will sabotage a career in the Church faster." Jerry squashed his cigarette forcefully into the ash tray, then looked up at me and added: "Truth? Much more damning for an ambitious cleric than faith, even."

CHAPTER 22

Minerva, California — 1970-1975

"Jack, let's get the flock outta here," the Bishop muttered after he'd slammed the car door on the mob of red-faced priests.

I had been driving him around for over a year by that time and he'd begun to let his guard down with me occasionally. I had learned how he detested these Confirmation visits to the parishes and the clergy gatherings — particularly the boozy roast beef dinners that always accompanied them. And I'd learned too, what a shrewd judge of men he was when it came to the pastors. Though he smiled at all of them equally, he was not taken in for a second by the time-servers and the phonies. He was, on the other hand, a friend and confidant to the good sincere men — someone they could rely on. How could he have been so taken in by me, I wondered. I couldn't be that good at pulling the wool, could I?

Upon my return to Minerva, brandishing a freshly-minted Doctorate in canon law, I had of course been assigned to The Chancery, and given the lofty-sounding titles of, "Judge of the Tribunal" and "Assistant Chancellor of the Diocese." These titles, however impressive, could not alter the reality: I had become what I had always despised: a priest who spent the better part of every day processing paperwork. I had maneuvered myself into a position where I was neither a parish priest nor a teacher nor much of anything else that mattered; I had schemed and manipulated until I had arrived in a job so unbelievably boring, so intellectually mind-numbing, that I might have jumped out my window — had there been one in my tiny office. And perhaps more galling than the boredom was the fact that, being now a diocesan official, to my friends I was seen as part of the reactionary establishment.

While Jerry was making the news every week protesting either the Vietnam war or our Bishop's lack of support for the striking farm workers, I was hunkered down in my office behind a stack of law books, working on the conservative legal opinions that would support the Bishop's position.

Part of my job was to go along as driver/chaplain when the Bishop was making his annual Confirmation visits to the parishes throughout the far-flung diocese. During the Spring and Fall Confirmation seasons I wrestled his ungainly Buick Electra along endless miles of winding roads in the Sierra foothills and up and down the Great Valley. For someone so ambivalent about religion in general and the hierarchy in particular, these hours spent with the Bishop and the old Irish pastors called on all the acting skill I had developed over my years as an impostor.

Ironically, my appointment as the Bishop's driver and flunky was regarded by the older Irish priests as a great promotion. Any position where one had ready access to the man in power was, by the reasoning of these old politicians, automatically a position of great influence.

"And who in the diocese has the Man's ear more to himself than young Jack Holland?"

"Ah! A sly wan that, make no mistake about it!"

The reality was quite different. Most days I felt I was within a whisker of being unmasked as a fraud myself. It's hard to believe you have an in with the sheriff when you feel the posse hot on your tail.

"C'mere a minit, Jack." Old Paddy Joe beckoned to me — he'd been waiting for me to come out of the john so he could put a word in my ear.

"Ye know that Phonsie O'Kane's retirin', Jack?"

"Is he now?" I asked — knowing full well that he had already submitted his letter and that it had been joyfully received by the Bishop — accepted by certified return mail, even.

"But surely he's far too young a man, far too healthy a man, to be retiring?" I added, faking sadness.

"Too young?" I thought one of the fat blood vessels on his forehead was going to burst. "The man's seventy if he's a day," he protested.

"A powerful man for his age, then." I'd say, innocent as the day's long.

"Well, Jack, like a good man now, would you put in a word for meself with himself?"

I looked at the broken blood vessels on his cheeks and on the flare of his nose. His small pale-blue eyes were darting about under the heavy thatch of eyebrows, cunning and mean as a rat's eyes. The Irish should never drink, I thought to myself. Their skin was never made for it — friggin' parchment, shows every capillary. Paddy Joe is still rattling on about how long he'd been stuck up there in Jack Ass Flats or some other god-forsaken shanty town and couldn't I persuade the boss to give him a nice, rich parish in the flatlands.

Of course he didn't use the words "nice" or "rich," but I knew exactly what he meant — politics comes with mother's milk to us Irish. Paddy Joe didn't deserve the one he had, never mind one with more responsibility, the way he'd been drinking. If the local sheriff hadn't been a parishioner it would have been a jail cell he'd be living in — instead of coveting a fat rich parish down in the flatlands.

"Well, if the matter comes up..." I tried not to lie. What I meant of course was, the day there'd be a cold snap in hell...

I found that having no brief for any of them worked as well for the Bishop as for me.

"Jack, me foin bucko! Let's get the flock out of here!" And he'd slam the heavy Buick door.

A knowing look, eyes twinkling, an exaggerated sigh of relief as I drove their Bishop away, waving and smiling, after the dinners they'd put on to show what wonderful chaps they were.

He'd say his goodbye's as soon as he decently could every time and we would leave with those flush-faced men of God and the tables littered with cold, greasy rib-roast bones and ranks of empty red wine bottles. He would use the excuse of age and the long journey back, to make his escape.

"Now they're free to bore the hell out of each other." He'd mutter to me or nobody in particular. "I just hope none of them get busted for drunk driving on their way home."

It was not an unfounded fear at all for just such a scandal often greeted us in the Chancery first thing in the morning.

The Bishop was past his prime now and the world had changed so much since his days as a young padre with the Eighth Air Force in England — even in the years since he'd become a bishop it had changed radically. He was looking tired. Helping him vest for yet another Confirmation, I often felt sorry for the poor old man, saddling up every day in that ridiculous get-up, to do those hundreds of repetitious anointings, for lines of giggling, unconscious teenagers.

I would wonder during those hour-long silences in the car, when he and I were alone with only our thoughts, how much he still believed after all these years. Was he just another of that dutiful generation, so grateful for surviving the war that any job where nobody was shooting at you; any job that was safe would do you just fine for the rest of your life — flipping hamburgers, pumping gas, anointing, blessing?

He would sometimes burst out of the sphere of silence with which he usually surrounded himself to talk about some priest who was having trouble with alcohol or who'd become embroiled in a messy sexual scandal. In these matters I was impressed by how understanding he was of human failings.

By contrast, where priests were involved in social activism that threatened large contributors, he was merciless. When he heard that priests had been organizing strikes against millionaire Catholic farmers in the Central Valley, he ranted from the pulpit about priests breaking their vow of obedience. It was immoral, he said, to upset the good Catholic farmers. The fact that the Mexican farm workers were also Catholic seemed unimportant to him

Though I had studiously avoided arguing with him on these matters, I was shocked once to hear him say I was "a man with his head screwed on straight." He had been bragging about me to a group of old Irish pastors while I was in the next room — telling them how proud they should be of me.

"Not like those young Bolsheviks that've been coming out from Ireland recently." He'd said and the assembled brethren wagged their heads sadly.

"What is the world comin' to anyway?" One of them wailed.

"Aye indeed. And from Ireland, too." Another lamented.

"Terrible, terrible!"

"A shame, a bloody shame, Your Excellency."

Theirs was a collective guilt. That their Ireland should have produced such an abomination: an independent minded priest —a veritable fart in church!

"That bunch is infecting the whole diocese — them with their damned Liberation Theology: Communism by another name, is all it is." He confided to them.

The assembled sages nodded sagely, glancing quickly at each other lest they put a foot in it — a canny bunch of poker players — they'd mutter approving grunts and "Aye 'deed's". Most of them wouldn't have recognized Liberation Theology if it had walked into the room and sat down on their laps.

"Indeed," one of the braver souls ventured an opinion. "That bunch of wee pups outta be shipped off ta Cuba where they belong."

"Cure them of their Liberatin' nonsense pretty damn quick! Eh, Bishop?" Another concurred. "They'd learn a thing or two about real life then, so they would — down there way aul Fidel!"

"By God!" they swore, as they drank their bourbon and Seven Up highballs. "If it wasn't for men like the Bishop himself here, sure wouldn't the Church be in a sorry state indeed."

The loud sucking sound had not escaped the old man. And in the car he'd laughed as he waved goodbye at them.

"Thirty years from now, Jack, if you play your cards right, you could have a nice little parish up here in the boonies."

I looked at him dismissively and gunned the Electra so the tires spun gravel. He laughed out loud..

"Sure ye'll be likin' the hills just grand." He guffawed as the momentum snapped his head back.

He didn't usually talk much in the car once we'd got under way, unless something was bothering him. At those times he would launch into a monologue that required no input at all from me. But mostly we just stared ahead at the road, each in his own world. Often we would go for hours at a stretch without a single word.

Chapter 23

Minerva, California — 1973

FATHER CASSIDY — the pastor of the parish where I was in residence—took Thursday's off. And every Thursday for over twenty years he had met with his three friends—old-country Irishmen like himself — for a round of golf followed by dinner.

Each time it was Cassidy's turn to have the "boys" over to St. Thomas' rectory, I made a point of being "out to dinner." This was not done out of hostility or snobbery on my part but simply because I'd found little to talk about any time I had joined them. One particular Thursday however, Cassidy had made a point of inviting me to join them for dinner.

"Sure we have the grandest *craic*, now, so we do. It's a pity you miss it every week."

So I had agreed — I would be there. Oh, God! I blush to recall it even at this distance.

Something urgent had come up in the Chancery that afternoon and I was running late. I had missed their cocktail hour and was forced to join the program already in progress — and without benefit of anesthetic. Madge, Cassidy's amazingly untalented housekeeper, had already called everyone to table with her famous "soup's on" battle cry before I arrived breathless at the table.

The evening's hilarity is already in full swing —*mots* zinging about the room and pinging off Waterford glasses filled with the best of Concannon's red — "He was Irish, you know, Father — wan o' the Galway Concannons — aye, 'deed and he was."

Pat Pat: "And I told him right out, any man didn't fill his Sunday envelopes wasn't worth the powder tae blow him tae hell, so did! Bloody knave, all he is. Bloody knave!"

Tom:	"A knave and scoundrel for sure."
John:	"Never a truer word was spoken — knave and scoundrel s'all he is."
Cassidy:	"Indeed, indeed!"
Pat Pat:	"Infernal, infernal nerve altogether."
John:	"A knave! Truly, a knave!"
Tom:	"Intolerable!"
Cassidy:	"O-o-oh! A knave indeed!"

(I make a hasty sign of the cross as I take my place at the far end of the table from the four older men).

Holland:	"Evening, everybody!"
Tom:	(leaning over towards Cassidy) "What did he say?"
Cassidy:	"Father, you're very late for dinner. We were expecting you to join us earlier."
John:	"We had given up on you. Thought you weren't coming at all. Isn't that right?"
Pat Pat:	"We've been sitting here waiting on you. We thought you were going to join us earlier."
Holland:	"I'm sorry. I got held up."
Tom:	"What did he say?"
Cassidy:	"He got held up.
Tom:	"Held up?" He makes his fist into a gun.
Cassidy:	"Delayed. You're a gas-man, Tom."
Tom:	"Oh! Delayed." (wriggles his eyebrows — somebody once told him he did it like Terry Thomas —so for fifty years he's been doing it every chance he gets).
Cassidy:	"Well gentlemen we can begin in earnest, now that Father Holland has seen fit to join us. Anyone care for a refresher on their drink?"
Pat Pat:	"No! No! No!"
John:	"A drink, is it? No! No!" Shakes his head adamantly. "Ah. Ha!"
Tom:	"No siree! Must work tonight yet. Converts, you know.
Pat Pat:	"Right! Right! The converts. The converts, it is."

John:	"Can't overdo! Eh Tom?"
Tom	"Noo oh! Wouldn't do to overdo. No siree!"
Cassidy:	"Moderation."
Pat Pat:	"Moderation. Moderation!"
John:	"In all things."
Tom:	"*Virtus in Media!*"
Pat Pat:	"Indeed! Indeed!"
John:	"*In media* it is! Indeed. That's where it's at!"
Pat Pat:	"In the middle indeed. Virtue lies there in the middle —between good and bad."
Cassidy:	"Wine anybody?"

(I'm not in the mood for drinking wine. The others pass their glasses to the head of the table and Cassidy fills them and opens a third bottle.)

John:	"Plenty."
Pat Pat:	"More than plenty. More indeed than plenty!"
Tom:	"Ah, great. Nice. Very nice!"

(Toasts Cassidy. The others join in the toast by holding up their glasses. Madge has served them soup.)

Cassidy:	"Don't you want some wine, Father?"
Holland:	"No. I'm fine. Thanks."

(I eat some of Madge's soup but it's thin and tastes like bouillon cubes dissolved in water. The others are slurping away heartily, dunking great fists-full of bread into the thin broth and washing the lot down their gullets with glugging slugs of red wine. Cassidy has already opened a fourth bottle —so there would be no stutter in the supply.)

Cassidy:	"Not having your soup, Father?"
Holland:	"Oh I am, indeed!" I am starting to sound like them.
Tom:	"Fine game today."

John:	"Absolutely *superbo!*"
Pat Pat:	"*Superbum! Superbum!*"
John:	"And a great day for it too, thank God!"
Cassidy:	"A fine day for a little exercise."
Tom:	"Ah, the clean fresh air!"
John:	"God's air!"
Pat Pat:	"Indeed. Indeed!"
Tom:	"The healthy life."
Pat Pat:	"Wonderful! Wonderful!"
John:	"What is it they say about *mens sana*, Father?"

(He looks meaningfully at Jack).

Holland:	"Ah. Yes." (I have to make a fucking effort to talk to these men). "How were the greens today?"
Tom:	(To Cassidy) "What did he say?"
Cassidy:	"He asked about the greens.'
Tom:	"What greens?" (To Cassidy) "I didn't know we were having greens. Madge knows that I can't stand greens. Why in God's name is that woman trying to get me to eat greens when she knows I can't stand the damned things — make me fart all night. If I'd wanted to eat greens every day of me life I'd have stayed behind there in Cashelber." (He farts a loud ripper that they all ignore).
Cassidy:	(Loudly into Tom's ear) "He was asking about the condition of the golf greens. What was it you wanted to know about the greens, Father?"
Holland:	"How were they today?"
Cassidy:	"Don't you want to finish your soup? Madge is ready to bring out the dinner if you're finished?"
Holland:	"Oh, that's fine. I'm done here."
John:	"Madge! We're all finished with our soup except for Father Holland."

(Cassidy rings a little hand bell and Madge bustles in carrying several covered dishes on a tray.)

Madge:	"Didn't you like my soup?"
Holland:	"It was fine, Madge, fine. I just wasn't very hungry. Late lunch."
Pat Pat:	"Delightful, Delightful!"
John:	"A great cook, Madge."
Pat Pat:	"The very best! The very best, indeed."

(I have reached the limit of my tolerance. In desperation, I decide I'd better join them in lotus land. Cassidy has begun passing around the wine bottle and this time I fill my glass to the brim with the raw red. But then, an even better idea strikes me and I excuse myself from the table for a moment. Going into the common room I pour a generous helping of Cassidy's Chivas into a glass and take it with me into the bathroom where I glug it down rapidly. Then I return to the table.

They're passing around the cover-dishes of those Irish favorites, mashed turnips with bacon crumbles on top and baked beans with bacon crumbles on top and, what meal would be complete without pork kidneys singed in butter, juicy with a faint tinge of pink in the ooze.)

Pat Pat:	*"Splendido! Splendido!"*
John:	"A true delicacy, indeed."

(Maybe I can eat some of the turnips and beans — pass myself — though my craw is convulsing at the sight of them mopping the oily pink gravy with dollops of bread cruelly ripped from the loaf.)

Tom:	"Pleasant companions, better than all the wine in the world!"
Cassidy:	"Good friends and good conversation. Truly a blessing. Didn't I tell you, Father? Did I not tell you they were great gas?
Pat Pat:	"Great *craic!* Great, Great *craic!*"
John:	"Good friends and great conversations!"
Pat Pat:	*"Dignum et justum!"*

(I am becoming more relaxed by the minute and have refilled my glass with red wine a second time).

Cassidy: "Before you arrived Father, John here was telling us a little story and I think we all would like to hear the rest of it. Isn't that right, fellas? Didn't it seem like a good one, Pat?"

Pat Pat: "A good one, indeed. It sounded like a good one to me."

Holland: "I'm sorry I interrupted your story, Father.
Let us swear an oath and keep it with an equal mind,
In the hollow Lotus-land to live and lie reclined
On the hills like Gods together, careless of mankind."

Tom: "What did he say?"

Cassidy: "Nothing. Go on with the story, man."

John: "It was nothing much. Not much to it at all, now."

Tom: "What's he going to do now?"

Holland: (To Cassidy) "So you had a pretty good round today, huh?"

Cassidy: "Father was about to tell us his story. Weren't you John?"

Holland: "Yeah, John. Let's hear this story of yours they've all been raving about.

(I refill my glass and take a generous pull from it.)

Pat Pat: "Come on John. Come on now."

Holland: "Yeah! By all means — out with it!"

John: "Well... I don't know..."

Holland: "Come on now. We're on the edge of our chairs, John."

(I top up my own glass after the most cursory wave of the bottle towards the others.)

Cassidy: "Let him tell it in his own way, Father."

John: "So . . . Where was I?"

Pat Pat: (prompting) "The second ten years had passed..."

John: "Ah, yes. Well, you see the second ten years had passed..."

Holland: "Is this a short story, John?"

John:	"Ah … Yes. I suppose you could say that."
Holland:	(I take a drink and smack my lips loudly —in appreciation of Mr. Concannon's art) "Good! Good! Nothing like a snappy short story to enliven the evening. Tell on, my man!"
John:	"Well. The second ten years have now passed. You see he's been a total of twenty years by this time, living in the rigors of the strictest form of monastic rule. O K? Well the big day finally arrives and in he comes to the Abbot's office to utter his two words …"
Holland:	"What's this about two words?"
John:	"The only words he's been permitted in ten years. You weren't here when I explained that he's only allowed two words every ten years."
Holland:	"So what had he said after the first ten?"
Cassidy:	"He said 'Feet Cold.' Isn't that right John?"
John:	"That's right. So now here he is and it's been twenty years."
Holland:	"Strict bunch! Worse'n the friggin' Trappists!"
Cassidy:	"Very possible. Go on John. Let John go on with his story, now. Why don't you stand up and tell us the story like you were doing earlier with gestures and everything."
Holland:	"He does gestures too?"
Cassidy:	"Father, please."
John:	(Stands and coughs dramatically) "So in he comes and gets ready to speak his two solitary words. What will they be I wonder?" (John affects a coy twinkle in the best Barry Fitzgerald tradition of stage-Oirishmen everywhere and, after a dramatic pause, says) … "'Feet cold!'"
Holland:	"He said the same words this time again? This guy was losing his marbles."
John	"No, no. That's not it." (He looks around the table —confused) "The second time the words are different."
Holland	"Good thing too. Nothing as boring as a man that keeps repeating himself."
Cassidy:	"Let the man tell his story, Father. Come on John, think about it. I have the feeling this is one of your good ones, John."

Pat Pat:	"It is. It is indeed. I've heard him tell this one before. It's a real corker altogether. Wait till you hear."
John:	"I've got it now. The second time he says 'Bed hard.'"
Holland:	(I explode with a great guffaw but then, noticing that no one else is laughing, stop suddenly). "Sorry. I … I thought that was very funny: 'Bed hard!'"
Cassidy:	"Go on John."
John:	"So." (He squares his shoulders) "Now then, ten more years pass. It's been thirty years in this place —thirty long silent years …"
Pat Pat:	"This is the good part!" He slaps the table with his hand. "This is the good part! Listen."
Tom:	"Hush up now, so we can hear the man. Go on John."
Holland:	"The suspense is killing me. I thought this was a short story?"
Cassidy:	"Go on John."
John:	"Finally …"
Pat Pat:	'Act it out John. Come on, now. Act it out like ye did for Breslin that night."
John:	(Pushing his chair into the table and leaning heavily on the back of it) "So. Finally the day of days arrives: the thirtieth anniversary of his solemn vows. Once again it's time for his two precious words. Two meager words after thirty years of devotion and self-denial. What will these words be, is the question? The Abbot waits expectantly at his desk. The monk takes a deep breath, for he can hardly trust his tongue to form the words, and he utters them:…"
Holland:	"He quits, huh?"
Tom:	"Shush up. You're going to spoil it! Go on John."
John:	(Looks resentfully at me but struggles back into character) "I quit."
Holland:	"I'm not surprised. All he's ever done was complain. The man wasn't happy, obviously."
Cassidy:	(To Holland) "Father, Please! Go on John. And what was it the Abbot said back to him?"
Tom:	"Yeah, John. What was his comeback to that?"

John:	(Looks crestfallen and sits down) "Huh!"
Cassidy:	"Come on John. Don't leave us hanging. What's wrong with him?" (Looks at Pat Pat).
Pat Pat:	"You see the Abbot said what Father Holland just said.'
Cassidy:	"That all he'd done was complain since he'd been there?"
Holland:	(I slap the table loudly with my hand.) "That's a damned good one John!

(I haven't noticed that the air has become decidedly frosty in the room. I swing the wine bottle around in a perfunctory offer before putting it to my mouth and glugging back the remaining wine.)

"Any of you guys know any good limericks?" (I take another swig from the already empty bottle and hold it upside down incredulous that it could be all gone.) "I ever tell you guys my all-time-favorite limerick?"

(The older men are stunned, watching my performance. When had they last seen someone so drunk and so rude?)

"How does it go? Let me see now.
'This girl from Bologna named Cass
With an incredibly talented ass
What she'd do with a buck
Besides ..."

Cassidy:	(Pushing his chair back noisily and standing up) "I think we're all finished here, gentlemen."

CHAPTER 24

Big Sur, California — 2004

It was a typical spring morning for the Central Coast of California, foggy with a cold nip still in the breezes blowing in off the Pacific. The water couldn't have been more than sixty degrees. They wouldn't see the sun till mid-afternoon, if it decided to show its face at all. What business had he living here, freezing his ass off, in the coldest part of the state? Nobody he cared about lived here — it was near time to head south. Holland turned for shore, having done the 'downhill' leg — grateful to be getting out. His shoulders had bothered him for the first ten minutes but his body, having long since given up on sending pain signals to his head, had gone numb instead. What's the point in sending the man signals, he never listens anyway.

But now it was his lower back that was bothering him, aching from the sag — friggin' sway-back, he grumbled when his feet finally found the sandy bottom. He bent forward painfully and stayed jackknifed — basking in the relief it brought — for a minute or more before straightening up. Felt so good! Isn't it a wonderful treat when you stop hitting your toe with a hammer?

He nagged himself for the hundredth time about doing more stretches.

Ah, sure who is listening, anyway? Never hear a word I say.

Pathetic old fart, rambling on to himself — the young surfers laughing at him, talking to himself.

He sat in the truck when he was dressed, savoring his Marlboro. The tourists were out on the road already, heading down the coast for Hearst's Castle. Most of those working their way north from San Luis Obispo wouldn't get up this far till much later in the day. A station wagon with Iowa plates was parked in front of him. A nice fat family from the mid-west, shivering in their shorts and cotton shirts.

They'd bought all the lightweight clothing they could find in Davenport for their trip to "Sunny California" — just like Lucy and Ricky.

Three or four surfer trucks were pulled in off the road too — optimists riding their planks in a glassed-out sea.

He stubbed out the cigarette and started the engine. Hanging a U, careful not to get clobbered by a Winnebago — that would take care of everybody's dilemma — he drove back up the hill to the monastery. He'd make a pot of coffee, wash the dishes, eat a bite. He was hungry after his swim.

Last night he had finished writing around midnight and, for a change, he had slept reasonably well till around five. While the breakfast Danish were in the cooling rack and the loaves of bread were proofing, he had hurried across to the monastery and pushed his latest pages under the door of Father James' office.

During his swim he'd been worrying that maybe the monk would take offense at what he'd written, that he'd think his description of the priests' dinner too frivolous — too cartoonish. But, after a couple of hours thinking about it, that was the only way he could come up with to give this American — a psychiatrist and a convert at that — the feel of something so utterly foreign to his experience as a gathering of elderly Irish priests.

He had made another nice bread for the monks today, fat and chewy, wheat berries and whole grains and enriched with a generous shot of malt. He cut a thick heel off one of the warm loaves but the coffee pot was gurgling still with his Sumatra — he would wait for it, have all his pleasures together.

He barely heard the knock — a tentative tapping. At first he thought the sound was coming from one of the compressors on top of the bank of refrigerators.

Was that it again — and from the door? He went to the door and opened it. Father James with a startled look on his face was standing there, knuckles poised for another tap.

"Morning Jack."

"Well?" He exclaimed. It was all that came out of his mouth. So surprised at seeing the monk out of context, he'd hardly recognized him. He looked shorter and younger over here in the kitchen. Let the man in — where's your manners? He scolded himself.

"Well, Father! Come on in."

The little monk looked around at the gleaming steel that was everywhere and drew in an appreciative breath.

"Isn't the smell of bread wonderfully friendly?" The priest went over to the rack where a dozen or so loaves were cooling and inhaled deeply. "You could get drunk on that," he said as he tapped one of the loaves with his fingertip.

Holland was pleased at having such an appreciative audience.

"Let me cut you a nice heel — it's at its best about now when it's still a wee bit warm." He offered.

"No. No. I couldn't let you spoil such a work of art."

"Don't be ridiculous. You can have a cup of good coffee and a heel of fresh bread — there isn't anything in the *Rule*, surely, forbidding that, now, is there?"

Holland took another mug from the drying rack and poured each of them a cup of the dark roast coffee. Going to one of the refrigerators, he took out a tin pitcher of milk and a tray with about five pounds of the butter he used for croissants. He laid them on the workbench by the mugs.

"Rough and ready," he apologized, signaling the priest to join him at the bench. He turned the loaf he'd been working on around and cut the other end off, nice and thick, and pushed it over the table to Father James.

"A knife!" Holland took a bread knife from the block on the side of the bench and slid it over.

"This is so good." Father James hadn't bothered with the butter — a small thing but something that pleased Holland inordinately. He was chewing slowly, appreciatively.

Neither said a word for a few minutes — just chewed and slurped the strong coffee in companionable silence.

"I wanted to ask you about that last thing you wrote." Father James broke the silence and the words sprung at Holland like a threat. He hoped the flicker of fear that swept over him, the dread of disapproval, hadn't been apparent. He said nothing but stared, unfocused, at the table top — white with the fine patina of flour from years as a baking bench. No amount of scrubbing could get flour out of the wood grain entirely. The priest was speaking to him but the voice came to him from a distance.

"I was wondering if that had really happened. Was it true, I wondered? Or was it just a device for story telling?"

Holland looked up finally and saw that the monk was not angry looking, as far as he could tell.

"That dinner scene?" The monk clarified his question. "Was it just like that?"

"It really was, just like that — well maybe not *verbatim* — but close. I did get progressively drunker during the dinner and John Meehan told that incredibly stupid story about the monk and the conversation at table sounded, or at least felt, exactly like that." Holland paused, considering for a moment, how to put the next bit.

"The Limerick bit I made up though, when I was writing it last night. That part wasn't strictly true. Fact is, I blacked out towards the end of dinner — remembered nothing till the next morning. Apparently though, I had recited something very vulgar that offended everybody. Cassidy wouldn't repeat it to me the next day, it was so disgusting, he said. I've just speculated that it was a dirty Limerick — I've been known to create such things, when in me cups, as they say."

"So, did you get in trouble for it?"

"Trouble? Sure wasn't I drunk when I did it? And, for what you do when you've drink taken, the Irish give a plenary indulgence the next morning. They might knock your teeth down your throat at the time, but next day, all is forgiven — otherwise nobody would be speaking to anybody else on the whole friggin' island."

"I liked the picture you painted of the priests."

"You didn't mind, then?"

"Not at all. You might try your hand at a play — writing a play, you know, someday."

"Well. I don't know." Holland was relieved and then flattered by what the man was saying. There had been a time… but that was long ago. He wouldn't bother the man with it.

"So, I'll see you again tomorrow?" The little monk had finished his bread and coffee and was obviously heading back to the monastery. "Thanks for the…" he waved his hand over the empty cup and the bench. "The bread was the best I've ever tasted."

Holland nodded and watched the little priest as he walked over to the door, where he waved briefly before leaving.

"Funny, isn't it?" He asked the empty kitchen. "Him coming over here like that?" Holland rinsed the cups and brushed the crumbs of the table. Back to his typewriter.

CHAPTER 25

Minerva, California — 1975

THOUGH THE TITLE "monsignor" may impress the average layperson, it has about as much real significance as a puca-shell necklace from Hawaii. Besides being a *Souvenir from Rome*, its principal effect is that the recipient may parade about in public decked out in red robes and lacy under-frocks — cross-dressed as a bishop. Being named a monsignor also means that one's name is still on the bishop's gift list when he's pushing his shopping cart through Ye Olde Vatican Gifte Shoppe — one's record is clean, so far as His Lordship knows.

It was this latter consideration that had most upset me when I realized I had not made the Bishop's list of honorees—that and the public humiliation. To honor others and not his right hand man — humiliating beyond words. My instincts told me I was in deep trouble. Time to get serious about that second career, I told myself. My mind scanned frantically all the most likely indiscretions that might have come back to haunt me. A body never knew who might have reported him and for what — and, god knows, there had been many indiscretions.

The Bishop had dropped the bomb on me the morning after returning from his biannual visit to Rome — just as he and I were setting out on another two-day Confirmation circuit.

"Jack, I want you, when we get back, to schedule the cathedral for an investiture of a new crop of *monsignori* — midweek, maybe three or four weeks from now."

I looked over at him but he was staring straight ahead at the highway. I could read nothing in his face. He glanced over then and noticing, I suppose, the question written loud on *my* face, he rattled off the names of the six honorees. Three of the six hadn't bothered me: old geezers being honored essentially for not dying, but the other three... These were my contemporaries — one was two years younger, even. I was so stunned I don't know how I kept the Buick from running off that narrow road in the Sierra foothills.

Granted, being named a "Papal Chamberlain" — the formal name for a monsignor — is a ridiculous anachronism in this age of indoor plumbing, but leaving his own chaplain off the list would be seen as an enormous slap in the face by my fellow priests. The least he could have done, after all the hours I'd spent driving the son-of-a-bitch around and waiting on him hand and foot, was spare me the humiliation.

After a sleepless night spent fretting and chain-smoking in the country rectory where we were staying, I managed, as dawn was breaking, to calm myself on the theory that he was merely rapping my knuckles. Rumors about me might have reached his desk but obviously there had been nothing provable — otherwise, wouldn't he have dropped me like a hot potato as his chaplain? I was still hurt and very embarrassed by the public disgrace but that I could endure — I wasn't that popular with the other priests at the best of times. I could hang on for awhile — till my next career move became clear.

When I came in for breakfast, the Bishop had smiled up at me — glad to see me. That was a good sign. As I usually did, that morning I provided him a little comic relief from the stilted platitudes of the awe-struck local priests gathered around the dining table.

"I hate places like this," I grumbled as I poured myself a cup of coffee. "Those damned birds — frigging racket — never closed an eye all night!"

He laughed out loud at that and I saw him wink at the others.

"And what makes you so bloody chirpy?" I asked him — shocking the locals with my disrespect.

"Ah, Jack, they say these parishes up here can grow on a man — you'll get to love it after you've been stationed here in the hills ten or twelve years. Isn't that right Father Brennan?" He winked at the Pastor.

I pulled a grimace and lighted a cigarette, pretending to be in a bad temper, though I was feeling far better than I had been only moments before. If he was still kidding me, I wasn't that badly in the doghouse. So, why then had he decided to humiliate me so publicly?

It was a difficult time for me, those weeks after the names of the honorees had been announced. It was hard being around the priests, particularly around groups of them, knowing what they would be saying behind my back — knowing what a backstabbing bunch of auld biddys they could be.

"There's somethin' goin' on way him we don't know about, you mark my words."

"Serves the wee shite right — suckin' up tae the Bishop like that."

"Oh, a'd say they caught him at somethin', finally, so ah would."

"Aye! Caught way hees pants down."

"Aye, round his ankles, if ye ask me."

But, worst of all would be their pity:

"Ah sure, the poor creature, 'tis a shame too, so it is — seeing him humiliated like dat."

It was nice at a time like that, feeling the love of your brethren — jammed right between your shoulder blades.

At the investiture ceremony I was in my usual place of course, on the altar by the Bishop's right hand, assisting those conceited sons-of-bitches into their silly little costumes: their lacy little nighties and those floor-length red capes and the watered-silk bellybands — a right bunch of ejits they looked, all rigged out like that.

"Let me help you with that. There you go! Lovely!"

And afterwards too, I forced myself to be the first in line, shaking their hands; and at the big dinner making a point of addressing each of them as "Monsignor;" and smiling all the frigging time, smiling till my jaws hurt from showing how ecstatic I was for them.

It was not an easy evening that, not with every priest in the diocese knowing I'd been passed over and a good half of them delighted at the thought. But of course to my face everybody was pretending they hadn't noticed a thing. And I was pretending too; pretending to be a good sport about the whole thing and hoping that my wine-red envy could not be detected.

How could the son-of-a-bitch have done this to me?

I had to survive several Confirmation circuits in the following three or four weeks and survive too, the endless hours in that big Buick with the Bishop; listening with half a mind to his ramblings about what they were saying in Rome— retailing the ecclesiastical gossip he'd picked up there.

It was strongly rumored in Rome that the Pope was in far worse health than they were pretending; might pop off at any moment; riddled with cancer, according to a priest who should know. The priest, you see, was a friend of this doctor who worked in the hospital where the tests had been run and he'd told this monsignor at the American College in Rome who'd told some bishop…, or something like that. I was hardly even listening as he rattled on.

Why hadn't this son-of-a-bitch picked me up one of those stupid monsignorships when he was at it? Cheap bastard!

"The Pope might drop dead at any moment." That was his big news from Rome. Did I care?

Maybe I should see if I could get to Rome — it might be fun, studying at the Gregorian for a couple of years with the Church in turmoil.

Nothing enlivened the souls of Roman priests like the death of a Pope. Nothing so brightened their bureaucratic little lives half so much as an upheaval in the Church's leadership. There would be weeks, months even, of gossip and speculation to look forward to. Time for the ambitious to do some serious sucking up to their patrons; time for favors to be called in and commitments lined up. The drama, the intrigue of it all. It would be fun, being in the middle of all that — more fun than driving this guy around.

"They'll never elect a non-Italian. Never!" He proclaimed as he stubbed his cigarette out.

I listened as he rambled on and mostly thought my own thoughts as we slogged from one dismal mining town to the next, from one white wood church to the next white wood church — all of them an indistinguishable blur of California's tawdry past.

"What the Church needs now," he was saying, "is a period of calm to recover from all the upheaval."

We had about half an hour's drive to the next one-horse town and I knew he'd go on playing the "What The Church Needs Now …," tape until we got there. I didn't need to listen, I knew it by heart.

I started thinking instead about my soul. Funny thing for a priest to be thinking about, but there you are. What I was thinking about specifically was how it was time to make an effort again at jump-starting some life into the poor thing. In seminary they told us that nothing beat daily meditation and prayer for restoring that rosy glow of spiritual health and I'd tried that several times in the past year—praying to the God everyone around me seemed to believe in — but nothing had come of it. To demonstrate my utter sincerity to any Higher Being that might be watching, I had even added a physical fitness program —the old *mens sana...*, working out with weights, running two or three miles in the morning and cutting back on whiskey and cigarettes. I had even gone so far as to practice a rigorous celibacy — alone and with others— that would have done credit to John of the Cross. But nary a pulse, my soul's breath would hardly mist a mirror.

You see the problem was this: no matter how hard I might try to reform, there lurked always the dismal reality that nothing I did mattered in the eyes of their God so long as I refused to unburden myself as a penitent in confession. In the calculations of the spiritual bean counters, I was "in the state of mortal sin" and in that condition any spiritual effort is cancelled out — null and void — worthless. By their reckoning, which I knew and understood only too well, I had been in the state of mortal sin ever since the day back in seminary when I had decided to exempt myself from the Church's moral theology in sexual matters. That day I had defied the *Senatus* and led my timid legions across the Rubicon, so to speak. And my spiritual debt had been compounding all those years; black stain heaped upon black stain, compounding with interest, sacrilege upon sacrilege. And, barring a stone-deaf confessor or a universal amnesty from Rome, my best hope of ever receiving absolution lay in a deathbed confession — one in which I would not be expected to go into much detail.

Apart from all that technical stuff, where was the logic in desiring absolution from a God in whom I didn't believe? Why should I so fear the judgment when I didn't believe in the Judge's existence? Wasn't the whole business just a primitive superstition clinging to me still like some fungus bred in the dank muck of Ireland? It could drive a body crazy, just thinking about such matters.

We were passing the sign welcoming us to the town of Who Cares, California, population 1,634 and, as I drove up Main Street with its wooden sidewalk and unpainted company houses, I tried not to picture my future: years in some god-forsaken town like this till mandatory retirement — or until I had lost myself in a bottle. And then there'd be the vague years; aimless years, doddering and drooling about the hallways of the Home for Senile Priests, sunny days gumming an orange on the porch — all the while trying not to shite in my paper diaper. Jack Holland, The Golden Years.

I should probably resign soon and do something useful with my life — before it gets too late. I'd hate to wind up one of these old frustrated drunks, rotting away in some one-horse town — someplace whose heyday was in the Gold Rush — in a parish where I'd sober up just long enough to get through the Sunday mass.

But what other kind of work was I fit for? The demand for canon lawyers was not great in the commercial world and what else did I know?

I could always get one of those royal blue leisure suits and a painted tie and do weddings in Reno, I suppose — a cassette tape of wedding music, a cardboard altar, a set of velour drapes and I'd be in business.

Or, I suppose I could offer my services to some other denomination — one that might not have what we called "valid, apostolic orders." I'd considered the Unitarians at one time on the grounds that most of them believed in almost nothing anyway, but still… Unitarians tended to be politically correct, clean-living types — hardly my speed either. To swap one absurdity for an even less coherent one? Hardly an improvement. And, as the Dubliner once said, "t'was my faith I'd lost; not my reason."

Hours of driving and ruminating; lines of sullen, indistinguishable teenagers; roast beef dinners and clerical trivia; godforsaken outposts with names like, Kudzu and Mount Pilot and Thalassa — "the sea," a wonderful name for a desert town, *"Thalassa"* — *Hoi!*

And every night enduring the mandatory Confirmation gathering of the district clergy — bad enough at any time, but nearly unbearable when every priest in the room was making a point of being kind to me. "In consideration of the snub, don't ye see." I could read that as the subtext of every conversation. It had been such a public slap in the face: not getting those stupid red robes with the others. There was no other way to look at such a public slight.

Being Irish, those old men of course loved me — now I was a loser too, like themselves. The Celtic beatitudes: "Love the loser" and "God help the poor bastard who dares aspire to anything above the mediocre, for him we will scorn and ridicule." Until after his death, of course. In his grave, where the "poor hoor" can no longer embarrass us with "that godless filth he writes," it becomes safe finally to celebrate him. It is then we will take full credit for having shaped and nurtured him in our moldy island and 'tis then we'll conduct watery-eyed tours of his birthplace for the tourists 'money — tours for the English or the French or whatever foreigners may have recognized and supported the poor bastard during his life in exile.

So, as an Irishman who knows what it means only too well, I slide into a slough of depression the minute I detect that sympathetic note in my countrymen's voices. It could mean only one of two things: either I have passed on to a better world or become a rank loser in this one.

There was no escaping those dinners either, for when we were up-the-country it was the time-sanctified custom to stay as overnight guests in the premier parish of that district — all part of the episcopal visitation ritual. God forbid you should take off down the highway to the comfort of the city, after the weeks they'd put in preparing for you!

Not only was I trapped into the roast beef and red wine part of the ceremony, but I had to remain a prisoner of their hospitality — near the foot of the long tables — sitting and listening and looking interested till the last bottle of Lodi Gold had been killed and the last fart had been uttered. I smiled and nodded as they talked and talked, those once-vigorous priests growing more maudlin and slurry as bottle after bottle went around the table. I drank enough gassy sodas during those dinners to float the Hindenburg — for it was my job to remain sober.

However, at one of our overnight stops during that trip I decided to try my hand at drinking a little; see if it made me feel more one of the boys; maybe numb out the hurt feelings and the humiliation a bit. With my career already in tatters, what the hell, I might as well "make friends amongst the mammon of iniquity." So that evening, when I was all done for the day with Confirmations and driving, I asked one of the drinker-golfer-priests to mix me one of the enormous ruby-hued concoctions he'd been passing around — a "Manhattan," he'd called it. It had to be a more effective anesthetic than the beer or Seven Up I usually drank on these occasions.

My request must have seemed a gift delivered into his lap by his rustic god: a golden opportunity for him — a lowly golfer-priest — to avenge himself on the wee aspiring shite from the big city of Minerva. He splashed whiskey into a jam-glass like it was water, then added various rose-colored condiments to what looked like a lethal depth-charge and gleefully dunked a cherry in the finished product before presenting me with his handicraft.

To see some bureaucratic prick from the hated Chancery falling drunk on his ass would make this man's life truly noteworthy in the minds of his fellows — it would become a legend, a story to be told and retold over clubhouse drinks down endless generations of country priests.

Suspicious by nature, I was leery of the drink at first and approached it with caution. It was actually quite a pleasant-tasting beverage, sweet and not at all fiery in the mouth; surprisingly smooth on the tongue in fact and it stroked my throat warmly going down in a way beer or wine never had. So, having discovered how agreeable it felt, I drank heartily from the huge glass and I was further delighted by the flush of unaccustomed well-being that spread throughout my body almost instantly.

And I discovered too, that my mind had become suddenly sharper, brighter and less cluttered. What a wonderfully clarifying effect this Manhattan was having on my thinking! No longer so self-conscious, I felt "ordinary" — a strange thing to feel — but "ordinary" as a freedom from most of the things that had been constraining me: things like ambition and pride and the need for approval.

I remember joining in some of their conversations then, talking animatedly to one group in particular about golf. And they were turning out to be a much friendlier bunch of fellows, these country priests, than I'd ever imagined. It was a shame, really, how badly I had misjudged these men all those years — we could have become the best of friends.

Compton MacKenzie's observation that: "…some men are just born a dram low…," came to mind. How true it was and what a tragedy that I had lived so many years before discovering the one ingredient missing in my personality: a single large Manhattan drink.

I had just told my newfound friend, the mixologist priest, that I simply had to have his recipe before I left for Minerva, when I was swept over suddenly by a great wave of a cold dampness — as though a light mizzle of rain had unexpectedly blown through the room and hit me in the face. I felt my brow and it had become indeed clammy-wet and the voices of those around me were growing fainter. Was I dying? Should I make my confession to one of these golfer-priests while I still had consciousness — avoid hellfire by the skin of my teeth?

With the last tatters of consciousness, I excused myself and headed for the bathroom. There I became violently sick.

Ten minutes or so later, after splashing my face with cold water, I realized that I had been struck completely sober again. Disappointing, finding that my social transformation had vanished with the Manhattan into the Mount Pilot sewage system. I grieved for that golden Manhattan moment when the world had been transformed and I had experienced the sweetness of brotherhood.

The huge bleeding slab of beef was congealing on my plate — an offense to my wounded stomach. I had begun sawing it up and dispersing the bloody bits under potatoes and turnips — like an axe-murderer disposing of a corpse — so as to not offend the hospitality of the parish.

I was lost in my own thoughts — remembering still that moment of grace when the Manhattan had worked its magic on my soul. Conversational volleys were coming at me from both sides and with only a small part of my attention I was lobbing replies from back at the baseline.

"Yes indeed, Father. The children were extremely well prepared. I overheard the Bishop himself remark on that very thing this afternoon."

What a marvelous and transforming sacrament alcohol might turn out to be: a sacrament that would forgive my compromised life and forge a sense of Christian oneness with these Sons of God as nothing else ever had.

"That's a very good one, Monsignor. No. No. I've never heard it before. Very, very funny! The Italians? I see."

"Yes indeed."

"In their sleevies. Ha, Ha! That's a very good one, Monsignor!"

"Yes, Monsignor, I got it —they keep their armies in their sleevies."

If I could become slightly intoxicated and stabilize there — titrate the alcohol dosage so precisely so as to neither get drunk nor relapse into my unredeemed personality. Surely there must have been a formula developed somewhere — in some university perhaps — an equation that would balance ingestion and oxidation so as to maintain a blissful equilibrium. Surely such a balance would be no more delicate to maintain than the state of grace. I could be at peace then in such a state and … I could *build there a hive for the honey bee…*

"Tyrone, Monsignor. Yes indeed. 'Among the bushes…' it is indeed."

"Yes sir! And the O'Neill's too."

"Indeed they were. Under Elizabeth."

"Yes. I have heard the rumor too. But don't they say she was the 'virgin queen'?"

"Well maybe that would be going a bit too far."

"Oh, well. You certainly are entitled to your opinion."

I needed to become an alcoholic — that's maybe what those country priests were aspiring to and I had never understood their goal. Unfortunately my tolerance for alcohol was not as great as theirs and that could present a problem. You didn't just get up out of your bed one day and discover that you had, as though by magic, become an alcoholic. It took work and a certain amount of innate ability. Mightn't be nearly as easy as it looked to an outsider. Calls probably for a special kind of grit — a grit I mightn't have in me.

"Yes, Father. It was a great drive up."

"I did indeed notice it. There's no way Mount Pilot could be overlooked."

"It certainly does.'

"Looms right up there." I pointed to a corner of the room and the gesture seemed to persuade him that I really had noticed the second highest mountain in California as I was driving past it.

We were both exhausted as we drove back after that last interminable week on the road but we were done with the Confirmation circuit till October and for that we were thankful. Ahead stretched a long, blessedly lazy summer: three months during which the schools would be closed and parish activity would slow to a crawl as the temperatures in the central valley crept upwards toward one hundred degrees. The valley was blazing hot as we came down into it from the foothills — too hot for May — and by the time we got to Minerva my eyes were dazzled and burning from driving with the heat shimmer that was rising off the road.

"Praise the Lord!" The Bishop sighed, when we finally turned in through the gates of the residence, rattling over the cattle guard and crunching along the gravel driveway to the garage. It was the first time he'd said a word since we'd driven off from the last parish.

"Let's get the flock outta here!" He'd said to me then — his usual, 'Hi, ho Silver, away!' as he continued smiling and waving at the assembled priests.

He had settled himself into his seat then and might have been asleep for all the company he'd been for the rest of the trip. I had tuned in a talk radio station finally to keep awake. It wasn't like him, closing down on me so completely. Wasn't he feeling well or had it something to do with me? It was hard to not take things like that personally — spending as much time together as we did.

My heart leapt up though, when I caught the first glimpse of my baby. Half-hidden by the giant rhododendron that grew next to the garage, there she sat, my pride and joy: my nearly-new, cherry-red Chevy step-side pickup — she of the lovely growling V8 and the twin chrome tailpipes. I had finally carried her over the threshold only ten days before and had had to abandon her almost immediately for the Confirmation circuit. It would be a joyous reunion, hitting the road with her again.

I eased the cumbersome Electra into its episcopal garage and gratefully stretched my back cramped from the hours driving — first signs of aging. I still had to lug the heavy vestment cases from the trunk and return each item to its proper drawer before I would be free to leave. His Nibs, hardly waiting for me to stop the damned car, had grabbed his overnight bag off the rear seat and practically sprinted for the front door. I never understood the man's urgency to start rooting through the basket of mail that awaited him at the end of these trips — as if there might be something that couldn't wait till the following morning. But it was his standing order: each day's mail must be brought to the residence that evening, so he could see it the minute he walked in the door from a trip.

Restocking the vestments in their proper drawers and hangers, with all the practice I'd had doing it, took me very little time and, with my lovely new truck calling to me, I was faster even than usual. I could already feel the power of her big motor throbbing in the seat of my pants as I thought of gunning her down the boulevard. I had called Jerry before leaving the last parish and arranged to meet him for dinner and recuperation over a beer at our favorite pizza joint. I had dreamed of this moment, the Confirmations finally done with, and us sitting over a leisurely dinner — the whole summer ahead. We would plan our vacation: that place in Pacific Grove again to escape the brutal valley heat and maybe a night or two in San Francisco for a concert or play, perhaps some other short trips to cooler places — it would be a long summer.

When I came out of the chapel I saw that the Bishop had already taken the mail basket from the hallstand into his study. He would be sorting the hundreds of pieces of mail — the majority consigned to the waste basket at his feet — until he was satisfied that he'd seen everything, if it should take him till midnight.

His door stood partially open so I rapped briefly on it and stuck my head in to wish him a quick "good night!"

He turned and shot an unusually sharp glance at me. He had seemed engrossed in one particular letter and my knock had apparently distracted him. He seemed vaguely annoyed. Rather than return my "good night" in his usual friendly, half-distracted way, he held up a finger imperiously — indicating that I was not yet free to leave.

"Would you plan to meet with me tomorrow morning at ten in my office," he said after I had waited a long few minutes, during which he had continued to read the letter.

Had his voice sounded unusually formal — even hostile? I couldn't swear to it but... And there had been none of his customary, "... bet you're glad to be done with the road-show," remarks.

Hadn't there been something decidedly unsettling about his manner since we had left the last parish — that ominous silence on the drive home and now this frosty distance. My antennae told me something was in the air; and that it was not something good.

"Yes, Bishop," I told him. Of course I would plan on it. Wasn't he the boss and if he wanted me to meet him at ten in the morning or ten at night, I'd be there at ten to any ten he wanted, for Christ's sake.

Did he want me to notify anyone else to attend? I inquired — the ever efficient lieutenant planning his own execution.

"No. That will not be necessary," he had replied, without so much as looking up at me again.

He waved a dismissive hand then and I left the presence with a heavy pre-monition — the strong and bowel-torquing kind of premonition that I had known so well as a child. It felt like Friday piano lessons, or the sight of St. Columb's across the Foyle after the holidays, or a hawthorn monster by a lane on a dark night — a lurking danger. I had not survived a youth, treacherous with emotional ambushes, without antennae finely tuned for danger — my radar would do credit to any field mouse.

In the shadow of my truck I changed into a pair of jeans, a tee shirt and my yellow Sears work boots. I hoped to look like an honest tradesman as I climbed behind the wheel of my honest truck. The motor turned over first time and set-tled then into a soul-comforting growl — sensuous, purring, bordering on erotic.

I eased my snarling baby from behind the rhododendron bush and let her roll gently down along the gravel driveway, coasted over the cattle guard, and then cautiously swung her out onto the wide boulevard that led into town. It was there I hit the hair-trigger throttle hard and heard all four barrels come on line. I popped through second, then peeled out in third before throwing her into a long-striding fourth at a screaming 4,500 R.P.M. Her thrust slammed me hard into the seat. I scanned the rearview mirror for the Minerva PD. All clear. I shoveled on a few more coals. God! She was a fucking truck and a half!

But shite! Within minutes, half the joy was being leached out of my soul again by the dread that had been set wriggling like a tapeworm in my gut. What in hell could have gotten into the old man's craw? Was it the same problem that had made him skip me in his honor's list — or was this something new that had been brought to his attention? Now we'd finished with Confirmations, I reasoned, he was replacing me —the timing made sense. I obsessed all the way to the restaurant. I might have been driving my old Ford Falcon for all the joy I was feeling.

Something was in the air and my antennae were telling me it was not good.

CHAPTER 26

Minerva, California — 1975

WITH NOTHING SPECIFIC to go on, it was hard explaining to Jerry why I was so worried. But he listened patiently anyway as I speculated about the Bishop's thinking.

We were sitting as usual over a huge pitcher of the gangster's thin beer and the crackling-hot pepperoni pizza that our personal gun moll had just plopped on the table between us.

"You haven't been caught with your weenie in the cookie jar lately, have you now, Father?" Jerry drew a triangle of pizza back over his shoulder — trying to break his personal cheese-stretching record. He gave me the gimlet eye of inquisition that teachers seem to have from birth — my father had often accused my mother of inheriting hers from her near-relative, the Prince of Darkness.

"Or, have you maybe been up to something else naughty — something you've been keeping secret from your aul auntie?" He took a healthy bite from the pointy end then and chewed it thoughtfully for a minute or two, never taking the eye off me.

I shrugged and shook my head, bewildered. I had been behaving better than usual in recent months, so it would be a cruel fate indeed to have some past sin catch up with me now.

"Keeping some romantic entanglement a secret from yer auntie would be damned near unforgivable, you know, given the celibate desert she's been inhabiting," he accused.

"I've racked my brain and there's nothing I can think of at all — recently," I assured him.

I had never for a moment pretended that my good behavior was due to virtue, there just hadn't been time, given my schedule. I took a long pull of the ice-cold beer for it was all I felt like. I had looked forward to this meal for days but now I had no appetite.

"God, this beer is awful piss!" I was depressed and the beer was not helping a bit. "I'm friggin tired of watery beer and runnin' to the john every twenty minutes and not feeling any better."

"Ah sure isn't it the faith itself that ye do be lackin'?" Jerry lamented and began to chant:

> *"If anyone thinks that I amn't divine,*
> *You'll get no free drinks when I'm makin' the wine*
> *But have tae drink wather and wish it were plain*
> *That I make when the wine becomes wather again."*

"Pish on you too!" I replied. Banter from seminary days.

"Maybe he's going to let me out of the whole driving thing." I speculated as I tried chewing on a corner of the latex-white goo. "I'd fuckin' love to get out of that." I mused. "God, how I hate those friggin' parishes and their damned dinners — worse every year, they're getting."

Jerry was being quiet, letting me ramble on.

"D'ye ever notice how those old rectories and churches up the country all smell alike — like woodworm?" I said. "It hits you in the nose the minute you go in the door. It's everywhere — even the beds smell musty — like ancient dried-up piss."

"You hate the musty smell and so you don't want to go there anymore?" He teased. "Rugged pioneer that oo are, boi!"

I said nothing but drank some more beer and stared at him.

"Maybe he's planning to send you away to school for another five years so you can live in a dormitory and screw your lights out — all over again."

He was teasing me — his favorite way to get me out of my Greek-tragedy mode.

"If he does send you off again you must take me with you — five long years as a war widow was too long. We could travel as a couple, The Reverend and Mrs. Jack Holland, DD, DCL."

"Seriously, though, what do you think it's about — this snit of his?" I asked without any hope that he'd have an answer. How could he?

"What kind of feelings did you pick up from him on the drive back? You had a few hours sitting beside him and with your instincts — like a friggin' jack rabbit — surely to God you'd have picked up any lurking hostility."

I shrugged. I hadn't noticed a thing till we'd got back to the residence. "Maybe he was quieter than usual in the car but he was very tired and he's not that strong anymore." I said. I told him then about the mail and this letter the Bishop was reading when I looked in to tell him good night.

"Something in that letter changed his attitude towards me, I'd swear," I said. "And then, when he asked me to meet him in the morning he was suddenly all business — cold, distant." Jerry shrugged and shook his head sympathetically.

"Shite! Where else did he think I'd be tomorrow at ten, the friggin' Phoenix park? There was something about me in that letter — somebody accusing me of something — and it's got him upset."

"I have an idea!" Jerry had been thinking, obviously, while I'd been fuming. He sounded like Mickey Rooney, or maybe Judy, planning a show.

"You go to that phone and call up Mick Cassidy right this minute. Tell him that you're not going to be home for mass tomorrow morning."

"And then what?" I asked.

"Then we'll go over to my place. We'll lock the door and hole up in my room for the evening and get wrecked — leave the rest of this pish for the waitress."

"You think…?"

"School lets out at noon tomorrow for teachers' in-service — I can teach four hours with a hangover, no sweat."

"You think it's a good idea?"

"I do. And here's the part that's so diabolically brilliant: when you appear bodily before his Excellency at ten o'clock precisely, you'll still be half anesthetized; you'll have all the mental competence of an oak stump, totally beyond caring what he does to you. He could cut your hand off and you'd hold out the other one. You see? It's brilliant, isn't it?"

I stared at him as my brain tried in vain to spot a single loophole in this deceptively simple plan for getting through what promised to be a painful interview. Actually, as a way of spending the final evening of my career as a diocesan official, it seemed unassailable.

"Well! Aren't you the fuckin' wee genius, thinkin' up sompin' 'ike 'at!" I exclaimed.

"So? What're you waiting for? Make your call!"

"You have a dime?" He gave me a dime and I called the rectory.

The endlessly tolerant Mick Cassidy, so used to my comings and goings anyway, never for a moment questioned my request. He would cover the convent mass in the morning.

I followed Jerry's car to the rundown part of the city where he and his equally hardworking Pastor served a population of mainly Mexican immigrants and a smattering of poor whites and blacks. The area had been a prosperous black subcity in a more segregated time, but in the 60's, with more integration, all the middle and upper class black families had moved out to suburbs like Wildwood and South Park, leaving only the poorest residents behind in the Oak Grove area. That remnant had been joined over the years by the Hispanic and white underclass in what was then referred to by city officials as "a very affordable neighborhood."

Jerry, who worked days and evenings as a math teacher, also accomplished more in the parish than most full-time parish priests. The salary he drew from the State College went into the parish collection, twice a month, in cash — anonymously. I was the only one privy to that piece of information and had been sworn to secrecy. I pulled my truck in off the street and parked in the open field that was their backyard.

Once in his rooms, he locked the outer door to his little study-cum-bedroom suite behind us. By comparison to my own sparsely furnished rooms, this was Appalachia. From a movie theater that had gone the way of all flesh, he and the Pastor had salvaged all the deco chairs, tables, lamps and sofas that had once adorned the lobby and mezzanine lounges. Their High Moderne lines and tattered upholstery created a unique air of decadence throughout the house — a fitting place for a debauched evening by the light of the fan-shaped sconces Jerry had installed on his study walls.

On the rare evenings we had been able to spend together in recent years, we had preserved our rituals from that earlier time — a time when we'd been in our twenties still and full of the excitement of rebellion. We still lighted the fat candles on the coffee table and played the old Joplin or Dylan LP's on the turntable, still passed a brain-numbing doobie back and forth between us and Jerry still got dressed up. But we were older now and not as angry. We had become the old men who ran the world and the Church — evenings such as this had become pilgrimages to a 60's shrine.

Though we usually drank wine I had decided it was a whiskey-drinking sort of night. I had picked up a bottle of Jack Daniel's Black Label, on the way over — fleeting thoughts of Julia and *The Flamingo*.

Jerry dressed for the occasion in his newest shift — off the five-dollar rack in the Salvation Army 'boutique' in San Francisco — set off by a blond shag wig, black hose and pumps.

He looked "fetching," I told him.

"You don't mean 'fetching' as in Fido?" He was as insecure about his appearance as the next girl.

"Definitely not." I assured him. "As in Novak."

And so we settled in for an evening of quiet and safe excess.

By ten o'clock, we were already nicely smashed and still there was half a bottle of whiskey to be drunk and a fat sandwich bag of buds that needed smoking.

I tended to get more lethargic the more I drank, while Jerry's reaction was the exact opposite. The conversation had been stimulating and fun for a couple of hours but it was flagging as I became increasingly stupefied.

I had been staring at the smoke spiraling up from my fingers. Something about it made me think of angels and of the letters my sister and I always wrote to Santa Claus, then burnt — so he would be sure to get them at the North Pole. I had begun to weep as I was telling Jerry how they had read my name out on Radio Eireann one Christmas Eve — one of the lucky children on Santa's list.

Jerry must have had enough of my wallowing in that maudlin swamp, for he got to his feet — rude of him — right in the middle of my touching Santa Claus story and started digging about in his stack of records.

"'S mather w' you?" I inquired soberly.

He didn't answer but continued instead flipping through the LP's till finally he pulled a record from its jacket and put it on the turntable. While it was leading in he spun the jacket over to me. I held it close to the candle and made out the title: "Monks of Solemne, Sing Gregorian Chant," or something to that effect.

"Soun's like fun ta me." I flourished an intricate pattern of smoke in the air with my cigarette and after admiring it for a moment, I instructed the phonograph to, "Play on!"

We joined the Benedictines then in a drunken twenty-minute sing-a-long of, *Kyries, Glorias* and *Sanctus*'s from *Missa de Angelis*. Jerry then— *a cappella* — intoned *Credo in Unum Deum...* and I continued it with him all the incredible way to the *Amen*.

We sang everything we could think of in Latin and then switched to those hymns in English we could remember from childhood — including of course the hymn, without which no Irish Catholic education would be complete, the ever-popular:

Oh, Mother, I could weep for mirth. Joy fills my heart so fast.
My soul today is heaven on earth,
Oh, could the transport last.

"Wow!" I exclaimed as I poured each of us refreshers from the square black bottle. "Wow! I said again for I was literally speechless. But Jerry was on his feet still — the drunker the more dramatic.

"So, mi Lords and Ladies we come now to the theatrical portion of the evening's program!" He was proclaiming in his Master of Ceremonies voice.

"The scene: Midmorning in the Chancery —off stage a clock strikes ten," he began.

"The Condemned — a gangly, big-boned country fellow — enters stage right. Bishop and Fitz-weasel huddle behind the heavy, ironbound doors of the inner sanctum — tum — tum — tum." Jerry did an echoing effect.

"Hold on!" He exclaimed, stepping out of character. He grabbed the badly tattered cassock that he had discarded in a heap on a chrome-bound theater chair pending the next ecclesiastical emergency and swung the sad remnant around his shoulders as a cape.

"Goes nicely with the dress and black tights!" I approved. "Even the heels. Very sharp, very new church!"

"Indeed, varlets!" He was back in character again. "Come gather 'round while I tell and foretell for ye the tale of young Jaques Holland."

Jerry was striding into his William Breakespeare character. One long ago day in first divinity, when we had been hunting in the library for ammunition —the better to torture some professor or other — we had come upon the story of a certain Nicholas Brakespeare. It seems that was the given name of Adrian IV, the only Englishman ever elected Pope — the same Adrian, incidentally, who had ordered the subjugation and "civilization" of the Irish. "Subjugation?" "Civilization?" Ha! Jerry had subsequently created a playwright brother for that Pope, named of course, William Breakespeare and for our "Fourth Divine Jack" had written a scene that had been performed to the greatest critical acclaim: it had caused the Senior Dean to threaten him with expulsion. He was reprising that scene for me with minor adjustments:

    "Fitz — The wretched soul awaits without, Mi'Lud."
    "Bishop — Ah! Good Fitzfellow. Loyal Fitzman.
               Let us ponder well what God
               would have us this day do."

Jerry was alternately crouching into a groveling Fitz and striding about, swaggering, as a pompous Bishop.

    "Bishop — Ah, would that God in his wisdom had
        Seen fit to vouchsafe this poor lad
        Ere now, the grace of sweet contrition.
        But failing that, there but remains his holy admonition."

    "Fitz —   "We root out sin in all it's forms and evil dispositions
        And give to man, unworthy though, this blessed Inquisition."

    "Bishop — 'Twould presumption be were we to strive
        His tainted sickly soul to shrive."

    "Fitz — And other do,
       Than follow through
  And at the stake
  His body bake."

    "Bishop — That never more would priestly man
        Befoul his soul or God's dear plan."

"Fitz —   Yeah!
By groping with anointed hand
In sewage ditch
Of female bitch,
Befouled by blood and devil's juices,
Unfit henceforth for sacred uses. (Echo — echo — echo)"

"Bishop — My sweet Chancellor, is every preparation made,
For this our sacred job:
The rack, the stake, the faggots and the ever- howling mob?"
"Fitz — 'Tis so, M'Lud."
"Bishop — Well done! Now comes the time
For us to grasp a chance divine
To flail *our* fleshy bodies vile
Lest they, us too, with lusts defile."

"Fitz — I've 'tained from off a quarried block
Some blessed, flinty, granite rock.
The which to kneel upon 'tis said
Will warrant all desire be dead."

"Bishop — And there with gleaming copper fang
A new flagellum whip doth hang."

"Fitz —   'Twould be my greatest pleasure, Lud,
If on my back these lashes first
would take the bight and quench their thirst
For human flesh and mortal blood. (Lashes loudly heard)
Ah, blessed lash! Ah, heavenly pain! (Ecstatic)
My Liege Lud, prithee. (pant — pant) Do it again!"

Chapter 27

Minerva, California — 1975

PREDICTABLY, I WAS barely conscious when I knocked on the door to the Bishop's office the following morning. I had slept, or passed out, for a few hours on the floor of Jerry's study and when his alarm had gone off it had hauled me back reluctantly from foggy unconsciousness to a barely conscious fogginess. A shower and coffee had helped only slightly. I'm sure I was legally drunk still as I was driving downtown.

My mind was hovering a few yards behind my body, watching warily like a child peeking from beneath a blanket tent, as I entered his office. It was precisely ten o'clock.

The Bishop was standing with a letter in his hand — presumably the same letter that had put him off his feed the previous evening. He pointed to a chair and seated himself behind his desk. I remained standing.

I remember noticing that the heavy wattles underneath his chin wagged as he shuffled his high-backed chair closer in to the desk. He seemed ill at ease as he raised his eyes to meet mine. He took a breath and started right in with what was obviously a prepared speech.

"You've probably been wondering, Jack, why you weren't made a monsignor in this last round of honorees."

It may have sounded like a question but, not knowing how to deal with it, I decided to hold my tongue till I got some idea where the conversation was headed. His face told me nothing.

I had been scared the previous evening, terrified that somebody had reported me for something scandalous. But, standing there in front of the man, still detoxifying, I couldn't feel the fear — I couldn't feel anything. My mind, though, was racing about like a rabbit trapped in its burrow by a ferret. I sat down on the edge of a straight-backed chair across from him.

He was still looking at me expectantly, waiting for a reply. Had I wondered about not being made a monsignor? Wasn't that what he'd asked? I was in big trouble but what the hell was there to lose at this point? What could I say? I answered as lightly as I could manage.

"I thought you'd just run out of money maybe, there in the Ye Olde *Curia* Gift Shoppe — all the other goodies you'd brought back."

He chuckled. He was chuckling?

"This might explain it to you." He spun the letter he'd been clutching across the desk to me. Up close I recognized immediately from the coat of arms on the letterhead: it was a *bulla* — an official Roman document —and in Latin. Of course! He wants a friggin' translation. God! And I'd been driving myself nuts. All he'd wanted was a formal document translated. The old man had never been any good with the Latin documents Rome was always sending out to the bishops. No wonder he looked worried when he'd opened it last night. He hadn't been able to figure out what it was saying.

"Read it," he insisted. He leaned over and stabbed it with his thick forefinger — looking at me as he did so.

"Now? Here?" I asked. God! I'd love a cup of coffee — or a cold beer.

"Yes, dammit!" He tapped the desk impatiently.

It took me a minute or two to realize what the document was saying. Oh! the Latin was easy enough to translate — it wasn't the words that were the problem. It was the meaning of the frigging words that I couldn't grasp.

Joannes Holland is hereby appointed to the office of Auxiliary Bishop of the diocese of Minerva, California and Titular Bishop of Praxitelensis, with all the rights and privileges thereof.

I reread the document several times, looking up at him puzzled between readings. My Latin had been good at one time but I was missing something in the translation of this. I wanted to take it to my office and figure it out under less pressure — some Latin friggin' idiom I was missing. Never could translate that classical poetry shite — the way they invert things at random. And me half-drunk still. This document *seemed* to be saying they were making me a bishop. Ridiculous!.

He continued looking at me and seemed to be expecting a reaction.

I didn't know what to tell him. What reaction should I have if it was true?

What are you supposed to say when they make you a bishop? Thanks? No thanks? This is wonderful! Is it sunny in Praxitelensis? Do they grow oranges there?

Instead, I just shook my head and said, "Oh, my God!!"

"I know this has taken you by surprise…" He prompted.

An understatement, to say the least.

I needed to get out of that office before I said something I would regret. My whiskey-soaked brain was refusing entrance to this piece of information. "Not possible," it kept insisting. "Not friggin' possible!"

I need to sober up so I can think. And I need to get a hold of Jerry as quickly as possible.

All I could do was shake my head and tell him I was overwhelmed and that I had never for a moment expected anything like this.

Actually I had known something like this was a possibility once I added that Doctorate in Canon Law degree to my resume — unless caught doing something non episcopal. But then, in recent years, I had given up on ambition as—slouching from season to season—the tedium of my life had wrestled me into surrender. I had trudged along year in, year out: soon it will be Christmas; then Lent with Easter just around the corner; schools are out and it's summer holidays and before you know it, All Saints, All Souls, Thanksgiving and back around again. So easy to piss away a decade — hand over hand, carrot by carrot — till it was too late to make your move and restart your life.

Somehow I got out of his office without making any commitments. I hoped I hadn't seemed rude in my lack of enthusiasm.

He said he understood how overwhelmed I felt. He had been pretty overwhelmed too that day the old Cardinal made him an Auxiliary in Los Angeles. I cut him off in mid recollection.

"Do you mind if I get some fresh air?" I didn't want to stick around just then and reminisce with him — maybe throw up on his rug.

He said he understood. He'd felt just like I did, overwhelmed.

The situations weren't at all analogous but I wasn't about to argue the point — I had to get away from the Chancery. It would have taken too long to explain the differences: that I was thinking about leaving the priesthood and the Church even, whereas he... I didn't feel like going into the fact that I didn't believe in any god he would recognize — let alone a lot of the other more arcane stuff in the Roman dogma book.

I would go out of my friggin' mind if I didn't get to discuss this with Jerry right away. How the fuck was I going to tell that nice old man that I didn't want this thing—this great honor?

Jerry would help me with the wording of it.

Ten minutes after I had read the document I was in my truck driving aimlessly. Jerry would know what to do about this but he wouldn't be home from school till shortly after noon. And on top of everything else, my hangover was pumping painful surges of blood through my temples and bringing on a skull-crushing headache. At a Seven Eleven I poured a cold 7-Up down into my stomach as a peace offering — rolling the cold, misty can on my sweaty forehead felt good.

I headed south paralleling the Minerva river — through the string of little levee villages — to a spot where the river was wide and smooth flowing, where the grassy bank was still green at that time of year and soft as a cat's fur from spring rains.

I had gone there often during my first years in Minerva — and it was here I had sat almost every day in those first weeks after I'd received the wire saying she had died. I couldn't cry for her but the tears trapped behind my face wanted to burst through my temples from the pressure. It was how I had always felt when I'd thought of her dying — even years before it happened. I hadn't cried for her till standing at her grave years later.

The day my sister had phoned from Ireland with the news, I had bought a six-pack of beer —the first time I had ever done that — and brought it down with me to that place by the slow moving river. I had sat on the wintry bank then, the grass damp on my trousers under the naked tree branches, the river gray and fog-shrouded — cigarettes bracing me against the pain, I was too numb to feel the cold. I had drunk all six beers rapidly, desperate and thirsty for anesthesia, and had sat, staring into the river till it was pitch-black night. I had bonded with the river then and with that place on its bank in particular. I would return to it later many times in those early years, to stretch out on the bank on hot summer evenings and listen — through the car window — to the ever-frustrating Giants or to sit in the quiet stillness and watch the river eddy and drift through the trailing willow tendrils on its way to the Pacific.

There was a stately house with its own landing wharf a hundred yards or so upriver from my spot on the bank. An avenue of windmill palms stretching up from the river to the front lawns recalled more gracious days when long-gone riverboats would stop there on their way to Minerva from San Francisco. That house had excited my imagination when I first saw her: a faded bride, neglected and in disrepair a delicate beauty in gray-white gingerbread, sickly and consumptive. But it had been restored since I had seen it last — wood gleaming white, lawn mowed, iron railings painted a deep green. I felt betrayed, as if Mimi had regained the full flower of health at the end of *La Boheme*.

I hadn't brought beer this time, but I had my Camels for comfort. A beer would have helped more than the 7-Up —too late to think of that.

The sun felt warm and the grass on the bank was green and dry enough to stretch out on. It was officially spring and the trees along the bank were clothed with newly unfurled leaves, the orchards behind the levee celebrated with a carnival of white and pink. She would have loved my river in spring.

I had just been appointed bishop of some place I had never heard of — some extinct diocese in Arabic Africa. They always gave these goofy titles to auxiliary bishops — bishops without a cause.

I must have dropped off to sleep for the horn of a riverboat awakened me. It was *The* Delta *Queen* herself, back where she had started, mighty stern-wheel churning the dark water as she pushed hard against the stream; white suits, pastel dresses, straw boaters, red, white and blue ribbons flying in the breeze, passengers in a holiday mood waving to me from the rail.

Barrels were lined up on the mansion's wharf ready for shipment, but no one was down on the dock — no workers. Who will load them? I fretted. Where were the people of the house? That's why *The Delta Queen* is blasting her horn — to warn them. They'd better get a move on.

"Father Holland? Are you all right?"

I looked up. The Highway Patrol car was pulled in close on the grass, only feet above my head and sounding its horn. The friendly grin of Sergeant Denny Meehan was framed in the window.

"I wondered who belonged to the truck," he said as he unfolded his lanky frame from the car and straightened up — he towered above me as I lay there looking up at him.

I hauled myself reluctantly to my feet and nodded to him.

"Denny."

"So this is how the clergy while away their days."

Denny had lived in the first parish I'd been in and we'd often run into each other in the years since. The day after I'd bought the truck he'd pulled me over outside the rectory — lights, siren and all — to get a look at it. I struggled up the bank and shook hands with him.

"Oh, I'm fine, really." I lied "Came down to be out of the way, think a bit — some news I got today. But, I'm all right."

"Sure?" There was concern in his question and he gave me a skeptical eye.

"I'll be all right."

"OK then, if ye'r sure." He chuckled then. "Och aye! 'Deed we keep the whole bunch of yez under close surveillance, don't ye know. Keep tabs on aal yez Irish rebels — subversives, like — the likes of yourself and me dad."

For a second generation he did a fair Northern accent.

He waved as he got back in the patrol car.

"You have this habit of coming down here when ye aren't too happy, Jack." He looked up into my face searchingly as he started the motor. I had told him about coming to the river after my mother died — he'd remembered.

I nodded thanks. He gave me a sharp look and a brief nod.

The big black and white pulled away scattering a spray of gravel that pinged off my hub-caps. He waved.

"Thanks Meehan." I shouted after him.

The nap, however short, had done my body good. I might tackle solid food again someday, but my mind was no better off than before. I sat in the truck awhile smoking a cigarette, reluctant to leave the soothing water, reluctant to face what I had to do next.

I tried to focus on what I might say to the Bishop but my brain spun dirt — getting no traction. Thinking would have to wait till I could talk to Jerry.

I started the truck, hung a U on the narrow levee road, and drove back the way I'd come. On the boulevard I pulled into the first gas station I came across and used the pay phone.

Jerry was back from school and yes, there was nothing he would rather do, at least that he could talk about, than spend some time visiting with me. Hadn't it been the outrageously long time since we'd seen each other — maybe six hours?

The rectory door opened even before I rang the bell. He was dressed in his wrinkled rag of a cassock — looking like an ecclesiastical tinker — his longish hair flying all over the place.

"My God! I could have mistaken you for a priest." I greeted him. "You're not going to do me another scene from Brakespeare, are you? My head couldn't stand it."

"Sure, I do be shocking myself now, when I do catch a glimpse of meself in the mirror, all rigged out like this, so I do." He smiled and bobbed in a servile curtsy, tugging at his forelock as our ancestors had been trained to do in the presence of their betters.

We went down the narrow hallway to his sparse two rooms and closed the door. The study smelled still of grass and cigarette smoke, a tang of alcohol lingering underneath — like the reek of an Irish pub in the early morning.

"So, Boyo? What takes ye out this way so early in the day — shouldn't you be deep in your red tape ministry at this hour?" He inquired. We sat on the theater chairs this time instead of the floor.

"I take it His Excellency didn't give you the old heave ho, this morning?"

"You're right." I said. "He didn't fire me — not exactly." I was having trouble breaking the news even to Jerry.

"So, let me guess. Ye'r out looking for a nicely demented priest to hear yer general confession?"

"Not bloody likely." I replied.

"I know what." He jumped to his feet and went to the side board. He held up the remnants of whiskey in the bottom of the Black Jack bottle.

"A hair o' the dog?"

"Sounds about right." I answered. I had been resisting the obvious cure all morning, but what the hell.

"So, you're thoroughly chastened and are now resolved to take the road less traveled?"

Jerry, I suspected, for all his kidding around, secretly hoped I would get straight with the Church some day. In spite of his own forays into the sexual demimonde, his faith in the institution continued to astonish me. Where I claimed that it kept people docile and exploitable, he would argue that religion — any religion, no matter how bizarre — gave people courage; the courage they needed to persevere, to get out of bed in the morning, to cope with problems and to accept the certainty of death. He was a big believer in *coeur-age* — the heart to face things.

He handed me a glass. After the first calming trickle burned its way down my throat and had begun to radiate its warmth, I was as ready as I'd ever be.

"I have something heavy I need to talk to you about." That was as much as I could get out in one gulp. I was embarrassed to tell him, I realized. I was ashamed of being chosen.

My tone of voice was enough to startle him. He looked into my face and sensed that I was struggling, unable to say what was pressing on me

"You met with the man..." he prompted. "...and, he didn't fire you... OK so far? I called your office twice on breaks, but they said you were out and didn't know when you'd be back."

"You won't believe what's happened." I said. He continued looking into my face. He was making me uncomfortable standing over me like that so I pointed to his chair and when he was seated I launched into it.

"There's something I have to make up my mind about but I have to keep complete secrecy about it. I'm not supposed to tell anybody, but I'm going to tell you ..." These conditions were stressed in the *bulla*. I didn't have to make him promise to keep it to himself, but he nodded anyway.

"So how long will I have to keep it secret?" He asked.

"Depends on what I decide, either everybody will know soon or nobody must ever know."

"God! It does sound heavy, all right!"

"What would you say if I told you they're planning to make me a bishop?" I rattled it all out fast so I wouldn't balk at the words.

"You're fuckin' kidding me!" He couldn't pretend — not even to be diplomatic. He looked more surprised than I had ever seen him and shook his head in disbelief. "A bishop? Well, fuck me!"

"The old man told me this morning. That's what that letter was — a *bulla* appointing me. I almost passed out when he told me and me half in the bag still.

"God almighty!" He looked at me for a few moments, shaking his head. "And here we thought you were in trouble."

"This is worse than trouble. I can't fucking do it! Ridiculous!"

I read compassion in his face, for the quandary I was in. He got up then and started scrounging about in his bookcase then, not finding whatever he was looking, he went into his bedroom. I heard him slamming cabinet doors and drawers.

"I think in the circumstances," he shouted, "we need another drap o' the crathur."

He came back tearing the Christmas wrap off a bottle of cognac. He poured us each glasses of the Martell.

"I don't know how to tell the old man that I don't want it." I said finally as the calming fire spread through my stomach "It would be a very bad joke, me, a fuckin' bishop... not believing in a damned thing. Who would I be representing anyway — the atheist faction?" I was trying to be rational, but the whole idea was crazy.

Jerry was nodding as I spoke.

"But then, on the other hand..." I continued. "Part of me..."

"'Deed, I know that part of you too," he interjected. "The part of you that's been angling for this since we were in Holy Trinity — up in that fourth floor icebox."

He was right in a way. Not that I was planning on being a bishop as far back as that, but I had played a good political game, even then. Instinctively, I'd always done the best political thing.

"It would be a fucking travesty, though, wouldn't it?.

"You're right. If you were to stand up there preaching things you didn't mean, it would definitely be a travesty."

"What?" I asked after a pause. He had begun smiling a sly smile and I didn't like that. I could see a light bulb had switched on somewhere in that large and complex brain of his. "What?" I demanded. "There's something going on in your friggin' mind and I just know I'll hate it — whatever it is."

"You're right. You are going to hate it and a part of you — that dishonest, connivin' Oirish ward-heeler in you — that part of you is going to start jiggling and squirming around it like an eel on a hook, wanting it and not wanting it."

"Come on. Out with it, whatever it is?"

"Who says that after they make you a bishop — let's say for the sake of argument that you go through with it — who says you can't then tell the truth about what you really believe?"

"You must be fucking kidding me?" I exclaimed. "Can't you just imagine what would happen if I were to tell people what I really thought about certain things?"

"It might be the best thing to happen Christianity in centuries."

"Didn't they crucify thon last ejit that tried it, or did I miss something in the Gospels? And besides, that's not even the real problem, is it? I can't be a bishop because I friggin' don't believe in God. That would seem to be an even more basic…!"

"What?" He interrupted me. He was up now and walking about the floor. "You're telling me you can't be a bishop because you don't believe in God? Don't be fuckin' ridiculous!" He snorted. "I've never met a bishop yet that believed in anything except rich Catholics and the Republican Party — maybe the Pope, some of them." He whipped his ripped cassock around him for dramatic effect. "Wrapped in tatters of a long-forgotten religion — that bunch!"

"And I'd be a great addition, wouldn't I, not having even the tatters left." I drank back my cognac in a great gulp. I lighted a cigarette and took a deep drag off it before I continued. "Running around the diocese all got up like some kind of friggin' holy man and not believing a damned thing I was saying. Crazy! Forget it. What I need your help with is, how to break the news to the old man."

"Wait a minute! Before you go off half-cocked." Jerry was pacing up and down, as though he was excited suddenly by an idea. He stopped in front of me and jabbed a finger into my forehead.

"Silly as it may seem…" He was speaking slowly, looking at me, studying my face for reaction — one eye closed. "There just might be a wondrous opportunity in this … something really exciting and revolutionary could be beckoning."

"I don't like it when you get that manic gleam and start going on about "wondrous" this and "revolutionary" that. Sounds like trouble."

"Just take a second and think about the possibilities. Look at it, is all I'm saying — before you say 'no'."

"That's all I've been doing, thinking about it, looking at it, ever since the man told me. Lying down on the riverbank, all I did was think. And still, I see nothing even faintly useful coming out of it. As far as I can make out it's a simple proposition: You don't believe in God, you don't become a bishop."

"You keep saying that 'I don't believe in God,' thing, as though it was an answer to something. What do we know for sure about this god thing? Tell me that?" He was standing in front of me, demanding an answer. "The only thing about the god we can know, for sure — what is it?"

"You're asking the wrong man."

"Truth!" He said and pounded on the arm of my cinema seat. "Hasn't everybody agreed that whatever sort of a thing this god is, it's *Truth* — that is, if it's anything?"

"It's what they say," I agreed. "'God is Truth'."

He was looking at me, his head cocked to one side, assessing the effect his argument was having on me. "You've heard that all your life, right?"

I nodded, but tentatively, for I felt a trap being sprung. Was he talking me into something I'd regret?

"And, if that proposition is true, who cares whether you believe in something the Pope calls 'God' or not?" He threw up his hands triumphantly — as in *Quod erat demonstandum.*

"What?" I hated the whine in my voice as I remonstrated with him. But he was pushing me towards the edge of a precipice and I was losing my grip.

"Make a commitment to the Truth, boyo, that's all I'm suggesting." He slammed his hand down on the arm of my chair again. He was really excited. "The world's full of bastards who say they believe in God, walk out of church, lie all week, back next Sunday — 'My God, I firmly believe.'"

He was crouching at my chair by this time and I was looking into his eyes — the fervent eyes of one inflamed by an idea.

"Maybe, if a certain man were to become a bishop and if maybe, if he were to then speak only the truth, isn't it likely that that man would be closer to God than most — closer than anybody I know."

"Become a bishop and tell the truth? That's the prescription?" I repeated the words and listened to my voice coming from a great distance.

"It's walking along the road towards God, anyway, don't you think?"

"You know what you're doing to me, don't you?"

'I do and I don't envy you." He went back to his chair then and sat down. "God only knows what lies ahead for you if you decide to go down that road." He drank some of his untouched cognac. I was ready for a second shot but decided it was a day to keep a clear head.

His logic was unassailable: tell the truth and you'll be close to whatever this "god" thing is. Could there be a way that I might salvage my life, after all?

"Telling the Truth." What a frigging concept.

I could feel his eyes on me as I sat with my head down on my chest pondering what he had put in front of me.

"I can see it all now," I began. "It's a sunny Friday afternoon —nice weekend for the beach and there I am, dangling from a cross by my metacarpals. Are you getting the picture?" With my arms I projected the scene onto the walls of his room, in front of the row of cinema seats. "Yes, it's coming in clearer now. Out there in the north area, near Orange Grove Heights, on this picturesque little hillock, I'm swinging in the afternoon Delta breeze and these sixteen-penny nails are ripping through the palms of my hands."

Jerry is smiling as I paint my little drama.

"Aye, and if it isn't me mither herself, alive and well too, leading that snarling mob of cat - lics — shouting at me they are, every epithet they can think of: 'amadan', 'ejit', 'cut-the-bags'! And me father himself, the chinless one, out there too, egging them on, handing them sharp, flinty stones to peg up at my bleeding head — stones and sally rods for skitin'. And he's challenging them. 'See if yez can ring ta bell on thon crown a thorns.' 'Ah, that'll learn ye ta tell ta truth, ye domned quizzlin', ye!' And Fitz too, there with a bunch of Kerrymen, playing poker at the foot of the scaffold — gambling for me aul cassock and me red truck."

"*The Suffering Servant,* himself!" Jerry sympathized "Let me know a bit ahead of time, I'll run out and pick up a few things, an outfit — something suitable for the occasion — the slut-look would be good. Always wanted to play Magdalene to an appreciative mob." He strikes a sluttish pose. "And at the foot of the cross, a tragic figure gazes up sadly; eye liner dramatically smeared from the crying; crotch length mini in black leather very with-it; cheeks radiant, yet damp with a widow's tears." He sighed longingly. "God, the soldiers'll love me!" He patted me playfully on the head. "I'd say, 'Go for it Baby!' Let's get ye anointed! Bring on them purple frocks!"

"Such a rich vein of merriment, my pathetic life." I couldn't help but laugh with him.

"Remember honey!" He had turned serious as sin suddenly and was hunkered down in front of me, looking into my eyes intently. "I've known you a very long time and you're not half as tough as you like to pretend. Underneath that Mick-politician façade, throbs an actual conscience. You'll be a grand bishop now, so ye will."

"Stand up for the truth?" I was checking — more with myself than with him.

"That's it, m'dear: Become a bishop who tells the truth. That's all there is to it."

CHAPTER 28

Minerva, California — 1975

THE NEXT DAY in the Chancery I formally accepted the appointment and I could tell from his face that the old man was relieved. He had half expected, I think, that I'd have turned it down. Then, after my formal acceptance, all sorts of official craziness was let loose in the diocese. Ordaining a bishop was a very big deal — and particularly so in such a small diocese.

The news release was composed and handed out to the press and then the phone calls started flooding in for me. And they kept coming without a break for days. I had phone calls congratulating me from people who wouldn't have given me the time of day twenty four hours earlier: calls from wealthy donors to the church and bankers who'd made millions off parish building loans; peddlers of all sorts of services, from insurance policies to church furnishings, from janitorial services to architects. I ought to join the Chamber of Commerce and be done with it, I told myself. Religion was big business.

Church law required that I go on a thirty-day silent retreat so I was mercifully spared the worst of the logistics that went into my ordination ceremonies. I chose a retreat house in Los Angeles so as to be well away from all the planning — only the Bishop and Jerry knew where I had gone.

I awoke very early the Tuesday of my ordination and, with hours to spare before the ceremony, I drove downtown and walked in the fresh cool of that late Spring morning under the trees in the City Center park and around the still-quiet streets, enjoying my last moments of anonymity.

The Cathedral had been splendidly decorated with colorful banners and flowers everywhere and, since I was not widely known there, I could still walk around admiring it all, unrecognized by either the sacristans or the altar society ladies. A young priest was saying mass on the high altar for a handful of the faithful — half a dozen spinsters and widows and two old men in raincoats. I sat in a back pew while the young man gave his homily on the gospel. It was a familiar passage and one that had deep resonance for me.

"Peter, seeing the winds and the waves, became afraid and began to sink."

It wasn't walking on water that scared him — easy on a calm day — but it was the water being sort of choppy, that and a stiff wind, that's what scared him. Good point, young fellow! Choppy water's a real bitch to walk on — give me a nice calm day on a glassy lake. It's a snap then, isn't it? I remembered O'Connell's bridge and the North Wall. Drowning in the dirty river or leaving for Liverpool — or becoming a frigging bishop.

Ordaining a bishop was a major event in the ecclesiastical world. Of course, it was a grand excuse too for the men stationed out in the remotest corners of the diocese to spend a few days in the lowlands, playing golf and poker — a few drinks with friends they hadn't seen in a while — the hell with the ceremony.

From the *predieu* where I, the Candidate, knelt — doing my best to look humbly prayerful — I watched this flotilla of neighboring bishops meander up the aisle. Like the tall ships of old — but broader in the beam — grave men they were, purple wattles wagging, portly men pushing lace-dripping stomachs, wizened men with silly comb-overs, all slouching lopsided, pudgy hands flaunting gaudy purple rings. How could they not be embarrassed, appearing in public, got up in such outlandish trappings? Or could it be from humility that they were willing to reenact this stylized drama?

Jerry, by my request, was serving as my chaplain for the ceremony, assisting me in all the newfangled vestings and un-vestings, leading me about the sanctuary 'like a blind donkey' — as he put it — during the lengthy ritual. And he would, I knew, continue holding my feet to the fire on my resolution, once I had become a bishop. I was counting on him, in fact — I was so frigging tired of feeling useless.

Now and again during the ceremony I caught Jerry's eye and he would wink back at me. Sometimes I even caught the faintest shadow of a smile playing on his lips as when I had to swear loyalty and obedience to the Pope as head of the Church. He had squeezed my arm so firmly then that it stung, reminding me as we had discussed after reviewing the ritual, that it was only to the God of Truth and not to some man in Rome, that I was pledging my fealty.

And also, typically, he helped me to a few lighter moments in the thick of all the anointings and blessings and swearings. Assisting me into a particularly lacy surplice that would have done honor to Madam DuBarry's boudoir, he looked at me appraisingly and eyebrow-raised, whispered,

"Oh, honey! I must borrow this one, some evening soon."

Best friend or no, it was obvious he was enjoying my predicament. How could he have watched and wondered at my crass ambition and not been amused seeing me 'hoist on my own petard'? I prayed he would be around when Fate demanded payment as it inevitably would if I were to keep my pledge.

When I try recalling that first summer I was a bishop, nothing of great significance leaps to mind. There were of course dinners in my honor throughout the diocese; a few evenings spent as the guest of various Irish pastors in scattered parts of the diocese, but little else had changed as far as my duties in the parish or the Chancery. The newfangled ness of being a bishop wore off sooner than I would have imagined. I often forgot about it entirely myself until someone addressed me by the title or I'd have to get all rigged out in the ridiculous costume.

When Confirmations resumed early in the Fall I had suggested doing those scheduled in the more remote areas, for I knew how much these trips had taken out of the old man. I think it was to be freed from them more than anything that he had requested an auxiliary. Since my rank didn't warrant either a car or a driver, I would drive from parish to parish in full episcopal splendor at the wheel of my cherry-red Chevy truck — a rhapsody in red.

The Pastors may have been disappointed at getting the second string bishop, but their pleasure at having one of their own as bishop seemed to compensate for any slight they might otherwise have felt. And I tried my hardest to be the bishop they wanted me to be: sitting with them for hours every night around their dinner tables, listening graciously in the way I imagined a bishop should listen to their reminiscences, laughing at jokes I had laughed at a hundred times before and dispensing what I hoped was sage advice to men who'd been priests before I was born.

I was the lead in a bad play that I had written myself — a *Jack*, more than a real play — I was a caricature of a bishop.

"That's a good one, Father."

"Ah, yes indeed. God bless old John Francis."

"Ah, sure isn't he in a better place."

"He was indeed. Truly a gas man, Father O'Sullivan was."

Every old priest, no matter that he was the biggest rogue or drunkard that ever pissed on God's green earth, was presumed to be resting in the bosom of Abraham, the arms of Jazus, or wit all the saints and our blissed mither, abive in te hivins — or some other fictional place. Never in the one locality where the old rip might get his just reward.

My performance throughout was flawless and my audience loved it.

The one event that stands out most in my mind that first summer was a brief trip I took back to Ireland. Though my sister still lived there, the trip was not to see her, but to take one last turn driving around the countryside   to see for myself whether it was truly as depressing a place as I had remembered. My sister and I were strangers — over the years since I'd left for America our correspondence had consisted entirely of notes hastily scratched inside Christmas cards — connected more by duty than affection. Neither of us had much nostalgia for our shared childhood and having disapproved of my decision to go to seminary, she had put a distance between us that had only widened with the years.

In jeans and pullover, I got off the plane and emerged from the Arrivals terminal into a cold and overcast, Shannon morning. A familiar shiver ran up my back. I was in Ireland all right. For the first time in months I felt invisible; another pathetic Yank rooting about in the countryside for spoor of his family in a Ryan U-Drive.

I turned off the main Derry-Omagh carriageway and drove down the short road that led to the Victoria Bridge station and the Nestle chocolate factory. The station seemed deserted and its once white fences and gates looked dirty gray and neglected. Few trains stopped at it anymore I guessed. I parked and walked up the incline to the platform and poked my head into the waiting room, painted still in the same yellow and brown I remembered from school days. A GNR teacup sat steaming on the ledge by the ticket window and a turf fire was flickering in the office behind — someone was still working there. I went back to the platform and jumped down onto the tracks, crossing to the down-line platform, feeling the familiar cinder-crunch under my shoes. "Watch for the trains," the porter had always warned. My bowel twisted with an old familiar fear and I shivered at the memory of St. Columb's. I needed to piss anyway, but it was good doing it there straddling the up-line. Piss on the Great Northern Railway or NIRTB or UTA or whatever it was they called themselves nowadays. And Best Wishes as well to the priest-bullies and that sadistic workhouse they ran!

Ah! Come the War Crimes Trials... I intoned as I relieved myself of a great burden.

It was on the down-line platform that I had last seen my father. I could feel, still, his stiff-fingered handshake and, not a day had gone by in the years since, that I hadn't seen him standing there, uncertain whether or not to wave at the train.

Yes. It was to you I was waving, and yes, you can now go back home and tell her you saw me off properly. It was the old man on the platform, pathetic and unsure, that I chose to remember and not a younger man, a strapping red-faced-with-rage man, a man with fists flailing about a boy's cheeks and ears. I crossed the tracks again and returned to the rental car that I'd left by the crossing gate.

I drove through Castlegorm town without stopping—the British military had erected barriers and fences blocking the downtown off—to keep the native Irish out, I suppose, as in ancient times. Bearing left at the school wall I headed out along the valley road and, after a few miles, turned right, up the narrow road that led onto the high moors where my people had been living for a couple of thousand years. I looked for the chimneys and the high-pitched slate roof to appear from behind the sally bushes as I approached the lane, but instead, only the jagged silhouette of ruined walls stood outlined against the sycamores on the hillside. I braked and pulled the car over onto the grassy verge. I stared up at the skeleton over the haw-thorn hedge. It had not been a happy place, yet for all that, it had been all I'd known of the world for so many years. It seemed wrong that it should have become this corpse of tumbled stone and gaunt walls pierced by sightless windows — a shame.

I decided to go up and look around — it had not been my intention to risk being seen by one of the thousand cousins who lived nearby. But I couldn't resist. I steered the little car into the once-familiar lane, now badly overgrown — briars and ferns resentfully scraped and flailed the doors as I forged through them up the hill. I shifted down at the last turn, getting up steam for the final steeper stretch, as my father had taught me, and on reaching the top I swung around into the deserted yard and stopped.

The house had lain empty for a decade or more and, with the inevitable collapse of its roof timbers from damp, little remained but a maze of ruined walls and forlorn rubble. The still creamy remains of her Aga—centerpiece of any post war modernization —lay abandoned alongside the barn steps and the heavy iron frame of the clothes mangle was unmistakable, rusting away in the nettles by the coal-house. I got out of the car and stretched my legs — the very paving stones recognized my feet.

I wandered through a mucky gap, well trampled by cows' hooves, where a fancy wrought-iron garden gate — featured in fifty years of family snaps — had once hung. The low boxwood hedges, that had once outlined her flower beds with neatly trimmed precision, had all but vanished; the privet hedge, separating her flower garden from the vegetable plot, untrimmed for decades, had developed into a line of straggly trees. Everything had died or gone wild and leggy, from lack of care. Her garden had been at once her safe place and her calendar: snowdrops and daffodil spears promised the end of winter darkness, crocus and phlox and a hedge of sweet-pea meant summer holidays from school and happiness; while cabbages and pruning foretold the approach of the dark winter tunnel once again. Her rhododendrons had swollen into huge groves, beautiful and unappreciated, usurping entire corners of the garden with their masses of reds and pinks. The roses had all grown yards of cane that she would never have tolerated, their flowers trailing sadly on the gravel paths, rusty petals scattered about the stones.

Only the peach tea rose by the front door, though badly overgrown too, was healthy as ever. This was her special rose. Others she would cut for the hall-stand or to scent the bedrooms after Saturday's laundry, but the tea rose was hers alone — worn by her with a reverence befitting a holy medal — consolation on school mornings and in celebration of the long, light days of summer holidays. I threaded a perfectly furled, peach-tinged bud into the weave of my sweater.

The vegetable garden had become a meadow choked with dockin leaves and nettles. The branches of gooseberry bushes were bent to the grass with hairy yellow fruit while farther down the garden, close by the vague outline of the bleaching green, red and black currants glistened in the sunlight begging to be gathered. Where the curly kale and cabbages had grown, the soil was red and slimy, fermented by damsons that had dropped unseen and unwanted.

Along the grass-covered lane behind the house I wandered like a man in a dream, picking and eating wild raspberries and blackberries, alert for the worm — still the country boy —till my fingers were purple with the juice.

Foolish Yank wringing his money's worth of nostalgia from a place of pain?

Not me. I was brimming with gratitude that I had not spent my life there as she had done. Perhaps, it was wrong to celebrate my escape from such a lovely place and perhaps even more wrong to have used the priesthood to effect that escape. But celebrate and give thanks I did that day to a survival instinct that had saved me from that beautiful grave. It had killed her — that lusciously landscaped hill with its dark winters and its un-grieved children.

I threw down the bunch of ferns and wild woodbine I had been gathering from habit and hurried back along the lane to where I had left the car. I drove quickly away before Fate could detect her bookkeeping error and force me to live out my days on that forlorn hill.

CHAPTER 29

Big Sur, California — 2004

HOLLAND HAD WRITTEN nothing in several days. It was as if some force field around the typewriter was actively repelling him. Twice now he'd cancelled sessions with the monk using the excuse of "feeling poorly." Where was the point in taking the man's time if he had nothing new to work on? He was confused by how suddenly the flow of writing, which he had come to enjoy, had shut down — like a faucet abruptly turned off.

What he did know was the next stuff was painful and, that it was the crux of the whole thing really. How could the psychiatrist make any sense of what he'd done later without knowing what really happened — what had led up to it. The man would still be basing his opinions on the stupid news clippings. God, those papers had made him look bad.

That afternoon the little monk surprised Holland by again showing up at the kitchen door and by again accepting a cup of coffee and slice of freshly baked loaf. He seemed so much more relaxed here — straddling a stool, drinking coffee, eating — than up in that damned office, Holland reflected

"It must have been very strange, starting all over again as a layman having once been a bishop —giving it all up," the monk said as he was accepting a second slice of bread.

Holland was standing at the table, one foot on the rung of a stool, an elbow resting on his knee. He smiled as he looked down at the monk.

"I can assure you, Father, becoming a bishop was far more of a shock to my system than was abdicating. That last day, after I had resigned — as I'm heading out of Minerva in my truck — it felt like I'd been let out of Folsom Prison. I realized that I was finally a free man; free for the first time in my whole life. But, with that freedom had come no feeling of elation. My life, my whole world, had lost value and meaning with the loss of…" Holland stopped in mid-sentence, suddenly short of breath — unable to finish the sentence.

The monk was quiet for a few moments, then very quietly said: "Jack, do you think we should maybe talk about what happened to Jerry?"

Though the question was posed so casually, it hit Holland hard —like a depth charge. Suddenly he was overwhelmed by a surge of powerful emotion, so powerful it threatened to cut off his breathing. He needed to sit down. The blood had rushed out of his head, as though a valve had been opened, and left him light-headed; his legs felt feeble, no longer able to support his weight. He rested his head on the tabletop, which seemed to help with the dizziness, but a hard mass had begun to pound as though trying to break through his diaphragm and suffocate him. He was frightened. Was this the heart attack that had done in so many of his relatives? His throat was already so tight he couldn't swallow or get air. Or, had the god of this place finally taken its revenge on him for the things he'd said? Suddenly, the dark thing inside him overcame whatever had been blocking it and it surged upwards, bursting out finally in great, body-wracking sobs. Breathing was hard and thinking impossible. He kept urging himself to Breathe! Breathe! You can't die if you keep breathing.

The little monk, seemed startled at first by the intensity of it all — by the heaving and tremors and by the suddenness of the outburst — but he regained his composure quickly and had become a doctor again.

"Good man, Jack," he murmured, his voice gentle and reassuring. "Let it come out, now. Bottled up for years, it needs to be released."

It had taken another fifteen minutes before Holland returned to something approaching normal. Nothing like this had ever happened him before and it had left him shaken. Such intensity of emotion, he'd never thought possible. Who'd have thought the stoic Jack Holland could be reduced to such a helpless state by emotion?

They'd talked afterwards for a time, sitting in the kitchen, Father James asking him more about Jerry and himself — he was curious still about the relationship — and Holland talking more openly about his feelings than he had ever imagined possible.

"I loved him more than anybody in my whole life but we never so much as hugged." Holland heard himself say. They were both silent then for what seemed to Holland a very long time — he glanced over to where the monk sat staring down at the table.

"Disappointed?" Holland asked and when the man in some confusion denied feeling anything of the sort, Holland had laughed. "You know what, Father, you're a hopeless romantic at heart. We're all looking for love but it was Jerry's tragedy that he came looking in an empty well like me."

The monk's face was sad when he looked up at Holland. He smiled ruefully.

"D'you think sitting up here on the top of this mountain... ?" Holland started to ask, but stopped himself — it was none of his damned business. "I hope you find what you're looking for," he said instead.

The monk stood up and pushed his stool back underneath the table neatly before looking at Holland.

"Jack, I suspect you were probably a far better bishop than you realize." Then, with a little nod towards the monastery he indicated he had to leave. "Thanks for the bread and the coffee."

"Anytime, my friend. Anytime."

Holland went back to his room and put another sheet into the typewriter.

He began:

"None of us in the Chancery could have foreseen the storm that the demon-god was brewing up for us that Friday morning in March, nor could we foresee how our lives would be turned on end forever by the chain of events set off by that letter. There had been no Gale Warning on the News-at-Eleven, nor 'Glass-be-falling' jeremiads — not even gulls circling too far inland. There was nothing that would have warned us of the disaster that was bearing down on us."

CHAPTER 30

Minerva, California — 1977

"Dan Pastorelli, molesting children? I don't friggin' buy that!" I'd snorted when I read the letter.

"You've been wrong before," Johnstone shot back at me from the easy chair into which he'd slumped after handing me a one-page typed letter in a plastic sleeve. "Remember saintly old Bill Hermann —old butter-wouldn't-melt Bill?"

I nodded, remembering how shocked I'd been when that nice, gentle old man had confessed in court to a thirty-year career of molestation — idiot me, thinking him fit for canonization. I read the letter again with a more open mind.

From one of the city parishes, an obviously anguished father was claiming that this young priest, Pastorelli, had molested his ten-year-old son and other boys from the school. The fondling had allegedly occurred after basketball practice. The parents, concerned over changes they'd noticed in the boy, had questioned him. And he had admitted—reluctantly, according to the father —that it had been going on for most of the year Pastorelli had been in their parish. He was writing to his Bishop, "…in the fervent hope that His Excellency would remove the unworthy priest from their wonderful parish community, quietly and quickly, so as to avoid any public scandal and further pain for the children."

"…quietly and quickly… What does he think we are, the friggin' Inquisition?" I looked over at Johnstone, the Tribunal Investigator, but could read nothing on his face. "You'd better open a file and look into it." I'd said finally. "How's your caseload?" I handed him back the letter.

"I can give it a day or so, see if there's a *prima facie* case, at least — get the guy off the streets." He started to get up but stopped halfway out of the chair and asked: "Wasn't Pastorelli out there for awhile with you guys in St. Thomas?

"Yeah, he lived with us for a couple of months when he was first ordained," I said. "Good kid, conscientious as far as I could see; reminded me of one of the old fashioned sanctuary priests, meditating every morning."

"Oh, well." Johnstone heard me out, made a note, then stood up quickly and stubbed out his cigarette in my ashtray.

"Got some calls to make." With this he had charged out of my office — a tornado, leaving in its wake an energy vacuum. Typical Johnstone, moving from one mode to another abruptly without apology. Every time I thought we were having a conversation, he was suddenly gone. I could hear the clatter of his boots as he pounded down the stairs to the parking lot. Our sleuth was on the case.

Hardly a week went by without a letter from somebody accusing some priest or other of some crime or other. The complaints covered the spectrum: from mispronouncing words at mass and failures in personal hygiene, through sins of reckless driving, intoxication and taking the name of "God" in vain, all the way to the theft of parish funds, being spotted entering or leaving a motel with a woman—or man —and the ever-horrifying, seemingly ever-present, child molestation. Which accusations were true and which false? It was impossible to tell from the letters themselves — we had to investigate each one to find out.

"Separating the fly shit from the pepper," was how Charlie Johnstone described his unenviable function.

Appointment as Judicial Investigator was not something many priests were vying for and in most dioceses they had trouble getting anyone to take it on at all. But we in Minerva were fortunate; we had a priest who was a born cop — from a long line of cops — a man who was flattered by the appointment. And the job of "snooper," as it was called by the other priests, suited him to a tee. In fact it would be hard to imagine any other priestly job Charlie Johnstone might be nearly so suited for — lacking as he did even the minimal social or pastoral skills. But there was something about him I liked. Maybe it was that athlete-gone-to-seed way he carried himself. As an investigator, I knew I could rely on him to be totally objective and even ruthless in uncovering wrongdoing. God help Pastorelli if he'd been doing any part of what the letter claimed.

Over the few months Pastorelli had been stationed with us, I found that he was anything but the frivolous boy he had first seemed. I was impressed by how he had revitalized some of the parish youth organizations, and by his spiritual practices. I was also fairly certain, that Danny was not only gay as pink ink, but quite sexually unsophisticated. It was hard to imagine him the sexual predator described in the letter. But, I had been wrong before.

I called Jerry that afternoon to ask him if he had picked up any rumors about Pastorelli. I was breaking protocol in doing this but I trusted Jerry so utterly that I regarded him as my expert consultant in many matters

He was in a playful mood when he came on the line and went immediately into one of his routines.

"Hi, honey!" He breathed in Marilyn's whispery, seductive voice.

"Jerry!" I was in no mood for playing.

"What are you wearing?" He insisted — more deep breathing.

"Hey, come on. Cut it out!"

"Want to know what I'm wearing?"

Sometimes I played along but not when I was sitting behind my desk in the Chancery with a problem like the one that was on my mind that day.

I told him about the letter and that Johnstone had been assigned to investigate.

"What do you think?" I asked him.

"God. He's the last in the world I'd have suspected. I mean, the boy's as gay as a day in May — anybody with half a brain could see that — but I honest to God think he's as innocent as the day's long. Not so much as a breath of rumor about him. And you know how the fruit-o-graph buzzes amongst us queer priests? But, of course, I forgot…"

There was a moment's dramatic pause before he continued in a mocking lisp: "A great big he-man, like Your Excellency's good self, wouldn't know anything about how we poor little gay boys behave, would he now?" He paused to allow my reaction — I said nothing.

He continued in his own voice. "Anyway, the word around the sissy-priests sorority could be summarized thusly: Danny's a very holy little boy; he works his little buns off trying to be the priest he's supposed to be; and, as far as anybody can determine, he still thinks it's a device for peeing out of."

"Well, he's going to need all the support from the sorority and everybody else you can think of if this thing turns nasty," I added grimly.

"I can't even imagine what an accusation like this will do to him! God help him, if the hounds of righteousness start yapping at his heels! And yourself…? If there's anything I can do…"

I knew I could count on Jerry — regardless of how the case against Pastorelli turned out and whatever action I might have to take.

"For now, all I need is that you'll be there." We hung up simultaneously.

I heard nothing from Johnstone on the Pastorelli case for several days.

"Jack, can I see you a minute." The Bishop had stuck his head around the door. As I entered his office he motioned for me to close the door and waved me into the armchair beside his desk.

Monsignor Hogan, out at St. John's, had just phoned him to warn him that a delegation from his parish was on its way down to the Chancery. He'd done every-thing he could think of to dissuade them, he claimed, but they were determined to have a showdown with the Bishop. They were adamant, Hogan said, in their demand that Father Pastorelli be removed from their parish, forthwith.

Hogan said he had explained all about due process "and all that stuff" to them, but they weren't about to be put off by what they'd called, "bureaucratic run-arounds." They were even threatening, he said, to wait out in the streets in front of the Chancery, if the Bishop wouldn't see them. He'd done his level best to dissuade them, he'd told the Bishop. What more could he do but let them go on?

The Bishop was under no illusions about Hogan's role in this. He might even have urged them take it to the Chancery or come up with the idea himself.

"… out in the streets" was of course a very effective threat —enough to put the wind up any bishop. You could just picture the front-page headline of the *Minerva Chronicle* that evening:

Diocese Shields Child-Molesting Priest

I went back to my office and as I waited for the delegation, I found myself thinking about Monsignor Hogan.

Like most of the pioneer priests in Minerva diocese, Hogan was a hard-work-ing, hard-driving, old Irishman who'd built a prosperous parish from what had been vacant fields only a decade earlier. Not for Hogan the well-intentioned bake sales and other "penny ante" money-raising schemes put on by parish ladies — he collected money from those who had plenty of it.

"Oi never seen a do-gooder tat done any good yet, boi!" He'd sermonize around the Confirmation tables. "Oo hafta' go to tem tat have it, boi and lean heavy on tem, and no apology."

The delegation, I felt confident, would be representative of the well-heeled, and the extremely well-heeled, saints of St. John's parish. Hogan was not a man who'd risk offending his best envelope using parishioners merely to save a junior priest's reputation.

The delegates had already seated themselves around the conference room table when the Bishop and I joined them, about a dozen of them, very respectable, very middle-class and very grim-looking.

A skinny, athletic-looking man sprang to his feet, evidently their spokesman. In his forties, skull-like head capped by cropped red hair, jaw-rippling tense, he stood poised on the balls of his feet, rocking with bottled energy.

He introduced the group and himself. He was Larry Bright, he said, and if we cared to call Monsignor Hogan over at St. John's we'd find out that he was "a pillar" of the parish. Monsignor had often called him that, he said. Not a hint of decent self-mockery. He looked around the table inviting confirmation. He was not disappointed: nods galore! Not even a smile of embarrassment nor an averted eye at retailing such obvious ass-kissing. Wealthy and naive too? No wonder Hogan had cultivated this poor bastard. "More dollars than sense," as they say.

"God bless Monsignor Hogan…" Mr. Bright announced. His right hand sliced the air, in a sort of psychic karate chop, maybe to prevent debate. "Now there's a priest for you!" A chorus of nods and affirming murmurs from around the table.

Bright listed his affiliations — parents' club for the school, building fund chairman, coach of basketball and baseball and sponsor of the CYO — before introducing the rest of the delegates. These were the heavy hitters you'd come across in any parish: good people, simple maybe, but folks without whom no parish would exist for long.

When all had identified themselves as worthies who should be listened to and I had made a careful note of their names—a good role, being seen as merely a secretary in sticky situations like this. The old man leaned over and asked me *sotto voce* whether the letter accusing Pastorelli had been signed by any of the people in this delegation.

It had not, I could tell him unequivocally.

I had checked with Johnstone before the meeting just to be doubly certain that I had remembered the name correctly. It had been written by someone named, James McKitterick, a name burnt into my mind, the name of that first traumatizing dentist I had been dragged to as a child. There was no McKitterick at this table.

Mr. Bright, the prosecutor, presented the state's case against Pastorelli and each sentence of his indictment evoked nods of concurrence from around the table. They were a well-trained lot, these good parishioners from St. John's: nod and they'd nod; frown and they'd frown.

The gist of their complaint was this: Pastorelli was an evil influence on the boys of the parish by his effeminate mannerisms.

I asked Bright to be more explicit as to the behaviors that threatened the morals of the children. He frowned and said nothing. Was the question maybe too difficult? Or, had he assumed we would take his word as adequate proof of guilt? He looked around the table at the others and threw up his hands, puzzled it seemed by my question.

Could I be so dense as not to find in his charges more than adequate grounds for a priest's removal? Wasn't "swishiness" proof enough? Surely he could rest his case on "swishiness." He seemed to be appealing to the others.

I had apparently thrown Mr. Bright's train off its track by asking for specifics. The tension in the room, already thick, had become positively electric when a short, heavy-set woman a few seats down from Bright leapt into the breach. I had been struck when I'd first looked around the table by her ruddy complexion and the nervous jangling of the half-dozen gold bangles on each pudgy wrist and the compulsive twisting of her many gold rings.

In a surprisingly deep voice she started by reminding us that she was still Mrs. Brachman. She explained that since "a blind man could see the young priest was a fairy," it was setting a bad example, "having that sort of pervert prancing about the church and school, saying he was a priest…" She exhaled loudly. "Such a sissy! You should see the swish of it up there on the altar… you'd think … Oh, it's awful! Just awful!" She emphatically twisted each of her rings then in turn — like the rosary of some very affluent religion.

"My God, if you could only see him!" Bright had found his voice at last. "The guy's an embarrassment even at a baseball game, can't throw a ball for nuts or swing a bat…"

"And when he tries throwing the ball, it's even worse!" Another man, a Mr. Sweeney, wanting to be accounted there on St. Crispin's Day. "A laughing-stock, is what he is! Might be a girl, from the way he goes about it. Coordination, huh! Couldn't catch a baseball if his life depended on it. Need's a physical, if you ask me — see if he's a man at all."

"And the way he dresses, huh!" Mrs. Brachman was wading back into the fray again, right up to her pudgy hips. "A real queer, not a doubt in the world about that."

Did this woman have any idea how offensive these terms were? Or, had she fully intended the offense?

"With his shorts and that cologne... You could tell he's a fairy a mile away — the stench of that stuff he splashes on himself. Must bathe in it — knock you down, so it would!" From another man, who'd been silent up till then.

"Told one of my boys he sees nothing wrong with getting an ear pierced — you know, like for an earring."

"That'll be the day!" One of the mothers volunteered.

"No son of mine will ever be caught wearing an earring, priest or no priest!" The Sweeney man added.

"Even the kids in the school laugh at him and call him a queer behind his back." Bright piled on.

"'Nellie Pastorelli', the kids call him. How d'ya like that, Bishop?" Mrs. Brachman taunted.

The Bishop looked over at me. He had that sad-eyed, pleading look which made the bags under his watery eyes look even more pronounced than usual. I knew the look well, it was his SOS — the seas were rough and he was foundering. What had I expected? That he might reveal some arcane episcopal mojo, some previously hidden leadership trick he'd picked up at some deeply secret Episcopal Command College—a place where they train the real bishops and give them special powers? Had I been waiting for some jewel, maybe, of Solomonic wisdom that would send these people home chastened but content? Or had I expected that he, like Moses, should confound them by turning a pointer into a snake — or Mrs. Brachman's rings into Cheerios?

But that was not our Bishop. No! There he sat instead, looking at me, eyes pleading with me to get him the hell away from these nasty people and back to the safety of his office.

Stall for time, it was all I could think to do.

"Was there evidence of anything more concrete than these, 'effeminate mannerisms' you mentioned?" I asked and let my eyes travel from one to the other around the table. I was met with blank stares all the way around. Hardly Bow Street Magistrates Court; not a Rumpole in sight; not a single quote from Wordsworth. They seemed dumbstruck and all heads turned as though on a silent signal towards Mr. Bright. But their spokesman was staring at me blank-eyed. Mrs. Brachman again charged to the front.

"Mannerisms? Huh!" She snorted. "The man's a raging homo and you'd need to be blind, deaf and dumb, not to see it." She was shouting now and her face had grown even redder.

"Mrs. Brachman," I was determined to keep an even tone. "I was merely asking whether there was any specific action on Father Pastorelli's part that anyone here can attest to — any action that can be proven to have brought harm to a single child in the parish?" Fountain pen poised over paper, ready to record the specifics. I had framed my question carefully, to not put words in their mouths. You had to be careful with a lynching party like this, for I believed they'd say whatever was necessary to get rid of Pastorelli — truth or proof be damned. And they'd do it, not because they were bad people or liars, but because they were convinced they were doing God's work. It was a crusade and no one has less regard for the truth than a man on a mission for his god.

"Look here, Bishop." Mrs. Brachman might have been using a racial or sexual slur the way she'd said the word, "Bishop."

"We're the people who have built St. John's parish from the ground up and neither you nor anybody else is going to stick us with a queer priest that's going to corrupt our children. So, we'll tolerate no more of this stalling, no more of this questioning — you'd think we were the ones that's been doing wrong."

Madame Lafarge in the front row with her knitting!

What was I doing in this room, surrounded by these right wing lunatics? Was it some demented play set in a New England colony? Or, was I maybe crazy Canute, commanding the ocean? I kept on plugging at them though, trying to wear them down, hoping to take the pressure off the old man.

"Father Pastorelli is a very devout young man," I declared with as much assurance as I could muster. "He would never, ever harm any of your children," I told them. "He has taken a vow of celibacy and, for a devout young man like him, that was a most sacred obligation," I asserted. I wasn't smitten by the deity for my hypocrisy. But, I might have held my tongue for all the good I was doing. They glowered at me with blank faces.

"Father Pastorelli would never violate his vows. Never!" I proclaimed with finality.

"What are you planning to do?" Rasped Mrs. B. "Heh? We should wait till one of the children has been molested maybe, and then come in with our lawyers and the police?" She glared around the mob — sweeping all in the room with her burning rage.

"Parishioners suing the diocese and a priest led off in handcuffs on the TV news, is that what you're waiting for?" She hurled this final well-aimed shaft at the real Bishop and slashed me with a glance meant to wound. She wasn't to be put off by some no-account auxiliary bishop, huh!

"The diocese plastered all over the front pages of *The Chronicle* and *The Union*. That what you want?" Bright filled in the picture as though the old man needed any help in visualizing such a disaster.

Nothing the Bishop feared more than those three modern plagues: priest arrested, molestation lawsuits and scandalous headlines. Those pale horsemen populated every bishop's nightmares.

The Bishop then did what he did best — maybe this was the specific episcopal skill they are taught in the command college — he bought us time with a promise of action. A firmly stated promise that the matter would get his full and prompt attention was enough to get them out the door. Back in his office he collapsed exhausted into the chair behind his desk.

"For the love of God, Jack, you got a Camel on you?"

I passed the pack to him and he gratefully lighted one, dragging the smoke deep into his lungs. I watched him smoke. I hadn't smoked all day and was dying for one but no, I wasn't going to start then.

"What did you think of all that?" He asked.

"The first thing we have to do is talk to Johnstone and find out what he's discovered."

This made sense to him, so I went down the hallway in search of our sleuth, but he wasn't in his office and no one had a clue where he might be found. He was hardly ever in his damned office and he never told the secretaries anything. Typical! I left a message on his answering machine and sent the old man home — I'd never seen him look so gray and tired.

CHAPTER 31

Minerva, California —1977

JOHNSTONE DIDN'T CALL me back till that evening after dinner. Surprisingly, he asked if he could come over to St. Thomas' right away and talk to me. Of course! I couldn't wait to see him. He knocked on the outer door of my suite around eight, having let himself in the back door using his credit card. He held it up by way of explanation.

"You should do something about those lousy locks — cheap shit! Credit card's as fast as a key on them." Wanted to avoid being seen by the housekeeper, he said. But doing things like that was just his way — stealth for its own sake; no unnecessary encounters with other priests who might answer the door.

I poured each of us a stiff one of Powers whiskey and we sat in my study. He looked around, taking in the unadorned walls, the bookcases made of bricks and pine planks that lined the walls, the two mismatched armchairs and the mixum gatherum of furniture — odd pieces Cassidy had bought from some parishioner who owned a salvage yard.

"Pretty fancy digs!" He sipped his whiskey and continued taking in the room. "They do nicely by you bishops." Not even a smile cracked his face — I admire a good deadpan.

"Yeah." I answered in the same spirit. "Work hard Charlie — you too can afford a nicely appointed place like this someday."

"Christ, Jack! Why don't you hit Cassidy up for some dacent furniture — all that cash he's been stuffin' into the parish investment accounts? This is a friggin' slum!"

He leaned forward and lowered his voice, "You'd never guess how much he has in them — in the parish accounts." He looked quickly around as though Cassidy might have installed a hidden camera or microphone. "Even in his personal account … Could afford a couple a dacent chairs!"

"Look Charlie, I haven't the foggiest what he's got in his bank accounts and I don't want to know." I was resenting, and not for the first time, the invasion of everyone's privacy that Johnstone took to be his right.

"He could afford more than this shite, that's for sure." He would have the last word.

I shrugged. Mick Cassidy wasn't a bad sort, as pastors go, and I didn't think it was from being cheap that he skimped on furnishings. The man set a good table — a highly regarded virtue amongst the older priests — better than most parishes. And he wasn't a bit skimpy with the bonus checks to the priests at Christmas. But, as they said about him, any taste he had was in his mouth. For Mick Cassidy, a chair was just something you sat upon.

Johnstone accepted a second drink, or ' the other half' as the Irish call it, before we got down to the reason for his visit.

"This business with Pastorelli," he began, "there's something rotten going on there but I haven't got all the way to the bottom of it yet."

He took out a reporter's notebook and started to leaf through it as he was speaking. "Just, take my word for it —something rotten is going on and it's not your man Pastorelli that's the culprit — not by an Irish mile." He leaned forward in the chair and, after again sweeping the room furtively with his eyes, he whispered: "I'd suggest you do nothing — take no action — for a bit, till I get clearer on this."

He fixed me with an unblinking stare. For a second, I thought he had asked a question that I'd missed, then I realized he was just thumbing through the card-files he kept in his mind, deciding what to say next.

"I spoke to a few of the people I know over in St. John's, and…"

"Lay people or priests?" I interrupted.

"Jack, for Christ's sake…!" He rolled his eyes to heaven at my apparent naïveté. "Parishioners! You think I'd ask Hogan? Shite!" He took a deep breath and continued. "Anyway, everybody I spoke to thinks the kid's the greatest thing since sliced bread." He pulled out his cigarettes. "You mind if I smoke?" I shrugged and he lighted a Benson & Hedges.

I had been trying to quit all week but the sight of that soothing, reassuring smoke, drawn deep into his lungs, was so alluring I dug out the pack of Camels I had thrown in the desk drawer with finality not an hour before. I lighted up and let myself enjoy the tingle as the lovely drug stroked and soothed my temples.

Johnstone went on with his report after consulting his notes.

"Appears the kid's a talented musician, plays piano and guitar and sax and what-the-fuck-have-you. The kids in the parish think he's a real cool guy." He flipped over some more pages. "Spoke to Liam Smith at diocesan CYO and he hears nothing but great stuff about him. The parish CYO out there was never more active, he says, with teams and trips and dances and what not."

Johnstone turned over another page but, instead of continuing his report, he ran his hand nervously through his stubbly hair and winced at me. It wasn't like him to be so fidgety and hesitant.

"What?" I prompted.

"I hope you don't take this wrong, Jack, but I came to ask a kind of favor from you — something that's kinda hard to put into words. Only a suggestion, mind you."

I nodded and he carried on.

"It could help my investigation a lot if you were to inquire of Jerry Egan whether he thinks this kid is really a queer or just appears to be one to the uninitiated—if you get my meaning?"

What he had just implied about Jerry shocked me. Was his "sexual orientation" such a given among the priests? I was afraid for him, knowing the trouble such a perception could cause him. But then, wasn't that vintage Johnstone, that guilty-until-proven-innocent pugnaciousness? Maybe that was just Johnstone. I took the offensive,

"Why on earth would I ask him that?" I asked. I wasn't going to tell Johnstone I'd already talked to Jerry. "And where in the hell do you get off, assuming that Egan's gay?" I made no attempt to hide my annoyance.

"Jack, please!" He rolled his eyes again in exasperation and took another deep drag of cigarette smoke, then exhaled in a sigh of frustration — at my unbelievable stupidity, it implied.

"For one thing," He pointed an accusing finger at me. "Let's, the two of us, stop kidding each other." He drew himself up straighter in the chair. "Look," he said, after a dramatic pause. "I've been rooting around in the dark creases of this diocese for a good many years now and I've received a heap of reports about your friend Egan in that time. It was worse a few years ago, but I still get at least half a dozen complaints a year about him." He straightened up before delivering his *coup de gras*: "He's become a bit more careful —about the dressing up, I mean—in recent times."

I was stunned. How was it that I, a bishop, had never seen any of these files nor been told about any of this? And working in the Chancery alongside them — the Bishop and Johnstone — and they'd been gathering dirt on everybody and keeping it a secret from me.

My stomach knotted with a familiar terror. What have they been saying about me over the years? I was worried suddenly for myself — I couldn't help it. I switched into survival mode for the first time in ages and Johnstone's predator radar must have picked it up.

"You're wondering about yourself now, aren't you?" He asked matter-of-factly —not a trace of mockery that I could detect. Suddenly chastened, I nodded.

"I haven't heard a peep about you at all in recent times — though there was a fair wee file on you a few years back. I think the old man pulled it back into his private collection when they canonized you. Probably fed it into his canonical shredder."

"Holy Christ!" I exclaimed aloud. My mind was racing all over the meadow like a hunted rabbit. What all was in that folder? I had been right! I'd sensed it all along. They'd been on to me! And still, he'd made me a bishop. Why would he have done that?

"And about Jerry...?" I prompted — as long as he was being so forthcoming ...

"The junk recently's been sort of harmless garbage. Semi-benign shite. This or that auld biddy spotted him coming out of a gay bar some place or other. What in hell the auld bitch was doing, casing a gay bar? Or, he was seen walking arm in arm with another man in the Castro. That sort of thing."

"Somebody had followed him to the Castro — how else had they *just happened* to be there?" I asked—humbled now in the face of this information.

"Could be somebody with a crush on him... stalking him." Johnstone suggested. "Or somebody making stuff up to get him in trouble. Who the frig knows? What do they think we're runnin' here — a friggin boarding school? When nobody's getting hurt, it's shredder time."

Johnstone lighted another cigarette and for something to do, something that might quiet my inner quiver, I lighted another of my Camels.

Johnstone leaned back in the chair, took a deep pensive drag on his cigarette and shook his head regretfully as the smoke trickled out his nose and mouth.

"So?" He inquired. "Will you speak to Egan about this?"

My earlier indignation on Jerry's behalf seemed foolish now in light of Johnstone's information.

"I had no idea…" I began lamely. "I didn't know about the files…"

"For Christ's sakes man! I haven' put a fraction of that stuff into Egan's file. Gimme credit for some common sense. Look…," he continued, holding both hands out in front of him palms down as though calming the waves. "Anybody with two eyes in his head could see that Pastorelli's a little pansy but, on the other hand, I haven't the slightest doubt but that he's as celibate as… Fuck! I can't think of an example, but you know what I mean."

I nodded.

"The biggest problem the kid has is that he's good looking enough to give some auld closet case a big dose of *delectatio*.. If Egan can help, I'd be obliged."

"You mean somebody may have tried something with the young guy… and then regretted it?"

"Yeah! Or got slapped down by him, more likely. Stranger things have happened, right?"

"Any idea who?"

"My suspicions, Bishop darling, don't bear repeatin' at this point in the proceedin's. I have a warped auld mind and I might just be seeing slime where none exists. But I think I'm onto something that reeks of foul play."

He paused and looked at me again with that quizzical look as though waiting for an answer. Had he asked a question and I'd somehow missed it? But no, as I found out, he'd just been flipping through those cards again — deciding whether or not to tell me more.

"I can tell you this much already: there's nobody named 'McKitterick' in St. John's parish." He nodded — more a sideways bob of his chin — and gave me a piercing stare, his lips pursed to emphasize the significance of the discovery. "In fact, I couldn't find anybody by that name in any of the neighboring parishes either." Again the chin bobbing off to the side.

"Somebody's trying to get that kid in trouble, for some reason, and I want to find out who that son-of-a-bitch is. And then I'd be most obliged, Bishop, if you'd string the fucker up by his bollocks!"

There seemed a glimmer of hope for Pastorelli in what he'd told me but I was puzzled still. "I still don't see what Jerry can do," I asked.

"Yeah, you may be right of course. Just thought there might be something to that 'gaydar' people joke about. Like maybe he has some innate talent for divining the closet cases; you know, like the boyos with the forked stick lookin' for water." He raised his eyebrows as though expecting a reaction from me to his suggestion. "Maybe take his sally rod or whatever they use and see if it quivers."

I said nothing and he continued.

"Somebody in St. John's is threatened by Pastorelli. That's my guess." He lighted another cigarette, never taking his eyes off my face as he did so. "What do you think?"

"Gaydar?" I had asked the question before I was aware I had said anything.

"Yeah. You know, like radar." He cupped his right hand over his head and rotated it in a crude imitation of a dish. "The way them fairies spot each other on the street."

Now he was being deliberately ignorant — perhaps his idea of a joke — or was he teasing me?

"Johnstone, what the fuck century did you crawl out of?"

He gave me a ferocious flash of teeth and shrugged off my protest as though he hadn't even heard me.

"I don't necessarily believe in any of it but… Can't hurt, can it? Don't have much faith in any of that paranormal, woo woo stuff, myself." He stubbed out his nearly new cigarette, slapped his knees with his hands, stood up and stretched his arms stiffly towards the ceiling, arching his back.

"Fuckin' age! A bitch! Well, I'm off."

"Huh? Oh!" I was as usual taken by surprise. With Johnstone there were no gradual transitions. No social graces. Machine-gunning bursts of facts. More Sam Spade than Father Brown —Bogart in a Roman collar.

He promised to keep me informed and I told him I would speak to Jerry for what it was worth.

Jerry wasn't home that evening, though I rang and left messages several times. I'd tell him about Johnstone in the morning — he'd laugh.

Arriving at my office the next morning earlier than usual, one of the secretaries told me Father Johnstone would like to see me as soon as possible. That was a surprise — it hadn't been twelve hours since he'd left me. Didn't the man sleep? I found him reading the morning paper, feet up on his own little-used desk, half-hidden in a cloud of cigarette smoke. I motioned him into my office while I went back to the coffee room and poured my first cup of the day.

He waited till I had sat down behind my desk before he back-kicked the door closed behind him — an emphatic slam. I looked up at him inquiringly but his face betrayed nothing. He had brought with him a bulging manila folder. He took the straight chair across from me and began to lay documents from the folder on the desk between us.

"Wait till Your Excellency sees what I've dragged in for him this morning — from out of the slime where his lowly and contemptible servant slithers for a living!" Johnstone was full of himself and unusually playful. He never called me by a formal title in private unless he was joking.

"You want to kiss it?" I held out my ring.

"Yeah, right!" He said and went back to the papers he'd taken from his folder. "Lookie here!" He pushed a few papers across the desk towards me.

"That plastic sleeve on top, that's the original letter from that McKitterick character."

It was the letter accusing Pastorelli. He pushed another document across the desk so that it rested alongside the letter.

"Next, Your Magnificence will discover a sample of type lifted from a certain typewriter that I managed to locate. A forensic expert will testify, in court if necessary, that the letter was written on said machine and he says so in the next document — what the farmers around home would call an 'affidavey.' Idiosyncratic irregularities, one machine to the next — as individual as fingerprints — especially on older machines."

I was scanning each sheet as he described it.

"The next document is a signed statement, notarized by me, from the secretary at St. John's Rectory. She states that this typewriter — on which the above identification was made — is, (a) the machine Monsignor Hogan keeps in his private study and, (b), that it is never used by anyone but Monsignor Hogan. The other priests all have machines of their own. She, by the way, was one of the righteous ladies in the little lynching party that paid a social call on you and the old man the other night."

I had hardly dared think the letter might have been written by Hogan himself.

"How did you get her to cooperate?" I was fascinated that Johnstone might have some previously unsuspected diplomatic skill.

"I didn't put the questions about the machine to her directly, you see." Johnstone winked. "I confided in her that I had been dispatched by the Bishop to see her especially — in response to the delegation's complaint don't ye see. She was flattered that such an important man—the Bishop's Chief Inquisitor—was spending so much time with her and being so nice to her."

"You even used the word, 'Inquisitor'?"

"Of course I did! Impressed the shite out of her too — there she was repeating it to herself: 'Inquisitor', 'Inquisitor' — like she was trying to remember it — to brag about it later to the other ladies."

Johnstone was blowing smoke over my desk and I was having a hard time not lighting up. I had once again sworn off the vile things for life at six o'clock that morning. While Johnstone was bragging, I was picturing the conference room and the woman sitting at the far end of the table, saying nothing. Dour nods of agreement to everything the vocal ones were saying — though not a word out of her. Might she have suspected something rotten even then?

Johnstone was explaining how he'd managed her cooperation: "When she answered the door and told me I'd just missed Hogan, she couldn't have known that I'd been waiting nearly two hours for the bastard to leave for his damned golf game. Sat in my car down the street a block, watching the driveway, smoked a pack of cigarettes —nearly ruptured my friggin' bladder too!"

"I thought you guys carried a soda bottle on stakeouts — they do in the movies."

"Yeah, well!"

Johnstone loved being in this position: the sole possessor of information that others badly wanted. The son-of-a-bitch had most of this evidence already when he'd been to see me the previous evening. That was Johnstone! Playing it close to the vest.

"So why didn't you tell me all this last night?" I leaned back and asked him.

He waved my question away impatiently.

"Never mind that! Go on. Back to the papers." He jabbed the next one with his forefinger.

I examined the next in the stack of documents. As far as I could make out it was an analysis of fingerprints. "What's this?"

"Just picked it up from the lab this morning." Johnstone hunched nearer to the desk and dropped his voice. "I had this guy with a forensic lab run some prints off McKitterick's letter and do comparisons. Guess whose prints are all over the letter."

"Hogan's, it says here."

"Yeah! Dumb fucker!" Johnstone shook his head in disgust — more, probably at Hogan's lack of criminal skills, than at the moral issue.

I reread the fingerprint report — it said the prints lifted off the letter were indeed Hogan's. "Then, if Your Serene Goodness would be so kind as to look at the next document."

"This one?"

"Now wouldn't ye be after knowin' that it's a copy of the Right Reverend gentleman's very own Baptismal Certificate. Wasn't he enrolled among the elect of Jesus Christ, Our Savior, through the holy sacrament of Baptism in St. Brigid's church, Ballymacdubh, County of Kerry. Ah, and isn't he the wonderful credit to the said Jesus?" He paused. "By the way, I found that document right here in the Chancery files."

I shook my head in amazement on reading the certificate.

"So," Johnstone grinned. "You've noticed what the stupid son-of-a-bitch's mother was called before she had the good fortune to marry his father — if in fact she did?"

I had noticed the name but, since I wasn't going to get any good lines in Johnstone's little drama anyway, I said nothing.

"Right! McFuckin' Kitterick. James McKitterick. Moron, using his own grandfather's name on a piece of criminal slander."

I was amazed too at such a piece of stupidity. I would have given Hogan credit for more brains than that.

"So, Yer Holiness, aman't I the great wan now, or what?"

Johnstone lighted another Benson & Hedges and blew a forceful cloud over towards my side of the desk.

"*Quod erat demonstrandum!*" He flourished his cigarette, making spirals of smoke that hung hypnotically in the air between us.

"No shit!" All I could do was shake my head. That vicious old bastard!

"So?" Johnstone leaned over the desk and inquired: "What does Yer Excellency plan to do to the Right Reverend Monsignor Hogan?" Johnstone was looking at me expectantly. He reminded me of a Border Collie that had brought all the sheep successfully down through the narrow gap. Good dog!

"I need to talk to the old man and see what he thinks about it all." I told him.

"So. I'll get out of your hair in that case and let you get out the thumbscrews and all that good stuff they never let me play with." Johnstone crushed his cigarette out in my ashtray and stood up suddenly.

"You do good work, Charlie." I said.

"Right!" He nodded awkwardly in acknowledgement and left me to my thoughts.

As the Presiding Judge of the diocese, sorting the whole matter out legally was my job. I had more than enough evidence on my desk to justify opening a formal investigation for what was considered a grave crime in canon law. Pastorelli could, of course, also sue in the state courts for the damage to his good name. But, for now, the onus was on me.

I'll have the bastard's ass for this if it can be proved, I told myself as I lighted up a Camel — I'll quit these things later. I was pacing back and forth behind my desk, muttering to myself. Make an example of him — a warning to the other bigots. Lot's of them out there. Hogan's not alone — more stupid maybe and naive than most. Fuck him!

My indignation was welling up in a way I hadn't felt it do in a long time and, for a change, I was on the side of the angels — stirred up for righteousness. Alleluia! Adrenaline was pumping blood through my temples in great hot rushes as I sat down and began to outline on a legal pad what needed doing as far as the canon law procedures.

I knew I should go next door and let the old man know the latest developments — as a courtesy — but I was not ready for that just yet. Instead, I called over to the cathedral rectory to speak to Norbert Meyer, the *Defensor Vinculi* or Prosecutor for the diocese. A Midwestern German, whose principal job title was Rector of the Cathedral, Norbert served regularly as a tribunal official as well. There was no love lost between the Native Sons and the Foreign Born priests, but Norbert was perhaps the one man in the whole diocese nobody could credibly accuse of bias.

I asked if I might come over and speak to him right away on a tribunal matter. As I expected, he said he would immediately make himself available.

The cathedral rectory was just across the yard from the Chancery and, in a matter of minutes, I was in his office filling him in on what we had discovered to date and passing along the sheaf of documents Johnstone had left with me. I watched his face as he was listening and reading through the narrative Johnstone had typed up explaining the documents. His face at the best of times looked grim — translucent skin tight-stretched over an ascetic's skull — but as I watched, I could see the muscles of his jaw struggling hard, fighting to contain his emotion. Though frighteningly stern-faced, Norbert was one of the kindliest men I knew and full of surprising fun and good humor. But his stern countenance that morning accurately reflected his inner feeling.

"An awful business! Awful!" He murmured as he finished reading and carefully shuffled the documents into a neat stack. He sat for a moment then, shaking his head slowly from side to side. He ran a bony hand down his face and shook it — as though slinging off something scummy.

"God Almighty! That a priest could do this to anybody, let alone another priest…"

I sat across from him and waited as he struggled to get his mind around the significance of what he had just read.

"If this happened in this way and if we establish that it has, you can't just let a thing like this go unpunished." He looked at me inquiringly.

"That's precisely why I'm here, Monsignor." I passed an envelope over to him containing a document I had prepared before leaving my office. "I'm afraid I have a most unpleasant assignment for you." I looked at him and he nodded sadly. "I am setting this canonical process in motion before informing the Bishop. No one knows about this yet — except Charlie Johnstone who dug the stuff up. You understand what I am doing and why?"

Norbert nodded.

"I agree with you completely on this," he said. "A matter of this gravity must be subjected to full judicial procedure — nothing brushed under the rug."

We were in agreement then, we were both afraid that the Bishop, in a misguided attempt to limit scandal, might insist on handling the whole matter *sub rosa*.

The document I had given Norbert ordered and empowered him to set up and chair a formal Committee of Inquiry. There was *prima facie* evidence that a crime had been committed and my appointment of him had set the legal ball rolling beyond recall. It would now run its course and not even the Bishop of the diocese could stop it.

He read the document and nodded. He looked at me and shook his head.

"Jack, I think what you are doing is absolutely the right thing but I'm sure you must realize what a firestorm you're unleashing here…" He paused and looked at me for a moment with his grim smile. "It's you, of course, they'll blame — your countrymen —for the whole mess and not Hogan."

"I know that only too well," I said

He chuckled. "There was a time I didn't think you had it in you to do something as courageous as this." His grimness dissolved suddenly in a toothy, tight-lipped smile. He shook his head in recollection.

"Are you thinking of that summer I was here — from Catholic U?"

He laughed and nodded.

"Bad time!" I agreed, embarrassed, remembering how unreliable I'd been then; the drinking, the late nights and oversleeping.

Sitting with him ten years later, I could appreciate his even temper and straightforward manner even more than I had then. The Church needed more men like Norbert Meyer.

"Norbert, I feel strongly that this is something we must do and do properly." I ticked off on my fingers then the two most compelling reasons I had for taking this matter into a formal process. "First, we must send a message to the priests, old and young, that this sort of thing brings serious consequences down on the head of the perpetrator. And secondly, we must assure the victims that there is recourse: that they can count on the legal process of the diocese to protect their rights."

He nodded as I spoke. "I agree with you completely, Bishop," he said.

"You know how to proceed from here?" I asked. Our tone had reverted automatically to one that was as solemn as the task ahead.

"Yes, Bishop, I do." He took his pen then and signed and dated his acceptance of the assignment on both copies of the document. He passed one back to me and, taking a manila folder from his desk, put his copy into it. He had opened a file on Hogan — and as he put it, I had just "unleashed a firestorm" and no one could stop it.

We both felt the weight of what we had begun as we shook hands in silence.

Now to break the news to the old man, I braced myself as I climbed the stairs into the Chancery.

CHAPTER 32

Big Sur, California — 2004

"I HAD THOUGHT you were going to start writing about Jerry," the monk said as Holland took his accustomed seat.

"You've read all that already?" Holland retorted. He'd written for hours yesterday after the monk had left the kitchen and had pushed them under the office door before finally lying down around 2:00 a.m. He was maybe a bit overly sensitive from lack of sleep — better watch his temper.

"Are you maybe practicing avoidance, telling me all this about how you handled the accusation against that young priest?"

The monk seemed to have once again taken refuge behind the psychiatrist persona. Holland was disappointed. Hadn't they come further than that?

"The answer to your question is, no," he said. The bastard wants to play being distant, I'm good at that one. See how he likes real distance.

"Regarding this, that I've just read," the monk said holding up the typed sheets. "I have some serious questions. I would like to hear why you decided to bypass the Bishop and set in motion a process you knew would sweep through the diocese like a firestorm? Normally, I would not expect a bishop to deliberately start something so destructive in his diocese."

"I thought I explained my motivations," Holland said defensively. "I needed to show the young priests — and the native sons — that they could count on due process from me."

"But you were anything but judicial in making the decision to go forward with this. You admit you were angry and determined to get Hogan and the others like him, right?" The monk raised his eyebrows. "You might want to think about your real motives, or at least what other motives, were propelling you in this matter."

Holland had been taken by surprise by the monk's criticism of actions that he had attributed to his new-found integrity. Flashes of Jerry's comments came to him. Had he just discovered another way to be self-destructive?

"Now," the monk began. He seemed to have changed gears. "I want us for the present to stay focused on the matter of Jerry."

"I need to tell the story in the way that makes sense to me," Holland retorted.

"Well, when I left you yesterday, I thought you'd decided it was time to talk about Jerry — after being rid of that emotional block? Seemed at the time you'd got past some repression."

Holland hated feeling as he did just then, sulking. He despised sulking and yet it was something he'd been doing a lot of recently. It was a weapon of the powerless, he'd read somewhere — pathetic! Grow up, he scolded himself.

"I'm sorry," he told the monk. "I guess I'm just too ready to take offense, childish this fear of criticism."

"So, tell me why I'm reading about this case from long ago?" The monk asked.

Holland could detect no change in the man's expression. Unrelenting little bastard, he muttered to himself. Get over it, he cautioned himself. You're not a child and he's not your parent.

"You'll just have to be patient," Holland looked the monk in the eye. "I'm getting to the crux of the matter but none of that would make any sense without knowing the context. Otherwise, you'd have no more understanding of the situation than those reporters you've been reading. I'll give you the whole story and you can judge for yourself when you've read it."

"And this is going to happen when?" The monk's face betrayed no emotion that Holland could detect.

"You can't wait, can you?" Holland teased. Might as well poke him a little, see if there's life there.

The monk smiled a grudging, minimalist smile.

"I've got you hooked," Holland persisted. "You can't stand not knowing what happened."

"All right," the monk conceded. "I really am impatient to hear the rest."

CHAPTER 33

Minerva, California — 1977

THE BISHOP LISTENED with pursed lips as I recounted for him what Johnstone had uncovered. He said nothing but I noticed that his cheeks became flushed in what, from experience of the man, I recognized as anger. He shifted uncomfortably in his chair as I told him about appointing the Committee of Inquiry.

"So what happens now?" He sounded skeptical. I knew him too well to think he would interfere with the legal process once I had set it in motion but, from his reluctant nods as I explained steps of the process, I sensed he wished I had not chosen such an irreversible course.

"Hogan will be notified today by currier of the investigation and he will be ordered to appear before the Committee of Inquiry at a given day and time." I explained

"My God! What a kettle of fish we have here!" He looked at me for a moment then and shook his head slowly. "You know they'll be like jackals after your hide, Jack? They'll want to tear you apart for doing this."

I knew what he meant. There was going to be trouble from the older Irishmen and I would be the lightening rod. An American bishop might be forgiven for taking such a legalistic stance, but one of their own… never! I might as well have joined the Black and Tans or the B Specials.

I hadn't long to wait for the reaction.

The bog-telegraph had obviously flashed the message that Hogan was under investigation, for I had no sooner returned to my office from lunch the following afternoon, than a call was put through to me from The Right Reverend Monsignor Michael A. Breen.

Micky Breen presided over a large and very wealthy parish in the south part of the city. Athough we had no Deaneries as such in Minerva, he enjoyed the status of quasi-Dean, ward-boss, or godfather, to a whole clique of older Irish priests: *primus inter pares* — but definitely *primus*. Many had been taken in over the years by his old country graciousness and charm, only to discover that both could be turned on and off at will. As a young man he'd been something of a scholar and, at a time when graduate degrees were a rarity in a small diocese like Minerva, he had brought masters degrees in both Philosophy and English Literature to his work in the diocesan high school. His tenure as Superintendent of Schools in the 50's had been a time of unprecedented growth in fund-raising and school building. Breen would be a far more formidable foe than an *amadan* like Hogan. And it was Breen I would be dealing with if he decided to champion Hogan's cause. I shuddered as I picked up the phone.

"Bishop Jack, and is it yerself tat does be in it?"

"'Tis indeed, now. And is it yourself Mickey that's after bein' in it?"

"Aw now. 'Tis indeed! 'Tis indeed!"

"And how are you doin' this lovely day, Monsignor?"

"Aw, sure just fine, just fine — thanks be ta God. And yer foine self, Bishop?"

This pseudo-Irish baloney was standard banter in any dealings I had with this older set, and not to engage in it would be considered uppity — "acting like a bloody Native Son." No worse epithet could be thrown at one of their own.

I knew, *as shoore as ta misht do be upon ta bog*, that the son-of-a-bitch had already heard about "poor Hogan's trouble" — and that's how his criminal act would be characterized by his supporters.

"And what can I be doin' for yourself the day, Monsignor?"

"Well, actually, Jack, I was wondering if you'd care to stop by our humble little parish on your way home tonight. Maybe we could have a little bite of dinner. Nothing big, at all. Nothing elaborate. Just me and my crew here. Haven't we been atin' bread and wather for weeks now, savin' up our pennies to buy a nice piece of beef against a special occasion like this — havin' our own foine bishop joinin' us at our humble board."

"That sounds fine, Mickey." I tried to sound eager, for I knew he would be weighing and parsing every shadow in my voice.

"I might even root around and lay me hands on a bit of the red to wash it down. Are ye on now for that?"

I had no illusions as to what he had in mind but decided, what the hell! Now or later.

"I'd be delighted," I told him. "Sixish?"

"Aw, sure that will be just grand now. I'll be after seein' you then 'round six."

Even as I hung up I knew he would already be on the phone, telling the rest of the Irish mafia that the first part of the job had gone off smoothly: the meet had been arranged. I would be walking into his trap this very evening and wouldn't springing it on me be a treat. He would of course give them a blow-by-blow afterwards — how he'd flexed his considerable muscle and how I had backed down rather than face his wrath. They may even have been sitting in his study while he was on the phone to me, listening to his end of the little performance. I could just hear him.

"Forgets where he comes from, the little shite. When I'm through with him he'll be singing a different tune."

"Don't you worry your head anymore about this thing," he'd be telling Hogan. "By tomorrow it'll be water under the bridge, so it will."

Everything about St. Finbar's parish spelled affluence: the tree-shaded streets and acres of well-tended park, the expansive ranch-style homes sprawling indulgently across double and triple lots, the Cadillacs, Lincolns and Mercedes. It was the sort of neighborhood where a man might enjoy God's abundance in peace and where the local priest could live like a gentleman.

Breen was a large man, in both height and girth, with florid cheeks, a small raw nose and a great turkey-wattle that lapped over his Roman collar like multicolored candle drippings. His lower face had slid into purple jowls and the whole visage was overhung by his most notable feature, a pair of enormous gray eyebrows — stiff as scrubber wire —that sprayed off in every direction. From beneath these jutting hedges, watery blue eyes peeked out from their deeply recessed caves like hunted wild things. His thinning gray hair he kept aggressively close-cut — flaunting rather than hiding his baldness.

I had always been slightly frightened of him perhaps because his eyes reminded me of my father's — deep-set, pale and watery.

Would he have set a trap for me? Would that whole gang of old men be waiting there to work on me? No! That would not be Breen's style. I fervently hoped my reading of him was right. And when I drove into the parking lot, I was relieved to see only Breen's Buick alongside the low-end cars of the assistants — not another Buick in sight. He would try working on me one-on-one, first.

I swung the truck into the slot next to Micky's shiny, navy blue Electra. He would be watching — so I was careful to park extra close. He would walk two blocks rather than park next to someone and have his paint chipped. I got out and breathed deeply for a moment before I walked up the short path leading to the front door. The door was opened before I was even on the doorstep.

"And, if it isn't His Excellency Jack, and him at the wheel of the episcopal truck?" He was the soul of joviality — fairly beaming with good fellowship — as he greeted me. But, the small watery eyes, mean beneath their wiry bushes, weren't smiling at all.

"It's red alright!" I volunteered.

He pumped my hand then and slapped me on the back as I passed him in the doorway — a great display of welcoming.

He whom I kiss ... that is he. Hold him fast.

In the common room, down the corridor straight ahead, I saw the three assistants awaiting the dinner bell, watching the TV News. Micky steered me off to the right into his study.

"We'll just duck in here for a minute, d'ye see, have a wee taste — the two of us. A drap before dinner never hurt a man." He started fussing-about then, looking for bottles and glasses in the sideboard — as though the performance had not all been fully staged in his mind hours before.

And every word out of my mouth would be retailed verbatim to the brethren. But I was doing well — so far I'd hardly said a thing.

"It'll be ready in about another half hour or so at the most, the dinner. So sit ye down there and I'll put something in yer hand in a sec."

I sat in one of the two wing-back chairs that were staged on either side of the elaborate fireplace and took in the room while he continued to fiddle with the glasses. Though we were in California's Central Valley, the study was more fitted to an Irish parochial house of the Thirties or Forties: a handsome fireplace of Connemara marble overhung by a mantelpiece of Irish oak; walnut paneled walls inset with bookshelves that were filled with impressive leather-bound volumes — so perfect they had "Interior Decorator" written all over them. Flames leaping off gas logs created an impression of a fire — it was at least eighty-five degrees outside. I was frankly surprised he would stoop that low.

"And what'd ye be havin' now, tae wet yer Lordship's whistle?"

I found it hard to enter into the spirit of bullshitting with him, knowing what was sure to follow. I said I'd have a scotch and water.

"Arragh, isn't it too much water that's in it as it is?"

He poured two generous drinks, baptizing mine slightly before handing it to me.

"Oi'll drink it just as God in his ineffable wisdom made it." The Paddy-the-Oirishman bit was annoying me — I wanted to throw the drink at him and leave, maybe go have a pizza. He took the other wingback and raised his glass.

"*Slainte!*" We agreed in toast. I was not a regular whiskey drinker and had forgotten how fast it could work its magic on me. Without thinking, I had taken a substantial swallow and could already feel the spreading warmth relax my body. If I'm to keep my wits about me, I thought, I'd better take it easy with the whiskey. My Manhattan fiasco came to mind.

"A good rule: never trust a priest pouring you a drink," the Bishop had told me after that one. It was an even more important rule for a bishop I was discovering.

I could see Mickey bracing himself. Was he maybe gauging the anesthetic's effect before getting down to business, like in the dentist's chair? Do you feel that, now? Is the lip numb yet? I wouldn't put it past him.

He coughed and leaned toward me in front of his phony flames.

"Jack…" he began. "We need to talk." The eyes peered out at me intently from their caves — none of the stage Irishman about him at all now.

"Something very serious is happening and I think you know what I'm referring to."

I had hardly said a word since coming into the room and the weight of my silence was forcing him to carry the conversation. That was fine with me — I wasn't interested in making things easy for him.

"We need to talk, you and I," he repeated, motioning with his finger back and forth between us, just in case I was in any doubt who it was he meant.

I would be patient and behave with as much judicial restraint as I could muster. This entailed setting the excellent single malt on the side table, lest under its seductive influence I might say what was on my mind.

"I'm not sure I follow?" I was being deliberately obtuse, but then isn't that what being judicial was all about?

"I'm speaking about what has happened over there in St. John's." He was keeping himself under tight rein but his face had turned redder and his voice taken on an edge. "It's only too well you know what I'm talking about, Jack. Don't go playing that coy stuff — not with old Micky Breen here!"

"If it's what I think you're talking about, there isn't anything I can say about the matter, Monsignor."

He straightened himself up in the chair then, lining his spine up against the high back as though recoiling from what I was telling him. I thought I'd best give him the official reason why I couldn't talk to him — maybe he could use it with the others.

"If you've heard something from someone who isn't bound by official confidentiality in the matter, that's one thing, but, as you yourself well know, I'd be the last person allowed to discuss a legal matter that's before the tribunal."

"Now don't be like that!" He sputtered and rubbed the air vigorously with his hand — to erase from it every trace of what I had just said. "Where are you off to with all this folderol about, 'legal matters' and 'tribunals' and such? Aren't the two of us talking here about something that's just between the priests and nobody else?" He was leaning forward now to bring the full brunt of his frowning eyebrows to bear on me. I managed to hold my tongue and, after an uncomfortable pause, he kept on grinding.

"And shouldn't things like that be settled as they have always been settled in the past, man-to-man, in private? A man has a right to his privacy, after all, hasn't he?"

"Well that would be fine in some cases." I agreed. I wasn't quite sure whether I should even go any further with explanations. But I thought — idiot that I was — maybe Breen deserved to be given a rationale he could promulgate to the others.

"Look, Monsignor." I began in as reasonable a tone as I could manage. "I can concede that if this were something that had happened man-to-man, 'in private,' as you say, it might very well be settled that way: man-to-man, in private. But then, what you're talking about here, as you know, did not happen that way at all now, did it?"

Breen, as far as I could make out, was genuinely puzzled by what I had just said and it was then I realized that Hogan hadn't told him half the story.

"Any time, Monsignor, that a priest incites a delegation of laity to storm the Chancery demanding the removal of another priest, the matter has got way past private, man-to-man issues. Don't you agree?"

Breen, though taken aback by this revelation, was undeterred.

"Look, Jack, maybe I don't know all the details — all the little ins and outs, of this matter. Never mind all that." He waved away as trivialities — banished like pesky gnats — the facts of the case.

"Jack, they've made you a bishop and we're all of us very proud that one of our own boys finally got all the way to the top." He paused and took out a pack of Camels and lighted one. I could taste it and feel the lovely fullness of it as I watched him inhale the first deep draught. I wasn't carrying any but I'd die before asking him for one. He was looking at me intently all the while through the curling smoke, his beady little animals darting about assessing me from their hedge-caves, appraising me, smelling out the chinks in my defenses.

"You haven't really been one of us much, socially though, have you?" He waved his hand in dismissal, tracing smoke trails in the air as he did so. "Aloof, like. Aye, a bit aloof, I'd call it." He took in another deep draw that swelled his chest for an instant before he blew the smoke out forcefully in my direction. I watched him and said nothing. He seemed to be staring now at something in the ornamental grate of the fireplace. I thought for a minute he might spit into it like the old men up at my grandfather's place, straddling their kitchen chairs. I wondered if gas logs sizzle like oak when spittle hits them.

"But the fact remains you're one of us and we're very proud of where you've got to." He looked up from under the eyebrows and made a patting motion with both hands as though keeping down some undesirable thoughts about me. "We'd all of us hate it though, if you used this new authority of yours to destroy one of the hardest working priests in this diocese."

I bit my tongue.

He braced his back against the high chair back so that he was drawn up to his fullest height again. Posturing, he was an impressive bull indeed. He shook his big head slowly and sadly from side to side so vigorously that his under chins swung about wildly like a luffed sail.

"A better priest this diocese never saw." He pointed at me with his crooked index finger and thrust his jaw out aggressively. "No sir! Not a better priest!" More head shaking. "And what that man did for the people of that parish. My God! Practically built that plant over there in St. John's single-handed. And the place so poor... wouldn't feed a mouse. For years, couldn't afford to keep an assistant to help him with the load."

I sat there and looked at him. There was nothing for me to say but keeping silent was becoming more difficult every second. I had to walk a fine line: to be unyielding, giving no false hope that I might relent in my decision regarding Hogan, while at the same time being sympathetic to the well intentioned loyalty of the many old Irishmen who'd truly been the backbone of the diocese.

"I understand Monsignor." I began. Walk that line, I cautioned myself. Be friendly — sympathetic even — but watch it. Do not open the door to hope, it's what Breen will be looking for. "I know how deeply you feel about your friend and I admire that in a man." I paused and stared into the fireplace — two can play at that game. I gazed into the silly gas flame and waited for about ten interminable seconds before continuing.

"No doubt about it, Monsignor Hogan has been a very hard worker." I looked over at Breen and shook my head a few times, sadly. "Has a lot to show for the years, as you point out." I paused again briefly before adding, "Very sad."

I stood up then suddenly. I was taking a page from Johnstone's book: the unexpected move. I could see the confusion on Breen's face as I began to walk slowly towards the door. "I don't think, Monsignor, that I should be sitting here drinking your whiskey while you're lobbying me about a matter that's before me in the diocesan court."

If I had struck him across the face he could not have looked more taken aback. He sat and stared up at me — speechless. Before he could find his voice, for I knew he would before long, I added. "I suggest we change the subject right away or join the others in the common room."

"Well I'll be damned!" His tone was ripe with sarcasm and his glare so full of menace as he raised himself slowly to his feet that I thought he was going to attack me physically.

"You really have forgotten who you are and where you've come from!" He thrust his large head at me so that his face was no more than a few feet from mine as he spat out the words. His half-closed eyes pulled tight furrows into his brow. He wagged the slabs of purple jowl ominously and a large nicotine-stained forefinger came within an inch of poking my chest.

"Look here you little shite…" He squeezed the words out through clenched teeth, flecks of foam forming at the corners of his lipless mouth. The finger didn't touch me but when I looked down at it pointedly he let the hand fall to his side.

Though filled with a terrible rage he was still not stupid. I had noticed the slight tremor in the finger before it dropped — Micky was getting old.

I began walking towards the door but he put himself directly in my path.

"Stand aside, Monsignor."

"I have a message for you." He stuck his chin out defiantly as though he might attempt to block my way. I was his height — maybe an inch taller — and twenty years younger, so I could have forced my way past him. But, how seemly would that be, a bishop getting in a fist fight with one of the senior pastors of the diocese? The Bishop would probably be amused when he heard about it. Breen stood there, a wall, determined to stop me long enough to deliver his message whether I liked it or not.

"We had a meeting here today in St. Finbar's," he began.

Hardly news to me, that.

"It was about this matter of Paddy Hogan, *Bishop*." Had the title sounded slightly mocking on his lips, or was it just my paranoia? I decided to let him say his piece.

"Many of the senior priests and I met here and we discussed this whole business…"

I interrupted him, "And you discussed it without benefit of the facts, it appears." I had guessed right: they had all sat around while their champion had set the trap — a trap baited with roastbeef.

"They are very disappointed in how you've handled this whole matter so far." He glowered and wagged the wattles and jowls solemnly, raising and lowering those bushy brows in what was intended as an intimidating display. I was past being intimidated by his theatrics.

"But, as disturbed and angry as they were, they agreed that I should try and talk some sense into you, man-to-man. If calm-headed reasoning worked we could all put this unfortunate business behind us and get on with the Lord's work."

His tone had become appeasing for an instant as he held out the sunny prospect of a life beyond this turmoil.

"But they were adamant." He wagged his head gravely in warning, glaring at me lest I mistake reasonableness for weakness. "Adamant, that we wouldn't plead with you like we were beggars. Never!"

"And what might they have meant by that, Monsignor?"

"It means we know more about you than you would ever want made public." His yellowed finger wagged in my direction and his jaw jutted with aggression.

"And believe you me, me foine bucko, if you go ahead with this 'canonical trial' of yours; torturing this good friend of ours, we'll have your episcopal ass before it's over."

"Do you mind moving out of my way, Monsignor Breen." I said in a low menacing voice. He moved out of my path then and stood at a safe distance, one arm resting on the mantelpiece.

"That is my solemn promise," he pronounced, running a hand through the stubbly remains of his hair. "You will regret the very day you ever set your foot in this diocese, boi." He pointed his finger at me in a most threatening way. I continued to stare at him and let a faint smile play on my lips for I knew that nothing would annoy him more than retaining my composure.

"We'll fucking destroy you, you little jumped-up shite, so we will!" His voice had become more shrill the more vicious the threats.

It was not at all subtle! I had expected a threat of some sort but thought a man of Breen's intelligence might have concealed the blade more skillfully. This had been more of a saber slash — crude — more Hogan's style.

"Well!" I said in my firmest voice: one I was told could be coldly intimidating — 'psychopathic' was how Jerry had once characterized it. "You can go back now to those who sent you and tell them that you have failed in your assignment. I wonder how many of those men knew when they delegated you that you would attempt to blackmail me in their name — putting their careers on the line. Your own, as you must know, is now hanging by a very slender thread."

He seemed rooted in place, now that I had raised my voice to him.

"You do not intimidate me and you will never intimidate me into any course of action, Monsignor. Just watch."

As I left the room, I glanced over my shoulder at Breen before slowly closing the door behind me — he was bent over, leaning on the mantelpiece, staring into his futile flames. He would soon have to get on the phone and report the failure of his diplomacy to his admirers. I wondered how that prospect was sitting with him.

I poked my head into the common room and waved to the three young priests still awaiting their dinner and still watching the TV. Already they would have heard all the gory details of the case on their grapevine. The damned Chancery leaked like a sieve and news, particularly scandalous news, traveled out from it at the speed of light.

They would, of course, have known about the meeting too and its purpose — nothing is a secret in a rectory either — and would have been speculating about the outcome. Of course Breen would have persuaded me, they'd guess. After all, they'd say, wasn't Holland part of the power structure? What could any young man expect from this diocese? Junior priests, particularly the young Americans, didn't stand a chance. And now, with the Paddys having their own tame bishop…

Once out in the parking lot, I stood a moment by the truck enjoying the warmth of the evening sun on my face — Breen's room had felt like a meat locker despite his decorative fire. My cigarettes were on the dashboard. At last I could have the smoke I had been longing for. I lighted the Camel and drew in a soothing chest-full, then let it stream out with exquisite slowness taking with it the tensions that were knotting my stomach. I could have used that great Glen malt I had left sitting by the fireplace. I leaned against the open door of the cab, watching for a long moment three boys in Catholic school uniforms playing catch alongside the church wall. I was careful not to appear in any hurry to leave, for I knew he would be watching from his study window for any sign that his intimidation was having effect. I walked around Micky's Buick then, deliberately provoking him, peered inside, shading my eyes as though examining it for something in particular. That would bother him simply because he wouldn't understand its purpose. He was the paranoid sort who would spend hours trying to puzzle out something like that. As I started my truck I became aware of a peculiar sense of relief — the relief of knowing for certain that the battle lines had been clearly drawn.

My original plan had been to meet Jerry after my dinner with Breen, but, since I had been done out of my roast-beef dinner, I phoned him from a gas station and arranged to meet for yet another pizza in our favorite Roaring 20's joint. I always kept a tee shirt in my truck for just such quick-change acts, the better to merge into the beer and pizza crowd. The bootlegger's decor matched my mood better anyway than an ersatz Irish parochial house that evening. Bullet riddled black sedans and the Thompson submachine guns décor seemed downright friendly after dealing with that cartel of priests. The pizza would have a thin crisp crust, the garlic would welcome me from half a block away, the pitcher of weak beer would be frosty and Jerry would be there, sitting across from me as usual, listening. I was very attached to my secular rituals. I found them more soothing than the church's liturgy. That pizza joint was a safer place by far than any rectory I could visit in Minerva that evening.

Over beer and triangles of stringy cheese, I filled Jerry in on the case and violated all the judicial constraints I had pretended to be bound by when talking to Breen. He looked at me throughout the story and at many points seemed on the point of interrupting to add something, but didn't. As I neared the end and was describing my confrontation with Breen, I was surprised to see tears welling up in his eyes.

"I know!" I said. "It must be hell for that poor kid."

Typical of Jerry, I was thinking, feeling for the victim in all this while the rest of us were fussing about rights and wrongs.

Jerry seemed too caught up in the emotion to even speak. I couldn't stand the awkward silence so I rambled on, vamping, till he could find his voice: "Can you imagine what a letdown the priesthood must be for him in his first year." I said. "I'm sure he got into it with some idealized picture of how priests …"

"That's not what I'm crying about." He wiped his eyes and seemed only slightly embarrassed by the tears.

"It's not?"

"No! God …" He looked at me and rolled his eyes dramatically as though I was being very dumb.

"What? What?" I prompted. "Don't do that 'tolerant-drama-queen bit'."

"It's you! I'm scared for you," he said. I must have looked puzzled for he went on to explain: "You know they're going to destroy you, don't you? And it's my fault you've got yourself into this mess. If it wasn't for me and my bright ideas you'd never have taken on this damned thing. I should have helped you that day, helped you to refuse it."

"You're out of your friggin' tree!" I told him with what little bravado I could call upon. His prediction of disasters-to-come hadn't helped any. It had only confirmed the paranoid thoughts I had been trying so hard to banish.

"Look!" I said in my most demanding voice. "Look at it from my point of view, for just a minute." That had got his attention. "This is the first thing I've ever done in my entire friggin' life that could maybe change something for the better. Right?"

He was looking at me, still crying and shaking his head, pitifully.

"Hey, Jerry, for Christ's sake…!" I decided that serious wasn't the way to go with him just then. "What the hell! I've never looked good in that episcopal drag anyway: the lacy nighties and red frocks … So, I go out with a bang, where's the harm? Fuck it!"

He was sniffling still but he held up his hand for me to be quiet.

"But I was the one talked you into it -- when you wanted to pass on it," he said.

"Yeah, so what? Remember that summer you spent with Chavez saying masses out in the strawberry fields and the vineyards and what not, and you and Carney yellin' 'Huelga! Huelga!' at those Mexican farmworkers from his plane over the Central Valley fields? Well I spent that summer shuffling papers in the Chancery — when I wasn't off in some motel getting laid." He was going to interrupt but I silenced him with my hand.

"And when that delegation of rich Catholic farmers came in demanding that the Bishop muzzle his troublemaking priests who were stirring up 'their Mexicans,' I was the one drafted that letter you all got, telling you to, 'cease and desist under penalty of censure.'"

"I never knew what that meant?" Jerry interjected.

"Neither did I. It sounded so official while being completely meaningless legally — the old man thought it struck the perfect note."

Jerry was quiet.

"What?" I asked but he still said nothing — just stared at me shaking his head sadly. After a long silence I continued.

"Carney invited me to go with him on one of those flights — I never told you. We'd both had too much to drink and I agreed to go but then called him in the morning and begged off. 'Lace-pantie liberal,' he called me that day."

I signaled the gun moll to bring another pitcher of beer. Neither of us had eaten more than a few bites of the pizza.

"A crazy man!" Jerry shook his head remembering Jim Carney, dead of a heart attack at forty. "That old yellow crop duster, farting and revving, yawing and rolling, and me hanging half-out, yelling through a bull horn and the farmers shaking their fists and threatening us with shotguns. He'd been so low over this one vineyard north of Merced we had vines trailing from the wheels."

We sat quiet then, each with his thoughts for a long moment.

"I'd have killed for his passion… or yours… a passion for anything." I said. "God! I envied that crazy bastard, even when I heard he'd died, that he'd had the balls to do something like that in his life. Anyhow… Maybe I can do this much at least."

Jerry had been stretching the cheese up past his shoulder to see when it would snap — he seemed to have little taste for eating it.

"I wish I could have pounded the shite out of your father." He blurted out with unexpected fury.

"Huh?" I replied. Where had that come from?

"I was watching you just now as you were talking. I've often watched you through the years and it makes me sad, looking at you."

"Huh?"

"At times I've watched Jack Holland nearly come alive; come almost all the way out into the sunlight. Times, I've seen a joyful enthusiasm start to bubble up in you. Then I've watched it stall and fall back to earth, like a fountain that seems about to burst into a magnificent plume but every time collapses, discouraged."

"What's all that about my father?"

"He's standing there still, off to the side, his big stick poised, waiting outside your shell ready to beat down anything authentic that bubbles up in you. You could've been so much more if you'd only taken the risk." Jerry looked angry as he said this.

"Well, maybe this time I've jumped off the cliff." I tried to sound breezy.

"I am scared for you," he said.

I looked up at the unashamed tears that were streaming down his cheeks. I reached over and very briefly let my fingers touch the back of his hand.

"Don't worry," I told him. "I'll be fine."

CHAPTER 34

Minerva, California — 1977

NOTHING MUCH HAPPENED on the case for the next few days except that the Committee of Inquiry sent me a notarized document saying it had held its first meeting. It had considered the submissions and was arranging to interview members of St. John's parish, clergy and laity, early the following week.

It had been a tough week and I was looking forward to Saturday morning's leisurely routine: reading the paper front to back, drinking multiple cups of coffee, dawdling over a late breakfast in the rectory dining room. I was pouring my first cup of coffee when Mick Cassidy placed the *Minerva Chronicle* in front of me.

"Oi don't tink you're goin' ta loike tat article tere!" He had folded the paper and pointed emphatically to a story below the fold on the front page.

BISHOP APPROVES GAY LIFESTYLE FOR PRIESTS.

The article described how my defense of priests who were "leading the homosexual lifestyle" was confusing and frustrating to the good laity and priests of Minerva. As evidence of this widespread confusion the reporter quoted several prominent lay folk. By some strange coincidence all of those quoted had been in the delegation seeking Pastorelli's ouster. A Mrs. Brachman it appeared, was "extremely frustrated" by my arrogance in defending homosexuals. A Mr. Bright was quoted at some length describing how "shocked and confused" he'd been, "... at hearing such abominations coming from the bishop's own lips."

I have seldom used anybody else's lips.

A Mr. Sweeney, self-styled lifelong Catholic, had been terribly confused by my new approach to morality -- not at all the sort of morality he and his wife had tried to inculcate into their children. I couldn't remember the morality of homosexuality even coming up for discussion that night. But then, what did facts have to do with anything?

And the *coup de gras* was dealt by none other than the saintly Monsignor Michael Breen himself and delivered in his best passive-aggressive style.

When asked for his opinion Monsignor Breen seemed reluctant to disagree openly with his Bishop but the good man shook his head sadly as he conceded, "I'm only a lowly parish priest and I'm not much good at all this new theology and such..." The good-natured Pastor smiled and waved to a group of children preparing for their First Holy Communion. "But it seems to me, at least," he continued, "that some of the old values are still worth defending. That's why I've devoted the whole of my life to the values of the Gospel."

The article concluded by remarking that Bishop Holland could not be reached for comment.

They hadn't tried very hard. I'd been in the Chancery all Friday morning and at a city parish doing Confirmations in the afternoon.

"Ah, sure Oi wouldn't worry me head a bit about some auld story like tat now, Jack." Cassidy was trying to console me.

"Sure ta hoors'd write anyting comes inta teir friggin' heads, so tey would!"

The Bishop called me while I was still at breakfast. He'd seen the article too and had already called the *Chronicle*'s city editor to correct the record. God help him!

I recognized the article for what it was: Mickey Breen firing a shot across my bow, using his press contacts to do his dirty work. There would be much tittering in many Minerva rectories at his cleverness -- sticking one to that upstart of a bishop. I had to be careful even around Cassidy — though not one of the Breen-Hogan gang, he was sure to be pumped by them on my reaction.

Breen had me over a barrel for the time being. He could say pretty much what he liked about me in public, while I was prohibited from divulging anything in my own defense without violating confidentiality. But if he thought such a tactic would soften me up, he didn't know me well at all. Though I have never considered myself the least bit courageous, there was one thing that never failed to stir my soul and that was defiance in the face of opposition. Stubbornness, or as my father had called it, "thrawnness," was as close to courage as I got, but when triggered it left courage in the dust — and prudence too, more often than not.

Saturday mornings, with the Chancery closed for the weekend, had become my time for catching up on the rivers of paperwork that flowed over my desk each week; a time when I could have three or four uninterrupted hours at my desk without phone calls or lunch engagements. But that Saturday was destined to be different.

I had already swung my truck into the parking lot before I spotted the gaggle of reporters lying in wait for me there. To back out at that point was unthinkable. For one fleeting moment, I hoped they might not recognize me in jeans and plaid shirt, but I had no sooner parked the truck than they were on me like flies, all talking at the same time; shouting and shoving, each one trying to get my attention. I felt sorry for them. It was a hard life, being a reporter's, scrambling every day for new stories, for a byline — no time to be polite. I was meat on the hoof. A swarm of questions came at me.

Had I really said I approved of priests leading a homosexual lifestyle?

Did I think homosexuality was a sin?

The questions flew so thick and fast I could hardly distinguish one from the other — let alone answer any of them.

Could a story about Jack Holland's opinions rate this amount of coverage? I wondered about this as I was trailing these eager youngsters after me and shoving them ahead of me towards the Chancery door. Or had they, maybe, been tipped off that there was more to this story than had come to light thus far?

They were being so damned persistent, with their microphones and questions. There was even a crew from a TV channel taking pictures of what I'm sure would be described as, "...the furtive-looking bishop," attempting to slink into his office. If I had known they'd be there I'd have dressed up a bit for the Eleven O'Clock News.

"Is it true, you think the Church's views on homosexuality are outdated?"

"Bishop, do you feel that a gay man should be ordained a priest?"

"Would you ordain a gay man?"

I had pushed my way almost to the Chancery door, trying to be tolerant and as good humored as possible with them. And I could probably have fled then into the safety of the office had not something in me balked at leaving them standing out there, frustrated; their legitimate questions still unanswered.

Truth? *Veritas.* What is truth? *Verbum Dei. Verbum Hollandis?* God is Truth.

Why shouldn't I answer their questions? It was cowardly, not answering. These were valid questions regardless of the motives behind the asking. What are you going to do? Run away and hide?

To their great surprise, I'm sure, instead of opening the door I turned around on the top step and faced them.

"Good!" I said. I was a little out of breath. "I thought for a minute there I wasn't going to make it past all of you. I'm not in as good a shape as you press people. Now…" I caught my breath and looked at each of them. They were all young — men and women in almost equal numbers — in their twenties or early thirties. Perhaps they would have more discernment than the old hacks in fedoras pecking at their Royals back in the city room — the old men Breen had in his pocket.

"Those were very good questions you were putting to me just now and if you could let me have them one at a time, I think I owe it to you — and to the Church for that matter — to answer them as honestly as I can."

I held up my hand before the barrage could start.

"One limitation! As you know, I cannot talk about anything privileged or confidential. I should, at the very least though, answer any questions you have about my views on moral theology and canon law."

"Bishop! They say you approve of gay men being ordained priests?" The question came from a young woman from the morning paper.

"They do, do they? I never recall having taken a position on this in public nor even addressing the issue." She was ready with a follow up, but I kept on going, again holding up my hand to silence them. "But I have no intention of avoiding the question." They were writing furiously, getting far more than they ever expected — never having met such a fool, most likely.

"As regards sexuality and the priesthood, the Church's only requirement is that a man remain celibate after he takes on the obligation. I recall no law in the Code of Canon Law stating the kind of sex he is to abstain from. A priest is required to lead a celibate life and abstain from sex. Period. That's all it says." I held up my hand again to stem the waves of follow-ups.

"The Church has not, to my knowledge, devised any test to establish sexual orientation of the candidate for ordination — nor has anyone else that I've heard of. The law simply is that he abstain from sex."

"Bishop! If it was discovered that a priest in this diocese was engaging in gay sexual activity what should happen to him, in your opinion?" Another woman reporter asked.

"The same as happens to a priest who engages in heterosexual sexual activity."

"No more?" She inquired.

"Why would it call for more?"

"Are you saying then that it makes no difference whether the man is heterosexual or homosexual as long as he is celibate?"

"Difference? Do you mean psychologically? Or spiritually? Or what? Each person brings his own gifts and background to the priesthood. I have no way of knowing who is a homosexual and who is heterosexual. If a man is a good priest and doing the work of the Church, how would anyone know his sexual orientation?"

"But if a man is obviously homosexual, Bishop?"

"Obviously? I don't know what you consider 'obvious' homosexual characteristics. Who has the definitive book on this? Are all effeminate men, for example, to be declared homosexuals? Are only effeminate men homosexuals? I think most of us know both these propositions to be silly assumptions — no educated person today would defend statements of that sort."

"Do you think the Church is behind the times in matters of sexuality?"

"The Church has its views on moral theology and they are not those of the present age in America, perhaps. But then, the opinions of this present age may be rejected by the next age that's just around the corner. The Church is attempting to be faithful to what it sees as it's mission: raising the moral standards, inviting us to aim higher."

"Would you ordain a gay man to the priesthood?" A young man from the TV News asked.

"I answered that already, I believe. I really do have to go and catch up on a few things."

"One last question, Bishop?" The woman reporter for the local daily seemed urgent in her request and I nodded to her.

"Do you think the Church should ordain women to the priesthood?"

I was on thin ice here. My personal opinion differed totally from that of Rome. But, it was yet another question that deserved an answer.

"You probably know that the Church's rule is that only men should be ordained priests, because, as they remind us, Jesus picked only men to be his Apostles. As a bishop of the Church I am expected to be faithful to this rule."

I was going to stop at that point — I had walked the fine line and not put a foot wrong — but to stop there would be cowardly. I would despise myself for it afterwards. I was tired of being cowardly and the dangers of walking that fine line were invigorating. I knew when I opened my mouth next I would be stepping off a cliff, hoping to fly. The reporters were silent — watching Humpty Dumpty do himself in with his big mouth.

"Should that rule be changed at some future time?" I asked rhetorically — charging ahead. "I think this is a very important question that will call for an answer in the near future. If that rule were to be changed, I for one, would be delighted to ordain women and to serve alongside them in the priesthood. I know many women who would make very fine priests."

The reporter scribbled furiously, having been given more red meat than she had ever counted on getting, I'm sure. I nodded to them then and this time made my escape through the door, into the safety of the Chancery — safe, from the reporters or from my own big mouth? Hard to tell which was the more dangerous.

They had seemed a polite enough lot, for reporters, and I felt confident, as I worked at my desk that afternoon, that I had acquitted myself well enough.

There was a snippet from my impromptu press conference on the TV News at Eleven, with a short piece on the national controversy over the ordination of gays. They had done a fair job with it and I felt sure the others would too. I had done a good thing, talking to them. Lulled by these reassuring delusions, I was totally unprepared for the page one headline in the *Sunday Chronicle*.

BISHOP WOULD ORDAIN GAYS AND WOMEN

The story was somewhat less sensational than the headline — if one were to bother reading it. But I knew the damage had been done by the headline.

I don't know how I got through three masses that morning — I remember little of them or what I had said in my homilies. But, when I had finished, I was in no mood for dawdling over a leisurely breakfast and reading any more of the Sunday papers. I was off newspapers. I called Jerry and arranged to meet at his rectory in about an hour. We'd go for a drive and I didn't much care where, so long as it was out of town.

The phone was ringing off the hook — reporters from everywhere, titillated by the story. I left a message on my answering machine saying I would be available for comment the following morning in the Chancery.

"Be Jazus, Boi, ye've fair pissed in the chalice this time! You, holding a friggin' press conference? As if you weren't in enough trouble already."

Consolation, from my best friend as he accelerated away from his parish yard where I had parked my all-too-recognizable truck. Reaching over, he nudged my shoulder and smiled.

"Fuck 'em! If they can't take a joke! Right?"

I couldn't help laughing. Jerry, feeding me my own line.

"What do you think? Didn't I make a right ejit out of myself telling them what I really thought?"

He chuckled and kept driving.

"I mean, I could have handled them a lot better if I'd just trotted out the party line. Right?"

He nodded.

"I should have stopped myself before I took on that question about women? Right?'

He shrugged and kept staring at the road ahead — more than I thought strictly necessary for driving. I knew Jerry too well.

"I'll call up the newspapers and have them talk to you, say it's all your idea, this truth-telling."

He grinned and cut his eyes at me briefly, then went back to staring at the road. I was becoming annoyed with this inscrutable act.

"So, does this God of yours — this God of Truth — show up in the last reel and *smite mine enemies*?" I asked.

He said nothing and we drove in silence for what seemed ages. I had begun thinking about the morning again and the Chancery tomorrow and the phone calls.

He spoke without looking at me. "Do you sometimes blame me for all this?"

"Well …" I began, but he cut me off.

"I wasn't the one did the politicking and ass-kissing that got you chosen, honey." He was laughing but I could feel sarcasm that wasn't typical of him. "Here! Take me! Take me!" He was mocking me.

I sat and watched him, surprised and hurt at his tone.

"It was embarrassing, watching you suck-up. Friggin' pathetic!" He added.

Something was bothering him, from the unaccustomed edge in his humor and it wasn't my sucking-up — that was old news.

"So?" I demanded. "How long are you going to keep this up, pretending you're just being funny? Tell me what's bothering you or take me back to my frigging truck. I'd rather drive into the fucking foothills by myself than be pecked to death with this passive-aggressive shite."

He didn't answer right away, but kept staring at the road. I could see the muscles in his cheek rippling.

"You're just trying, every way you can think of, to get yourself into trouble — that's what's bothering me."

"What? The 'press conference,' as you call it?"

"You could have seen that coming." He was sounding pouty now. "You've stopped giving a damn. What role are you playing this week? Samson pulling the temple down around his ears?"

I shrugged. There had indeed been something fatalistic in my recent behavior — starting with the action I had initiated against Hogan.

"Is it this heretic-bishop act, Holland the iconoclast, that's gone to your head?" He was angry at me — scolding and sobbing at the same time.

"Ah! Now I get it." I said. His superior attitude was annoying me. "I wasn't supposed to take that, 'Truth is the road leading to God,' stuff so much to heart? Is that what you're saying? Not something to go practicing — more like a joke, maybe — a joke that I didn't get? Is that what you're telling me? That I'm too stupid to be turned loose with a dangerous weapon like Truth? A child running with scissors, I could hurt myself?"

He wasn't saying anything but tears were running down his cheeks.

"And don't act as though you thought it would turn out differently." I told him.

"Come on! It wasn't that hard talking you into those fancy robes — closet drag queen that you are." His voice had softened and he had laughed through the sobs as he said this. He wiped his eyes. "I was feeling a bit guilty, though, when I read the papers this morning and yesterday — if that's any consolation to you. It's hardly Golgotha though, is it?"

"Not yet it isn't, but it's going to get worse, you know that? So keep your hopes up and your makeup dry."

"I have to admit I was proud of you when I read what you had actually told the reporters."

"They want to destroy me, I think." I said.

"You've committed the one unforgivable sin: you've said what you really think about things — it will cause you a lot of trouble but it may also save your soul."

"I've stepped in it every time I've put a foot down the last few days."

"You pulled the covers off one of the darlin' auld Micks and exposed him as, not only a liar and slanderer, but a queer, into the bargain. And, for that, boyo, they'll have your ass. Remember Ham? He exposed Noah's shame, they say, and look what happened to him?"

"God sent him to Africa, as far as I recall. And isn't that where Praxitelensis is anyway? What more can they do to me?"

"I just wish you hadn't provoked such a mean hive of bastards." He wiped his eyes and his cheeks. "Never mind me," he sniffed. "You're doing the only honest thing anyone could do in the circumstances, going ahead with the investigation."

"I wish to God I'd had the nerve to quit back in seminary, could have got a job, maybe traveling for a distillery or fixing cars, something useful…"

"You'd have been no good at anything practical like that." He was laughing and sobbing.

"And I'm such a raging success as a bishop?"

We were driving through the Central Valley farm country. Dusky women huddled at sorting machines in the cruel sun; brown-eyed children playing tag around dusty cars alongside the grassy verge. Trucks high-stacked, wobbling over the rutted field — wooden boxes with gaudy labels — fruits and vegetables. A different fragrance every mile: cantaloupe, peaches, lettuce and broccoli, strawberries and pears — fertile mothers all around.

What had I done that was useful since I'd weighed out bluestone and soda for the potato farmers behind my father's shop?

"I don't give a shite what they do to me," I protested aloud. "Who the fuck needs bishops anyway?"

Jerry nodded and pointed his finger at me. "You've got that right!"

"Who the fuck needs priests, either, for that matter?"

"So, now that we've got our values straightened out, where'd you like to eat?"

"Let's sit at the counter in Vanessi's?"

"And we'll split an order of *saltimbocca* and *canneloni?*"

"And one of their monster banana fritters?"

Jerry, to distract me, started describing some of his wilder cross-dressing esca-pades while he was living in Berkeley — escapades he'd kept from me for fear of my reaction. The "straight" man whose roving hand had detected the penis when they were making-out.

"You'd have thought he'd struck gold, he was so excited. We were stopped alongside the Marina green and this guy is under the dashboard having the time of his life. God! If a cop had seen us…"

I was petrified — just hearing about it. But I said nothing.

And the Halloween he won the "Drag Queen of the Silver Screen," category at the Hookers' Ball and had to do this exhibition waltz, backwards in ball gown and six inch heels, with the butch-lesbian Grand Marshall.

"In front of that whole gaggle of queens and closet gawkers. It was lovely! Truly grand! Ginger Rogers was right: dancing backward in heels is much harder than what Fred was doing."

It was an unusually clear day in The City and as we came across the Bay Bridge the afternoon sun was glistening on the orange towers of the Golden Gate in the distance and reflecting off the flashing windows of the financial district. It was a magic carpet for me.

Another five minutes and we were pulling into the familiar parking lot on Broadway. Problems? Dinner in Vanessi's took care of everything. What problems? To hell with them! What's the worst they can do to me anyway? So what if I'm going to be an out-of-work bishop.

We henched up onto the familiar stools — ringside to the action.

"I'd love to have been a cook," Jerry mused as we drank the glasses of Valpollicello the counter waiter had brought us.

"I've thought that at times too. I'd get bored though, making the same stuff all the time — need a new menu everyday for variety."

We watched the action at the stoves — one of the cooks was coming on to a young woman a few stools down from us.

"He does it with everybody, that son-of-a-bitch!" The same cook had come on to him one night he'd been at the counter in drag. The cook hadn't been faithful to him — he was hurt.

"You can tell to look at him." I suggested.

"Tell what?" Jerry asked and looked over at me.

"He's been suffering from a broken heart."

Jerry punched me. Had there been a momentary delay before he realized I was having him on?

"I've sometimes thought I'd like to open a shop carrying clothes just for drag queens," he said. "A safe place where they could find large sizes and not feel so damned queer."

We were silent for a few minutes and then the counter waiter took our order.

"I think he recognized me." Jerry nudged me, worried.

"Never! Your own mother wouldn't recognize you when you're dressed up."

"I could always say I have this twin sister."

"Forget it!" I said. "About the shop...?"

"Problem with a shop like that, it'd be packed from morning till night, queens trying stuff on and not buying a frigging thing. Once they've strutted a bit and got it out of their system, why buy."

"Still, might be interesting." I was encouraged that he had thought of something other than being a priest. "Think you'd make enough to live on?" I didn't think his future lay in the diocese of Minerva.

What if Breen and those other bastards knew about Jerry? The thought flashed across my mind fully formed — no part of it had ever been in my conscious thinking before that moment. I must have turned pale but no one noticed.

"Might be fun — doing that for a while anyway. I'd call it, 'Ju Ju's Closet.'" He was prattling on about his fantasy career.

"Sound's good, where'd the name come from — Ju Ju?" I tried to keep my mind on what he was excited about. "As in sweets: *bijou, joujou, pou* ...?"

"It's my name on the street, so to speak. "Ju Ju" is what I call myself when I'm dressed. If I were to leave I'd live as that."

"You'll never leave though, will you?" I challenged.

"You're no fun at all tonight!" He elbowed me, calling me back into the escapist mood he had intended for the evening. This was Vanessi's on Broadway Street in San Francisco — Oz.

"When we've had our fritters," he said. "I'll take you over to the Castro, introduce you to some nice boys I know there. They'll have your head set straight before the sun comes up. Make you forget women forever, those boys."

The maestro was finishing our fritters with dollops of whipped cream.

We didn't go to the Castro, but we did drive out to Land's End. He knew I loved to stand by the low wall there and feel the wind, fresh and untainted after it's long flight from the Orient. It was cool and damp against my skin and I could taste the salt kiss of it on my lips and tongue. Tasting the sea, I was a child again, thrilled and terrified by it's power; excited by its immensity. From Bundoran I had seen New York in the waves of Donegal Bay and heard the yellow taxi horns noisy on the Rogey rocks. I would draw the Empire State and the Statue of Liberty in the Irish sand to welcome the Yankee waves, homeless and tempest-tossed — make them feel at home.

Jerry shivered and I realized I was cold too. Without a word we got in the car and headed back along Geary and through the city, home.

CHAPTER 35

Minerva, California — 1977

I HAD BEEN planning to meet with the Bishop anyway that Monday morning but he phoned me even before I went over to say the early mass for the parish nuns. Best we meet and talk at his home rather than in the office, he said. I got through mass on autopilot and took off right afterwards without waiting for breakfast. I was in no mood for small talk with Cassidy or his assistant, Finoocan, that morning.

The old man met me at the door wearing the same dilapidated cassock he had worn around the house all the years I had known him, despite all my hints that he donate it to the trash can. Years of egg yolk and cereal milk had trailed, Pollock-style, over the red buttons that lined the front while the skirts were crusty with dog food and slobber from Calvin, his 15 year-old Basset hound. He had been eating breakfast and without a word waved me into the dining room with his napkin. I joined him at the table, poured myself a cup of nearly-cold coffee and watched his morning toast ritual. In my years as his driver/assistant, I had always wondered at the hypnotic trance he seemed to enter when eating at home. It wasn't that he ate so much — oatmeal, a boiled egg, two slices of wheat toast and coffee. But it took him so damned long to eat it — most of an hour on a good morning — longer when he was stressed.

I noticed that the cloudy film that had been forming for years on his blue eyes seemed to have grown whiter and that the shaky right hand, when he raised his cup, had become shakier in the past year. He had always cut his toast in small pieces, European style, then slathered each small rusk with a heap of Kelleher's marmalade. Now though, he was smearing as much jam on his finger and thumb as on the toast. Pouring his coffee refill, he had so overfilled his cup that it had spilt into the saucer and onto the damask tablecloth before I grasped his hand.

"Damned cataracts," he explained. "One of these days must have them cut off." He smiled sheepishly. "When I don't have company," he winked, "I put one finger into the cup so I'll know when it's near the top."

"I'm company now?"

He reached over and squeezed my arm without saying anything. I was shocked to see how old and gray his skin looked. I had never thought of him dying before that moment.

"Jack, I don't know what to do about all this that's happening." He was staring with his vague cataract-fogged eyes across the room at the dreary painting of a Madonna on the far wall.

"I had a call last night from Archbishop Kelly in San Francisco asking if I needed his help; and then this morning, before I called you, I had this call from the Papal Nuntio, in D C." He paused and shook his head regretfully. "They haven't heard a word in Rome, it seems, about the slander trial and how the whole damned mess got started. Oh no! All he wanted to talk to me about — rattling along in his 'guinea' English — was, 'this a bishops that's a wan a make a womens and a homosesuals a priests. What a for he wan a go talking cont a da teach off a Holy Fata?'"

"So what did you tell him?"

"I tried to tell him that it was all a big misunderstanding started by the newspapers, but he was all wound up about what you told those reporters. Afraid he'll get his tit in a ringer at the Holy Office — or whatever the frig they're calling the Inquisition these days."

The old man looked at me as he continued to slather more marmalade on his fingers. "Jack, you know I'd never for a minute second-guess you, but tell me this one thing: why in God's name did you give those vultures all that ammunition to shoot you with?"

"I was just trying to answer their legitimate questions," I said, knowing even as the words were coming out of my mouth how false it sounded.

He chewed his toast and licked his thumb and forefinger clean of the jam before he looked over at me. Suddenly his eyes didn't look so vague and feeble anymore.

"Don't you bullshit me, Jack Holland." He pointed the wedge-shaped marmalade knife at me for emphasis. "I knew you when you were a young greenhorn not long off the boat, and you wouldn't have been that stupid even then."

He fished in his pocket and took out a battered pack of the Camels he smoked in private when he was stressed. He lighted a cigarette. As an afterthought, I took one from his pack and he lighted mine.

"I thought you'd quit," he nagged.

"Yeah! So had you."

"So?" He grinned as he looked over at me. "Do you want to be a martyr for the cause of change? Is that what you're after? Or are you just bored with this whole unwieldy Rube Goldberg we call the Church?"

I couldn't help laughing. He knew me better than I'd even given him credit for.

"Maybe a bit of both and some other things too," I replied. "I get pissed off that the Church always has to be dragged kicking and screaming into change. Look how long it took them after the Reformation to permit the vernacular. And all those things that were so wrong for so long, suddenly they're OK. Four hundred years from now they'll decide that it's positively virtuous to ordain women and we'll look like a bunch of morons."

He wasn't saying anything.

"It's true though isn't it?" I prompted.

He was nodding and staring off into the corner of the room above the Madonna.

"I never had you pegged as an idealist; never saw you bucking for sainthood."

I was going to respond but he held up his hand to silence me.

"When I got the notion to make you a bishop, it struck me as a very far out idea at the time. I had a laugh to myself when I came up with it. I'd thought about some of the other more likely choices, men who'd never given me any trouble, far better behaved, probably far holier men. I'd look over at you when you'd be driving me around and I'd think to myself, 'Now there's the consummate politician, if ever I saw one.' Sometimes I'd have trouble keeping from laughing, watching your face as I was sounding off about something that I could tell was getting your goat, and you'd just sit there, biting your tongue not to get in an argument with me. I'm right, aren't I?"

"Yeah. I was the politician all right."

"So what in God's name happened to that guy? He'd have made a great bloody bishop! Why in hell did you change him? What's gotten into you anyway?"

"If I told you, you'd be convinced, more than ever, that I'm nuts."

"Try me. Down deep, underneath all this episcopal pomposity, I'm not a total idiot, you know."

I told him about the panic I'd felt when he picked me to be a bishop — even though it was everything the politician in me could have hoped for. I recounted how I'd decided to decline the appointment as too far-fetched, given my spiritual condition. I told him everything: how I doubted Christianity and the Church's usefulness; even told that I doubted the existence of his God. How could I become a bishop while practically a pagan?

Without naming my advisor, I explained then how this man had suggested a way I could reconcile my spiritual emptiness with the role of a bishop: the "Truth as the path to God" hypothesis — how I could represent God by trying to always say the truth.

While I was speaking he continued smoking and sipping his coffee, giving me only the occasional sidelong glance if I were to pause for an instant. I could see he was following what I was saying intently.

He shook his head when I finally stopped talking, as though mystified.

"Well God almighty!" He paused then and gave a slight chuckle. "I never thought I'd see the day a man would get struck down with religion on the road to becoming a bishop." He looked at me then and smiled.

'Felled by the Spirit', my grandmother would have called it. She was a Pentecostal till her dying day, you know — living in a den of papists and her only daughter gone over to the papists too. You didn't know that I was practically a Protestant, did you?" He slurped the rest of his coffee before he continued.

"It's hardly the Road to Damascus for most men that are picked to be bishops — the opposite in most cases, I'd guess." He sat back in his chair and inhaled and slowly exhaled a lung-full of smoke. His tone was of a lecturer — lecturing a class of fast track junior executives.

"Mostly, you understand, a bishop is the product of years and years of crass ambition and well calculated social climbing. It's only in mythology or the fictitious biography of saints that Rome reaches out into some parish and, moved by the Spirit of God, drags to the episcopate some obscure and reluctant saint." He inhaled deeply then blew a cloud of smoke down the length of the table in frustration.

"Dammit! I could have sworn I'd picked a real good candidate in you, Jack." He laughed at the irony of the situation I had landed us both in and slapped the stained tablecloth hard.

"You'll make me the laughing-stock of the province." He wiped his eyes with a large, not very clean, white handkerchief.

"Sorry I've been such a disappointment…" I couldn't help laughing with him. "and I could have been the perfect bishop without trying at all, is what you're telling me."

"Strange how things turn out," he declared with finality as he stood and brushed crumbs and ashes off his cassock.

"Jack, me boyo, you're a far better man than I thought, so don't let the bastards burn you!" He placed a large hand firmly on my shoulder and squeezed. I had never felt such a fatherly gesture in my life and was unexpectedly moved by it. Tears? Christ! I'm coming apart at the seams from a little love.

"Let's get down to the office and see whose nose you've tweaked this week." He stubbed out his cigarette forcefully, punctuating his determination to face the day's challenges.

I held the dining room door open for him, but he stopped suddenly and pushed the door closed very deliberately instead. He lowered his voice then so that neither the housekeeper nor the secretary could overhear.

"Before you do anything else, make sure you nail that evil bastard, Hogan. The instant you have the goods on him, let me know. I'm going to throw the book at him first and then have a serious heart-to-heart with Breen about the rest of his little gang. I'll suggest that he and they might consider an early retirement in the auld sod or Timbuktu — or some other garden spot well out of my sight."

He shook his finger at me.

"They've pissed me off and they're about to discover they cannot do that to their Ordinary and get away with it."

I had seen him take off into towering rages before on a few occasions and had been more embarrassed by them than anything else. But this rage seemed to give him renewed vigor — it was good to see. His face was redder than usual and he seemed to shake with the power of his emotion. No longer the frail old man I'd seen fumbling over his toast just moments before, he was a bull of a man now.

"I'll check with Norbert Meyer and see what progress his committee is making and let you know right away."

As it happened, Monsignor Meyer was waiting for me in the outer office when I arrived at the Chancery not twenty minutes later and reliable old Norbert was armed with a stack of depositions and a report from the committee giving its conclusions.

Thank God for that Midwestern German work ethic, I thought to myself.

I glanced through the authenticating documents on top of the stack and, as I expected, they had been meticulously prepared. Norbert had drawn up careful and clever interrogatories and his committee had followed the canonical procedures to the letter.

I asked Norbert to come with me into the Bishop's office — there seemed little point in having him deliver his report twice. I brought a notebook to keep a written record of the meeting.

Hogan had admitted to the Committee of Inquiry, when confronted by Johnstone's evidence that he had had indeed written the letter pretending to be the father of a child molested by Pastorelli. When faced with the depositions of Mrs. Brachman and Mr. Bright, he had admitted to spreading the rumors about Pastorelli's child molesting and to persuading his key parishioners to demand the young priest's removal. The delegation to the Chancery had, as I suspected, been Hogan's idea from the start.

The housekeeper at St. John's rectory had put two and two together herself and when questioned by the committee had told about hearing an altercation in Father Pastorelli's room one night around eleven. When she ran to investigate she was in time to see Monsignor Hogan scurrying back to his room naked and an enraged Father Pastorelli shouting after him that he was going to report him to the Bishop. She said she had pleaded with the young man to forgive the Monsignor, swearing that he'd never done anything like that before. She admitted telling lies and remaining silent to protect her employer but her Franciscan confessor had instructed her to tell the committee exactly what she knew. It seems Hogan had tried the same thing with several of the young men who'd been assigned there. A few years before, a Father Quigley had put him in the hospital with a fractured jaw.

The committee interviewed all the previous assistants then and their stories supported that of the housekeeper. They had brushed it off at the time as, "the way he is when he's had a drink or two."

With Pastorelli in the room, Hogan admitted to the Committee that he had made sexual advances to the young man on several occasions. And once, "with drink taken," even attempting to climb into his bed. Having been rebuffed and threatened by Pastorelli, he had set out to discredit him.

We listened for the next twenty minutes as Meyer read out to us the findings of his committee. When he had done reading his report and looked up, the Bishop surprised me by suddenly assuming a formal manner of address. I recorded his words verbatim for the case record.

"Monsignor Meyer, we thank you for the carefully prepared report delivered to myself, the Ordinary and to Bishop Holland, the *Officialis* of this diocese. This is in the matter of The Right Reverend Monsignor Patrick Hogan, brought before the Diocesan Tribunal of which Bishop Holland is the Presiding Judge. Having heard the result of the judicial investigation I, as the Ordinary of this Diocese, am asserting my authority and hereby reserving the disposition of the matter from this point forward to myself."

He turned to me then.

"Bishop Holland, would you be so good as to summon Monsignor Hogan to meet me here in my office promptly at two o'clock today."

"Yes, Bishop."

"Monsignor Meyer you are witness to this action I am taking and I order that you, as *Defensor Vinculi*, also draft a memorandum for the file recording what I have just done in reserving this matter."

"Yes, Bishop."

That was how it went down. At two o'clock precisely, a very shaken Hogan was led into the Bishop's office by one of the secretaries, there to stand alone and suffer the consequences of his crime. The secretary told me later she was scared he would faint on her, he was so pale.

The Bishop's deep, angry voice that not even the stout oak door could muffle, rumbled up and down the narrow hallway, causing spine-shivers in all who heard it. None of the secretaries dared look up from their desks as Hogan, treading with unsteady steps, walked out past them. It seems he stumbled several times on the stairs as he made his way out to the street. It was probably his last time to be in the Chancery of the diocese of Minerva — or of any other diocese for that matter.

The administrative punishment the old man had imposed was a tough one. Hogan was immediately removed from his parish and ordered to vacate the rectory that very day. He was to find residence elsewhere at his own personal expense and not in ecclesiastical property anywhere, i.e. not in the rectory of any of his friends. He would no longer be allowed to perform any public religious function in the diocese and his "faculties were suspended" which would, in effect, prevent his functioning as a priest anywhere again—ever. Without a document of "good-standing" no diocese in the world would touch him. It was a very tough sentence, leaving him in effect without either a livelihood or a place to live.

He had signed a document that Meyer's Committee of Inquiry had prepared admitting to the exact details of his offense. This document would be read from the pulpit at every mass on three successive Sundays in St. John's parish and the five adjoining parishes. In that letter he made a public retraction of the calumnies he had uttered and promulgated against Pastorelli and he begged forgiveness from him and from the people whom he had misled.

When Hogan had left the building, the Bishop called his secretary in to take down the formal details of the sentence and instructed her to give me one copy and put the only other one in Hogan's personnel file. She had never experienced anything like this in all her years as his faithful scribe and when she delivered the document to my desk, she stood and watched as I read it. I had never seen her so shaken.

"The Bishop did exactly the right thing, so don't worry." I reassured her.

She nodded and without a word left my office. She was very fond of the Bishop and had confided in me more than once how she worried about him, fearing that the strain of the job was becoming too much for him.

A little later I ventured into his office when he'd had a chance to calm down a bit. The cigarette smoke was thick in the air but the old man looked pleased with himself as he sat back in his chair.

"Do you think he got the message?"

"Oh, yes! I think he did. I'm just wondering what the others are going to do about it." I said.

"Well I have an appointment with your good friend Breen out at my house this evening as soon as I get home. I'm going to give him a piece of my mind and I'm toying with the idea of offering him a smaller parish up in the high country — something suitable for a man in his declining years." The old man had a twinkle in his eye as he said this. I knew he'd love to do just that, but would not consider it wise politically to provoke the Irish dragon further.

"I dare you!" I teased.

He shook his head and began to gather his things together into his briefcase.

"I'd be in as much trouble with them then, as you are now, me foine bucko!" He looked at me and chuckled. "There has to be at least one bishop around here in good standing with the priests."

I wished him a good night.

Back in my office again, I began working my way through the reams of paperwork that would keep me at my desk till late into the evening. It was nice, I remember thinking, to come out into a patch of calm water after such a stormy passage. A few quiet hours spent on routine administrative tasks would be the very thing to help me relax.

Occasionally during the evening my mind wandered from the mind-glazing stack of Pauline Privileges and formal annulment petitions, the banns dispensations and record searches, to the meeting between the Bishop and Monsignor Breen.

There would be none of that, "Ye wee shite," business with the "real Bishop" or he'd find himself out on his ear without a pot to piss in, just like his friend Hogan.

At times like that I felt the impotence of my position acutely. I caught myself wishing again for the powers of a real bishop, a man who'd be boss in his own diocese — a bishop with "Ordinary Power." As an auxiliary, my only authority was what was given to me by the Ordinary. I had no real clout in dealing with these older pastors — and they knew it. Coveting more authority was of course insanity for someone with one foot out of the Church but, there you are… the illogic of blind ambition again.

Jerry, just in from school, phoned around four-thirty. Was I on for a movie and pizza? Much as I would have enjoyed it, I had far too much catching up to do. I took a rain check.

He was in the mood for celebrating what he called "a skirmish in which truth enjoyed a rare, though minor victory." He had already heard about Hogan, and had somehow learned all the terms of the censure. How had the word got around so fast? Hogan? Not likely. And if Jerry had heard it, everyone in the diocese had too for he was almost gossip-proof.

He had sounded bubbly — I almost called him back. An evening with him might be fun. Relax, after all that stress it'll be good for you, a voice said. Then remembering how far behind I had fallen in my work, I silenced it.

CHAPTER 36

Minerva, California — 1977

I SURRENDERED TO an overwhelming fatigue finally around ten-thirty. My eyes were having trouble focusing and the underside of my eyelids felt dry and grainy. I had been staring at the same page for several minutes without a clue as to what it said. The phone in the front office had been ringing sporadically for the past ten minutes but since it wasn't on my private line I let it ring. Nut case, more than likely. People call their parish in emergency, not the Chancery. Time to go home. It had been a very long, very stressful day. It seemed a week since I'd said mass for the nuns that morning. But, at least the Hogan matter was finally settled.

Once in my truck, I felt home already; leaning back in the seat, my head resting against the rear of the cab, I closed my eyes. I would have readily spent the night there, but for the scandal. *"Bishop Sleeps One Off In Truck."*

I stirred myself and started the motor. You'll be in bed in twenty minutes, I promised myself.

I had driven a few blocks through the downtown before I punched the radio to catch the scores and the too predictable valley weather.

A news bulletin was just coming in:

"A Minerva priest is being held tonight in San Francisco charged with lewd conduct in public and with soliciting for prostitution. The announcer trumpeted the headline. Then, after a dramatic pause, he elaborated:

Tonight, police in San Francisco are holding in custody a man they describe as a priest of the Minerva diocese, on charges that, while dressed as a woman, he was soliciting patrons leaving a gay bar in San Francisco's Castro district. Police identify the man as Reverend Jeremiah Egan of Minerva. No further details on the case are available at this time."

I drove a few more blocks on autopilot before I realized that I had to do something about what I had just heard. I had to talk to Jerry; I had to call him; had to get him out of jail. My God! My worst fears. The Chancery was the closest place where I could use the phone. I swung the truck around and was back in my office less than ten minutes after I leaving it.

I called the rectory first and asked if I'd had any calls.

"A man called several times but left no number," the housekeeper said.

I left my private office number in case he should call again.

The phone in the eerie emptiness of the front office started to ring again and I punched the blinking button on my phone.

"Hello?" I answered cautiously, half expecting to find a reporter on the line.

"Jack? Is that you, Jack?"

"Jerry? Where in the hell are you? I just heard the news. Do you need to be bailed out? Do they have you in the jail?"

"Jack, please! Listen! No questions. I've only got a few minutes and there's a line of others waiting to get to the phone. They're going to release me in the morning after I make a court appearance. If you could get someone to post bail for me, or pay the fine or whatever needs doing in court, that would be a great help."

"Of course I'll do that. No problem! Anything else?"

"Yes! Listen to me carefully! You stay away from me and this whole scene. I want you to promise me that above everything else. They were waiting for me tonight in the Castro, so I'm sure they had me followed. They want to get to you through me. I know that's what's behind it. Such an ejit, walking straight into their trap!"

He sounded distraught and his mind seemed to be playing tricks on him. I'd never heard him so neurotic. I'm sure the shock and humiliation must have pushed him near breaking point.

"I'll be careful but don't worry about me. What's important is that we get you out of there."

"You stay the fuck away from this mess or it's going to get splashed all over you! Do you hear me?"

"I hear you. But, for the moment, you try to stay calm and I'll have someone there to help you with the court appearance and the bail and whatever."

"Thanks! But Jack, don't be stupid. Stay away — be extremely careful!"

He hung up and I got on the phone to San Francisco right away. I was able to ask a big favor from an old friend, Bernie Klein, who'd worked for years in the San Francisco DA's office and knew his way around the Hall of Justice. He was now in private practice, but once I explained the matter he took complete charge of the legal arrangements.

He and I had killed many an evening at the bar in Trader Vic's when we were much younger and he was single — Hawaiian rum drinks and fried oysters and great arguments. He hadn't a prudish bone in his body and, as I expected, never turned a hair when I explained the circumstances — just reassured me it would get handled; not to worry.

I arranged to meet him at his home in the Sunset and to bring some less dramatic clothes for Jerry to wear at his court appearance. He would arrange with the jailers for him to get dressed in them before court.

Less than twenty minutes earlier I had been falling asleep in my paperwork, now, with a busy night's work ahead of me, I was so wired I could hardly sit still.

I called over to Jerry's residence and told the Pastor I would be coming by shortly to get some of his things; I arranged with Cassidy to cover mass for the nuns in the morning and finally I called the Bishop. It was the last thing I wanted to lay on his plate, on this of all days, but he needed to know so as to not be sandbagged in the morning by some reporter.

"Oh, God help us!" was his response. "Is he all right? They didn't harm him, did they? Ah! The poor little fellow."

I told him all Jerry had said.

"He's right about who's behind it too, I can feel that in my bones," he fumed. "That son-of-a-bitch needs skinnin'!" He was as convinced as Jerry, it seemed, that I was their target. It rattled me, hearing it from him too.

"Will you see what you can do for Jerry and try not to get set up yourself?"

I promised I would do both and told him what I had arranged. Then I left him to his thoughts and prayers. Poor old man. When I'm his age I hope I'll be leading a quieter life, I reflected as I hung up the phone.

I gassed up my truck on Broad Street before getting on the Interstate. I had a bag with some masculine civvies from Jerry's closet and two hundred dollars that I'd been keeping in my sock drawer for emergencies. Days that try men's souls are not a good time to quit Camels. I bought a pack and a cup of coffee that had been burning for hours in the pot, black acid — it might keep me awake for the hour or more I had to drive.

I spent that night at Bernie's. His wife, whom I knew only slightly, graciously made up a futon in the living room for me. Bernie, as he left for the court appearance in the morning, recommended that I not be seen anywhere around the jail or the courtroom.

"Wait here," he'd said, "and stop worrying." He would call me when he had handled the legal part and Jerry had been released.

Jerry and I could meet someplace for lunch, like Joe's of Westlake, he suggested, some place well away from downtown where we were unlikely to run into anyone who would recognize either of us. Bernie's confident tone was reassuring. I would wait for his call.

In a surprisingly short time he rang from a pay phone on Bryant street to say they were all done in court and were off to look for Jerry's car, hoping it was still where he'd parked it the previous night. Jerry got on the phone then. I tried to be casual.

"So, Jerry? How does Joe's of Westlake sound, for a bite?"

"Jack, for Christ's sake! Haven't you got the message yet? It's your friggin' scalp they're after."

"Huh?" I seemed to be the only person having trouble accepting that I was the real target.

"Look, Jack! I don't want you to be seen anywhere in my vicinity. Forget lunch! You get your ass back in that truck of yours. You'd better be found sitting at your desk in the Chancery this afternoon. Do you hear me?"

"Yeah. I hear you," I said. He was scaring me. "But don't you think you're being just a wee bit paranoid?"

"Paranoid, my ass! I was set up by Hogan's friends and the cop who just happened to catch me was that cousin of Breen's -- that big *amadan* that's always sucking around him at the clergy golf tournaments."

"Oh shite! How'd they know you'd be there?"

"I suppose the word is out about me — more than I knew."

I remembered what Johnstone had said and even Breen's threats. There were few real secrets among the clergy.

"I saw the big red face of him — recognized him right away as I came out of The Elephant Walk -- and thought to myself, what's he doing over in the Castro?

Look Jack, I've gotta go now." Jerry's tone became more urgent. "Thanks for everything, the clothes and for Bernie here, especially! And now, you waste no more time getting back to your friggin' desk. They're going to be calling you from every newspaper in the country looking for a comment about me this afternoon. So watch your mouth. Don't forget for a second that it's you Breen's really striking at."

I still thought he was being a bit too paranoid, but one thing he said was dead right: the press would be calling me, looking for a comment that afternoon. I took his advice and headed for Minerva.

I drove directly to the office and was hardly at my desk before I was handed a stack of call-slips — the phone had been jumping all morning, mainly from reporters. One message aroused some curiosity in me and gave me a rush of adrenaline the moment I saw it. I couldn't resist dialing the number.

"Good afternoon, St. Finbar's Parish."

"Monsignor Breen?"

"Speaking."

"This is Bishop Holland. You called while I was out?"

"Ah, yes, Bishop Holland. Yes, indeed." I could hear him take a deep breath. "Yes, indeed, Bishop, I did call you earlier. Isn't it an awful thing that happened to poor Father Egan, the poor misfortunate creature. Sure it must be the curse of God Himself that he's bent in that way. Don't you think so, now?"

"Were you calling about that, Monsignor? Or was there something else you needed?"

"Ah, sure isn't it a shame, the way some things happen? I'd say you had a busy morning yourself, taking care of things, and all?"

The old bastard seemed to be principally interested in gloating over what he'd achieved. I was becoming convinced that Jerry was right about him.

"What can I do for you, then, Monsignor?"

"Sure it's not a thing I need done for myself, at all then. It's like this, ye see..." Again I could hear the deep breath wheezily drawn into his chest.

"There's this whole business with my good friend, Paddy Hogan — as fine a priest as ever set foot on an altar — and there he is now, after all his years of faithful service to the people of this diocese, a destroyed man. A destroyed and broken man is what's in it. Now I think that's a crying shame! And all over what? Over some little misunderstanding. I put it to you, was it anything worth destroying a good man over?"

"You mean, was it worth destroying Father Pastorelli?"

"Ah, now! Nobody wanted to destroy that young fella at all, at all. I think it was just a big misunderstanding was what it was." He took another deep breath — he was smoking a cigarette, that's what the wheezing was. He tried a different tack.

"You know, Jack, between you and me, these Americans hate us Irish. They're as jealous as can be of us, you see. I'd hate to tell you some of the things they're saying about you being made a bishop, and all. They fair hate us, I'm tellin' you."

My response was far more episcopal than my instincts were urging.

"I'm afraid the matter of Father Hogan has been decided, Monsignor. The Bishop was adamant in his determination to punish the criminal slander, the character assassination, and the forgery. But of course, you've had occasion to hear from the Bishop first-hand on this matter yourself, have you not? The Bishop was under the impression that he'd made his position very clear to you at his house last evening."

I paused to let him react, but he said nothing so I went on. "But, Monsignor, if there's some part of what he said to you then that you didn't understand, I'll ask him to clarify it for you."

There was a muffled sound from the other end of the phone; he was covering the mouthpiece and relaying my message to someone in the room. The whole gang of them was there, I suspected.

"I'm sorry." I asked. "I didn't quite hear what you just said."

"What was that?" Breen seemed afraid I'd heard his comments to the others.

"Did the Bishop not explain to you how he feels about this matter of ruining a young priest's good name and criminally forging documents aimed at destroying a fellow priest?"

"That he did! That he did!"

"Well, I find it hard to credit the reports that a man of your intelligence is giving aid and comfort to such a villain — against the express wishes of his Ordinary." I guessed that Hogan was staying there.

"Now let's not get too far afield on this, young man. I heard what the Bishop told me just fine, but it's you we're calling now, though isn't it, Bishop Holland? It seems to us hereabouts, that you're the only man could change his mind. That is, if you were to decide to."

The threat was obvious.

"I have thought about it all very long and very carefully, Monsignor." There was a deathly silence from the other end of the phone. "I feel that Monsignor Hogan is fortunate in the leniency of his punishment."

I paused so Breen could relay what I was saying to his audience, for I sensed rather than heard the muffled voices through the covered mouthpiece.

"Perhaps, instead of holding out false hopes to him, you should be reminding him that this minute he could be facing a civil suit for damages in Superior Court were Father Pastorelli of such a mind."

I again paused to let him relay the sound bites to the Irish wake I felt was in progress around his beautiful gas logs.

"Or maybe, Monsignor, if you were to remind Pat Hogan what he has admitted to in writing: first of all, slandering a priest before an entire parish and, secondly, forging a letter of complaint to the Chancery about this priest's alleged sexual deviance. Both of which vicious steps were taken, he admits, to cover up his own sexual advances toward and attempted rape of Father Pastorelli."

I would swear that someone was listening on an extension phone there in the rectory. Hogan? Or could it be one of Breen's young American assistants? That would be interesting.

"I'm sure, Monsignor Breen, that the District Attorney would gladly bring criminal charges too, if Father Pastorelli were to file a complaint. I seriously doubt, for all your bluster, that you would be caught dead taking the stand as a character witness for Hogan in such a trial. Imagine the headlines then?"

I felt sure he would not relay this latter part *verbatim*. I could only hope Hogan was on the extension.

"The Bishop was much less severe than I would have been, had it been up to me." I added. Even as I said the words I felt the shivers of fear feathering along my spine.

"Well then! So that's that, you say?" For once, Breen seemed at a loss.

"Was there anything else, now, Monsignor?"

The phone connection had been broken and I was left listening to empty air for a few seconds before the line disconnected. Someone had very quietly replaced the other phone — one of the assistants in St. Finbar's had heard it all, was my guess. I was pleased at this, for now, without my deliberately violating confidentiality, the truth of the matter would be already spreading like wildfire amongst the younger priests from border to border.

I understood Breen's call to be a floundering, face-saving spasm by Hogan's champion — a Hail Mary pass in the final second. I felt we would hear no more pleas on Hogan's behalf.

I leafed through the remaining call slips on my desk. They were mostly from the same few reporters who had been calling repeatedly all morning, clambering for comment — probably trying to meet a deadline. The old man had apparently stayed out of circulation all day.

I took a deep breath and decided to throw them some red meat. The meat would probably be mine when they were through editing my words, but I was sick and tired of walking on eggshells around issues and facts. The whole damned Catholic Church was as bad as any conglomerate when it came to spin-doctoring the truth for public relations.

With adrenaline pumping courage through me, I was a daredevil — fearless. Bring on the press! Bring in the clown! Where was the harm in a headline or two? And if it gets the Papal Nuntio worried, wasn't that just sauce on the pudding? I would be forthright with these reporters and say exactly what I meant. The old man didn't seem to mind me raising a bit of dust. Diplomacy made me feel dirty and timid; thinking up half-truths was exhausting work.

I arranged to meet with the reporters in half an hour, plenty of time to get their stuff on the evening news and the Late Final edition of the paper.

I began the briefing with a short statement acknowledging the fact that, yes, Father Egan had been arrested by the San Francisco police the previous evening and that he had been released that morning after a court appearance. I truthfully did not know exactly what charges had been brought against him and, yes, I felt sure he would report to the Chancery when he returned from San Francisco. So far, so good.

"Bishop?"

"Yes?"

"It has been widely reported that he was arrested outside a gay bar and that he was dressed in women's clothes at the time."

"I have heard those reports too. I can neither confirm nor deny them. I'm sure the police report would contain that information, but I haven't seen it nor Father Egan himself for that matter, since the arrest."

"Do you think your recent remarks favoring gay priests may have contributed to this behavior on Father Egan's part?"

"No."

"Bishop? Do you feel that Father Egan should be barred from working as a priest because of this?"

"Nothing has been proven against the man at this time. Let's not get ahead of the facts."

"But, if those rumors were proven to be facts?"

"You'll have to ask me then, is all I can suggest."

"Bishop? Is it not true that Father Egan has been your closest friend in the diocese?"

"That is true. He and I first met in seminary many years ago and we have been very close friends ever since."

"How is it possible that you were not aware of his cross-dressing?"

"Some things, a person keeps private — even from friends." I evaded.

The floodgates then opened.

"Bishop? Have you ever seen him when he was dressed as a woman?"

"Is it true that he and you would go to San Francisco together as a couple, posing as man and woman?"

"Would he dress up especially for you?"

I tried to maintain my dignity but the session was devolving into a tabloid nightmare: no longer waiting for answers, the reporters were creating their own event, making their own story with questions that were really statements and accusations.

"If you have no more questions…"

The threat of ending the session caused a momentary return to order and for that moment I clung to the hope I might yet salvage something from the train-wreck.

"Bishop? Would you say that Father Egan was a good priest? Could you say that in all honesty?"

"I feel that Father Egan has been a good and dedicated priest. A much better priest than I have ever been, myself. A man of great spiritual depth and strong faith. He has often been the one who prodded and encouraged me to strive for higher values."

I could feel the pressure building out there in front of me, behind a flimsy dam of self-restraint. I held up my hand to beg a few more seconds. Canute on the beach again. Would he ever learn?

"My fervent hope is that Father Egan can return here and resume his duties or we in Minerva will all be much the worse off."

I knew I'd better make my escape on that note and, amid a barrage of shouted questions and statements, I left them tearing and clawing at the meat they'd already stuffed into their notepads.

As I went back to the office I felt that in the final statements I had perhaps retrieved what had threatened to be a disaster. We'd have to see how it played at six and eleven when the TV editors got through with it.

Back in the office, I finished off the work I had neglected that morning and dialed Jerry's private number to see if he was back in town yet. Though I was exhausted from stress and lack of sleep, I could still swing by his place with some Chinese take-out and spend an hour or so with him. My heart was hurting for him, imagining what he would face coming back to work — and in a high school of all places. He'd need all the support I could give him.

There was no answer yet. I dialed again and let it ring — still nothing.

The upcoming days and weeks promised to be one long-drawn-out exercise in damage control for the Bishop and myself. I wasn't looking forward to any of it.

Jerry would be crushed by this whole business. I would have to think of something — I was a friggin' bishop after all, wasn't I? I would suggest he take an extended leave of absence, maybe till the new school year — time to think things over. Maybe leave the diocese altogether and open that shop for drag queens. Despite what I had said at the press conference, what future could he hope to have in the diocese after all this? Of course, if he was willing to try it, I'd stand behind him to the last.

Still no answer on Jerry's line. I'd try again from home.

I was already back in the rectory when the six o'clock news came on. I had been sandbagged again. Jerry's arrest was the lead item on the local news as I had expected. It was reported as a voice-over to a full screen color photo of Jerry, taken in the moment of his arrest.

"The bastards had been lying in wait for him with a cameraman, to ambush him." I growled to Cassidy who was watching with me in the common room. With regrettable clarity the still-shot showed Jerry in drag. His wig had already been snatched off by the arresting officer — not shown, of course. Without the wig, Jerry's made-up face, startled by the flash, looked as clownish as a Halloween mask.

"Breen's cousin the cop was the arresting officer," I told Cassidy. "You should know who was behind this." I was pulling no punches now with Cassidy.

A recording of my statement praising his character as a man and a priest ran as simultaneous commentary to another close-up of his face, lipstick and eye liner smudged, his hair in that damned net. I couldn't imagine the torture he would be suffering if he were watching this program. Cassidy had the evening paper open on his lap.

"Te've done a job on yous bot on tis one, ta bastards."

I looked at him and thought I detected compassion in his watery eyes.

"Which bastards do you mean — the reporters or the Irish priests?" Was all I could reply.

He handed me the front section of the paper and there on the front page was the same shot of Jerry being arrested as had just been on television, thanks no doubt to the Breen news service.

"Somebody's trying ta make bot a yous look bad."

"And a blind man could see who that is." I told him. "But that man will have his just desserts before this is all done. Mark my words!"

The word was out, obviously, that they were getting back at me for Hogan.

"Aren't they a credit to their country and church, now, the whole bunch of them?" I said.

"Ah now, I hope ye don't tink we're all agreeing wit what tey're doin'."

"Ah, Mick shut up for Christ's sake!" I was shouting and I didn't give a shite. Cassidy had pressed himself hard against the back of his armchair, clutching on to the arms till his fingers were white claws.

"Why don't you quit with your fuckin' whining and hand washing?" Angry, I was a dreadful sight, Jerry had told me.

"If even one of you had two balls hanging down between your legs, you'd take your integrity back from the Hogans and Breens of the diocese. But I don't see one of you with the courage of a friggin' mouse." I kicked the ottoman, sending it skiting across the room and crashing into the fireplace screen. "Flock of bloody sheep!" I muttered as I left the room.

I could feel rage tightening my stomach muscles and stretching the cords of my neck. I was so wound up it wouldn't take much to set me at somebody's throat. I thought it best to go to my own room. I had seen a blinding rage exactly like this come over my father too often not to recognize the fury and violence it could unleash. I needed to cool down. It was a time for clear thinking — not rash impulses. Whether I liked it or not, I was a bishop and had responsibilities and I needed to keep my head. In the past when I would become upset like this and sense the Holland madness rising in me, threatening to overtake my mind and reduce my thinking to a mere instrument of its vengeance, I could count on Jerry to be a voice of reason, calming me back to my senses. I needed his strength more at that moment than ever before.

I began phoning his private number every few minutes and continued for the next hour or so but there was still no answer. Hadn't he come home or was he just refusing to pick up the phone from embarrassment, not knowing who it might be? I was worried. I couldn't think of food or do anything else until I'd heard from him.

He must have arrived home by now, if he was coming home at all. My rage was being rapidly upstaged by worry as the time dragged on. It was nearly seven-thirty and still no word. I had called the main rectory phone too a number of times, and no one had picked that up either. Had the Pastor, maybe, decided to spare everyone the inevitable harassment?

I had already waited as long as my nerves would allow; I couldn't stand it another minute. I would drive over there and see for myself.

CHAPTER 37

Minerva, California — 1977

THE SIMPLE TRACT house that served as a rectory for this, the poorest parish in the city, was in total darkness when I drove up. I tried the doorbell and there was no answer. I rang several times and listened as the buzzing echoed throughout the little house. A phone started to ring in one of the rooms. It was ringing in only one room — Jerry's phone — the parish phone hanging on the kitchen wall had several extensions.

The phone rang and rang and finally stopped. The house which looked half-deserted at the best of times, that night looked particularly desolate.

After waiting on the front porch for as long as I could bear I walked around the side of the house. There were lights on in the Quonset hut that served as the parish church. Odd, a service at dinnertime? Benediction? It wasn't a Friday night.

Curious, I walked down the gravel path that connected the rectory to the church and quietly opened the back door. Up in the front pews a dozen or so adults were kneeling. I could hear the hum of prayers, the rosary obviously, from the alternating verse and response.

I stopped halfway up the center aisle several people were sobbing. Pete Carton, the Pastor, was kneeling at the communion rail leading the rosary. His shoulders were heaving painfully, his voice muffled and raspy — on the verge of breaking — as he forced out the words.

My stomach was instantly a knot tight-clenched. I quietly joined those kneeling in the third row and whispered to the woman kneeling next to me: "What's happened?"

"It's poor Father Egan," she sobbed. "He's been found." Her eyes and nose were red-raw and swollen from crying.

"Found?" I hadn't needed to ask but the question came out on its own.

"His body… it's been found… off the Golden Gate, this evening, finally."

Another woman leaned over the speaker to fill in further details.

"Hadn't you heard, Father? They found his poor body about an hour ago and called Father Carton. We'd been waiting here, praying all evening, since they found his car near the bridge — in the parking lot — around four o'clock."

I knelt there for a while — I have no idea for how long — listening to the comforting drone of the familiar prayers. My mother, kneeling on the seat of her arm chair, leaning over its back, her head pressed against the speaker of the Cossar radio on the shelf. The ritual drone of the family rosary marking every night of childhood. But I couldn't pray these familiar prayers with these people. Nor could I let myself think of the dead body stretched out somewhere on a steel table, wet and gray — a cold stiff thing like that was not Jerry. I had no interest in that dead body and the religious fuss and hypocrisy it would attract in the days to come.

Jerry cold and gray. Shivering cold, he and I in our room, soutanes and bedclothes wrapped around us — Jerry warmer in his tights — First Divines in Holy Trinity… The thoughts and associations paraded before my mind's eye, induced by the hypnotic buzz: *"Hail Mary full of grace…" "Holy Mary, Mother of God…"*

I can see now that it was the calm before the storm, that trance-like interval kneeling there, lulled by ritual. I was the numb spectator of a slide show programmed by a stranger-god.

I'm back at the family rosary, my sister and I, heads buried in the seats of our chairs, cushions warm from our bottoms still, automatically scoring on the Catholic abacus till our fingers feel the spacer links before the *"Glory be's. . ."* Calm and peaceful, the fireplace-glow warming our behinds and the backs of our thighs — my mother's voice: *Hail Mary…*

Soothed by the droning.

"Bee-loud" I'd loved that as a child. She had recited the poem as she and I were climbing Glencar waterfall. At the top she'd done, *"When you are old and gray and full of sleep…"* I had tried to not let her see me cry.

I am walking with Jerry up the bridge from the visitors' center. I hadn't realized till then that you walked *up* the bridge from the toll plaza. Standing at the rail we had looked back at the Bay with Alcatraz off to our left and the City gleaming white on the hills to our right. And leaning over the rail we had looked down below the orange steel roadbed, down to the dark gray-green water of the Pacific dashing against the slime-green concrete footings below.

"I have always been terrified of the ocean," he'd said as he spat and watched the spittle drift down into the angry water. The wind, cold and blustery rushing under the roadway, had blown the white gob out far from the footings.

"When I look down into it I know its going to reach up and snatch me in with a wave," he'd mused.

"But you swim so well," I'd said. He was a strong open-water swimmer.

He had begun to shiver then, I remember.

"Do you ever picture what it would be like, jumping from up here?" I'd asked him. The thought of a leap like that — going off the top of Rogey Rock, for example — had been in my nightmares as long as I could remember.

"Not bloody likely!" He was emphatic.

"Wouldn't it be a great ride, going down, though?" I'd joked, not meaning a word of it, for I was scared even looking down.

"Nothing has ever terrified me so much as the thought of drowning." He had shivered just thinking about it. "The worst way I could think of to die, drowning!"

He had shivered so hard then his teeth were chattering. I began to worry he was running a fever or something.

"I've always been terrified of being buried alive, myself," I'd told him. "Had nightmares about that when I was little — woke the house up screaming at least once a week. They'd bury me, thinking I was dead and I'd only be paralyzed by some disease they didn't know about and then I'd wake up already in my grave. I'd start clawing, desperate, till my fingernails were broken and bloody trying to open the coffin lid. The wallpaper by my bedside was torn to shreds."

He had been staring over the rail as though mesmerized by the rowdy water but looked at me when I stopped speaking. I could see the fear in his eyes. He said nothing, just looked at me as though I was a stranger.

"You'd damned well better check and make sure I'm really dead." I nudged him, trying for a response. "You hear me?"

"I'll check very carefully for any undetected diseases." He spat once more out into the wind and watched it float all the way down till it was lost in the leaping green water before he turned and without a word began walking quickly back to the toll plaza.

"Let's get off this friggin' thing as fast as we can," he'd muttered when I caught up with him. "It's scaring the shite out of me." He was breathless when we got into the car, whether from the terror or the hurried walk back, I couldn't decide.

That had been our first year in America and our first year in the priesthood. We had eaten dinner later that day in Alfred's on Broadway and had walked down the street after dinner to catch the show at Finocchio's where some of the best female impersonators in the country performed. He had met one of the "girls" standing at the urinal and quizzed him on specialty stores in The City. Driving back to Minerva that evening, all he could talk about was the show and how it had inspired him to achieve greater realism. He would go shopping in San Francisco, he said, with loads of new ideas from seeing the impersonators. I just wouldn't believe how much he had learned talking to that man in the bathroom — in just ten minutes. He seemed to have put the bridge out of his mind completely and had never mentioned the subject again.

My mind had been drifting about like an untethered balloon, far from the Quonset church and the rosary-buzz of the little congregation. The woman beside me began sobbing and keening louder than before. It was this that had reached up and dragged me back to earth.

I saw him dropping down and down and drifting in the wind like his white spittle, watching, as one of the mossy concrete footings grew larger, plummeting towards it, the orange metal rows of rivets flashing past as he dove into the whitecaps.

What do we think about as we leave?

I had nothing to say to any of those people praying for Jerry's soul and against their own fear of the stalking monster-god. So, before they could finish the Fifth Sorrowful Mystery, I left the church and walked back along the gravel path to where I had parked my truck.

I had no sooner settled myself behind the familiar wheel than the dam broke and the grief of years began pouring out of me. I had always known that love was the lure and that grief was lurking with its hot irons behind the arras. I'd seen it in her shadowed face and heard it in her voice; in that minor mode, banshee-keening,

Celtic voice of hers. I had not cried in years, not even when I'd heard of her death, nor on the morning I had left her waving after me from the green door. I cried for her and Jerry and myself as I sat in my truck outside the rectory. I couldn't see to drive for the tears blinding my eyes and the hurt in my head from the grief and the loneliness and the confusion. Who would I talk to now — who would understand?

We could have made it, the two of us. We could have made it in the world, damn it — gone off together somewhere; made it in another town — in Southern California maybe. He had always said we should have chosen the other end of the state in the first place; it rained less there and the beaches were whiter and the water warmer.

Fuck it Jerry, you didn't have to do this! Fuck the bastard that drove you to this! Fuck him! Fuck him! Fuck him!

I realized suddenly that I had been pounding my head against the steering wheel and my forehead was sore and bruised from the beating. I had been clenching the wheel so hard my forearms were knotted hard as steel — my fingers were white and bloodless clutching the rim.

The people would be coming out of the church soon and I couldn't bear to meet anyone just then. I had to get away. I dried my eyes and shook my head to clear it.

I started the truck and drove without conscious purpose along streets that had become familiar over the years. But this town was no longer my home — never had been, really. My arms and jaw were still tight and my head hurt from the pressure of tears and grief and from banging it on the wheel, but as I drove the tears had ceased and the grief had subsided into a lower region of my brain. Something cold and clear was taking up a position near the front of my mind — something that gave form and purpose to the emotions and the energy that had been coiling inside me for weeks.

I thought of the old man sitting alone out in the Bishop's mansion. He would have heard by now the news of Jerry's death. I could go there and be with him. But then, what could I do for a man who'd known so much pain in his life? He would weather this in his little chapel as he had weathered the death of airmen in the war and his parents and siblings. He would be in his chapel now and he would be praying in his old fashioned way for Jerry's soul — and for mine too. He knew how close we'd been and would be worried for me — not a twinge of pity for himself.

I was to blame for most of the problems that had landed on his plate recently. If I had not been so bullheaded and impulsive in pursuing Hogan… He would never say it, but he'd have been so much better off without my help.

I listened to News-on-the-Hour and there was today's sensational story, sure enough: the Minerva priest, arrested yesterday for soliciting, today dragged out of the Bay — a suicide — the Bridge Captain gave the exact time some man was seen to jump.

I had not imagined it then. That stranger had said it on the radio just now: Jerry is dead — forever.

In my seemingly aimless drive through the darkened streets I had come within a few blocks of St. Finbar's parish before I realized where I was. Perhaps I had been headed there all along, controlled by some primitive instinct of a blue-painted Celtic ancestor or of that wild, hairy man of the northern glaciers. My heart was thumping against my rib cage and blood was surging hot through my temples, pulsing, pumping, as I had never felt it pump before. My mind, however, was cold and merciless as spring steel. I swung my truck into the parking spot alongside the big Buick. Breen was at home — in his oak paneled Irish study, enjoying his gas log.

The elderly housekeeper, an old-country woman, answered the door. Delighted to see her "Darlin' little Irish Bishop", she practically curtseying before me, then bid me follow her to Monsignor's study. She knocked and held the door open for me to enter. I paused outside and motioned for her to leave. I gave her a friendly smile of thanks and she took off, back to her kitchen. Everything seemed fine, she'd say afterwards, for hadn't the bishop smiled a nice smile at her.

Breen was standing at his desk, talking and gesturing emphatically at someone on the phone. He ended the conversation as soon as I came into the room, his face immediately assuming a mask of sad gravity as he came towards me. He made no effort though to shake my hand.

"Ah, Jack, Jack! God save us! Sure didn't I just hear the tragic news about poor, poor Jerry!" He looked at me as he said that, his face all scrunched up in an imitation of grief — but I saw more fear than sadness in his eyes. He kept wringing his hands as he stood there. Was he washing them or maybe cringing? Pilate — or was it Uriah Heep?

310

"Ah, the poor young fella!" He keened.

Fuckin' hypocrite! I didn't say a word though, but stood there watching the play of his guilty conscience across his face — cloud-shadows drifting over a winter bog.

"Sure isn't it a terrible thing all together? An awful, awful thing indeed!" He wailed.

I just stood there and looked at him and the longer I remained silent, the more unnerved he became. It was taking every bit of constraint that was in me to play the waiting game with him.

"Ah, sure we had no idea things would come to this, none at all, at all, so we didn't." He was pleading, his little eyes darting about under those wild, wiry tufts — rats reading the wind.

He never saw the fist that caught him squarely on the bridge of his nose, just beneath those furtive rodents. I felt the crunch as the bridge-bone shattered under my knuckles. I had knocked him to the floor — flat on his back. He raised himself painfully onto his elbow and blood started pouring out of his nose and dripping from his chin onto the expensive moss-green Berber carpet. I dropkicked him in the ribs then and heard glasses from his pocket skite off in pieces across the Connemara marble hearth. He groaned and squealed but said nothing. Bloody and stupid-faced he looked up at me, confused by the violence that had invaded his comfortable life.

"Fuck you, Breen! Fuck you!" My voice came out low and grave.

He looked up at me with small cowardly eyes. Had he thought himself immune from physical retaliation?

I kicked him again, between his splayed out legs this time, hard into his genitals and felt a jarring crunch as my foot struck bone. He curled into a fetal position whining in agony. I stood astride him, my enemy vanquished, my insanity spent.

I took a handful of his expensive alpaca jacket and hauled him to his feet. He was surprisingly light for such a big man or perhaps my rage had made me stronger. I threw him into one of the matching wingback chairs by the fireplace. He sat bent over from the pain of his groin — blood from his nose ruining the expensive limousine cloth of his chair. He looked up at me, cowering from me, whining wordlessly, his lower lip quivering. I looked at the sulky face, contorted by pain and self-pity, and saw only the cold gray thing lying on a stainless table and I slapped the fat purple cheek hard.

"You were right, Breen! Let's forget all that legalistic nonsense! You killed my best friend and I am now going to destroy you. 'Man to man' you said. Right, then! Man to man!"

I pulled the other chair over closer and sat almost knee to knee with him.

"We are going to have a talk, Monsignor, man to man. Do you understand me?"

He looked at me dumbly. I slapped him hard — so hard that my palm stung from the slap against the fat jowls. The bloody snot was sticky on my hands.

"You and your thick Micks killed a good man tonight — after you had gone and destroyed his good name. Do you hear what I'm saying?"

He stared at me loose lipped. Drool and blood seeping down his chin was staining the chair seat where it dripped between his legs. I slapped his face again and he nodded.

"And none of you even dreamed you would be made to pay for it, did you? Hogan never dreamed he would have to pay either."

I couldn't help but think that I was a pretty thick Mick myself at that moment. I didn't care.

"I've come to tell you that you were very mistaken. You are going to pay, and pay dearly too. Do you hear me?"

He said nothing and I slapped his face again. I could see the blue and purple blood vessels behind his loose-flapped lower lip.

"Do you understand what I am telling you? Nod if you understand me." He nodded.

"You and I are going to draw up a letter tonight in which you tender your resignation from this diocese. You will inform the Bishop that you are retiring immediately and going off to live in Ireland; and furthermore, you are donating all of your vested assets in the Priests' Retirement Fund to a charity of the Bishop's choosing. You will similarly notify the Pension Fund and the Personnel Board. Do you understand what I am telling you?"

He just stared. I slapped his face and he nodded.

"You are also going to write a letter in which you take full responsibility for organizing the trap that caught Jerry Egan and admitting that you did this to retaliate against me for punishing Hogan for his crime. Your cousin on the San Francisco police force, who acted on your orders in arresting Jerry, will roll over on you the instant charges are brought against him by the D. A. for abusing police authority for personal purposes. That will put his twenty-five year police pension at risk. He doesn't like you that much. And do you think for one second that the photographer he used will protect you and your cousin when he's offered immunity for his part of the stalking and ambush? Do you understand what I am telling you?"

He nodded this time without prompting. Pavlov was on to something.

"Oh! And, one more thing: This confession will be addressed to the *Minerva Chronicle:* an open letter to be published over your name."

He stared at me dumbly.

"So. You sit where you are for just a few minutes. I'm going to type these letters and when you have read them over you are going to sign them and then you may start your packing. Do you understand me?"

He nodded.

I typed up his letter of resignation for the Bishop and the Personnel Board and the instructions to the Pension Fund Trustees regarding the disposal of his assets. I suspected that the crafty bastard had salted away plenty over the years in his rich parish so that he'd never starve. The final document, the confession addressed to the newspaper, I typed with two carbon copies.

He read what I had written and signed all of them without a whimper, addressing the envelopes by hand when I asked him to.

He had not said a word to me since I'd first hit him. He sat still where I had thrown him, slightly hunched over in his wingback chair. I had given him a hardcover book to lean on while he signed the letters and addressed the envelopes — he clutched it now to his stomach like a shield as I stood in front of him. There was terror in his eyes as he looked up at me — fearing another physical assault. Shame swept over me suddenly, leeching the last of the rage out of me.

I told myself I should feel no remorse for what I had just done but, for the terror I had put into the man's eyes, I knew I would ever afterwards be ashamed.

There was nothing but emptiness in me as I let myself out of the front door and walked along the peaceful leafy street to the mailbox I had remembered seeing. The walk was calming, but I felt as though I was moving through a dream world. Having mailed Breen's letters I realized that there was one more letter I had still to write. My decision had been arrived at without any mediation of the conscious mind, but I had not the slightest doubt that it was a correct one.

Vere, dignum et justum… equum et salutare. Right and fitting, truly!

I drove to my office so as to compose it in peace. I had imagined it would be hard, finding the right words for such a delicate piece of correspondence. But that was not the case; the proper words streamed out onto the paper with surprising ease once I had begun to type. I read over what I had written and was satisfied that it was free of rationalizations, justifications and other forms of dishonesty. I thanked him for his kindness and apologized for my failures.

I would have to deliver it personally in the morning — I owed him that. For the last time I left the office with its blond wood paneling and the familiar ecclesiastical smells of wax candles and cigarettes. I stopped at the Safeway a few blocks from the rectory and threw a dozen or so discarded produce boxes into my truck.

Back in my rooms I looked around at the few things I had accumulated in the years I had been a priest: books that I would never read again if I lived to be a hundred — philosophy, history, theology, canon law and liturgy. I had been promising myself to reread them "someday," but time had run out. There was a fair stereo and some albums I had enjoyed, but I didn't need to lug those around with me. I packed everything into boxes and carried them down to the storeroom. Aside from a few clothes — most of mine were impractical unless I was planning to start in the wedding chapel business — that was it.

My bank balance, when I balanced the check stubs, amounted to around four hundred and some dollars. There might be fifty more at most in a dusty savings book I hadn't looked at in years and then I had the two hundred in emergency cash — the stash I had brought with me to The City in case Jerry had needed it. In the bathroom, a nearly full bottle of Powers from the cabinet under the washbasin, a toothbrush, my safety razor and the engraved shaving mug Jerry had given me — *"The Head Bombadier of Praxitelensis,"* it joked in Latin — these I'd take in my new leather bag. I had bought another pack of Camels on the way home. What else could an ex-bishop need besides a bottle of Irish whiskey and a pack of Camels?

The Bishop would call Cassidy and tell him all he needed to know, so I was spared the bother of goodbyes in the rectory — we had never really become friends in all the time I'd been living there.

God almighty! I thought, when I had poured a generous drink into a coffee cup and drawn deep from my first cigarette in hours. What a fuckin' cock-up I've made of my life so far! I fell asleep sitting there in my grand, salvaged armchair in that stripped-down ruin of a room.

I awoke with the first glimmer of light shining through the window of the study. The frogs down in the swampy land at the back of the playing field were loud at that hour and far in the distance the Western Pacific freight whooped sadly as it charged down the valley. I sat a few minutes in the familiar lumpy chair wondering if it was time to get moving — too lethargic to even check my wrist watch, I nodded off again.

The automated lawn sprinklers beating gently on the study window brought me to the surface again — that would be five o'clock — the convent mass was at six-thirty.

I would shower and finish whatever packing I still had to do before going over to say mass for the last time. It was only five-thirty when I let myself into the darkened church and without turning on any lights, I took a seat in the first pew. Then, for the first time in many years and for the last time to this present writing, I sat in meditation as they had advised all good priests to do before approaching the altar.

Introibo ad altare dei, ad deum qui laetificat iuventutem meam.

I will go to the altar of God; to the God who gives joy to my youth.

Chapter 38

Big Sur, California — 2004

THE MONK WAS engrossed in reading when Holland rapped on the open door. Without looking up he motioned for him to come in and, holding a finger up, signaled that he would be only a minute.

Holland had shoved the pages under the office door that morning as soon as he was sure the monks had gone to chapel. He had not been to bed all night but had forced himself to keep writing till he was done.

Let the Prior do his worst, he had told himself repeatedly in the course of the night.

It was with the same fatalism that he approached this meeting with the monk, though now that he was here and the man was reading what amounted to his confession, a snake was writhing and constricting in his gut.

"Well!" The monk exclaimed finally, looking up from his reading.

Though he tried, Holland could read nothing in his face. He would be silent and let the man set the agenda.

"So that's what really happened." It was a statement not a question.

Holland was unaccountably relieved that the monk was not seeming to doubt him. He nodded.

The monk rubbed his eyes hard with his finger and thumb underneath his glasses. He looked young and bewildered when he stopped rubbing, as though he didn't know where to go next.

"And, since that morning when you left Minerva…?" He asked after a long silence.

"What have I done?"

The monk nodded.

316

"I've survived mainly and wandered. I drove over to San Francisco that first day and took a room in a single-men's residential club. From the classified, I got a job in a specialty grocery store on Union Street, delivered orders to the nobs in Pacific Heights in my truck — the truck's what got me the job. Next door to the grocery there was this bakery run by a gregarious Swede — gregarious, that is, when we'd have a few beers together after work. I volunteered to give him a hand Sunday mornings when he'd be in there alone baking — he supplied the breakfast croissants for a lot of the big hotels: The Fairmont, The Mark and the like. Soon after that he hired me and taught me everything he knew about baking, or tried to. I worked on the bench alongside him and a couple of hardworking Mexican bakers for a few years and suffered from baker's knee and baker's back and baker's arms. Standing at a bench is the best way I know to ruin your body."

Holland straightened out his long back and winced as though talking about it had renewed the aches of a day's baking. The monk seemed reluctant to break into the narrative, merely nodded for him to continue.

"Finally, I got tired of The City and its fog and the cold, dark four o'clock bakery mornings. I told Bo Swensen good-bye, piled my stuff into the truck and headed south on Highway *101*—seeking a place where the days were sunnier, the ocean warmer..."

"... and oranges grow alongside the road." The monk finished it for him. "Finally?" He smiled.

"Finally." Holland agreed. "Finally I had become the total beach bum — fulfillment of my father's prophesy that I would 'go to the dogs.' Behold the dogs!"

"You shouldn't get superstitious about him. I don't think he was right about you at all."

"Maybe it's more than superstition. The Israelites, you know, took that whole business of blessing and cursing their children very seriously. Jacob stole the blessing intended for Isaac and even that worked. Blessings were powerful charms to them."

"Jack, you're a strange one." He shook his head slowly and kept looking at Holland till the latter finally raised his head — curious.

"There was this one other question that I've been meaning to ask you," the monk began hesitantly. "Has there been anyone else — a lover or such — someone with whom you've become involved since you've been free to, so to speak?"

"Not a solitary soul, man or woman, has shown the slightest interest. Even when I was still relatively young and a lot less broken down than I am now, not so much as a nibble. And to tell you the truth, I haven't had much heart for it myself either — pretty disastrous track record."

The monk said nothing but continued looking at him — what was going on?

"So?" Holland cleared his throat. "Is this the day you deliver your verdict? Or do I have to stand before the bench while Father Prior passes sentence? You haven't noticed him cutting out a square of black velvet, have you?"

"I don't understand…"

"The condemned will be taken from that place in which he is held and brought to a place of execution… And may God have mercy on his soul!"

"Jack, do you want to stay on here? That's the only question from my point of view."

"As a breakfast cook, I'd love to; as a brother, I couldn't, even if I wanted to." Holland looked down for a minute before continuing. "I hate to be a smart ass, Father, but I do still remember a fair bit of canon law even after these many years."

"I know. You were a Doctor of Canon Law."

"Well, canon law prohibits a religious order from receiving a man as a lay brother who has ever been ordained to holy orders. *Sacerdos in aeternum, secundum ordinem Melchisidech* and all that…"

"You've known this all along?"

"I'm afraid I have — but the weather was still cold when we started this and the Prior was being such a know-it-all." He scratched his head apologetically. "Who was I to teach a man like himself canon law?"

Holland became aware of a quiet sucking sound and looked up. It was the monk's version of laughing his head off — that and scratching his jaw wildly with his thumb.

"The rest of this that you've been writing for me has been the truth, though?" He asked as he simmered down. There was a skeptical note in the question.

"As the Gospels." Holland replied, but then had a second thought — he looked into the monk's face. "Given my views on religion, let me say instead: everything I wrote for you is as truthful a telling of what happened as my memory allows."

Holland stood up and walked the few feet separating himself from the little monk. Until he stretched out his hand the priest had looked puzzled — maybe even a bit startled.

"I'll be off then." Holland reached out his hand. The monk extended a slender white hand — a weak moist hand — in which the knucklebones rolled in the big man's grip as they shook hands.

"Don't think I'm up to another session with Father Prior. But please tell the Abbot good-bye for me. I will write him later to thank him for his great kindness."

"Jack. I wish you wouldn't go like this. We could spin these sessions out for another month — more even — till you've got something else lined up." There seemed to be a fleck of moisture in the monk's eye.

"Will you walk me out past the gander?" Holland headed for the door and held it open for the priest. They walked down the stairs side by side, out through the tiled lobby into the afternoon breeze.

The fountain in the center of the quadrangle was splashing silver in the sunlight and underneath it a dozen or so small brown birds were enjoying the spray — the men walked around the path to not disturb them.

"Everything's in the truck already." Holland said as they came to the kitchen door. He noticed that his swim trunks was still hanging on the nail where he'd left it earlier that morning — it was nearly dry. "Can't forget that." He slung it over onto the front seat, let off the handbrake and shifted the gearstick to neutral.

The monk watched as Holland laboriously pushed the faded old pickup out along the gravel to where the road sloped downhill, then lent a hand to the fender as it passed.

"Where are you headed?" He looked back at the big gray man as they strained.

Holland inclined his head in a sideways nod that could have indicated anything from the Golden Gate to Mission Bay.

"...To sail beyond the sunset, and the baths of all the western stars, until I die....it may be we shall touch the Happy Isles,..."

"Tennyson," the monk smiled.

The truck was beginning to roll more easily now.

"Right you are," Holland nodded.

"Where the days are sunny, the ocean is warmer and the oranges grow wild along the roadside." The monk repeated the litany and looked at Holland. He was rewarded with a slow wink.

"There's room for two in this thing," Holland invited.

The monk stood back and let the truck and Holland pass him by. The roped muscles on the tanned arms pushing were beginning to relax. The truck was rolling almost on its own now and picking up speed. Holland gave a final quick wave before leaping aboard.

"Like a child, full of excitement always, at heading out," she'd said. His mother had been right in that. The engine stumbled into life.

Coda

THE MONK STOOD at the head of the lane waving till Holland had gone past the first bend. Had he waved back? Hard to tell. He shook his head sadly and walked over to the edge of the mesa. He stood by the low stone wall there and watched as the dusty red truck turned south onto the highway far below and disappeared behind the jutting cliffs.

The bell had just begun to ring, calling the monks to chapel for the Small Hours. He turned and walked slowly back to the monastery.

Made in the USA
San Bernardino, CA
26 May 2019